SCATTERGOOD BAINES
RETURNS

Scattergood Baines Returns

By

Clarence Budington Kelland

CONTENTS

HOW COME?

SCATTERGOOD BAINES came into being in 1915 while I was in Vermont inefficiently helping my brother-in-law to manufacture clothespins. He was no Minerva to spring full panoplied to life, but has been a development through the nearly twenty-five years that he has been appearing in the magazines of this country. There was no human original, but rather he expressed my notion of what a true Vermonter was like. Bit by bit was added to his character as new phases presented themselves until he was pretty well set as an individual.

The first three stories of his exploits appeared in *The Saturday Evening Post.* Then John Siddell, of *The American Magazine* took him over, and he had continued to inhabit the *American's* pages through the reign of the present editor, Sumner Blossom. In the *American* he has appeared in at least a hundred short stories and in one novel; so you will see that he has been a very good friend to his inventor. Probably he has been the most persistent example of longevity in the history of American fiction.

He had, as I say, no original in the flesh, and I thought of him as typical of Vermont, but to my surprise and to my pleasure I have had news of his existence in nearly every state of the union. So it may be that his character expresses something wider than the characteristics of New England, and that his peculiarities and virtues and meddlesomeness are properties of our entire people from coast to coast.

I have been sent photographs of him and descriptions of him. I have been introduced to him many times so that it has seemed to me that almost every village in America has its Scattergood, and that, pleasantly to me, these local characters are not offended by the comparison.

We are accustomed to believe that there is little similarity between the people who live north and south of the Mason and Dixon line. Nevertheless I have met and been informed of Scattergoods in Alabama and Florida and Georgia and Texas. So it may be that we are not so different basically as we think we are, and that it is a fact that the same kind of people, living the same kind of lives and holding the same kind of ideals, inhabit all sections of our land. Which seems to me to be a step in the right direction.

"It is not Scattergood alone who seems to have gotten on friendly terms with American readers. If a few stories go by in which Mandy Baines is not mentioned there come demands for her reappearance; Pliny Pickett and the Elder and the Deacon have fixed themselves in the stories, and Johnny Bones. They, too, seem to fit into the American scheme of things."

To me the continued acceptance of the Scattergood stories has been a great satisfaction and a notable reward. A vastly important, if imponderable, part of the returns to a writer from his work lies in the knowledge that there exist here and there friends whom his work has made for him. It may be that in the Scattergood stories there is little literary merit visible to the critical eye, but nevertheless I am content with them and even a little proud to have been the conduit through which they flowed. It seems to me that the business of writing may have more than one purpose and more than one result. To satisfy the demanding eye of those who read alone to discover literary excellence is a fine thing; to satisfy the homely, decent emotions and to give pleasure to millions is also a splendid thing. To combine the two is a miracle.

If I were compelled to choose between the two, being impotent to work miracles, I believe I would with deliberation choose the latter.

CLARENCE BUDINGTON KELLAND

Port Washington
November, 1939

SCATTERGOOD BAINES
RETURNS

I

The Young Man Who Was Prepared for Everything

CRANE and Keith, lumbermen on a very large scale indeed, had been lifelong enemies of Scattergood Baines. In his beginnings, Crane, who was the active head of the firm, had tried to crush him; as he grew, Crane had done all in his power to impede his progress. Even today, when opportunity occurred, Scattergood found that firm meddling in his affairs. Probably the old hardware merchant would have missed them, for they had become a sort of habit.

There had come a period of years during which the warfare was quiescent. Crane was aging, and perhaps less aggressive. Then, Scattergood heard, young Crane had climbed in the business. He was an able young man, according to stories, and the concern was stirred to new life and activity. It was no longer content to run along in comparative placidity, wealthy and powerful. The new blood was all for expansion, and the only way it could expand with profit and efficiency was up the Coldriver Valley. And, as all men know, Coldriver Valley was Scattergood Baines' especial principality.

There had been vague rumblings of young Crane's activity, but no overt acts. Then, suddenly, of a summer morning, young Crane got off the train and walked to

1

Scattergood's store, where he found the old man sitting on his piazza gazing at the always interesting activities of Coldriver.

The chair, especially reinforced to sustain Scattergood's bulk, creaked as he sat upright to regard his visitor, whom he knew by sight. A nice-looking young man, Scattergood thought, able, brainy, perhaps a trifle excited over his own success and importance; but by no means negligible.

"Good morning, Mr. Baines," said Crane. "I've come up to talk business."

"Set," said Scattergood, "and talk it to your heart's content."

Crane took a seat on the step, below the level of Scattergood's eye, and assumed a look of mature sternness and gravity.

"I am now," he said, "the virtual head of Crane and Keith. Father is in Europe, and things are left in my hands."

"Look like capable hands," said Scattergood.

"This," said the young man, "is an age of expansion. A firm cannot stand still. It must grow or decline."

"Seems as though I heard that some'eres before. Hain't sure, but it's got a familiar ring to it."

"We," said Crane, "have been standing still. I was not satisfied. I've been urging expansion, and at last the older men have consented to my carrying out my plans."

"Hope ye have good luck," said Scattergood.

"Luck," said the young man, "has nothing to do with it. I have planned efficiently. I know where I'm going, and I'm prepared for everything."

"Most folks is," said Scattergood, "till it commences to rain, and then the's a leak in the roof, and they go scurryin' around for pans to set on the floor to ketch the leak."

"My roof," said Crane, "is water-tight."

"Glad to hear it. But you better keep a bundle of shingles handy."

"I imagine," said Crane smoothly, "you are reaching an age where retirement tempts you."

"It's funny what folks imagine sometimes."

"So I have come to offer you an opportunity. Crane and Keith would like to confer with you on the subject of taking over your holdings in Coldriver Valley—mills, timber, railroad rights, and whatever other property you own."

"Um. . . . Includin' this here hardware store?"

"We would be willing," said Crane, with a smile, "to include that in the transaction."

"Offerin' me a partnership?"

"No. I want to buy. I want to combine under one management and ownership the timber and mills of this locality, as well as the water power. Does the idea appeal to you?"

"Prob'ly," said Scattergood, "you figger on a lot of financin'. Bonds and stock to be sold to the public, and all sich?"

"We propose to form a new corporation to take over the holdings of Crane and Keith, yourself, and certain others. A certain amount of stock will be offered to the public. That end of the matter is provided for."

"Um. . . . Be ye a married man, young feller?"

"Not yet," said Crane, with the first touch of boyishness he had exhibited. "But I am to be married in September."

"Hope ye got you a good gal."

"Very good and very lovely," said Crane, and something in his voice as he spoke made Scattergood like him a trifle better than before.

"Runnin' a fam'ly is quite an undertakin'," said Scattergood. "Mebbe you better put off this here expansion till ye see if it don't take up more of your time 'n what ye kin spare."

Crane wrenched the conversation back to the original subject.

"I've checked up on your holdings. Roughly, you have in this valley a hundred and twenty-five thousand acres of timber, worth, say, twelve dollars an acre; making a million and a half dollars."

"Ye kin do arithmetic," said Scattergood.

"Your mills, the three of them, I figure as going concerns, to be worth around half a million, and I believe the tax commission valued your railroad at four hundred thousand."

"So they did."

"Besides which are your dam and boom companies and other sundries—river rights, water-power sites and the like— say a couple of hundred thousand."

"Looks like I was perty well off," said Scattergood. "How about the hardware store, eh? What figger you set on that?"

Crane laughed. "Oh, say five thousand dollars," he said. "But, to get down to business: According to my figures, which are reasonably fair, your holdings are worth, say, two million six hundred thousand. And here's my proposition: We'll take them, lock, stock, and barrel, and give you a million and a half in cash and a million and a half in the seven per cent preferred stock of the new corporation. A clear profit to you of around four hundred thousand."

"Includin' the hardware store?" asked Scattergood.

"Including that," said Crane.

"Now, I tell ye," said Scattergood. "I might sell, but it's got to be everythin'. Won't omit nothin'. Clean sweep. Ye can't buy part and leave part. So I tell ye what. I'll sell ye all my holdin's in timber and mills and the like fur your three million; but then we come to this here store. Fur that I'll take a million extry."

"You're joking!" exclaimed Crane.

"Nary joke. One million round, hard dollars fur the store."

"Why, that's just plain crazy."

"Not from my p'int of view," said Scattergood. "This here store's my first business. It's the first grip I got onto life. I've allus had it and allus run it. Seems like it's about the most important thing the' is. I set here and the folks come along. I git pleasure out of sellin' a pound of nails or a jack-knife. Occupies my mind, like. No, I wouldn't part with jest this front piazza to set on for less 'n a million dollars."

"I suppose," said Crane darkly, "this is your eccentric way of refusing my offer."

"Hain't refusin' nothin'. I'm jest statin'. Ye kin take it or leave it."

"But, won't you listen to reason? Four hundred thousand profit is ——"

"What," asked Scattergood, "would I do with it? Kin I spend it? Kin I commence to spend what I got now? Most of the money I made I made fur the pleasure of makin' it. I enj'yed managin' and contrivin'. Mebbe you won't credit it, young feller, but Mandy 'n' me has lived comfortable all these years on less 'n what this here hardware store earns. We don't need no more. Why, the' never was a year I didn't lay by suthin' out of the earnin's of this store. Yes, sir, we've kind of pertended it was all we had, and we've laid by out of it enough to care fur our old age. All the rest was kind of extry, and didn't mean nothin' special. It was just like all that there timber and what-not wasn't real at all."

"But," exclaimed Crane, impressed in spite of himself, "you've made big money out of this and that. Your mills have made as high as a quarter of a million in good years."

"Better 'n that."

"For goodness' sake, Mr. Baines, what have you done with it?"

"Oh," said Scattergood, "jest put it here 'n' there."

Crane found himself face to face with something he could not understand, and until his very sane young mind put it down to eccentricity—or even insanity—he was nonplused. Scattergood regarded him soberly, but with eyes that twinkled.

"W-al?" he asked.

"Is this your last word? Am I to understand you refuse definitely to deal with me?"

"Seems as though," said Scattergood.

The young man arose, frowning. "No man can stand in the way of progress," he said.

"Depends on what progress is," said Scattergood.

"Your holdings are essential to my plans, and to an efficient reorganization of the lumber industry in the East. I had hoped to do business with you in a friendly way—a manner profitable to both of us."

"Too bad ye can't," said Scattergood.

"I prophesy," said Crane, "that within six months you will be glad to accept a million dollars less than I am offering."

"Um . . . kind of reminds me of your pa. He used to flare up and talk so. Kind of threatenin' like. Dunno's I been in a good war fur quite a spell. I guess mebbe, young feller, you better turn loose your dog."

"You may depend upon it—I shall," said Crane.

Johnny Bones, senator, and for years Scattergood's lawyer, was home from Washington, and Scattergood ambled across the square to see him.

"Johnny," he said, "old times is comin' back. Crane and Keith has come to life ag'in."

"Old Crane's kitten, I suppose," said Johnny.

"Him," said Scattergood. "He's got to feelin' perty sizable for his bigness. Looks like he can't rest content till he's kind of busted loose and chopped down the front steps with a hatchet."

"What's on his mind?"

"He aims to buy me out," said Scattergood, "and if he can't buy, he calc'lates on forcin' me to sell. Offered me three millions."

"How does he size up?"

"Capable," said Scattergood, "but he acts like he's been readin' a book."

"What sort of book?"

"About one of these here ruthless captains of industry you hear about, that goes around crushin' whatever gits in their way. Smart boy, I figger, and maybe he comes under the head of crusher. Can't tell till he tries."

"Didn't say how he was goin' about it?"

"Jest let off a kind of a gen'al threat," said Scattergood.

"And what do you propose to do?"

"W-al, I don't propose to git crushed," said Scattergood amiably, "and I ain't figgerin' to sell out. I don't want no price-cuttin' war. Looks like you 'n' me's got to take steps, Johnny."

"For instance?" Johnny asked.

"What we been doin' with our surplus?" Scattergood asked.

"Putting it in waterworks and electric lighting companies around the state, mostly grouped in the south. You started that years ago, when you got the idea that water-power development was going to have so much to do with the future of the country."

"C'rrect," said Scattergood. "And, as I figger it, we own

kind of a sizable chunk. Scattered around, kind of. Um. . . .
Combine 'em, Johnny, combine 'em. Git up a holdin'
comp'ny and collect 'em all under one head. I hain't ap-
pearin' in it. Hide me as complete as ye kin."

"Done," said Johnny.

"And," said Scattergood, "you better tie up all my Coldriver Valley holdin's in another corporation. Kind of group
'em so they kin be swung as a single club."

"Easy," said Johnny.

"G'-by," said Scattergood, with his usual abruptness.

"G'-by, Mr. Baines."

The practical results of these two combinations were,
first, The Coldriver Company, owned by Scattergood Baines,
and the Mountain Water and Electric Company, in which
Scattergood Baines' name did not appear at all. Forty-eight
per cent of the stock in this latter concern was held by a
gentleman in Boston named Middleton, as trustee.

The balance appeared on the stock books of the company as scattering, in small blocks, held by scores of stockholders in the original companies. To all intents and purposes, a concentration of forty-eight per centum of stock in
a single hand represents perfect control of such an organi-
zation; for proxies from the small stockholders are readily
obtainable. Most of the great corporations are controlled by
a much smaller concentration of stock than this.

News of this combination was not long in reaching young
Crane—Scattergood saw to that—nor was a rumor that the
Mountain Water and Electric Company had an option on
the stock of Scattergood's Coldriver Company slow in getting to him. And Crane saw his opportunity.

He journeyed to Boston. Mr. Middleton received him.

"Mr. Middleton," he said, very businesslike, "you have
been arranging a nice little combination of companies."

"So-so. Successful so far."

"You hold, according to records, forty-eight per cent of the stock."

"I do, as trustee."

"With power to transfer?"

"Certainly."

"I have heard rumors that a further extension is contemplated."

"Why," asked Mr. Middleton, "do you ask?"

"Because," said Crane, "I want you to entertain an offer for your holdings—which are practical control. You have never found difficulty in getting enough options, have you?"

"I've voted as high as ninety-four per cent of the stock."

"Excellent. Now, first, will you consider an offer?"

"I'm here to make money for my clients."

"Then, before I get down to figures, will you answer one question. Have you an option on Mr. Baines' Coldriver Company?"

"We have. A ninety-day option."

"May I ask the figure?"

"Three millions of dollars."

"Cash?"

"No. He has agreed to accept half in six per cent bonds and half in seven per cent preferred stock."

"I don't," said Crane, "see how you contrived it. No cash! I think you are a better negotiator than I, Mr. Middleton."

"Mr. Baines seemed to have some pressing reason for desiring to sell."

Crane smiled. He fancied he knew what that reason was: First, the old man did not want Crane and Keith to get his properties; and, second, fear of a contest. Age, he thought, was commencing to tell on Scattergood Baines.

"In which case," he said affably, "let us get down to business. Even your company is somewhat smaller than Crane and Keith, and our resources are large. We aim to expand. The fact of the matter is, we wish to control the timber, but more especially the water power of this region. We wish to concentrate under one management, thus cutting down overhead, reducing rates, and in the end making splendid profits for everybody concerned."

"I follow you. But any offer made for my stock must be in cash."

"I think I am prepared for that eventuality. We have a nice reserve. I believe you are incorporated for a million and a half."

"Which capitalization will be largely increased when we take over the Coldriver properties. To five millions at least."

"Exactly. But, perhaps unnecessary—except for the issuance of non-voting preferred stock and of bonds."

"Exactly."

"Any deal we enter into will be kept private," said Crane.

"Except from the people for whom I am trustee," said Middleton.

"Then, let's get out our pencils and figure," Crane said genially.

They figured. Nor did they go out to lunch, but sat over the desk until four o'clock in the afternoon. At the end of that time Mr. Crane went away. He had succeeded in purchasing the Middleton holdings for one million dollars cash, a profit to the trustee's principals of two hundred and fifty thousand dollars, but nevertheless an excellent piece of business for Crane.

It gave him possession of efficient control of the Mountain Water and Electric Company, and with it an option on Scattergood's holdings upon terms which required the payment of no cash. It is true he had gone far toward depleting the money reserve of Crane and Keith, but he had succeeded in his main object and won a triumph which he considered to be nothing short of remarkable.

"And now," he said, "all I've got to do is buy three per cent of this scattered and outstanding stock to have the whole thing tied in my fist."

The transfer was made next day, and the day following that Crane took the train to Coldriver. As usual, Scattergood Baines sat in his reinforced chair before the hardware store.

"A fine day," Crane said, by way of greeting.

"Middlin'," said Scattergood.

"I just ran up again to have a talk with you about buying your properties in the valley," said Crane.

"Thought we finished that up."

"Possibly you thought so," said Crane, "but when I make up my mind I want a thing I'm not easily discouraged."

"Kind of stubborn, eh?"

"I'm afraid I'm stubborn. But it pays."

"The's times when it does. But I've seen folks set a fire under a mule and singe the hair off'n his belly. Mebbe he got satisfaction out of bein' stubborn, but he come out of it with a sore skin."

"But I've come out of it with something better than a sore skin," said Crane. "I've come out with control of the Mountain Water and Electric Company—and a perfectly legal option on your properties. On terms, incidentally, much more favorable than those I offered you."

"Eh?" said Scattergood, sitting suddenly erect. "You what?"

"I have bought, for cash, Mr. Middleton's stock."

Scattergood frowned, and the young man watched him with amusement. He had heard much of this old man's reputation for shrewdness. Perhaps he had been adroit in days gone by—in the day of the elder Crane, but even the astuteness of the last generation was no match for the cleverness of the new. Young blood will tell. In that moment young Crane thought very highly of himself. He almost felt sorry for Scattergood in this moment of his defeat.

"You mustn't take it too hard," he said. "After all, you are coming out very well. It isn't as if you were taking a loss."

" 'Tain't loss that worries me," said Scattergood. "But your pa and me fit fur years. Seems like I gen'ally had perty good luck gittin' the best of him. He never wanted to see me grow, but I contrived to git bigger jest the same. And now he and his fam'ly look like they was comin' into possession of all I built up. I don't mind sayin' it's a kind of a shock. It's more 'n upsettin'."

"But, after all," said Crane, "no man can expect to stand in the way of progress and modern methods."

"Seems as though," Scattergood said dolefully. "Um. . . . W-al, an option's an option. No way of gittin' out of it. I hain't a-goin' to whine, nor to wiggle out. If I'm licked, why, I'm licked. 'Tain't no pleasant dose, but I calc'late I got to stummick it."

"That's the spirit," Crane said. "We'll be ready to do business in two weeks."

"You young fellers is hustlers!"

"You have to move fast nowadays."

"It's a perty big thing you're a-goin' to swing," said Scattergood.

"I'll swing it," said Crane. "And now let's shake hands and have no ill feeling."

"Hain't got a mite," said Scattergood. "Hope you feel the same way—and keep on feelin' so to the end of it."

"End of what, Mr. Baines?"

"End of everythin'," said Scattergood.

"Don't you ever worry about me."

"I hain't. It's me I'm worryin' about. Goin', eh? W-al, g'-by. Hope you keep on bein' satisfied with your bargain."

"I shall," said Crane.

He got on the train again, jubilant. Not that he had anticipated any difficulty over the option, but Scattergood might have made trouble and forced him to resort to law. Now all was smooth sailing.

"I'll just step out and pick up that three per cent of stock," he said, "and that's that."

On his return to his office he wired his brokers to buy enough of the outstanding stock to give him actual control instead of the practical control he held. Then he lost himself in the details of reorganization. In order to carry through, it became necessary to call a meeting of the stockholders, to ratify certain acts and to empower certain others. Notices in legal form were got out and mailed. Then he bethought of calling up his brokers.

"How about that stock I told you to buy?" he asked over the wire.

"Haven't managed it yet," said the broker. "Folks seem to like the investment. Haven't been able to pick up a share. We've written and called on a hundred people. But we'll get it. Just have patience."

This was a trifle disappointing, but, after all, it was a compliment that his stockholders should regard so highly their investment in his company that they would not part with their little holdings.

However, after ten days had passed and no proxies arrived, he experienced a vague annoyance, that was not quite a worry. It was queer that not a single proxy came in. Not one from all the scores of persons who should have sent them. Still, it was nothing to worry about. Forty-eight per cent would dominate the meeting. Small stockholders never troubled to come and vote in person. He shrugged his shoulders, wondered a little at the peculiarity of human beings, and went ahead.

The meeting was called at the main offices, legally situated in Boston. This he proposed to change today. He entered the room, to which, presently, came the dummy directors, men scarcely known to him, and the other officers who would be giving up office that day. In all, they represented more than enough stock to make the meeting legal.

"Shall we come to order?" he asked.

"Better wait a minute," said a director. "It isn't quite the official time."

Then the clock struck two, and almost upon the stroke the door opened and Scattergood Baines came in. Crane stared.

"How do you do, Mr. Baines," he said. "Have you made a mistake? This is a stockholders' meeting, and you're not a stockholder, are you?"

"Kind of," said Scattergood.

"Your name's not on the books."

"Calc'late it will be," said Scattergood. "What stock I come by was too late to transfer to my name before the meetin'. But I got me proxies fur it, so's I kin vote."

"Very good. Mr. President, suppose we come to order and go ahead with business. By the way, Mr. Baines, how many shares do you vote?"

"Quite a few," said Scattergood. "I jest counted 'em up, and I find I got what amounts to fifty-two per cent of the hull caboodle. What ye might call a controllin' interest. Here they be. Now ye kin git to whizzin'."

"But"—young Mr. Crane suffered from sudden shock,

5

and could not at once realize what had happened to him—
"but you can't have. I've forty-eight per cent myself."

"To be sure," said Scattergood. "I ought to know. I sold
it to ye. But not till I'd gone around and bought up all the
rest."

"You didn't sell to me. I bought from Mr. Middleton."

"Representin' me as trustee," said Scattergood. "Yeah, he
sold ye them shares fur a million cash. I got it in the bank.
I bought up what shares I got fur considerable less 'n a
million. Jest figgerin' par, you paid me a kind of a profit of
a quarter of a million and up'ard."

"But that was for control."

"You figgered the control yourself, young feller. You figgered forty-eight per cent was control a hundred times out
of a hundred. 'Tain't. It's that jest ninety-nine times out of
a hundred—and here's the hundre'th time."

"But you said—when I saw you in Coldriver, you admitted I had beaten you."

"Don't recall it. No, you kind of made a threat you was
a-goin' to have my propities whether I wanted or not. You
figgered you got 'em. No. This here Mountain Water and
Electric Comp'ny's got 'em, and I control it. They kind of
remain where they be, and if you're a-lookin' fur more fight,
why, I got a million dollars of your cash to do the fightin'
with."

Young Crane sagged. He was looking into the future,
listening to what his father would say to him when he came
home from Europe. He was listening to business men of
his acquaintance, who would tell this story with relish. He
was humiliated, beaten, and felt himself to be disgraced.
Scattergood watched him gravely, rubbing his cheek with
his horny hand. Presently he spoke.

"Young feller," he said, "your fam'ly and me's been enemies up'ard of forty year. The's been times when your pa didn't play jest fair with me. But he's kind of put a tang in life fur me. You're jest startin' out in life, and you figgered to start by tryin' to be smarter 'n somebody else. Now, I hain't got no enmity to'ard you. Not a mite. I kind of valued your pa as an enemy. But I didn't ever hate him."

There was a brief silence.

"If ye got an enemy," said Scattergood, "it hain't allus wise to lick him more 'n he can bear. 'Tain't a good thing to crush folks, nor to outmaneuver 'em more 'n what's good business. Now, if you was jest a stranger, I dunno but what I'd do my best to down ye—if you started in fust to down me. But you hain't. You inherit this here war. So I calc'late to treat ye different than as if ye was a stranger or a friend. I'm a-goin' to deal with ye like I figger an enemy ought to be dealt with."

"What do you mean?" asked the boy through white lips.

"Why," said Scattergood, "here's a certified check fur one million dollars. It's what ye paid fur this stock. Jest sign it back to me, and the money's yourn—and we stand back where we was, with nobuddy damaged any. I calc'late I could derive a good profit off'n ye, and kind of punish ye fur meddlin' with me. But I hain't a mind to."

"I don't—understand," said Crane.

"You was startin' out wrong. And I don't need no more money 'n what I got. This hull rumpus was jest to show ye. You was commencin' too big fur your bigness. Now, go on home, and the next time do kind of different."

Pride got the better of the young man. "I won't take it," he said. "I won't take anything from you."

Scattergood shook his head kindly. "Don't be no more of a fool 'n what ye kin help. I've watched ye. You're smart. You'll go a long ways. Don't commence it by lettin' your vanity burn a hole in your pants. And kind of remember this: An enemy's a good thing to have. He's mighty valuable. He teaches ye a lot. Here, boy, take this here check, and call it a day."

Crane took the little piece of paper.

"Tell your pa," said Scattergood, "that I'm doin' this fur his sake. Kind of in remembrance of them old days. Just a mark of gratefulness to him fur makin' life int'restin'."

He paused, and his old eyes grew kindly.

"The meanest thing ye kin do to an enemy," he said, "is not to hate him as much as he thinks he ought to be hated!"

II

Scattergood Uses an Eraser

SCATTERGOOD BAINES sat on the piazza of his hardware store watching with interest an approaching cloud of dust; or, to be more accurate, two clouds of dust. One cloud advanced in a more or less sedate manner down the middle of the road; the other cloud was given to sudden darts and forays and venturings toward the four quarters of the compass.

As these phenomena came nearer, Scattergood made out in the center of the larger cloud a boy who trudged stead-fastly, but, nevertheless, could not restrain his bare feet from kicking up the dust, from digging his toes into the warm sand—as barefoot boys have done from time immemorial—and letting its pleasant warmth filter between his digits.

The second and more erratic cloud contained a dog. One arrived at the conclusion that it was a dog by elimination; by that process of logic known as the *reductio ad absurdum*. Namely, there was nothing else in the world the creature could possibly be, so it must be a dog. It was not a yellow dog, but before the dust of the road painted it gray it had been a sort of black. Not a sleek, jet black, but a kind of dingy, moth-eaten black.

Its hair was long where it should have been short; it seemed to be higher behind than before; one ear stood

18

erect, while the other was what prize fighters call a cauliflower—and it was very thin. None of which interfered with its good spirits nor with its energy.

The boy carried a bundle on a stick, and was very lean. Scattergood decided that he was small for his age, whatever his age might be. Just what sort of face he had could not be guessed, for the layer of dust which clung to his eyelashes and brows was streaked by perspiration into a species of war paint. He looked neither to the right nor to the left, but plodded straight ahead, only pausing now and then to kick an especially alluring mound of powdered sand into the air.

There was something unusual about this boy. He did not whistle.

Scattergood noticed this at once, and squinted. Boys plodding along the road with dogs should whistle. And, though Scattergood was sure this particular boy never had been in Coldriver before, he did not exhibit any curiosity. He was not conducting himself, thought the old hardware merchant, the way a normal boy should. Therefore, when the procession came abreast of the store, Scattergood leaned forward and called, "Hey, bub!"

"Me?" asked the boy, stopping and poking an index finger at himself.

"Don't see nobuddy else in sight," said Scattergood. "Goin' some'eres?"

"Calc'late to," said the boy.

"Walked fur?"

"Quite a piece."

"That critter yourn?"

"Folks," said the boy, "has made fun of my dawg before today."

"Don't recollect makin' fun of him," said Scattergood. "Jest asked a question."

"He kin fight," said the boy. "He kin lick any dawg in the state."

"Who's your folks?" asked Scattergood.

"I hain't got no reason to answer questions."

"Mebbe so. Mebbe so. But s'posin' the deppity was to git the idea you was a suspicious character, eh? Or a vagrant, mebbe, or a runaway?"

"If you was to git me took up," said the boy, with curious deliberation, "I'd contrive to git away, and then you'd be sorry. I'd prob'ly come and bust all your winders."

"I got some cold drinkin' water here," said Scattergood.

"I hain't comin' in reach," said the boy. "Anyhow, if you was to grab me, my dawg 'ud chaw ye 'most to pieces."

"Hain't calc'latin' to grab ye," said Scattergood. He whistled to the dog, which came to a halt and regarded him suspiciously. "Come here, feller," said Scattergood, holding out his hand, palm down, as only men who understand dogs are wise enough to do. "Tongue's kind of lollin' out, feller, like you was dry."

The dog drew nearer, and finally mounted the steps warily, ready to whisk back at the first hostile move. Scattergood continued to talk to him, but remained motionless. The dog sniffed his legs and then sniffed the extended hand—and his tail commenced to sway. Then Scattergood scratched him behind the ear, and the dog looked back at his young master significantly.

"I guess I'll git that drink," said the boy.

"Set," said Scattergood, "and I'll fetch it."

Presently he returned with a dipper for the boy and a pan for the dog.

"Hungry?" he asked.

"A body kin take a drink of water 'thout beggin'," said the boy.

"Kind of proud, hain't ye?"

"I don't take nothin' costly off of nobody. Not if I was starvin'."

"Even the proudest folks," said Scattergood, "goes to each other's houses for dinner. If somebody was to invite me over fer turkey and cranberry jell, I dunno's I'd climb up on my high hoss and refuse."

"That's different," said the boy.

"Different how?"

"That's jest bein' neighborly back and forth."

"Any good reason why I shouldn't be neighborly?" asked Scattergood.

"I don't know ye," said the boy. "I don't know ye from a side of sole leather."

"My name's Baines—Scattergood Baines."

"Mine's Spotty Mott," said the boy.

"You be freckled up some," said Scattergood. "Now we've both got kind of introduced and all, hain't we?"

"If I kin earn it," said Spotty, "I'll take it."

Scattergood nodded. "I got some odd jobs. They been kind of accumulatin' on me. Kin ye handle a broom?"

"Yes, and I kin handle an ax," said the boy with some pride, "and I kin hold my end of a crosscut with most men."

"I bet ye," said Scattergood. "Object to takin' pay in advance?"

Spotty hesitated. But Scattergood was adroit. "Your dawg's mighty nigh starved, seems as though," he said.

"You promise I kin earn it?"

"Hope to die," said Scattergood gravely.

"All right," said Spotty, "but Emp'ror's got to git his fust."

"Who?" asked Scattergood.

"Emp'ror—that's my dawg."

"Um. . . . I allus kind of craved to see what a emp'ror looked like," said Scattergood. "Hoped to see one in Europe when me and Mandy was there, but they had mostly been reduced to privates or shot afore we got there. But I dunno's they'd let a dog into the dinin'-room to the tavern. So you jest set a spell and I'll fetch you 'n' him suthin' to eat right here."

Scattergood found enough plausible labor to keep Spotty Mott busy through the afternoon, and then suggested that boy and dog stay overnight to clean the cellar the next day. The old man succeeded in convincing Spotty that he had been trying to get that cellar cleaned for months, without success.

"Ye kin sleep in the store, if you got a mind to—and hain't scairt of the dark," said Scattergood.

Spotty snorted. "I dast sleep in a ha'nted house," he said firmly.

"This here store hain't ha'nted to speak of," said Scattergood. "And I kin fix ye up with a cot and beddin'. I find ye turn out to be a stiddy worker, mebbe it'll take two-three days to get rid of all the jobs I got hangin' around. If ye kin contrive to stay that long."

"I calc'lated on stoppin' in this neighborhood fer a spell," said Spotty; but Scattergood was not ready yet to ask why.

His first business was to establish confidence; to induce by his behavior a trust which would bring voluntary disclosures of history and purpose. Well he knew that one hint of prying would send Emperor and Spotty down the highroad in a cloud of dust.

Matters continued on this footing for some days. Each morning more essential work developed, and each evening something was found to hold the wanderers for yet another

day. It was on the afternoon of the fifth day that Spotty relaxed his suspicions sufficiently to ask a question; and that
was enough for the adroit Scattergood. Before the conversation was over he had possessed himself of the kernel of the
mystery.

It was four o'clock when Spotty paused in his rearrange-
ment of a shelf to regard Scattergood calculatingly. Apparently, he made up his hard little mind favorably.

"Mr. Baines," he said, "ye hain't heard tell of a stranger
comin' to these parts, have ye?"

"Man or woman?" asked Scattergood.

"He's—he's a man," said Spotty, "and I calc'late he's about
the biggest man around anywheres. I bet you he's the
strongest man in this here state, and he kin lick any two
that's a mind to try it. He kin lift a barrel of flour 'thout
even bustin' a gallus." There was a deep organ note of
pride in the lad's voice.

"I dunno's I've heard of sich a stranger. The' hain't been
no onusual liftin' nor no onusual fightin' recent."

"He wouldn't be friendly with nobuddy," said the boy.
"He wouldn't have nothin' to do with folks. That's what
makes him so hard to find."

"I'm allus sorry fer a man that don't have to do with
folks," said Scattergood. "He gits to be mighty lonesome."

"I guess he's the lonesomest man the' is, what with one
thing and another, and me not bein' there."

"Yes," said Scattergood; "you ought to be there, hadn't
ye?"

"He don't want me," said Spotty. And then, as if he could
bear no misunderstanding of this, he said quickly, "I mean
he prob'ly wants me like tunket, only he figgers I hadn't
ought to be along."

"He's thinkin' of your good, mebbe," said Scattergood

with understanding, and this one sentence did much to open wide the closed gates of Spotty's confession.

"What's gallin' me," said Spotty, "is that I bet you it 'ud be good fer him to have me. What I care about me! But he jest won't have nobuddy know I b'long to him. That. was the word he sent out to me."

"I calc'late he was perty proud, eh? 'Most as proud as you be,' said Scattergood.

"He's the proudest man in the world," said Spotty, "and he can't git over it. Yes, sir; he sent me out word I mustn't never come near to visit him whilst he was in. And that when he got out I wasn't never to own up to him or recker- nize him, or anythin'. And he says it might be hard fer me to git along, but it was better I should starve than git to be known as the son of a—a jailbird."

"He was tryin'," said Scattergood, "to think fer your good."

"Don't I know that!" said Spotty resentfully. "But I don't care nothin' about that. I'm a-huntin' him, and when I find him I calc'late to stick to him like a bur. I'd ruther be a son of a jailbird about a thousand times over, an' be along with him. I hain't ashamed. I kin lick any feller twice-t as big as me that says I'm ashamed of him jest 'cause he was shet up in a jail. And they hadn't no business to, neither, but he was a stranger there and didn't git no fair show."

"I've knowed it to happen like that," said Scattergood.

"They said he was drunk, and he don't never even take a drink," said Spotty; "and one of these here men kicked me fer nothin', and the' was two of 'em, and when he got through with 'em they took what was left off to a horspittle. He like to have killed the both of 'em. And so they shet him up in the cooler. And they grabbed me and took me to one of them farms, but I contrived to git away. But I hain't been able to ketch up with him."

Scattergood painted for himself a picture of this big, rough, two-fisted, simple man who was Spotty's father. He could see him, bewildered by his catastrophe, seeking for the better way, and finding it in this desertion of his child; finding it in the tearing of his own heart and of the boy's heart, that his son might not be soiled with the stigma that clings to the ex-convict. He could see the man, alone, embittered, dangerous; and he saw that, if there were to be a salvation, it lay in the hands of a small boy with freckles on his cheeks.

"If ye was to come on him, Spotty, what d'ye calc'late he'd do?"

"Drive me off," said Spotty. "But I'd hang right on and foller him, no matter how he lambasted me, or what he done. Him and me," he said in a voice that came close to trembling, "was allus together. I got to show him I hain't ashamed."

"To be sure ye hain't ashamed," said Scattergood. "What makes ye think he's near here?"

"I kind of traced him," said Spotty.

"I'll kind of inquire around," said Scattergood. "I got ways of findin' things out. If he's in this here caounty I'll come to hear of it."

"And then we'll go git him," said Spotty.

Scattergood shook his head. "Not till we git it all planned out how we're going to hang on to him," he said. "Got to convince him he won't be no disgrace to you, seems as though."

"He's been in the cooler," said Spotty; "and our folks allus thought that was the wust disgrace the' is."

"Bein' in the cooler," said Scattergood, "is kind of like

droppin' a lot of ink onto a clean sheet of paper. It looks like mebbe the sheet was ruined till a body remembers about erasers. I calc'late what we got to do is to git your pa an eraser."

The population of Coldriver County was not so dense that a newcomer, no matter how humble, could pass along without notice. Scattergood was confident that if Spotty Mott's father were in the locality some random word of it would come to his ears, even if he made no effort toward locating him. And so it proved.

"They got a gang of swampers into Crane's Camp Six," said Pliny Pickett, whose position as conductor of Scattergood's train gave him unusual opportunities for news-gathering. "Cuttin' a tote road through to the railroad."

"Um. . . ."

"Makin' some talk about their blacksmith," said Pliny. "Claim he kin pull a ten-inch spruce up by the roots, or suthin'. But he hain't sociable, accordin' to accounts. Won't have nothin' to do with nobuddy."

"Mebbe he runs so much to muscle," said Scattergood, "he hain't had time to develop no tongue. How clost kin ye drive to Camp Six?"

"The's what passes fer a road right in," said Pliny. "It's an axle buster, but a body kin git there."

"Hey, Spotty," Scattergood called. "Where's Emp'ror?"

"Sleepin' under the caounter."

"Calc'late he needs air? Eh? Figger you could contrive to run this here store while Emp'ror and me takes a buggy ride?"

"I could run a bigger store 'n this," said Spotty.

"Sell fer cash," said Scattergood. "Sell fer cash—and *git it*."

There was insufficient room on the buggy seat for Scattergood's breadth and Emperor's proportions but, both being companionable persons, they made the best of it. It was after the luncheon hour. when they arrived at the camp, so Scattergood went at once to the cook shanty.

After he had fed himself and Emperor he strolled through the rising camp. A new and enlarged bunkhouse was going up; the hovel for the horses was being enlarged; the black-smith shop occupied an eligible site by itself. Scattergood strolled in this direction, and through the open door saw a huge man striking sparks from a curving piece of red iron.

"How be ye?" he asked from the doorway. "Weather's kind of seasonable, hain't it, eh?"

The giant grunted, but cast an eye in Scattergood's direction. The old man saw that the blacksmith was not many years past his youth, that his face was dark and dour, but not evil, and that the big blue eyes were the eyes of a very simple man, who never would think in a devious path but always straight ahead, like a bull charging.

No exchange of the time of day was to be had here. Scattergood stood watching the skilled hands for a few moments; then he whistled to Emperor, who came and stood, tail wagging, at his side. The hammer struck a blow, then another, then it lagged and became still while the big blue eyes regarded the dog. The blacksmith wet his lips with his tongue.

"Where," he demanded, "did ye git that dawg?"

"Come to me," said Scattergood. "Calc'late he's one of them tramp dawgs."

Emperor, at the sound of the voice, tore his collar from Scattergood's fingers and leaped upon the big man with ostentatious joy.

"Um," said Scattergood. " 'Pears to know ye."

"Never see him before," said the blacksmith heavily. "Dawgs is fools."

"Not sich fools as men," said Scattergood.

"When he come to ye," asked the blacksmith, "was he alone?"

"He fetched a-plenty of fleas," said Scattergood non-committally.

"I hain't got no time to talk about dawgs," said the blacksmith.

"G'-by," said Scattergood, but there was no response to his farewell.

As Scattergood drove back to Coldriver he advised with Emperor as to the situation. "The trouble is," said the old hardware merchant, "he hain't got no self-respect left. Kind of despises himself, like you might say, and that's a turrible bad disease."

Emperor wagged his tail in agreement.

On the following day Scattergood met in the bank Dan Brown, boss of the camp for which Spotty's father was blacksmith.

"How be ye, Dan?" he asked.

"Middlin'."

"Dan, I hain't never asked no favors of ye, have I? If I was to consider askin' suthin' of ye, how'd ye feel to'ard it?"

"Favorable," said Dan.

"Got a blacksmith, hain't ye? Seems as though I heard ye put one to work."

"Fust-class man," said Dan.

"Ever send him to town fer a new hammer or a bar of iron or suthin'?"

"I hain't."

"Could ye?"

"Dunno why not. When?"

"About four minutes after I telephone ye," said Scatter-good.

"To be sure," said Dan.

"G'-by, Dan."

"Afternoon, Scattergood."

So matters stood while Scattergood scanned passing events with a calculating eye, awaiting the arrival of some happening which he could turn to account—to Spotty's account.

And then fate took a hand. It rained. It was no clement, reasonable rain, but a relentless downpour which lasted through the day and night and another day. Brooks swelled and rivers commenced to lift their currents and their voices in sullen threat. Toward the second evening Cold River was six feet nearer the planking of the bridge than it had been three hours before. Scattergood leaned over the railing, surrounded by other wise men of the village, and grew apprehensive.

"This here," he said, "is more onusual 'n usual."

"Seems as though," said Elder Hooper, "it's goin' to git wuss 'fore it gits better. A heap sight wuss, and more 'n that, if dams start goin' out."

"Um," said Scattergood. "I dunno but what you're right. Calc'late this here's goin' down in hist'ry as a flood. Wa-al, if we got to have a flood, I dunno but what we might's well figger to make use of it."

He walked back to the store and used the telephone.

"That you, Dan?" he asked when the connection was made.

"What's left of me."

"Ye kin send along that there blacksmith."

"Doubt if he kin git there."

"If he can't," said Scattergood, "he hain't the feller I want. G'-by."

He turned away, wagging his head. "All I kin do," he said, "is to give him his chance-t. I calc'late the'll be opportunities for the right feller 'fore another sundown."

At six o'clock the dam at the Red Mill went out, and then the bridge below, cutting Coldriver into parts. Mountain brooks poured their torrents into the river above the town; the saturated ground could absorb no more, and streams formed where none had been before. Already the streets were knee-deep with swirling water, and all was darkness and terror and confusion.

But Spotty's father had come through—to buy a hammer. Spotty did not see him when he waded into the store, for Scattergood had long ago sent the boy back to the high safety of the farm.

"Seems as though we need men around here," Scattergood said. "Things is kind of confused-like. I calc'late I better do some organizin'."

"Kin I do anythin'?" asked Ben Mott.

"You kin," said Scattergood; "pervidin' ye *kin*."

Word, frantic word, came from up and down the valley of this or that family imprisoned by the water in houses whose security was threatened. Families perched on roofs; sick people were carried to attics without food or fire.

In the midst of this, Scattergood organized. But his forlorn hope was Spotty's father.

The man, with his huge, tireless body, was built for the emergency; he went about the business as he would go about fashioning a horseshoe, deliberately, without excitement. It was a job of work which had been assigned to him, and he went at it as he would have gone at any other task. That he performed prodigies he did not know; that he displayed heroism he was unconscious. It was a pleasure to pit his young strength against the furious waters; but he did it all in so matter-of-fact, almost phlegmatic a manner that even those he rescued from extreme peril failed to realize what he had done.

Yet, in those few days, by his own efforts alone, he saved from extreme peril of death no less than twenty-one persons.

Then, when the danger was past and the waters subsided, he came back to Scattergood.

"Gimme that hammer," he said simply; "I got to git back."

"Here's the hammer," said Scattergood. "G'-by."

And so Ben Mott went back to camp, and there was an end to it so far as he was concerned. But not so far as Cold-river was concerned.

"That one big feller," said Pliny Pickett, "must 'a' saved ten-twelve folks."

"I kin name twenty-one," said Scattergood, "to say nothin' of other things."

"Sakes alive!" said Old Man Weldon's wife. "Who 'n tunket was he?"

"Name of Mott," said Scattergood.

"Suthin' ought to be done about it, seems as though."

"Fer instance," said Scattergood, "what?"

"Under obligations, hain't we, as a town and as individuals?"

"Calc'late so."

"Huh. You hain't overanxious about it, be ye? W-al, I'm goin' to talk it up among the ladies."

It was talked up among the ladies and among the men, until the common opinion manifested itself that Coldriver was obligated to show its gratitude. Scattergood hid behind the fence and egged it on until it became a popular movement with a definite object.

And when all was ready Scattergood called up the camp boss again.

"Send the blacksmith in fer another hammer," he said. "In time fer supper."

Presently he summoned Spotty from his labors. "The's goin' to be doin's to the hall tonight," he said. "I want ye should go. I'll contrive to git ye a seat way up front. And after the meetin's over, the's a-goin' to be a chicken-pie supper."

"What'll I do with Emp'ror?"

"He kin come too," Scattergood said.

So, when it was time for what Coldriver called the exercises, Mandy took Spotty to the hall and sat with him in the front row. In good season the blacksmith arrived for his hammer.

"'Fore ye go back," said Scattergood, "I got a job of work fer ye. 'Twon't take long. It's over to the hall."

He walked down the street with the unsuspecting Ben Mott, and into the crowded hall. The young man would have been terribly self-conscious walking down the aisle through that sea of faces had he arrived as one of them; but, curiously, as a blacksmith come to do a piece of work, he was utterly unconcerned. He was unaware of his working clothes or of the mud on his boots, and even when he was taken out upon the stage he was without self-consciousness. He was there to make a repair.

But, quite unexpectedly, Scattergood took him by the arm and led him to the front of the platform.

"Folks," he said, "here he is—the feller that all of us owes so much to. Name of Mott. Kin ye holler?"

They could. The hall rocked with the shock of it, but piercing through the mass of sound of that cheer came a treble, a boy's voice which reached the stage:

"Pal . . . Pal . . . It's Spotty. I'm right here!"

Ben Mott blinked and scowled and looked at Scattergood and then at Spotty and Emperor.

"What's the hullabaloo?" he asked.

"This here meetin'," said Scattergood, "'s called in your honor, jest to show ye what the folks of this town think of ye, and what store they set by ye for what ye done durin' the flood. We calc'lated we couldn't do no more ner no less. And so we jest kind of called together this here meetin' to ask ye if ye wouldn't move to Coldriver and be a citizen of it."

"Me?" said Mott.

"Nobuddy else. And, jest by way of sayin' much obleeged fer what ye done and fer the lives and proppity ye saved, the hull town kind of got together and put up a blacksmith shop and fitted her up with everythin' a fust-class blacksmith could ask fer, and there it sets a-waitin' fer you."

Slowly the thing penetrated the blacksmith's slow-moving understanding.

"I can't do it," he said finally. "When I see that dawg I sh'u'd 'a' knowed Spotty was around. I hain't fit to be near him, nor nobuddy. I been a-hidin' away."

"Why?" asked Scattergood.

"Because," he said, "I'm a jailbird!"

"Oh, *that*," said Scattergood. "I thought mebbe it was suthin' important. Um. . . . Ever hear of a eraser? One of them rubber things that rubs out marks? Wa-al, mebbe you was in jail, but bein' in jail fer lickin' a couple men hain't so tarnation awful. But, admittin' it was, it hain't nothin' but a mark. And so all of us—us that wants to be your neighbors, we kind of figgered out what you done durin' the flood was plenty big eraser, and it's rubbed over the page so as there hain't hide or hair of the mark showin' this evenin'. It's gone fer good. Hain't it, everybuddy?"

Everybody assented loudly.

"So," said Scattergood, "here's the deed and the bill of sale to the shop and the little house fer you 'n' Spotty."

Spotty leaped to his feet. "Pa! . . . It's so! The' never was no disgrace. I never held nothin' ag'in' ye. I hain't done nothin' but hunt fer ye, to stay with ye. Won't ye stay, Pa? Won't ye *stay*?"

Mott's big hands were working; his broad face was working, too. He struggled for words. "D'ye—mean it?" he said at last. "Ye mean ye won't hold it ag'in' me ner throw it up to me? And ye'll be willin' to neighbor with me, side by side?"

"More 'n willin'," said Scattergood. "Proud!" ,

"Please, Pa!" shrieked Spotty.

"Dog-gone," said Ben Mott. "Dog-gone! I wouldn't never of b'lieved it!"

III

Scattergood Takes to His Bed

SCATTERGOOD BAINES lounged· in his big chair, especially reinforced with iron rods to bear his restless weight, and regarded the life of Coldriver from the piazza of his hardware store. He drowsed with eyes half shut, but very little went on which those half-shut eyes did not see. No one would have guessed that he was waiting and watching for someone to appear.

But presently, as a young man—a gangling, homely young man with a black bag in his hand—came along slowly, with head down and face very grave and set, Scattergood cleared his throat. It was the young doctor who had moved to Coldriver during the winter on the invitation of the old doctor, and who by his kindliness and his efficiency had been winning rapidly a place in the regard of the community.

"Mornin', Doc," said Scattergood. "How be ye? Mornin'.'"

"Good morning, Mr. Baines," said Doctor Judd.

"Goin' some place or jest walkin'?" Scattergood asked.

"It looks," said the young man, "as if I'd better be going some place—a long way off."

"Dew tell," said Scattergood with interest. "I been a-hearin' talk. Folks says this and that. Doctors and ministers draws gossip like molasses does flies."

35

"Mr. Baines," said the young man, "either I'm not fit to practice medicine or there's been something pretty malignant going on."

"What d'ye think, eh? Which? Kind of like to git your idees about it."

"It doesn't matter what I think, sir. It's what other people think. Titus Benjamin is dead. He was poisoned. The town believes I gave it to him by mistake. Even if I escape a prosecution for malpractice, I'm ruined as a doctor."

"Mebby so. Mebby so. Kind of like to git your idees jest the same. Ever ketch yourself bein' careless before? Make a habit of it?"

"I've thought, sir, that I was a careful man."

" 'Twa'n't a prescription filled at the drug store?"

"No. I gave him the medicine myself."

"Out of that there bag?"

"Yes, sir."

"What ailed him, eh? What was he sick of?"

"Nothing was wrong with him but a little touch of indigestion. I gave him something to fix that up—and in two hours he was dead."

"What of?" asked Scattergood.

"Strychnine poisoning," said the doctor.

"Have any in your bag?"

"Yes, sir."

"Know how much you had?"

"I certainly do. We have to be pretty careful in such matters."

"And that," said Scattergood, "is what's worryin' ye, eh? Know how much ye had, but it turns out ye hain't got it. Some's missin'. When this come out, the fust thing ye did was to look and make sure—and some of this here pizen was gone."

"How did you know?" asked the doctor. "I —"

· "You was a-keepin' that part of it quiet, wa'n't ye? Don't blame ye. Kind of a deep hole you're into, seems as though. Law'll make ye account fur all the strychnine ye had—and ye can't do it."

"That," said Doctor Judd, "is the situation."

"What's Ann think?" asked Scattergood.

The young doctor's eyes glowed. "She wants," he said, "to marry me right away."

"Wimmin is funny that way—the best kind," said Scattergood. "And ye'd be s'prised to know how many is the best kind. The's lots of things I like about wimmin. Um . . . me 'n' Ann, we kind of had a sort of a talk."

"About me?"

"You was mentioned," said Scattergood dryly. "Now, young feller, what d'ye aim to do? Goin' to uptail and run, or be ye plannin' to dig in your toenails and see it out?"

"It's pretty hopeless," said Doctor Judd.

"Nothin's hopeless exceptin' bein' hopeless," said Scattergood.

"When," said the doctor, "it is found out enough strychnine is missing from my supply to have killed a horse, there won't be much chance for me. And it must be known. You knew it."

" 'Tain't everybuddy in Coldriver's as good a guesser as I be," said Scattergood. "Be ye certain you didn't reach fur the wrong bottle by mistake?"

"Since this happened I've thought of nothing else. I've tried to remember and to place every detail of that visit. Right now I can see my bag open on the chair by the bed. I can see the rows of little bottles. I can see every detail of it. I can see myself taking a bottle out of its leather loop and holding it up to the light to read the label. Then I arranged it in doses in little spills of paper."

"Sure it was the right bottle?"

"I'd stake my life on it."

"Um. . . . Could somebuddy have shifted bottles on ye?"

"They were all in their correct places when I got back to the office."

"When," said Scattergood, "a feller is the kind of a feller that probably wouldn't do a thing, then most gen'ally he probably didn't do it."

"I don't think I did do it, sir. But I can't see how anyone else could have done it, either."

"Ever see a feller yank a rabbit out of a silk hat? Ever see one of them magicians?"

"I've seen them."

"Know how they did it, eh? Know how the rabbit got into that there hat? What I'm a-gettin' at," said Scattergood, "is that mebby all the tricks hain't done on the stage. A trick could be done off'm the stage, couldn't it? Now, couldn't it?"

"Why, yes. It could."

"G'-by," said Scattergood.

"But I'm not going away. I've decided to stay—and see it through."

"G'-by," said Scattergood.

"Good-by, Mr. Baines," said the young doctor, accepting dismissal as all Coldriver had been accepting it this forty years back.

Scattergood waggled his head a couple of times and settled back comfortably in his chair. Automatically his hand went to his foot and he commenced to unlace his shoe. The time had come for thinking, and the old hardware merchant did it much better when his toes were not confined in leather.

The chair creaked and groaned as Scattergood shifted his weight. Presently he put his shoes on, and then got up and ambled down the street toward the dry-goods store, where he found a young woman—very young and slender and homelike and dependable to look at.

"Mornin', Ann," he said.

"Good morning, Mr. Baines."

"Jest seen the doc, Ann. Jest had a mite of talk with him. Kind of low in his mind, seems as though."

"Is he going away, Mr. Baines?"

"Calc'late he plans to stay around. Him and me, we discussed that."

"But what will happen, Mr. Baines?" she asked gravely. "It—it sounds horrible to accuse a doctor of killing by carelessness a patient who puts his life in the doctor's hands."

"Perty bad," said Scattergood. "What I can't figger is the reason fur it."

"For what, Mr. Baines?"

"Fur Titus Benjamin to die. Now, a body kin die of sickness and not have any reason fur it except bein' sick. He kin git killed by the cars without no reason back of it. He kin fall off a precipice. But pizen's different. The reason could be that the doc was heedless, but we know that he hain't a heedless feller."

"He's very, very careful and conscientious," said Ann.

"But if he didn't make no mistake, then I can't see no reason fur it. Titus didn't have no money to speak of. I don't calc'late he left no life insurance, and the farm wa'n't wuth a dose of pizen. And, so fur's I know, Titus never done nothin' anybuddy wanted to git revenge fur."

"Do you mean, Mr. Baines, you think he was murdered?"

"If Doc wa'n't careless, the' hain't no other explanation of it, is the'? Don't seem as though. But the's got to be a reason fur a murder."

"But who? Who?"

"The reasons back of killin' a man," said Scattergood, "is money or wimmin or revenge or suddin rage or fear."

"Yes," said Ann.

"I calc'late we kin strike out money, and pizen hain't used in no sudden rages, and Titus was along about thutty year past excitin' interest in any woman. So we got left revenge and fear. Now, take old Titus. He was a kind of a slipshod, easy-goin', kind-hearted feller. That kind of a man don't stir up folks to git revenge onto him. So what we got left is fear. But who'd be afraid of Titus, eh? Jest rear back and tell me that, young woman."

"Certainly his old housekeeper wasn't afraid of him," said Ann soberly. "She had lived there twenty years."

Scattergood's eyes twinkled. "Don't calc'late Mis' Fox would git scared by a tribe of scalpin' Injuns."

"And," said Ann, "Jake Benjamin wouldn't be afraid of his uncle. Titus always gave him a home and was good to him."

"Them's my idees," said Scattergood. "But the' must 'a' been somebuddy that was so scairt of Titus that they planned and contrived and snooped to kill him."

"If," said Ann, "Doctor Judd didn't give him that poison by mistake, then someone else must have been in the house to give him the dose. Was anybody there besides Jake and Mrs. Fox?"

"I dunno," said Scattergood. "G'-by, Ann. Keep stiddy on your feet. G'-by."

"Good-by, Mr. Baines," she said, and there was hope in her eyes for the first time in forty-eight hours.

The noon train was in by the time Scattergood reached his store again, and he seated himself in his chair to await the appearance of Pliny Pickett, ex-stage-driver, but now for many years conductor on the one passenger train which plied the twenty-odd miles of railroad owned by the old hardware merchant. Pliny came around the corner and marched down the street with as exact an imitation of Scattergood's walk as could be achieved by a man of half Scattergood's weight.

"Mornin', Mr. Baines," he said.

"Mornin', Pliny. How's business? Folks a-ridin' care-free and hearty?"

"Wa'n't but six passengers. We're a-feelin' the dee-pression."

"Um. . . . Goin' anywheres, Pliny?"

"Home, mebby."

"No idee of stoppin' to the pust office?"

"Gen'ally do," said Pliny.

"If a dozen ol' coots was a-talkin', Pliny, what d'ye calc'late ye'd do?"

"Listen," said Pliny.

"If they was to mention, say, Titus Benjamin, would ye be apt to remember what they said?"

"Never forgit nothin'," said Pliny.

"I calc'late to set here fur some time," said Scattergood. "G'-by, Pliny."

"G'-by, Mr. Baines."

In half an hour Pliny was back again.

"Been to the pust office," he said.

"Dew tell!" said Scattergood with every outward sign of astonishment.

"Lots of folks there. More 'n usual, seems as though. Come

to hear and to tell. Some holds the doc ought to be rid out of taown on a rail."

"Some would," said Scattergood.

"The's them that hints the doc done it a-purpose."

"I swan to man," said Scattergood.

"Titus Benjamin wa'n't one to keep his teeth clamped together."

"Seems as though," agreed Scattergood.

"He let on not more 'n a week ago that if he was to tell all he knowed folks 'ud be s'prised. And he says, says he, that if he was to talk, he says, the'd be somebuddy that would up and skedaddle betwixt dark and dawn. That's what he says."

"And folks is guessin' he meant the doc, eh? That's the opinion folks is hazardin'?"

"They're hintin' it," said Pliny.

"G'-by, Pliny," Scattergood said.

"G'-by, Mr. Baines."

Scattergood leaned back and closed his eyes and considered the population of Coldriver. He knew it, including cats, dogs, chickens, and pet woodchucks. He had seen it born and raised and married. He had seen its children born and raised and married, and he had watched with interest the coming of a third generation. Few strangers moved to Coldriver, but within twenty-four hours of their arrival there was little about them that Scattergood did not learn. Now he studied that population for possibilities. Who of it was capable of committing some act which would, if disclosed, make him skedaddle betwixt dark and dawn?

"Ye can't most allus tell," he said to himself. "Folks with no leanin' to'ards crime'll sometimes up and commit one when they git pushed."

He puffed out his cheeks and pinched his nose and wrung the lobe of his ear.

"No," he went on in his discussion with himself, "we got to find a feller that done suthin' on purpose in the fust place—suthin' perty bad. Then we got to find a feller that knowed the ins and outs of this here taown, and the habits of folks like ol' Titus and the young doc. And we got to find a feller that's capable of bein' cruel and doin' a ruthlessness—and all in a slinkin', schemin' kind of way with darin' mixed up in it. And the' hain't many sich. Kind of narrers it daown."

Presently Scattergood stirred himself to go home to the midday meal, and he walked heavily down the street; but on the corner in front of the bank he encountered Jabez Post, uncle to Ann.

"How be ye, Jabe?" he asked.

"No complaint, Scattergood."

"Ann's kind of worried, Jabe."

"About Doc Judd?"

Scattergood nodded. "How old's Ann?" he asked.

"Twenty-one come October," said Jabez. And then, "The's perty mean talk goin' on about Doc Judd. Dunno but what he deserves it. Folks don't pay doctors to give 'em doses of pizen. Dunno but what the grand jury ought to take cognizance."

Scattergood looked at Jabez under shaggy brows. "Um . . ." he grunted.

"'Tain't likely it will," said Jabez gloomily. "Folks in this here taown is backward about makin' complaints."

"So the' be," agreed Scattergood. "Ye might make the complaint yourself."

"'Twouldn't look good fur me to do it, bein' Ann's uncle and guardeen and all."

"Folks'd talk," said Scattergood. "On the other hand, mebby the doc never give that dose of pizen."

"Couldn't be no other way," said Jabez.

"Could be," said Scattergood, "if 'twa'n't accident but murder."

"What d'ye mean, Scattergood?"

"I mean if a body had a reason for gittin' rid of Titus and stole that there strychnine out of the doc's bag."

"Who'd have a reason?" asked Jabez.

"G'-by, Jabe," Scattergood said abruptly.

"G'-by, Scattergood."

The old hardware merchant toiled up the hill and tramped on toward his house on the edge of town, where Mandy's dinner and irate tongue awaited him.

"There ye be," she said acidly. "Dinner's sp'iled a'waitin' fur ye while ye stopped and gossiped all along the road. Seems like the' hain't no use fur a woman to work and slave."

"Mandy, I hain't a-feelin' jest right," he said lugubriously.

"What ails ye?" she demanded with counterfeit truculence.

"Stummick, seems as though."

"Stick out your tongue."

Scattergood obeyed and Mandy eyed that organ with interest. "Looks all right to me. Hain't been piecin', have ye?"

"Didn't touch a snack since breakfast."

"Mebby you're comin' daown with suthin'," she said. "Better git the doctor to look at ye."

"Mebby I will on the way back," he said, and then sat down to the table, where, for an ailing man, he did complete justice to the meal Mandy had prepared.

After his second piece of pie he got up from the table

and moved to the door. "If anybuddy inquires how I be," he said, "you tell 'em I hain't so good."

"Nobuddy's apt to ask," she snapped.

"They might," he said mildly. "G'-by, Mandy."

He stopped at the post office on his way to the store and again took occasion to mention his physical condition to the assemblage. "Dunno what ails me," he complained. "Mandy says I'm comin' daown with suthin'."

"Mebby it's suthin' ye et," guessed Elder Hooper.

"When a body's mind gits upset," said Scattergood, "it's apt to affect his liver or suthin'."

"What ye upset about?" asked Jabez Post.

"Suthin's kind of preyin' onto me," Scattergood replied. "I wisht I didn't git to know things like I do sometimes."

"What kind of things?" asked the elder.

"Things that's apt to git folks in trouble," said Scattergood, "and mebby jail or, if wust comes to wust, a halter around their neck."

"Hain't meanin' young Doc Judd, be ye?" asked the deacon.

"Doc Judd, he hain't in no danger," said Scattergood in an odd, evasive voice.

"What d'ye mean he hain't in no danger?" asked Jabez Post. "I'd say he was in consid'able."

"Trouble is," said Scattergood, "you don't know what I know. No, siree; Doc Judd hain't got no good cause to worry, but somebuddy else has."

"Meanin' what?" asked the deacon.

"Meanin' I calc'late to keep my mouth shet till I git things figgered out and make up my mind," said Scattergood. Then he made a grimace of pain. "Dunno but what I better drop in and see the doc."

"What doc?" asked Elder Hooper.

"Young Doc Judd."

"Me," said the deacon, "I wouldn't let him doctor a cow."

"Nuther would I," said Scattergood, "but then he don't specialize on cows. G'-by, everybuddy. Guess I'll step up to his office right now."

He climbed the stairs in the post office building and consulted with Doctor Judd for half an hour; then he went across the road to the bank, which, in common with most of Coldriver, was an enterprise controlled by himself, and spent more than two hours consulting its books and records. The rest of the afternoon he sat on the piazza of his hardware store and groaned and grimaced.

In the morning, to Mandy's perturbation, Scattergood refused to arise. He mentioned pains and pointed out their locality.

"I'm a-goin' to call in the doctor," said Mandy with determination.

"Calc'late ye better," Scattergood said pitifully. "Mebby ye better telephone. Only trouble is, if ye telephone, the hull taown'll know it in fifteen minutes, what with nine folks on this here party line, all runnin' to listen when you ring the bell. But I calc'late it's got to be endured."

"I'll call him right now," said Mandy.

In twenty minutes Doctor Judd entered the house and was led by Mandy to the bedroom. He seated himself in professional manner while she stood by anxiously, wiping her hands over and over again on her apron.

Doctor Judd did his best. He felt of pulse, listened through stethoscope, scrutinized tongue. He thumped and prodded and listened. Having exhausted these resources, he asked questions which gave him little more actual enlightenment than his explorations. He could, as a matter of fact, find nothing whatever the matter. But one cannot tell a patient nothing ails him. So, in his most professional voice, he cast his vote in favor of a bilious attack, and proceeded to fill numerous spills of paper with harmless white powders to be taken on the tongue and followed by water every hour.

"I'm sure you'll be quite all right in a day or two," he said.

"Calc'late to," said Scattergood. "G'-by, Doc."

"Good-by, Mr. Baines."

When he was gone, Scattergood called Mandy. "If folks drops in to see me," he said, "ye might let 'em in. Kind of lonesome a-layin' here."

People did come. There were Elder Hooper and the deacon; there were Pliny Pickett and Senator Bones and a dozen others, who came and lingered and went. While Scattergood was gossiping with the senator, Mandy announced the arrival of Jabez Post.

"Skedaddle, Johnny," said Scattergood to the senator. "Might drop around this evenin', eh? Kind of lonely—evenin's."

"To be sure, Scattergood. Right after supper." He turned to shake hands with Jabez as he came through the door, and Post advanced to the bed and looked down at Scattergood.

"Never expected to see ye sick in bed, Scattergood."

"Never expected so to be," said Scattergood, "but it comes to everybuddy soon or late. Set."

Jabez sat in the bedside chair, and they discussed crops and politics in droning voices until, at the end of half an hour, Scattergood's eyes grew heavy and more than once he started from the very verge of sleep. Jabez droned on. Heavier grew Scattergood's eyes, until they closed, but still Jabez's voice mumbled along, but now his body was tense in the chair. He leaned over Scattergood to peer into his face and to catch the regular rhythm of his breath.

The old hardware merchant clearly was asleep. Then, slowly, cautiously, Jabez picked up one by one the little spills of paper containing Scattergood's hourly powders, and thrust them in his pocket. His hand moved to another pocket and withdrew from it a handful of identical containers, and this hand he stretched out to drop them on the little table. But before his fingers could open, he found his wrist seized suddenly and twisted so that he uttered a cry of pain and fear. Scattergood was sitting up in bed, his face grim, his great paw holding Jabez by the wrist.

"Much obleeged, Jabe," he said. "Much obleeged. Jest set stiddy. Don't wiggle or I'll have to twist it plumb off of ye." Then he raised his voice. "Hey, Sheriff! Hey, Towne! I calc'late ye kin come in naow. Got a present fur ye."

The form of Sheriff Marvin Towne appeared in the door of the adjoining room.

"Was ye able to see it all?" Scattergood asked.

"I seen it clear," said the sheriff.

"Better collect them little parcels of Jabe's," said Scattergood. "Come in handy fur evidence. Liable to be strychnine. To be sure. The balance of what he stole outa Doc Judd's little bag and didn't use fur pizenin' Titus Benjamin."

"I never . . . I never . . . It's a lie, Scattergood. I never meant to do nothin'."

"Two killin's with strychnine 'ud 'a' made it bad fur Doc Judd," said Scattergood. "Um . . . funny how a feller sticks to a way he's proved he kin use. I figgered Jabe 'ud do jest that. Everythin' was arranged handy fur him to kill a couple of birds with one stone. To be sure. Git rid of Titus so as he couldn't talk, and kind of ruin Doc Judd so as he couldn't marry Ann."

"But what'd he want to kill ol' Titus fur?" asked Sheriff Towne.

"You tell him, Jabe," said Scattergood. "I don't want to monopolize the talk. Jabe's Ann Post's guardeen and trustee, Sheriff. If Ann got married, her husband 'ud be askin' questions about Ann's proppity. And, Jabe, I was tinkerin' around the bank all yestiddy afternoon. Sheriff, ye might not b'lieve it, but Jabe was about ready to put fur some'eres with every cent Ann's pa left her."

Jabez sat rubbing his wrist where Scattergood's powerful fingers had wrenched it. "If 'twa'n't fur that meddlin' ol' fool," he grated between set teeth.

"Meanin' Titus?"

"Him," said Jabez. "I sold him a farm of Ann's, and somehow he got onto what I done with the money. Threatenin' to talk. If it hadn't of been fur him . . ."

"If it hadn't of been fur him, Jabe," said Scattergood, "it 'ud 'a' been somebuddy else. And so ye stole that strychnine out of Doc's bag, and ye waited your chance and ye was watchin' when the doc called, and then ye switched pizen fur medicine. Jest like ye aimed to do with me. And like I figgered you'd do. Wa-al, Sheriff, hand me them pants. I'm gittin' up."

"Guess we better be a-goin', Jabe," said Sheriff Towne. "But how about the money, Scattergood? Did Jabe make away with it?"

"Had things fixed and ready, but he didn't dast make no move till the Titus Benjamin thing settled daown. No, Ann's proppity's all there. G'-by, Sheriff. G'-by, Jabe. Never do a thing the second time jest because the fust time worked. Gits to be a kind of a trade-mark. And, Sheriff, ye might call the doc on the phone and tell him he's cleared and all. Ann'll like to know it, too."

"Why don't ye tell him yourself?" asked the sheriff.

"I'll be busy," said Scattergood, "explainin' my capers to Mandy. She hain't a-goin' to relish bein' bamboozled."

Mandy came bristling into the room. "I heard ye, ye old skeezicks. Up to your tricks. Next time ye git sick ye'll lay there, fur all of me. Makin' me worry myself to the bone. And gittin' me all upset without no need."

"No need!" Scattergood's voice was surprised. "Didn't I have to find out how ye'd act when ye learned ye was apt to be a widder? And ye was joyful, Mandy. It come to ye as a boon and a relief. I seen the glitter in your eyes."

"If 'twa'n't fur this and that," Mandy said, "I dunno but what I'd pizen ye myself."

"But," said Scattergood dryly, "there's sich a heap of this and that, hain't the', Mandy? Any pie left?"

IV

Scattergood Makes a Deal

JOHNNY BONES was a very poor lawyer, indeed, when he came first to Coldriver, but Scattergood Baines, the old hardware merchant and the town's leading citizen, discovered in him qualities and attributes, and Johnny prospered. Scattergood, who wielded authority in such matters, made a senator of him presently, and a senator he had remained for more than a generation. He would remain a senator until he died if he so desired, because the state was both proud and fond of him, and he represented it in the way it wished to be represented.

Johnny was a very human and unassuming man. When he was absent from Coldriver he dressed in sack suits and soft hats; but when he came home he wore a black frock coat and a high silk hat. Not to win votes or to impress the populace, but because it was the wish of his neighbors. Coldriver desired its senator to look like a senator, and Johnny, having ample sense of humor, did as they desired.

Now his silk hat was gaping up at the sun from the piazza of Scattergood Baines's hardware store, as Johnny sat with tails tucked out of harm's way discussing this and that with Scattergood.

"I don't know about letting him go into politics," the senator said.

"Politics hain't done you no special hurt," Scattergood said. "If it hadn't been fur politics I don't calc'late ye'd ever 'a' got to own a silk hat."

"Would you want your son to choose it as a career?" asked Johnny.

"Depends on the son," Scattergood said. "If a boy's a-goin' to go bad in politics, most likely he'd go jest as bad as an undertaker. It ain't politics ruins good men; it's bad men that ruins politics."

"Vote-getting is a tough business," said Johnny.

"So's money-gittin'. Um. . . . Trouble with politics is too much democracy. And gittin' more 'n' more so. Allus veerin' to'ards givin' more responsibility to everybody and takin' it away from anybody. Look what's happened to the Senate since we got to electin' direct. Gone to pot."

"Well! Well!" exclaimed Johnny. "And I always thought you were all for the people!"

"I be. So be I fur sheep, but you wouldn't git no'eres lettin' the flock elect a shepherd. I hold that votin' hain't a divine right but a kind of a privilege that ought to be earned so as it'd be valued."

"You favor limiting the ballot?"

"To be sure. As it is now, every Tom, Dick, and Harry kin shove his vote into the box. What's the result, eh? Wa-al, I'll tell ye: The unfit is herded to vote by politicians, and the fit, that can't be herded, forgits to come or is too busy to come a-tall. So eight elections out of ten is decided by the scum, so to speak, and not the responsible citizen, and there ye be. And the character of the voters decides the character of the politics.

"And more 'n that. Folks is allus sayin' ye can't git good men to run fur office. Ye kin, but ye don't. And the reason ye don't git good men to vote fur is because ye don't have good men a-votin' fur 'em. It's the character of the voters decides the character of the candidates. If we didn't have nothin' but first-class citizens votin' we wouldn't have nothin' but first-class candidates. Ye can't expect cream to rise on skimmed milk."

Johnny laughed and shook his head. "Maybe you're right, Scattergood, but who'd dare propose a limiting of the ballot?"

"Nobuddy," said Scattergood, "and we're goin' to keep on rarin' along and gittin' more 'n' more democratic, till we end up in a mess and have to start all over ag'in. And there ye be. And so, if young Johnny wants to git into politics I dunno but what I'd encourage him. What's he want to run fur?"

"State legislature," said the senator.

"Johnny's a good boy," Scattergood said ruminatively. "If he's as good as I jedge, politics won't hurt him, and, what's more important, he won't hurt politics."

"And," said Johnny, "he's got to make his own decisions."

"The sooner he gits started to makin' 'em," said Scattergood, "the sooner he'll git through makin' the same old mistakes. Give him a shove out of the nest, Johnny, and watch him try to fly."

Johnny sighed. "He was a baby just the other day," he said wistfully.

"So was you," said Scattergood. "I recall ye when ye didn't have a pinfeather." He paused. "Them old Revolutionary Fathers was a perty able lot," he said presently, "only they kind of got drunk on the sound of words. One thing they let off in the Declaration of Independence has caused a sight more trouble 'n what line fences or blond wimmin has done."

"What's that?" asked Johnny, amused at Scattergood's oligarchical tendencies.

"The one where they said: 'That all men are created equal; that they are endowed by their Creator with certain unalienable rights; that among these are life, liberty, and the pursuit of happiness.'"

"What's wrong with that?" asked Johnny.

"It's flavored the whole hist'ry of this nation like a dipper of vanilla in a tub of milk. It wa'n't true, and they knowed it wa'n't, and they didn't live up to it themselves. No two men is created equal; but because it's in the Declaration, the ones that is the most unequal hugs it to their breasts and insists on it. The only feller that ever hollers about how equal he is is one that knows in his heart he hain't equal a-tall. If they'd of said that one of man's unalienable rights was to git equal if he had the ability, then they'd of said suthin', instid of that nonsense about the pursuit of happiness. If they'd of said it was man's unalienable right to pursue anything he wanted that was decent and lawful. Um. . . . Givin' a man a right to chase suthin' don't guarantee he's a-goin' to ketch it. But about ninety-nine per cent of the folks jedges it does. Yeah, them Signers bogged down in a mess of fine words, and the country's been reapin' the harvest ever since."

"How would you have written it?" asked Johnny.

"I," said Scattergood, "would have set it down suthin' like this: 'We hold that nothin' is created so unequal as man; that they wa'n't endowed by their Creator with anythin' but two arms and two laigs and a stummick; and that if they want to git anythin' or git anywheres they got to git out and stir their stumps to earn it. And that the pursuit of happiness is a lot more fun and a lot more important than ketchin' it.'"

"Your Declaration would have been a peculiar document," said Johnny.

"It would," said Scattergood, "but it would have let out a couple of facts."

The result of this conversation was that young Johnny Bones came before the electorate and was sent by an overwhelming majority to represent his district in the capital of the state. This being accomplished, Scattergood settled back in his specially reinforced chair to watch what should ensue. . . .

It was Scattergood's custom, during sessions of the legislature, to visit the capital unexpectedly and to remain there for indefinite periods. He preferred keeping his own eye on events rather than trusting to the reports of lieutenants. But this time he had a special reason: He wished to observe how young Johnny Bones was conducting himself in this first foray into public life. He sent for Johnny, who called at Scattergood's room in the hotel.

"Wa-al, Johnny," said Scattergood, "how d'ye like addin' to the troubles of mankind by pilin' up more laws onto their backs?"

"It's rather confusing at first, Mr. Baines."

"After that," said Scattergood, "it gits bewilderin', and in the end you git so's you can't make head nor tail of it."

"That's a tough outlook," Johnny said, with a youthful and charmingly disarming smile.

"Hain't been jostlin' ye around, have they, Johnny? Kind of pushin' and shovin'?"

"Nobody pays the slightest attention to me."

"Um. . . . They will. Important legislation comin' up this session. Rate bill and what not. Wa-al, Johnny, I hain't a-goin' to give ye no advice nor nothin'. Sometimes we have to let on to these representatives what's expected of 'em, and keep 'em in line. But your pa 'n' me's decided to give ye your head and see where it'll lead ye. Been a-studyin' up any?"

"I've been doing my best to learn something about this rate bill," said Johnny.

"As to the rights and wrongs of it?" Scattergood asked. "Or as to how it'll affect your political future?"

"I hope," Johnny said earnestly, "I will never be influenced by my personal advantage."

"That's noble," Scattergood said, and wagged his head. "It's awful noble, Johnny. If a feller could allus vote in a legislature with nothin' to consider but the rights and wrongs of the bill he was considerin' it 'ud be perty smooth sailin'. But 'tain't practical. Anyhow, 'tain't practical till fifty-one per cent of the representatives does the same. Nope, Johnny; the feller that serves the people best hain't the one that allus does what he knows is right; it's the feller that knows jest how much to concede so as he kin git the most possible of what he knows ought to be got."

"Surely, Mr. Baines, you aren't suggesting that I compromise with my conscience!"

"I told your pa you'd be noble," said Scattergood dryly. "The younger ye be the nobler ye be. I hain't suggestin' ye compromise with your conscience; I'm p'intin' out it's advisable to compromise with the Member from Suffolk. Mebby your conscience tells ye his bill fur ketchin' all silver cats and paintin' 'em blue is evil and opprobrious, but he won't vote fur your bill to cure all the evils of the railroads. So ye got your choice of seeing your bill fail or of votin' for blue sliver cats. And there ye be."

"I don't like it," said Johnny.

"Neither does anybuddy like smallpox," said Scattergood, "but we git outbreaks of it. Um. . . . . G'-by, Johnny."

"Good-by, Mr. Baines."

"I'd like fur ye to have supper with me around six."

"Sorry, Mr. Baines; I've a dinner engagement."

"I calc'late," said Scattergood, "that the feller who thought of callin' supper dinner was the one that invented twin beds. What's her name, Johnny?"

"Miss James."

"Meet her since ye came here, eh? New acquaintance?"

"Yes."

"Perty?"

"Very."

"Mention the rate bill, Johnny? Seem kind of interested in it?"

"Not in the least."

"G'-by, Johnny," Scattergood said again, and this time permitted the boy to take his departure. . . .

There was only one place in the capital where a young gentleman could take a beautiful young lady to dine. Scattergood, always curious about the affairs of his acquaintances, put on his coat—a considerable concession that warm night—and went to this restaurant, where he took a table in a corner and ordered steak smothered in onions. It was half past seven when Johnny appeared with a young woman whose clothes unquestionably were expensive, and who was endowed with hair and eyes and a very noteworthy nose. On the whole, Scattergood liked her looks and decided she was what Coldriver referred to as "a sma't gal."

Presently a Mr. Bailey, representative from the town of Dover, strolled nonchalantly into the place. He was very nonchalant, indeed, and highly and dramatically surprised to see Scattergood Baines, whom he had been pursuing for an hour.

"Wa-al, I never!" he exclaimed. "Calc'late you're the last feller in the world I'd expect to see here."

"Seems as though," said Scattergood dryly. "I wouldn't be too s'prised, though, Bailey. I seen you ploddin' after me."

Not abashed, Mr. Bailey grinned. "Ye see most everythin', don't ye, Mr. Baines?"

"When a bill's up that means as much to the boys as this one," said Scattergood.

"She's seethin'," said Mr. Bailey. "Is it goin' to git took out of committee?"

"If I was in the legislature," said Scattergood, "mebby I'd know."

"Be you a-backin' it?"

"Ye might say I was more fur 'n what I am ag'in'," said Scattergood.

"It's a-goin' to be close't. This here lobby's got influence."

Scattergood blinked. "Ever use a telephone, Bailey?"

"Got one into the house to home."

"Dew tell! See any members of the legislature in this eatin' house?"

Mr. Bailey surveyed the scene. "Nobuddy but young Johnny Bones yonder."

"Any telephones in the neighborhood, Bailey? Eh? Handy-like across the street?"

"Calc'late the'd be one in the cigar store."

"Thinkin' of usin' it?" asked Scattergood. "Feel moved to call somebuddy up?"

"I could be," said Mr. Bailey, who had been long enough in public life to know something of Scattergood Baines's methods of procedure.

"Um. . . . Now, who might ye be thinkin' of callin'?"

"I might call up Johnny Bones."

"What fur?" asked Scattergood.

"Fur about ten minutes," said Mr. Bailey, who enjoyed a reputation as a humorist.

"G'-by, Bailey," said Scattergood.

"G'-by, Scattergood."

Mr. Bailey went out, and in a couple of minutes a waiter stopped at Johnny's table and summoned him to the telephone, which was in a booth in the rear of the room. As he entered it Scattergood rose and walked across to the chair Johnny had vacated.

"Evenin'," he said to the young lady, who looked up at him big-eyed but in no manner disconcerted.

"Good evening," she replied interrogatively.

"Lemme see," said Scattergood; "I call to mind meetin' ye durin' the session of 1880. Dressed some different ye was. Kept right on a-meetin' ye, seems as though, every session since. Ye don't git no older, but I hain't sure but what ye do git sightlier."

"I wouldn't know what you're talking about," said Miss James.

"Ye never did," said Scattergood, "not when your name was Williams and ye was a blonde, nor when ye was Miss Scoggins, with red hair, nor in '90, when ye was Miss Wood and was darker 'n a gypsy."

"I wasn't born in 1890," said Miss James.

"Mebby not," said Scattergood, "but you're like this here lama feller over in Asia some'eres, that don't never die. The's allus a lama in Thibet, and the's allus you around the legislature. . . . How d'ye find Johnny Bones?"

"Pleasant and courteous," she said.

"And kind of young and not too doggone' discernin'," said Scattergood. "Um. . . ." He appraised her shrewdly.

"I dunno but what you'll do as well as somebuddy else fur him to cut his eyeteeth on."

"Come to the point," said Miss James.

"The' hain't none. Johnny's a free agent, out learnin' what makes the wheels go 'round. I jest wanted ye should know I knew you was a wheel with teeth onto it. I don't aim to interfere none. Johnny's got to paddle his own canoe. If ye can gaffle onto him fair and square, that's your business. If he kin come through it 'thout bein' took in, that's his business."

"But?" asked Miss James.

"The' hain't no but. Jest wanted ye should know I was lookin' on and admirin'. My name's Baines, by the way."

She smiled. "I was told to look out for you," she said frankly.

"I hain't much to look out fur—eh?" said Scattergood.

"You mean you're going to keep hands off?" she asked curiously. "Why?"

"Wa-al," he said, "Johnny's pa and me calc'late to find out if Johnny's sound and free from knots or windshakes."

"And if he isn't?" she asked.

"We'll be perty sorry, miss, seems as though." He smiled down at her genially. "Perty gals has got to earn a livin'," he said. "Most everybuddy has got compellin' reasons fur what they do. I bet yourn seems good to you, and mebby they be. The's a heap sight wuss things 'n bein' a lady lobbyist. Um. . . . G'-by, Miss James."

"Good-by, Mr. Baines."

"I seen a good joke come to pass in the legislature of '93," said Scattergood.

"What was it, Mr. Baines?"

"The ball," said Scattergood, "bounced back and knocked the lady lobbyist flatter 'n a pancake."

She looked after him as he walked back to his table and resumed his meal; and then she glanced up at Johnny with a quick smile as he returned.

"Isn't that Scattergood Baines over there?" she asked. "The one they say is Boss of the state?"

"It is," said Johnny.

"Even," said Miss James with maidenly innocence, "if he is a wicked politician, I like his looks."

It was some two weeks later that the rate bill, after a prodigious struggle, was reported out by the committee and the battle transferred to the floor of the legislature. No lobby of such size or influence or power had infested the capital within the memory of man. The so-called predatory interests meant to defeat this bill, and their every force was marshaled in the trenches.

In those days Scattergood Baines was a very busy old man. He had scant time to give to the affairs of young Johnny Bones. And at that time Johnny was seriously in need of attention.

The young man was seen more and more often in the company of Miss James, but this caused no uneasiness in the minds of his friends who were aware of it, because Miss James was not suspect. She was not known to have any affiliation with the opposition, nor did she devote the slightest attention to any other member of the legislature—as undoubtedly she would were she a beautiful lobbyist of the good old-fashioned sort. And Johnny, who was an extraordinarily intelligent boy himself, was charmed by her quickness of mind, her *savoir faire*, her unruffled efficiency, as well as by her clean-cut beauty. Nor did a suspicion ever enter his head.

So, on an evening, when she suggested that instead of dining in town he should drive with her in her little runabout to a place in the country where rather pleasing chicken dinners were served, he was delighted to go. During the drive Miss James seemed distraught.

"Don't you feel so well?" he asked.

"Splendid," she said.

"But you run so to words of one syllable," he objected.

"Even a girl has to think sometimes," she said shortly.

"She wouldn't be thinking about me, would she?" Johnny asked.

She did not reply, but bent over the wheel and drove with reckless disregard of straying chickens.

"Because," said Johnny, "I want you to think about me a lot. Maybe I'm in a bit of a hurry, because I've known you only a few weeks—but that's plenty long for me. I'm—I'm up in the air about you. Way up. So why fiddle around when I'm sure?" He paused and looked at her set face. "How about marrying me?" he asked.

She uttered a little sound through set teeth, but did not turn her head to look at him. "Don't," she said in a whisper.

"Why not?"

"Don't!" she cried. "Don't say another word or I'll turn around and go back."

"All right," said Johnny, "if this is the wrong night for it. But I'll be asking again—and again."

She made no answer, and he did not speak again for some time. Then she said harshly, "I hate life. I hate being a woman. I hate being good to look at."

"We'll change all that," he said gayly.

Again there was a pause and again it was Miss James who broke it.

"I wonder," she said, "how many people do wicked things on purpose—and how many are compelled to do them— *compelled to.*"

"I calc'late," he said, in gay imitation of the genial speech of Coldriver, "that them that does bad is bad. I jest can't see how a body could be made to do suthin' that was ag'in' his nature."

"Young men," said Miss James, "are so young!"

She turned the car sharply and drove through open gates into the yard of a farmhouse which had been enlarged and decorated, that it might devote itself to the service of the eating, and, more privately, of the drinking, public.

"Run in," said Miss James, "and order dinner while I park the car. They're pretty slow."

"So long as you're here I don't care how slow they are," said Johnny, and, leaping from the runabout, he went up on the porch and opened the door.

The place did not seem lively; the hall was gloomy, and no one was in sight. Johnny entered, took a couple of steps forward, and called. From that moment he remembered little. In the morning there was a confused recollection of a smothering cloth, of a startled struggle—and that was all. He awakened in a small room upon a rumpled bed, half clothed and with a splitting headache.

He sat upon the edge of the bed holding his head and trying to think, trying to remember what had happened, where he was, how he came to be there. Then, with sudden alarm, he thought of Miss James! What had happened to her?

He rushed to the door and shouted, jerking on his clothes as he descended the stairs. At the bottom a hard-faced woman scowled at him.

"Clear out of here," she said. "A nice mess you got us into. Clear out of here."

"Where's Miss James? Where's the girl I came with?"

"Don't know. Clear out."

Two men now appeared. They propelled Johnny to the front door, gave him a vigorous shove which sent him flying down the steps, and slammed the door behind him. He picked himself up to return and to batter and batter upon the unyielding barrier.

Bewildered and frightened, Johnny had not ceased pounding on the door when a Mr. Wrenn, unfavorably known in legislative circles, rapped for admission to Scattergood Baines's room in the hotel.

"Come in," called Scattergood, and when he saw his visitor, "Mornin', Wrenn."

"Morning, Mr. Baines. May I see you privately?"

"Buyin' or sellin'?" asked Scattergood.

"Swapping—possibly," said Wrenn.

"Clear out, boys," Scattergood said. "It's my day fur listenin' to anybuddy."

When the other occupants of the room took their hurried departure Scattergood turned to Wrenn.

"Let's see your samples," he said.

"I just dropped in," said Wrenn, "to ask you and Senator Bones to drop out of the picture."

"Want me 'n' Johnny Bones out, eh? Wa-al, now! What gives ye a notion we might, eh? Suthin' convincin'?"

"Very," said Wrenn, and he tossed an envelope on the table. "Looks like you stuck your necks out when you sent a lamb to the slaughterhouse."

"Meanin'?"

"Young Johnny," said Wrenn.

"Um. . . ." Scattergood glanced at Wrenn sidewise. "Young Johnny, eh? Wa-al, I swan to man!"

"Look 'em over," said Wrenn, gesturing to the envelope. "The camera don't lie?"

There were pictures—flashlights—of Johnny Bones in what

might well be termed compromising positions. Coatless, and in what was to all appearances a drunken stupor, he sat at a table with four men playing what obviously was a game of poker, and before Johnny was a great stack of chips—but also a considerable huddle of currency. The picture showed the denomination of one of these bills to be a thousand dollars.

"Recognize any of the men?" asked Wrenn. "Thought you might know Tompkins, there, who's a kind of a professional pay-off man. And as any politician knows, a poker game is as good a blind as there is for handing over a bribe. And Tompkins'll turn state's evidence. Those pictures won't look so good in the papers nor in court. Kind of bad all around—even for the senator himself, I'd say."

"Seems as though," said Scattergood.

"The day the House defeats the rate bill," said Wrenn, "these pictures, together with the negatives, will be placed in your hands."

"G'-by, Wrenn," said Scattergood.

Scattergood was direct and not at all oblique when Wrenn left the room. To Pliny Pickett, who always accompanied Scattergood on any extended stay in the capital, he said shortly, "Fetch young Johnny," and Pliny sped out of the room. To another man the old hardware merchant said with almost equal succinctness, "Fetch that Miss James that Johnny's been eatin' around with."

Having issued these orders, he sat back in his creaking chair and closed his eyes. Here, indeed, was a problem which required solving.

Presently the telephone rang, and a voice said in Scattergood's ear, "She won't come."

"Won't eh? Um. . . . Is she there?"

"Yes."

"Put her on."

Scattergood waited until Miss James said "Hello."

"Gen'ally when I send fur folks," said Scattergood, "they come."

"No," she answered.

"If ye hain't here," the hardware merchant said, "in five minutes, what ye come to the capital to git done won't never be done."

"You know?" she asked.

"Young woman," said Scattergood, "I learned my A B C's when your ma 'n' pa was a-layin' in their cradles."

Before the five minutes expired Miss James rapped on the door. Scattergood received her gravely.

"Got suthin' to show ye," he said, and tossed toward her the envelope Wrenn had left him. "Was ye figgerin' on jest sich a happenin'?"

Miss James looked at the photographs and uttered a little protesting cry. "Oh, he couldn't. He couldn't."

"Couldn't what?"

"Couldn't do—what these pictures show."

"They was took last night," Scattergood said. "You went a-drivin' off with him and come home alone. Tell me jest what happened. Come to think of it, ye don't need to tell me. I'll tell you. You drove him out some place and then you sent him in ahead. And as soon's he was inside you drove back to taown."

She stood silent.

"But d'ye know what happened when Johnny got inside? These pictures shows. Johnny, all unsuspectin', steps through the door, and he's grabbed and suthin's shoved over his nose 'fore he kin holler. In a picture the' hain't much difference betwixt a boy that's dead drunk and that's been put under with chloroform. And next off they fix things to look like they want 'em and take pictures. And it was you tolled Johnny out to that mess."

"No," she cried. "No."

"Ya-as," said Scattergood.

"But they told me—that all they wanted was a private talk. And all I had to do was—was get him out where they could—talk to him alone."

"And if you done that," asked Scattergood, "what?"

"They'd get a pardon for my stepbrother."

"Which," said Scattergood, "they couldn't by no manner of means do. And so you've meddled in and ruined the life of as nice a boy as I ever see. And one that thought ye was a fine gal. Wouldn't care to be in your shoes, seems as though."

"But I—I promised I'd take care of my stepbrother——"

"Calc'late it's a good idee to ruin a fine, upstandin', honest boy, jest to git a scalawag out of the penitentiary?"

"I—I never meant to do that. I—I wouldn't. Oh, I wouldn't." She paused and stood rigid, with her hands clenched.

"Hold your hosses," Scattergood said.

"He—he asked me to marry him on the way out there," she said.

"And what did ye think of that?" Scattergood asked.

"I didn't dare think."

"Um. . . . Seems like ye been done bad by. On the other hand, it seems like ye was willin' to take perty dangerous chances. And look how it come out."

"If I'd known," she said in a taut, still voice, "I'd have died before I did it."

"And Johnny's such a nice boy," said Scattergood.

"He— Oh, Mr. Baines, what can I do? I didn't know it—

I didn't realize it—but I love him. I love him. I'll do anything—anything!—to undo what I've done."

"Young woman," said Scattergood, "politics hain't no
place fur a gal like you—no matter what fetched ye into 'em.
Ye won't do nothin' but git your hands dirtier and dirtier
until it won't never come off. You got into this mess from
motives that looked decent to ye, and now, fur even better
motives, you're willin' to wade into mud ag'in. But you just
go off some place and wait and see what'll come of it."

"But Johnny—he'll think ——"

"Johnny," said Scattergood, "hain't old enough to have
anythin' to think with yit. Jest kind of leave it to me."

No sooner had she gone than Scattergood summoned
Pliny Pickett.

"Know Toopy White?" asked the old man.

"Calc'late to. Runs errands fur Seth Bradley."

Seth was a power in the northern portion of the state,
representative, himself, from Brockton, and reputed to control the votes of the ten northernmost towns.

"Hain't seen him tonight, have ye?"

"I hain't," said Pliny.

"Could ye?" asked Scattergood.

"Dunno why not," said Pliny.

"If ye was to happen to see him would ye speak up to
him?"

"Him 'n' me's friendly," said Pliny.

"Any idee what you'd say to him?"

"I'd tell him you was wantin' to see him," said Pliny.

"G'-by, Pliny."

"G'-by, Scattergood."

At ten o'clock that evening the telephone of Macy Cushman, generalissimo of the forces opposed to the rate bill,

rang insistently. Mr. Cushman was president of that great holding corporation which had most at stake in the battle.

"Toopy White speakin'," said a cracked voice over the wire.

"I remember the name," said Cushman.

"Feel like talkin'?" asked Mr. White.

"About what?"

"The northern towns has got ten votes," said Toopy.

"I'll send someone to see you," said Mr. Cushman.

"Dunno's I could talk to somebuddy else," Toopy said. "And I figger it's a sight more important than playin' checkers."

"Very well," said Cushman. "I will leave here in my car at once and drive around Capitol Park. It's a closed car."

"I'll be in the shadders by the statue on the east side in ten minutes," said Toopy.

At the designated time Cushman's car slackened speed in the darkness abreast of the statue. A shadow darted out from the shrubbery and entered the car.

"What's the big idea?" asked Cushman.

"Seth Bradley let on I should tell ye the potater crop up north was a failure this year."

"So. And Seth and the ten towns need money."

"Perty bad," said Toopy.

"Is Seth willing to talk reason?"

"Calc'late so," said Toopy. "Seth he says that when he's paid fur seeds and barrels and labor he figgers to lose nigh twenty-five hundred on his crop, and that fellers in the other towns'll each of 'em lose about the same."

"So what?" asked Cushman.

"Seth won't discuss potaters with nobody but you. If you agree he's losin' the right amount on his potaters."

"It's about what I'd judge his loss to be," said Cushman.

"Seth's brother-in-law's got a farm about two mile out. But the family is away. Seth's kind of lookin' after the house fur 'em. I hear tell he'll be there at nine o'clock tomorrer night."

"If you happen to see Seth," said Mr. Cushman, "tell him I regret his loss exceedingly, and that I know where his brother-in-law's farm is, and that my watch keeps good time."

"I'll be gittin' out here," said Toopy.

Ten votes—the ten solid northern towns! Cushman felt well satisfied. It would be enough, added to what he already had, to defeat the bill—but it would be more: It would spell the end of the power of Scattergood Baines in the state. If Baines could no longer control the northern towns, Baines was done as a political power—and that was very excellent, indeed.

Mr. Cushman was not without caution. On the following day he spied out the land and arrived at the conclusion that no more favorable spot for a secret conference and for trafficking in votes and the payment of illegal money could have been found within twenty miles. Therefore, some time before the hour of the rendezvous he drove his car past the farm, returned again in half an hour, and ran up the lane to park behind the farmhouse. The back door was open, and Cushman entered the kitchen. He walked through into the parlor, where an oil lamp burned smokily. Seth Bradley sat in a rocking-chair smoking his pipe.

"Evenin'," he said.

"Good evening," responded Mr. Cushman.

"Got it?" asked Seth.

"Twenty-five thousand—in the bag here."

"Aim to buy suthin' with it?" asked Seth.

"I'm told," Cushman said humorously, "you can deliver the votes of the ten northern towns."

"It's been said."

"At twenty-five hundred dollars a town," said Cushman. "The figger's low, but times is hard. Now, let's git this straight, Cushman. For twenty-five thousand I agree to throw my vote and nine others ag'in' the rate bill. But the' hain't no ensuin' obligations."

"Right," said Cushman.

"I b'lieve in countin'," said Seth.

"Count ahead—you'll find it right."

Seth opened the bag and covered the table with packets of currency. "Ye might hand me that other one; my hands is full," he said, and Cushman picked up and extended the remaining packet. On that instant the room was illuminated as by a flash of lightning, there was a faint boom, followed by the odor of the smoke of flash powder, and before the blindness left Cushman's eyes Scattergood Baines stepped through the dining-room door.

"Evenin', Cushman," he said amiably. "Goin' in fur politics? Wa-al, fetched some out to ye, seems as though. To be sure. Got a record of that there conversation you 'n' Seth was havin'—and got it onto one of these here phonygraph plates. And I calc'late that there picture of you handin' Seth a package of money'll come in handy. Kind of rouse the state, won't it—you fellers a-tamperin' with the legislature? Don't figger ye got a valid explanation?"

Scattergood waited, but Cushman seemed to have no words with which to express himself.

"Now, I tell ye—I don't gen'ally set out to put up no jobs on folks, but the's times when you got to set a backfire to stop a blaze. You folks done a kind of a low trick onto Johnny Bones which ye might 'a' had sense enough to know

I wouldn't tolerate. And ye wasn't awful bright thinkin' Seth could be bought up."

"Seth!" Cushman saw a ray of hope. "It was a frame-up. You can't get at me without getting at Seth."

"Calc'late I kin. Ye see, Seth he give the governor a statement lettin' on what he was a-doin' and why. So the' hain't nobuddy but you in this here mess. I'm kind of sorry I got to let ye wiggle out."

"Wiggle out?"

"To be sure. We're waitin' here till you write a letter to Wrenn tellin' him to come out with them photographs of Johnny and the negatives and all. Which we'll swap ye fur what we got. And that'll kind of wind up the clock, as ye might say. After which ye kin go back home and forget the rate bill, which is a-goin' to pass tomorrer with twenty votes to spare. Is it a deal?"

Cushman did not hesitate. "It's a deal," he said. . . .

It was eleven o'clock when Scattergood got back to his room, where young Johnny Bones was awaiting him.

"Kind of figgered you'd want the fun of destroyin' these here," he said, handing a package to the boy. "And now ye kin figger you've got a glimmerin' of what politics kin be and how careful a body's got to walk."

"I have, indeed," said Johnny glumly.

"And suthin' ye don't know yit—Miss James didn't have the slightest idee that she was. a-goin' to git ye into sech a pickle, and she's been a-worried sick ever since— She ought to be rappin' onto the door in a minute. Ye kin talk it over here if ye got a mind to. Mebby it'll kind of give ye a head start if I was to tell ye she let on she was in love with ye; and if I let on that your pa 'n' me's looked her up thorough and is fur it."

Light knuckles rapped on the door, and Scattergood

opened it. "Looks like the's a lady lobbyist to see ye, Johnny," he said. "And I'll be goin'. Dunno how ye kin fail to git on in this state, young feller, with what you got added to what this young woman's got. Um. . . ."

He paused in the door.

"G'-by, folks," he said.

"Good night, Mr. Baines," said Miss James.

"He'll be out on parole tomorrer, that brother of yourn," said Scattergood. "What amazes me is how the old tricks work. A body don't have to think. All he's got to do is reach into the bag. The' hain't been nothin' new invented in a hundred years—and there don't need to be for another thousand. No, siree. Ye don't have to have brains in politics—all ye need is to know the old standard contrivances."

He paused and looked at them, but they were paying no attention to him.

"Um. . . ." He puffed out his cheeks. "And nothin' new's been diskivered about love since the Garden of Eden."

V

Patron of Arts

SCATTERGOOD BAINES, as almost everybody knows, was the elder statesman of Coldriver. Aging now, but sturdy and rather more than ordinarily interested in the common affairs of men, he was accustomed to sit on the piazza of his hardware store and meddle with the lives of his fellow townsmen. It would be an understatement to say he was the most powerful political figure in his state—and if he seemed to be only a fat hardware man it was because he wished it so, for Scattergood's possessions were multifarious. He had a finger in everything. Even according to urban standards he was a wealthy man.

Just now he was returning from an extended trip, the first he and his wife, Mandy, had taken in many a year. The trip had been pleasant and they had enjoyed it, but Scattergood was more than glad to know that their train was nearing Coldriver and he would soon be able to go on with his sitting and meddling.

Pliny Pickett went about the business of collecting tickets from the passengers on the train that day in such an engrossed manner that Scattergood Baines knew he had something on his mind. He was ostentatiously efficient and avoided Scattergood's eye, so that the old hardware merchant nudged Mandy, his wife.

74

"Notice Pliny?" he asked.

"Not special."

"Um. . . . Dunno's I ever see him so all-fired official. Kind of noble, hain't it?"

Mandy sniffed and looked out of the window.

Pliny was moving back through the train. His official duties were done and he had no excuse for avoiding Scattergood further. But he came slowly, reluctantly, with the leaden feet of one who bears evil tidings.

"How be ye, Pliny?" asked Scattergood. "How be ye?"

"Hain't complainin'—much," said Pliny. "How be ye?"

"Who done what, and why?" asked Scattergood directly.

"Um. . . . When ye got suthin' onto your mind, Pliny, best thing's to come to the p'int."

"I kind of hate to tell ye, Scattergood."

"F'r goodness sake," exclaimed Mandy testily, "don't be keepin' a body on tenterhooks."

"Wa-al," said Pliny, "ye know Luther Boody?"

"Calc'late to," said Scattergood, "seein's I was a-settin' on the front stoop when he was bein' born."

"Ye know he was a-lookin' after the hardware store while ye was gallivantin', don't ye?"

"Hired him to do it, didn't I? Eh? Been a-payin' his wages?"

"Seems as though," said Pliny, and then came to a dead halt.

"He hain't dead?" Mandy asked, growing very excited by this time.

"Wuss," said Pliny.

"Sakes alive!" Mandy exclaimed.

"Ye know travelin' men?" asked Pliny. "Them fellers 't come sellin' things."

"Heard 'em mentioned. Calc'late I even seen one once.

They ketched him down near Higgins Bridge and had him chained in the park— What about travelin' men?"

"The' was one come to Coldriver," Pliny said reluctantly.

"He run off with Luther's wife," guessed Mandy.

"He never," said Pliny. "Wuss."

"I swan to man!" said Scattergood. "Dunno's I got any more guesses."

"He wa'n't travelin' fur hardware—not exactly."

"What fur, then?"

"Idols," said Pliny. "Heathen idols and sich."

"Doggone!" said Scattergood.

"Yessir—idols and statues and sich. Come from Boston. The' was nekkid wimmin and sheep and fellers dancin' with goat's laigs, and fat babies, and fellers with wings onto their heels, and the dangdest, all-firedest lot of doodads and contraptions. That's what he was a-travelin' fur."

"Dunno how that pertains to me," said Scattergood.

"You'll find out," said Pliny.

"I been a-tryin' to," said Scattergood patiently.

Pliny braced himself, drew a long breath, swallowed, and then announced, "Luther bought 'em. Honest Injun. A gross of 'em. Twelve dozen. A hundred and forty-four. And all of 'em along about two foot high."

"Fur the store?" asked Scattergood. "Fur my hardware store?"

"Seems as though," said Pliny. "And they was delivered. And Luther's got 'em distributed around. Used up the hull top shelf. The's a line of 'em from the front of the store to the left, and it runs right slap around to the front of the store on the right. A hundred and forty-four of them leapin' and prancin' heathen idols. And sich a sight was never seen in Coldriver."

"Um . . ." said Scattergood.

"The's mothers in taown won't even let their daughters walk past," said Pliny.

"And," said Scattergood, "the's others that comes in and buys two cents' wuth of putty four times a day. Wa-al, seems like Luther kind of distinguished himself, eh?"

"They're made out of plaster Paris," said Pliny.

"Dew tell," said Scattergood.

"Luther says he got 'em cheaper by buyin' a gross."

"Anyhow," said Scattergood, "they hain't hand-painted paintin's."

"I warrant," said Mandy, "the Congo preacher's up in arms."

"So's the M.E.," said Pliny, "and the Baptist. Adventists 'n' Christian Science hain't quite made up their minds yit."

"It'll teach ye to go gallivantin'," said Mandy to Scattergood.

When they alighted from the train in Coldriver, Scattergood turned over his baggage and checks and climbed into a jitney with Mandy, who was eager to get home to see if there had been any leaks. At the bridge he got out to walk the few steps to investigate the enormity of the calamity that had befallen his business, while Mandy went on to their home on the edge of the village.

Luther Boody was trying to make himself invisible at the back of the store when his employer came in, but Scattergood did not look for the young man. Instead of that he stood and let his eyes follow the top shelf as it meandered around the room—the top shelf cumbered with a hundred and forty-four plaster-of-Paris replicas of classic statues.

"Huh . . ." observed Scattergood after a lengthy examination. "Huh . . ."

He lowered his eyes, so that they fell upon Luther Boody,

who was trying to look as if he were not there; indeed, he was trying to look as if he never had been there.

"How be ye, Luther?" asked Scattergood.

"No complaints, seems as though."

"Fort'nate," observed Scattergood. "Them that has no complaints is members of the lucky minority. How's business, Luther?"

"Slack. All-fired slack."

"Dew tell. How's your ma?"

"No complaints."

"Onusual family—you Boodys," said Scattergood. "Kind of endowed by your Creator, hain't ye?"

"Mr. Baines—" Luther commenced apprehensively, but his employer interrupted him.

"Proba'ly," said Scattergood, "it's jest because ye got happy natures. Huh. . . . Mebbe ye don't notice troubles like other folks. It could be that."

"Mr. Baines, I got to help Pa on the farm. He's been needin' me."

"Luther," said Scattergood, "I wouldn't stand in the way of your betterin' yourself, not fur a plugged nickel."

Luther waved a reluctant hand at the array of statues. "About them ——"

"Guess I'll fetch my chair out onto the front stoop," Scattergood said. "G'-by, Luther."

"Don't ye want to know ——"

"G'-by, Luther."

"G'-by Mr. Baines," Luther said, and he put on his coat and went out into the teeming life of Coldriver, abandoning with sweet relief his temporary employment as manager of a hardware store. But something other than relief accompanied his rapid steps—and this something else was bewilderment.

"He never," said Luther to his mother, "so much as mentioned them there statues. He never. He jest stood and talked about which and tother, and never so much as alluded. It beats me."

Scattergood settled back in his specially reinforced chair, with his face to the street, and considered the catastrophe that had darkened his life. It is true the hardware store was but a minute fraction of his business interests; it is a fact that it was an insignificant trifle of his very considerable fortune. But it is also true that it was the apple of his eye and that he would rather make a dime of profit *in* his store than a thousand dollars *out* of it. He could view with equanimity a loss in timber lands, or a deficit in a mill, or the shrinkage of an investment in bonds, but anything that adversely touched his hardware store rankled in the very depths of his soul.

Here he was, saddled with a hundred and forty-four statues which would mean a financial loss; but in addition to that his store had been made ridiculous. Not only was it a laughingstock, but it was a scandal, as he was presently to learn from Elder Hooper and Deacon Pettibone.

These pillars of the church and guardians of public morals bore down upon him as soon as they became aware of his return. Grimly they advanced down the street, the deacon hobbling on his peg leg and the elder clicking his cane. They stopped at the lower step, and their faces were implacable.

"How be ye, Deacon? How be ye, Elder? Eh?"

"This here hain't no time for shilly-shallyin', Scattergood Baines," the deacon said sternly. "The elder 'n' me come to pertest."

"What's hinderin' ye?" asked Scattergood.

"Pollutin' morals and debauchin' youth," said the elder.

"Who? Me? Jest what pollutin' and debauchin' have I been up to?"

"Them statues," said the elder.

"Didn't buy 'em," said Scattergood.

"Ye tolerate 'em," said the deacon.

"Dum nigh all of 'em heathen idols," said the elder, "and what ain't is nekkid wimmin."

"How d'ye know? Eh? How come ye to be familiar with 'em?"

"We went in and seen," said the deacon.

"We was aghast," said the elder.

"Ye owe me suthin' fur that, seems as though. I jest looked them sculpturin's over myself. I admit I was suthin', but aghast don't describe my feelin's. A hunderd and forty-four ——"

The elder snorted. "Be ye a-goin' to demolish 'em?" he demanded.

"Hain't reached a mature conclusion yit."

"Church folks'll boycut your store so long's them lewd idols is to be seen inside."

"They don't boycut the Library because the's a statue of a soldier leanin' onto a gun in front of it."

"He's got his pants on," said the elder.

"We'll give ye twenty-four hours to consider," said the deacon. "Then we aim to take action."

"Um. . . . Nothin' hasty about ye, is the'? Now, seems to me, some of them statues was kind of perty."

"If they be," said the deacon, "it's a evil beauty."

"Kind of hard fur me," said Scattergood, "to see how beauty kin be evil. If it's evil it hain't perty; and, on the other hand, if it's beautiful it jest can't be evil. G'-by, Deacon. G'-by, Elder."

When they were gone he slid down in his chair com-

fortably and closed his eyes. Automatically, his hand slid
down to his shoe and unlaced it. Presently his toes were
exposed to the balmy air, and he wriggled them rhyth-
mically. After a time he opened his eyes, replaced his shoe,
and sat erect in his protesting chair.

"Mebbe I could give 'em away," he said to himself.
"Mebbe I could use 'em fur premiums." But before he could
follow this line of speculation a young woman, hardly more
than a girl, came across the bridge and was passing with
downcast eyes when Scattergood spoke to her.

"How be ye, Isabel?" he asked.

"How do you do, Mr. Baines. When did you come home?"

"Hain't hardly got here yit. Hain't married yit, be ye?"

"How could I get married, or ever hope to, when everybody's against him so, and laughs at him and calls him no
good?"

"Oh, turned out to be another of them gals that falls in
love with the wrong feller, eh? What wrong feller did you
pick out?"

"Seneca Craw," she said simply, as if that explained
everything.

"Um . . . Seneca, eh? What ails him? Morals bad?"

"No."

"Got his health?"

"Oh, yes. He's very healthy."

"Wa-al, what does ail him, Isabel?"

"He wants," said the girl, "to be an artist."

"Dew tell. Seems as though I remember him always
gallivantin' around drawin' things onto a piece of paper."

"Everybody says he's shiftless and no good. They say he
won't ever amount to anything. Mother and Father for-
bade me to have anything to do with him."

"What d'ye have to do to git to be an artist? Dunno much

about them professions 'n' callin's, savin' 'n' exceptin' I hear tell all artists starve to death in attics."

"You have to study and study," said Isabel. "You have to go to Paris."

"I see a lot of pictures one place and another," said Scattergood. "Looks like some artists don't starve. Mebbe it's jest them that hain't good artists that starves, like the's poor hardware merchants that goes busted."

"People who know have seen his work, and—and they say he has great promise. If only he could get a chance. But it don't seem right everybody should want to keep us apart. If—if Seneca's going to starve I—I would—would like to help him do it."

"Starvin' sounds better 'n it tastes," said Scattergood.

"For just a few thousand dollars he could go to Paris and study. And I could go with him. And his father and my father could give it to us, but they won't. His father offered to buy him a farm."

"But Seneca he didn't want that?"

"No."

"Different people is hardly ever the same," said Scattergood. "Um. . . . Calc'late to see Seneca?"

"Nobody can stop me from seeing or from loving Seneca."

"I bet ye think you're the fust girl ever said them words," said Scattergood. "Um. . . . If ye was to happen to see Seneca, would ye mention me?"

"Why—possibly."

"What would ye say? Eh? About me?"

"I've no idea."

"You wouldn't jest happen to mention, would ye, that it wouldn't be sich a bad idee if he was to stop past?"

"I might, Mr. Baines."

"It could be today," said Scattergood. "G'-by."

It was some two hours later when young Seneca Craw approached the hardware store and stood before Scattergood. "How be ye?" Scattergood asked. "What kin I do fur ye?"

"I'm Seneca Craw. Isabel said you wanted to see me."

"Wa-al, you're the nearest I kin git to expert opinion around here. I got some statues. Figger ye could look at 'em 'thout gettin' all corrupted?"

"Where are they, Mr. Baines?"

"Clutterin' up the top shelf. Go inside 'n' look at 'em."

In half an hour the young man reappeared. "I know almost all those statues," he said. "Of course I haven't seen them, but I've seen pictures of them. I know them by name —and—well just to look at those replicas in plaster-of-Paris makes you feel kind of happy. I—wouldn't it be wonderful to see the real ones?"

"I dunno," said Scattergood. "D'ye figger they're wicked?"

"They're beautiful," said Seneca. "Wouldn't you like to make beautiful things, Mr. Baines?"

"Makin' money's more in my line, seems as though. Huh. What d'ye want to git to be an artist fur?"

This was opening the floodgates. For half an hour Seneca talked. As a boy sometimes will, when caught unawares by a sympathetic elder, he laid bare his soul. Scattergood saw it was a nice soul. Somehow Seneca was able to make him understand why it was that a human being would rather paint pictures, or carve statues, or make music, than buy and sell or delve and dig.

"Huh," he grunted, at the end. "So them statues hain't just so much rubbage."

"I suppose they're poor imitations and cheap—but—but it meant more to me just to stand and look at them and imagine—imagine the beauty of the real statues—than anything I almost ever did."

"And ye hain't polluted, nor nothin' like that?"

"Only a person with a mind like a sewer," said Seneca hotly, "could think anything but fine thoughts as he looked at those figures."

"I betcha that there observation would tickle the elder nigh to death," Scattergood said. "G'-by, Seneca."

It was perhaps four o'clock when he surveyed the village again. Before Sam Kettleman's store stood a very ornate and splendid motorcar, with chauffeur in livery. Scattergood reared to his feet and ambled across the road. As he reached the other walk a majestic figure emerged from the store.

"How be ye, Mrs. Minturn?" asked Scattergood. "Up kind of early in the season, hain't ye?"

"I," said Mrs. Minturn grandly, "am overseeing some alterations."

"Goin' to have that there classic dancin' in the dew this summer?"

Mrs. Minturn frowned. "The people were not educated up to it," she said.

"Um. . . . Kind of sad to contemplate—how folks hain't eddicated up to things. Did ye ever stop to think, Mrs. Minturn, what a chance't the' was fur a body with public spirit to kind of uplift the folks?"

"Ah," said Mrs. Minturn.

"Take Coldriver. Who in Coldriver ever seen a paintin'? Mrs. Minturn, how is folks that never seen art goin' to be able to set and think about it, come winter?"

"How indeed?"

"Saddenin'," said Scattergood lugubriously. "I git all melancholy-like when I figger how much beauty 'n' art the' is scattered around the world, and that none of it ever gits to Coldriver. Ma'am, you're perty fond of Coldriver, hain't ye?"

"Exceedingly," said Mrs. Minturn.

"The's folks in the world don't dast dodge their respon-sibilities," said Scattergood. "The's folks born to lead. Yes'm. Sich folks has got to do their duty."

"Sometimes," said Mrs. Minturn, "I have felt myself to be that sort of person."

"Ma'am, I don't marvel at it," said Scattergood. "Wa'al, g'-by, Mrs. Minturn. Nice to see ye. G'-by."

"You have given me food for thought," said the majestic lady.

Scattergood walked along until he came to the stairs which mounted to Johnny Bones's law office. Though Scat-tergood had elevated Johnny to the position of United States Senator, that youngish man still maintained his old office over the post office. Johnny was behind his desk.

"Afternoon, Johnny," said Scattergood.

"Welcome home. I was just coming over."

"Um. . . . Seen a perty ornamental automobeel down-stairs."

"That would be Mrs. Minturn. I wonder what caper she'll cut up this summer. Classic dancing, yogis, cockeyed music?"

"Huh. . . . A woman given to servin' tea, hain't she?"

"Every day at five."

"Hain't goin' out to Minturn's to git a cup of tea, be ye?"

"I could," said Johnny.

"Senators is oracles," observed Scattergood.

"I agree, enthusiastically."

"If a senator was to happen to mention to a woman like Mrs. Minturn that Coldriver's cryin' need was Art—"

"Listen, Scattergood; what are you up to?"

"Jest upliftin'. Aimin' to shine light in dark places. It's

perty murky in the neighborhood of the elder 'n' the deacon."

Johnny pushed back his chair. "By the way," he said with a guileless expression, "you'll have to excuse me. I've got to go out and drink tea with Mrs. Minturn."

"Dew tell!" exclaimed Scattergood. "G'-by, Johnny."

Evidently Johnny Bones performed his errand efficiently, because in the next issue of the Coldriver paper appeared a notice that, under the auspices of Mrs. Minturn, there would be a lecture on Art in the Town Hall on Wednesday evening . . . no admission. It also stated that this was but the first of a series of instructive talks to be given weekly.

The village turned out for the event; first, because it was free; second, because there was nothing else to do. It was an illustrated talk by a man able to popularize his subject, and by the following noon a number of Coldriver ladies discovered an avid interest in the finer things of life.

It had been some time since Coldriver ladies had had anything to go into mild frenzy about. Now the Thursday Afternoon Club took up Art, and the Congo Ladies' Aid considered redecorating the Sunday-school room.

As for Scattergood, in unnoticeable ways he fanned the flame of culture. Nor did he neglect business altogether, for again he approached Johnny Bones.

"Johnny," he asked, "got twenty-five dollars?"

"Possibly."

"Um. . . . Ever figger to make a loan to Seneca Craw?"

"He never asked me."

"Mebbe," suggested Scattergood, "he dunno he wants to borrow."

"So," asked Johnny, "what?"

"Winters estate owns the proppity next the hotel."

"So I believe."

"Eatin' its head off with taxes 'n' insurance."

"It is."

"Cost a sight of money when Ol' Man Winters got that idee of hisn. Estate 'ud sell fur a song."

"Who'd sing it?"

"Seneca might. I dunno. Seems as though. Mebbe they'd like to git it off their hands fur three-four thousand. Wuth ten-fifteen—if it turned out to be wuth anythin'."

"Why twenty-five dollars, though?"

"If ye was a mind, ye might git an option onto it in Seneca's name."

"I hear," said Johnny, "that you've sort of branched out down at the store. Elder and deacon stopped in. I gathered they wanted me to throw the might of the government against you and some immoral statuary you have in stock."

"A hundred and forty-four of 'em," said Scattergood lugubriously. "I'm. . . . Attend Mrs. Minturn's lecture?"

"I did."

"So did several," said Scattergood. "G'-by, Johnny." . . .

The deacon and the elder were industrious. They were carrying with them the more ancient members of their respective churches, and decrepit hornets buzzed around Scattergood's ears. But, simultaneously, Mrs. Minturn fought valiantly her campaign to bring Art to Coldriver. The town divided.

Mrs. Minturn, a very stubborn and majestic lady, got the idea that the deacon and the elder were running a war against Art itself. It was no great step from this for her to come to the belief that the whole thing was gotten up in opposition to her and to her plans. Consequently she seethed.

On a Monday afternoon Scattergood got into his buggy and drove westward out of town. He jogged along until he reached the Minturn place. Mrs. Minturn sat in lonely majesty upon the shady porch.

"How's them alterations a-comin'?"

"Satisfactorily."

"Glad to hear it. Hain't met with no opposition?"

"Opposition to what?"

"Alterin' your house. Coldriver kind of objects to changes 'n' innovations."

"I should like to see Coldriver object to anything I choose to do."

"Yeah. Yes'm. I hear the deacon and them don't take so awfully kindly to prettyin' up the taown. The elder's special vindictive. Word came to me he's gittin' the selectmen to call a taown meetin'.'"

"I," said Mrs. Minturn, "am moved by motives they fail to understand. I am trying to make better and brighter the lives of these people. With what result?" She paused oratorically. "Abuse, Mr. Baines. Abuse!"

"Don't seem jest right to me. Um. . . . Jest the same, it looks to me like ye was inculcatin' some. The younger folks seems kind of eager to git beauty and sich-like."

"There are hopeful signs."

"Folks," said Scattergood, "is like a grass lawn. Ye kin sow your grass seed and it'll come up spindlin'. But come summer and it'll yellow up and kind of die on you. Yes'm. Ye got to keep at it with water 'n' lawn mowers and sich."

"I see what you mean. Art must be kept before their eyes. They must be constantly reminded. It must be a continuing effort."

"Yes'm. I been a-wonderin' what keeps Art alive in big cities."

"It is," said Mrs. Minturn, "in large part the possession

of art treasures, of great paintings and sculptures. So that people may always go to see them."

"Coldriver couldn't git none of this great art," said Scattergood. "But I tell ye what—it could git better art 'n what they got at Higgins Bridge or any other taown around."

"Mr. Baines, that is a splendid idea. Imagine making Coldriver the art center of the region!"

"Yes'm, but it can't be done. Even if we got us some art, we hain't got no place to put it."

"No place to put it! Ah. Very true. . . . Ah. The Minturn Museum of Fine Arts. . . . Ah."

"The's a lot of fambly pride here," said Scattergood. "Yes'm. Folks takes pride in their lineage. If we had a place to put it, we could kind of git some second-class art and scratch this here fambly pride. Paintin's and statues—and hist'ry, like ye might say."

"I see your point."

"If, say, every family that has lived in Coldriver more 'n a hunderd years was to hand up a crayon picture or a daguerreotype of a couple of prom'nent ancestors, they'd be fur it."

"Mr. Baines, you have given me a splendid idea—and—ah—a noble opportunity. I—ah—you being a practical man and one acquainted with local matters, I should like to consult you regarding certain details."

For more than an hour Mrs. Minturn and Scattergood Baines remained in conference.

After that Scattergood did errands. He ambled about Coldriver, first interviewing Pliny Pickett.

"Goin' to be a taown meetin', hain't the'? Eh? Consid'able of a taown meetin'."

"I hear talk."

"It's apt to take a turn folks mebbe don't anticipate," said

Scattergood. "Um. Goin' to move around a good deal, Pliny?"

"Aim to."

"The's right folks and wrong folks, but they all have a vote in meetin'. It wouldn't occur to ye, Pliny, to kind of see to it that them that can be depended on to vote like they ought to was present?"

"I git the idee," said Pliny.

"If ye figger ye need two," Scattergood said, "git four. It don't make no difference if ye lick the other feller wuss 'n what ye need to. The main idee's to keep him from lickin' you at all."

When Scattergood returned to his store, news was brought to him that the Village Fathers had called a town meeting for Friday night, the purpose of which was to take up the matter of public morals. There was even talk of reviving the Committee of Public Safety. Scattergood found himself in an exceedingly delicate position, but, for all that, his broad face wore an expression of blandness. He sat and regarded a hostile town with unjaundiced eye.

On the great night the town was crowded. Freemen from the surrounding country embraced in the limits of the Town of Coldriver, drove into the village and gathered on corners.

Johnny Bones stopped at the hardware store.

"Set and buttoned up?" asked Scattergood.

"Ready," said Johnny, and together they walked across to the Town Hall, which was rapidly filling. At eight o'clock the first selectman called the meeting to order. Instantly Elder Hooper got on his feet and launched into a philippic. No sooner had his voice died down than the deacon embarked upon his attack. Scattergood was aware of unfriendly looks. Hostility was in the air. But, as the deacon sank into his seat, mopping his brow, Mrs. Minturn arose.

She was not contented merely to rise, she walked to the platform.

She was a firm woman and she spoke with authority. "You have been," she said, "listening to a lot of twaddle." The meeting gasped. "It is high time," she said, "that such a benighted influence was scotched. Men such as those who have just spoken are a menace to the life of any community."

After that, in a truly Minturnly manner, she paid her respects to deacon and elder. Then she arrived at her topic, and told them about Art. And, building to her climax, she said, "What this village needs, what it must have, what I, in short, shall provide for it, is something which shall be a constant reminder of local pride."

She paused. "Tonight," she went on, "I am presenting to this village a property—land ,and building—which shall be used as a museum of fine arts and as a memorial to the sturdy ancestors of this generation. It is a free gift. As to the memorial: Any family which has resided here continuously for upwards of a hundred years may hang in the museum portraits of their ancestors. An historic treasure."

There was silence while the town digested this.

"We cannot have great original paintings and statues," she said, "but we shall have the next best thing. I shall provide them, in order that your citizens and your children and their children may see and appreciate the great art of the ages. Replicas . . ." Again she paused.

"One of your citizens has assisted. Tonight he has been held up to scorn and obloquy—and why? Because he has formed a collection of statues—replicas, it is true, but replicas of nearly a hundred and fifty of the greatest pieces of sculpture in the world. . . . I speak of Scattergood Baines."

The silence was tense. "Not one piece in his collection but is a masterpiece. With characteristic self-sacrifice, he has sold them to me, and I include them in my gift to you. . . . And with this gift I salute your fellow townsman, Scattergood Baines, Patron of the Arts."

"Gosh!" exclaimed Pliny Pickett aloud.

"The museum shall be housed in the structure known locally as Winters' Folly. I have purchased it. I have deeded it to Coldriver. In addition, I have provided a fund for the purchase of art and for the perpetual maintenance of the museum and memorial. The Minturn Memorial and Museum of Fine Arts. . . . I thank you."

She sat down amid tumult. Johnny Bones rose and moved the acceptance of the munificent gift. The freemen, a bit subdued, voted their acceptance. The meeting adjourned, and the first selectman approached Scattergood.

"So them things was Art?" he asked. "Huh, I might 'a' knowed they was suthin'."

Scattergood, accompanied by Johnny, walked across the street.

"Now," Johnny said, "let me in on all this. What was the ——?"

"Wa-al," said Scattergood, "you couldn't expect me to take a loss on all them statues, could ye?"

"Just how much did they cost?"

"The bill I paid come to seventy-six dollars 'n' forty-three cents."

"And how much profit did you make?"

"Twenty-seven cents apiece," said Scattergood with great satisfaction. "Makin' a grand total of thirty-eight dollars 'n' eighty-eight cents."

"You've put in three weeks' work. You've almost torn this

town apart. You've wangled Mrs. Minturn into spending thousands of dollars—and for what? Less than forty dollars."

"Ye don't git the p'int," said Scattergood. "That was the money I wanted to make. It was a kind of a problem I had to solve. I druther have that thirty-eight dollars, got like it was, 'n I would to have thirty-eight thousand I didn't *have* to git."

"Maybe I understand. But what about Seneca Craw?"

"Oh, him! Seneca he wants to be a artist. Mebbe he is one. He wants to git married to Isabel. Might be a good idee. Artists got to study in Paris. Wa-al, I kind of figgered if Mrs. Minturn wanted to do suthin' fur Art, mebbe Seneca was as good as givin' a museum. So I kind of let her pay about five thousand dollars so as Seneca 'n' his gal could marry and go to France fur a couple of years. Yeah. Difference between Seneca's option price 'n' what she paid fur the Winters proppity."

"You make forty dollars. Seneca makes five thousand!"

" 'N' me, through Mrs. Minturn, 'll git credit in heaven for perducin' another Michelangelo. Me, I got what I want. Seneca gits what he wants. Mrs. Minturn gits what she wants."

He paused and smiled blandly.

"I kind of like a deal where everybuddy comes out ahead."

VI

Scattergood Breaks into Society

"MANDY," said Scattergood, flopping an envelope in his wife's general direction, "it looks like you got to buy you one of them there lipsticks."

"Shet up and wash fur supper," said Mandy.

"And, more 'n likely, we'll be seein' you paradin' around in one of them there dresses that commences at the floor and ends just no'th of the stummick."

"What's gittin' into ye, ye old coot?" Mandy asked. "Lost what senses ye ever had?"

"We been took up," said Scattergood. "We been took up social by society. Yes'm. I'm a-lookin' forrud to seein' our pictures in the Bostin papers: Mr. and Mrs. Scattergood Baines up and entertains at a hoss-shoe pitchin' party in their palatial summer residence adjoinin' the environs and suburbs of Coldriver."

"I've kind of looked ahead," said Mandy, "to you losin' your mind. Anyhow, it'll be a kind of a change."

"See this here envelope? Know what 'tis? Huh?"

"Proba'ly," said Mandy ironically, "I'll find out along about the time the news is stale."

"It's an invitation," said Scattergood.

"To what?"

"To a week end," said Scattergood. "Out on the Handle

94

amongst the swell summer folks. A week end," he explained, "is a kind of a party that starts in of a Friday or Sattidy, and goes on continuous without pausin' or haltin' till Monday mornin'."

"In the fust place," said Mandy, "I calc'late you're lyin'. In the second place, what 'ud them folks invite us fur? And in the third place, I wouldn't go if they did."

"It's the Carboys. And we're asked to come the end of this here actual and i-dentical week. Guess they're havin' others, too. Dunno's I jest exactly penetrate into the underlyin' idea behind it, neither."

"We hain't a-goin'," said Mandy.

"Mebbe not," said Scattergood, "but we kin reason it over —can't we?—and kind of seek to peer into the darkness of it. Off and on I've had occasion to kind of take notice that nobody does nothin' onusual and startlin' without havin' a purpose."

"Most likely they want to git ye to git their taxes lowered," said Mandy.

"That hain't important enough, seems as though," said Scattergood. "Fur a favor like that Carboy'd figger orderin' an icebox or a couple kitchen stoves to the hardware store 'ud about be the ticket. You kin gen'ally read how big a favor a feller's goin' to ask ye by the nature of what it is he does fur you before he gits down to askin'. As soon as a body does suthin' for me gratuitous I start figgerin' what it's a-goin' to cost me."

"We hain't a-goin'," Mandy said.

"The other guests," said Scattergood, "is a-goin' to be the Chessmans 'n' them Pullingers 'n' Miss Cate 'n' Pete Gowan. Been talk about the Pullinger woman."

"Her 'n' Peter Gowan was seen —"

"'Tain't good society to go gossipin' about your feller

week-end guests," said Scattergood. "Not unless ye kin remember suthin' p'tic'larly disgraceful. Huh. . . . Now,
what in tunket does Carboy want you 'n' me lurkin' around
his premises fur?"

"You won't never know," Mandy said, "because we hain't
a-goin' to lurk."

"My curiosity's gittin' a mite the best of me," Scattergood said. "Um. . . . It could be suthin' to do with utility
legislation up to the Capitol. It could be."

Scattergood washed up for supper and sat down at the
table. Mandy bustled in from the kitchen and plumped
down into the chair opposite.

"We've gotten to see a sight of life since we was married,"
Scattergood observed. "Um. . . . I call to mind the day I
walked into taown. Yes'm. I recall the very feelin' of the
dust oozin' through my bare toes. Wa-al, we hain't done
bad fur folks abidin' in this here part of the country. We
got us a good hardware store."

Mandy sniffed. Scattergood's pretense that his hardware
store was his sole and only important business annoyed her.
It annoyed her that he regarded everything else as sec-
ondary to it—his railroad, his reaches of timber, his bank—
his many and diverse interests. To him these were but
avocations, and the fact that he was, to all intents and
purposes, the political ruler of his state was a sort of hobby
indulged in for pleasure.

"It's a kind of a dare," Scattergood said.

"What is?"

"The way this here Carboy figgers he's got some kind
of a scheme to outsmart me. It's like settin' a trap in the
woods 'n' leavin' your tobacco pipe alongside so as the
animal'll be sure to smell it."

"Hain't it possible he wants ye to smell it?" asked Mandy.

"Sometimes," said Scattergood, "it almost seems to me like mebbe you're smarter 'n you be other times. H'm. Pullingers 'n' Chessmans. Them couples could be in suthin', but where 'n tunket do them two young folks come in?"

"They could," said Mandy, "be jest decorations to make it look pertier."

"I knowed you couldn't resist goin'," said Scattergood.

"I can't abide fancy cookin'," said Mandy. "And I been tellin' ye fur years you ought to git ye one of them full-dress suits if you're set on gallivantin'."

Scattergood grunted. "Pigs is constructed to give pork and wear curly tails. A hog 'ud look kind of foolish if it come out of the pen some mornin' wearin' wool like a sheep. Huh. . . . Next you'll be urgin' me to git a set of these here pyjammies to sleep in."

The result of these discussions was that at the end of the week Scattergood and Mandy drove out to the Handle, some five dusty miles, in a ramshackle car borrowed for the event. It took them through beautiful mountain country to the estate of the Carboys on a ridge overlooking a stretch of forest and hill. It was a huge, rambling house from whose face a broad lawn sloped down to the cliff and the lake, a gentleman's country home designed for leisure.

The car drew up before the main entrance, and Scattergood and Mandy mounted the steps. Mr. Carboy appeared in the door and advanced with extended hand.

"Mighty fine of you to come up here, Mr. Baines. Mrs. Carboy has been looking forward to meeting Mrs. Baines. Hope the drive was not uncomfortable."

"I feel," said Mandy, "as if I'd et a pound of grit." She smiled comfortably at Mrs. Carboy, who had come out to stand by her husband's side and welcome the arrivals. With the self-possession of the perfect hostess she concealed the fact that Mandy's jet bonnet had taken her between wind and water.

"You'll be wanting to bathe and change," she said. "I'll have you shown to your rooms. Then if you'll come down I think the other guests will have appeared."

"I dunno what I'd change to," Scattergood said amiably, "but I wouldn't mind gittin' my shoes off fur a couple of minutes."

Mandy puffed as she climbed the stairs, and when the bedroom door closed behind them she sank into a chair and snapped at her husband. "I wisht to goodness we hadn't come," she said. "I got a feelin' the's suthin' wrong in this house. I kin kind of smell it. A cold chill run up and down my spine."

"Shucks," said her husband.

"Suthin's a-goin' to happen," she insisted.

"Suthin' allus does happen," he said. "That's what makes life wuth observin'."

He sat down in a large chair and removed his shoes and his socks. He leaned back, closed his eyes, and almost instantly was snoring placidly. After a time Mandy shook him.

"It's goin' on half past six," she said. "We'll be late fur supper."

Docilely he put on his footgear and looked approvingly at her. She was wearing her black silk and to his way of thinking she presented a pretty dazzling appearance.

"Mandy," he said, "I dunno's you'd take a prize fur beauty, but you're kind of satisfyin' to the eye. The's some substance to ye."

Presently they ambled down the stairs and, hearing voices and laughter, found their hosts and the other guests on the veranda, where cocktails were being served. They were presented to Mr. and Mrs. Chessman, a tall, thin, saturnine man and a blond, vivacious young woman; to Mr. Pullinger, chubby and inane; to Miss Cate, dark and piquant and very lovely indeed; and to Mr. Gowan, who was a large young man with nice eyes and an extraordinarily homely but likable face. These elegant personages had been warned, and received the Baineses courteously if curiously.

"Cocktail, Mrs. Baines?" asked her host.

"Hain't never tetched licker yit," said Mandy uncompromisingly.

"Now, take me," said Scattergood. "When I was young I couldn't afford it, and when I got so as I could afford it—I couldn't afford it."

It was a curious thing, but this fat old man in wrinkled, ill-fitting clothes dominated the group from that instant— dominated that group, all in evening dress, the women lovely in gowns from correct shops. With one sentence, dryly spoken, he had ceased to be a figure of fun, had impressed himself upon them, had even charmed them. He had no manners, but he had a dignity and a personality which did quite as well. Every individual there felt drawn toward him, and what restraint there had been evaporated before his keen, shining old eyes and his understanding grin. Even his hostess heaved a sigh of relief.

"Where's your wife, Pullinger?" asked Carboy.

"She chased me out. I was the first one down," said Mr. Pullinger. "She's always chasing me out." He said this rather sulkily.

"I'll send a maid up to see if she needs anything," said Mrs. Carboy.

The clatter of light talk continued until it was stilled

suddenly by the voice of a hysterical maid calling, "Mr. Carboy, Mr. Carboy!"

She appeared in the door, ashen, terrified, grasping the doorjamb for support.

Everyone was on his feet. Carboy gripped the maid's shoulder. "What is it, Edna? What's the matter?"

"Mrs. Pullinger—she—she's dead!" cried the girl shrilly.

There was an instant of awful silence; then, with a common motion, they all moved toward the stairs, jostling each other, on the verge of hysteria.

"I knew it," said Mandy.

At the door of Mrs. Pullinger's room they halted—it was Scattergood's voice that halted them.

"I wouldn't go a-tramplin' in if I was everybody," he said. "S'posin' jest Mr. Pullinger and Mr. Carboy goes."

"And you," said Carboy.

"I'll kind of stand in the door," said Scattergood.

Mr. Carboy turned the knob and entered with Pullinger. Mrs. Pullinger sat before the dressing table, bending forward, with her face among the cosmetics. After one swift glance Scattergood closed the door behind him.

"Don't tetch her," he said sternly. "Don't tetch nothin'. Come back here, both of ye."

For Mrs. Pullinger had not died from natural causes, nor could there be any suspicion that she had taken her own life. Protruding from her back, just beneath the left shoulder blade, was an object which had no place near a lady's dressing table. There was very little blood.

"Murder!" whispered Mr. Carboy.

"Seems as though," said Scattergood.

Mr. Pullinger took a tottering step forward and then slumped to the rug.

"What will we do?" Carboy asked helplessly.

"Haul Pullinger out, lock up the door, and telephone the authorities," said Scattergood.

"But who—who could have done it?"

"That," said Scattergood dryly, "is what I call a pertinent question." He bent over Pullinger. "Take his feet," he said, and, as they lifted the man, Scattergood kicked the door open. "Where do you want us to lay him?"

"Across the hall," said Carboy.

They bore him through the silent, apprehensive people in the hall and laid him on the bed in the opposite room. Scattergood came back and stood in the door.

"Somebuddy," he said, "up and killed Mrs. Pullinger. Jammed a knife into her. We're a-sendin' fur the sheriff. Whilst we're a-waitin' I calc'late we better git together in one room and stay put."

"I'm going home," said Mrs. Chessman tremulously.

"It's a sight easier to stay than to git fetched back," said Scattergood mildly. " 'Tain't nice. But murderin' hain't nice, either."

"The sheriff will be here in ten minutes," said Mr. Carboy, coming back from the telephone.

"Sheriff Fox is gen'ally prompt," said Scattergood.

"But who—who—could have done it?" asked Miss Cate.

"Calc'late we better jest possess our souls in patience till the sheriff gits here," Scattergood said.

The room was heavy with an unpleasant silence until a car honked before the door, and Sheriff Fox, accompanied by a deputy, was shown in. He was a big, rangy man with a kindly face. His deputy was a pudgy, broad-shouldered individual with big blue eyes that wore a perpetually startled expression.

"How be ye, Mr. Carboy?" said the sheriff. "Kind of an awful thing, hain't it?" His brown eyes alighted on the old hardware merchant. "If 'tain't Scattergood Baines!" He heaved a sigh. "Was you here when it happened?"

"We was," said Mandy bitterly.

"Let's you 'n' me step out in the hall and talk," said the sheriff.

Scattergood followed him out of the room, and Fox turned with a worried look in his eyes. "I hain't exactly what ye could pernounce an expert on murders. Willin' to take a hand?"

"Dunno's I kin avoid it," said Scattergood.

"I'd take it in the right spirit," said Fox, "if you was to do the talkin' and askin'. I'll deputize ye."

They returned to the library, and Scattergood addressed the company.

"I hain't a guest no more," he said. "I'm a deppity. Sheriff here's asked me to kind of conduct the services. Let's start in by establishin' two, three facts."

"Such as?" asked Mr. Carboy.

"Who was where, when," said Scattergood. "That's the fust set." He turned to the sheriff. "Coroner a-comin'?"

"To be sure."

"Wa-al, we kin start out with the time this here was discovered. When the hired gal let out that yawp it was ten minutes past seven. When was the last time Mrs. Pullinger was seen before that, and by who?" He glanced at Mr. Pullinger, who had been revived.

"It was just six-thirty when I left the room," said that gentleman. "My wife had bathed and was dressing."

"When did ye git down onto the front stoop?" asked Scattergood.

"Mr. Pullinger was first of the guests to come down," said Carboy. "It was only a moment after six-thirty."

"Um. . . . Anybody have a room next to the Pullingers?"

"I," said young Mr. Gowan.

"See anythin'? Hear anythin'?"

"No."

"What time you leave your room?"

"I arrived on the porch just before you did, Mr. Baines."

"Where's Mr. and Mrs. Chessman sleepin'?"

"Next to Mr. Gowan," said Carboy.

"Anythin' to offer?" asked Scattergood.

"Nothing. We dressed and were ready to come down at—say, six-forty-five."

"Together every minnit?"

"Yes."

"Um. . . . How about Miss Cate?"

"I came down just after Mr. and Mrs. Chessman."

"How about you 'n' your wife, Carboy?"

"I was dressed shortly after six, and came down to do some telephoning. Mrs. Carboy was dressing."

"I was down just before six-thirty," said the hostess.

"Wa-al, wa-al. From them stories hain't nobuddy got an alibi but the Chessmans, and mebbe Carboy. Anybuddy see ye telephonin'? Anybuddy see ye from six till the fust guest come down?"

"I haven't the least idea."

"Pullinger, got any notion?"

"None, Mr. Baines."

"How many hired gals and sich?" asked Scattergood.

"A butler, cook, laundress, Mrs. Carboy's maid, two housemaids, chauffeur, superintendent, and three men outside."

"Nobuddy kin say ye hain't got copious help," said Scattergood. "Um. . . . Sheriff, you see none of the help don't go gallivantin' off before they're wanted. Sounds like the coroner comin'. Doc Crafts?"

"Yeah."

"Then we'll kind of go up and see what kin be diskivered in Mrs. Pullinger's room."

They joined the coroner and went to the room where Mrs. Pullinger met her death.

"Don't trample around before we git a look," said Scattergood.

"Prob'ly her husband done it," said Sheriff Fox.

"He could of," Scattergood agreed.

"Now, let's see. Pullinger could of, and then went downstairs like nothin' happened. Or somebuddy could 'a' come in the door—somebuddy she knowed real well, and stood behind and talked. Or"—he walked to the window—"somebuddy could 'a' crep' along the roof of this here stoop from one of the other rooms. Huh. . . . Know anythin' about stabbin', Sheriff?"

"Not a smidgin."

"Huh. Wa-al, the's two ways of doin' a stabbin'. A feller that jest grabs a knife and lets her go most gen'ally takes it by the haft with the blade on the side of his little finger and hits down like you'd hit with a hammer. The one that's used to it takes hold like a knife was a sword."

"Yeah?"

"This here feller was used to knives," said Scattergood. "Mrs. Pullinger was sittin' upright. Whoever done it stood behind and swung from low down. He never raised his arm, and that's why she didn't see what he was a-doin' in the lookin' glass."

"Right," said Dr. Crafts.

"Mebbe we kin identify the knife," suggested the sheriff.

"Mebbe. See anythin', Doc?"

"Nothing."

"Um. . . . Mebbe we better move her." They placed

Mrs. Pullinger on the bed, and there, where her skirts had spread over the carpet, Scattergood saw something small and glittering. He picked it up.

"What's this here gadget?" he asked.

"Fraternity emblem," said the coroner. "Epsilon Tau Epsilon. Rubies and sapphires. Looks as if it came off a watch or a cigarette case."

"Guess we're finished here," said the old hardware merchant. "Better see what we can contrive to git out of the hired help."

The servants were assembled, and Scattergood spoke to them without preamble.

"I've allus found out," he said, "that the hired gals know more about the fambly 'n what the fambly does itself. Any rumors creepin' around why somebuddy might want to git rid of Mrs. Pullinger?"

"She makes an awful fool out of her husband," said a maid tartly.

"Last summer it was that young Mr. Gowan," contributed the cook, "but this year he's traipsin' after Miss Cate."

"Rich folks, be they? Eh?"

"If they are," said the pert maid, "they hang on to it. Stingiest tips of any guests come to this house."

"Um. . . . Mrs. Pullinger goes rovin' around and they're close, eh?"

"What money they have belongs to her," said the chauffeur, "and the story was going around she lost a lot. A chauffeur sees a lot drivin' around the country."

"Sich as?" asked Scattergood.

"Who's sittin' in cars in lonesome spots with who," said the man.

"And she was a-sittin' with young Gowan?"

"Last summer—him among others. . . . There's times their servants have to wait for their pay."

"Dew tell. And when they git money to pay up where's it come from?"

"Their chauffeur says none of them can guess."

"Now, folks, about this here murder. Anybuddy know anythin' about it?"

"I was down by the lake, Mr. Baines," said the superintendent of the estate. "This was around half past six. I saw a man step out of a window on the second floor and sort of dodge along the roof of the piazza and go into another window."

"My goodness," said Scattergood. "Recognize him? Eh?"

"Mr. Gowan," said the superintendent.

"And what winder did he go into?"

"It was the next window."

"Pullingers' room was next to hisn," Scattergood said. He turned to Fox. "Sheriff, you see if ye kin git any more tidin's from these folks. Calc'late I'll go 'n' have words with Mr. Gowan."

Scattergood made his way to the front hall, where he encountered Miss Cate.

"Mr. Baines," she said. "Mr. Baines!"

"Yes'm."

"He didn't do it. I know he didn't!"

"That clears up a p'int," said Scattergood. "Who didn't?"

"Peter didn't—Mr. Gowan."

"What makes ye think I figger he did? Huh? What's your fust name?"

"Linda."

"Wa-al, Lindy. How d'ye know he never?"

"I—I love him," she said.

"Dunno's I ever heard better logic. Engaged to marry this here young feller?"

"Yes."

"Um. . . . Calc'late you 'n' me better go 'n' have it out with your young man."

Scattergood rapped on Gowan's door, and the young man opened it. His face was gray, but his eyes were steady.

"How be ye?" Scattergood asked.

"Reasonably well, Mr. Baines. Linda, what are you doing here?"

"We're huntin' in couples," said Scattergood. "She lets on you didn't do it. Did ye?"

"No."

"B'long to one of these here college fraternities?"

"I do."

"What's its name?"

"Epsilon Tau Epsilon."

"I figgered it would be. Um. . . . I'll betcha ye got a good reason for amblin' along roofs an' gittin' into winders."

"So I was seen," said young Mr. Gowan.

"Seen? Seen! What does he mean, Mr. Baines?" Linda Cate wrung her hands.

"Jest about the right minute he took it into his head to scramble along the roof of the front stoop and crawl through the winder into Mrs. Pullinger's room. How d'ye calc'late to make folks figger it was jest an innocent caper?"

"I guess I'd better say nothing."

"Sich a course is best sometimes, young feller, but I dunno's it's best now. Huh. . . . It wouldn't turn out you was an experienced feller in the handlin' of knives?"

"Father has a ranch in Mexico. I've gone there ever since I was a small boy. Everybody knows I can do tricks with knives."

"To be sure. Kind of expected it. And now, if it turns out ye had a grudge ag'in' Mrs. Pullinger, things would be most startlin'ly jim-dandy fur you."

Gowan looked at Linda with distress in his eyes. "Maybe you'd better go," he said.

"Don't," she said sharply, "be a dumb cluck. If you think I don't know that woman made a play for you last summer then you must believe I lead a pretty sheltered life."

"I made a complete fool of myself," he said.

"Naturally," she responded briskly.

"What kind of a fool did you make of yourself?" Scattergood asked, and then he nodded his head and answered himself: "Took your pen in hand, hey?"

"Yes."

"So she was a-goin' to pass your letters on to Lindy here?"

"Yes."

"If ye didn't up and render financial assistance?"

"Yes."

"And ye couldn't raise it?"

"No."

"And so ye contrived to git into her room as soon's her husband went out. Your story bein' that you calc'lated to plead with her. And you're a-goin' to say she turned out to be reasonable and give ye a breathin' spell."

"She gave me until Monday night."

"And then you come away peaceable, 'thout layin' a finger onto her?"

"I did," said Gowan.

"Didn't I tell you he was dumb?" demanded Linda. "If he'd had a trace of brains he'd have told me the whole mess, and I'd have gone and scratched Mrs. Pullinger's eyes out, and everything would have been nice and friendly.

Mr. Baines, if I don't marry this amoeba and look after him, he's coming to a bad end."

"He's a-standin' with one foot over the end right here 'n' now," said Scattergood.

"Do you think he did it?"

"I figger that he's almighty apt to git himself hung fur it. How come ye to drop this in there? And where was she when ye done it?" Scattergood exhibited the fraternity emblem.

"But I didn't drop that in there, Mr. Baines. That could be the emblem that was on my cigarette case. It must have come loose, but I don't know just when. All I know is I missed it a week ago."

"Was she dressed and settin' in front of her lookin' glass?"

"Yes."

"Skirts billowin' around the chair, touchin' the floor?"

"I think so, Mr. Baines."

"Well, this here was hid by her skirt. It was close to where her feet was. If somebuddy dropped it accidental, however did it git way under her skirts like that?"

"But I lost it. I don't know how it could have gotten in that room."

"That there story," said Scattergood, "is so incredible it might almost be true."

Linda stood watching his face. She caught her breath convulsively.

"What will they do?" she asked. "Arrest him?"

"Calc'late mebbe," said Scattergood.

"He didn't do it."

"Only one thing's any good in front of a jury, and that's evidence. Young feller, if it turns out you hain't guilty, it's a-goin' to be perty self-evident you been a ree-markable example of a dum fool."

"What are you going to do?" asked Linda.

"Snoop," said Scattergood. "G'-by."

Downstairs he found Carboy alone in the library. "Wa-al," he said, "hain't no reason the livin' should starve. Kin the cook rescue any hunks of the dinner? If she kin, we better git folks together 'n' eat."

Mr. Pullinger was the only one of the group who did not appear at the table. Scattergood scrutinized the faces as food was brought in. They were all serious, strained. Nothing was to be learned from them. Mrs. Carboy was the first to speak:

"Is there anything you can tell us, Mr. Baines?"

"Hain't nothin' happened. Don't seem's if she was robbed. Looks to me like one of them mysteries."

"The sheriff thinks someone came in from outside?" asked Mr. Chessman.

"Either that or one of you folks at this here table."

"It's nonsense to suppose anyone at this table would have harmed Lily Pullinger," said Mrs. Carboy.

"Seems as though," Scattergood agreed.

"It wouldn't be difficult for someone to climb the piazza and enter the window," said Mr. Carboy.

"But Lily would have seen him and given the alarm," objected Mr. Chessman.

"Calc'late you're right," agreed Scattergood in a discouraged tone.

"Unless it was someone she knew and expected," said Chessman.

"Yeah," said Scattergood, "but seems to me she'd 'a' let out a holler when she seen the knife. Even if she wa'n't lookin' at the feller, she'd see him in her lookin' glass."

"That's what puzzles me," said Carboy.

"It's got me floppin' around helpless," admitted Scattergood. "When his hand come up with the knife, she'd of seen it sure's shootin'." He illustrated the knifestroke by lifting his dinner implement above his head and striking downward.

"Land sakes!" exclaimed Mandy. "Sich talk at the table's enough to make a body's vittles curdle in her stummick." She snorted. "You 'n' the sheriff is goin' at this all lefthanded, seems to me."

"How'd you make a fist to do it, Mandy?"

"Fust off," said Mandy, "I'd find out what dreadful thing this here woman done to drive a man to murder her. The's eight of us at this table. Don't stand to reason the hull eight of us wanted her dead."

"You seem certain one of us is guilty," said Mr. Chessman.

"Stands to reason," said Mandy sharply.

"But it *couldn't* be one of us. We've all known one another so long." Mrs. Carboy twisted her long, slender hands together.

"I calc'late we got to face facts," Scattergood said. "It must 'a' been one of us here, or else Mr. Pullinger, upstairs."

"Oh!" exclaimed Mrs. Carboy.

"One of the things in this here life it's hard to git used to," said Scattergood, "is that folks ye know kin be jest like folks ye read about in the paper."

Mrs. Chessman seemed on the verge of breaking down. "We—we all know there was gossip about Lily. I—oh, it looks as if her husband must have heard it and——"

"The' was two people in that room after Mr. Pullinger left it," said Scattergood.

"Two!"

"A couple, Carboy. Yeah. She was alive when her husband come down. She was alive when one of them others left the room, but she wa'n't alive to speak of when the last feller went away."

"Who were they?" demanded Carboy.

"That's a-puzzlin' me some," Scattergood said.

"Two! What were two men doing in Lily Pullinger's room?" Carboy was frowning and obviously disquieted.

"They was tryin'," said Scattergood, "to git off'm the hook. Thrashin' around like a couple of trout whilst she dabbed at 'em with a landin' net."

"Just what do you mean?"

"This here Pullinger woman," said Scattergood, "wa'n't what ye might call highminded. Didn't none of you folks wonder how them Pullingers held up their end?"

"Yes." Carboy half rose from his chair. "Are you hinting at blackmail, Mr. Baines?"

"I can't believe it! Not Lily!" exclaimed Mrs. Carboy.

"The's eight of us at this table," Scattergood said. "To two of us—and mebbe more—it don't come as no astoundin' s'prise."

"This is not guesswork, Mr. Baines?" asked Carboy.

"Never met with no stouter a fact," said Scattergood. "Um. . . . Way it looks to me, Pullinger's the gist of the argyment. Yeah. Seems as though. Now, f'r instance, if the's letters or documents or sich, Pullinger's apt to know where they be. Mebbe he wa'n't wholly in his wife's confidence, but I warrant he knows a lot. Knows enough to be able to say who them two persons was. All we got to do is to prove which went in to see Mrs. Pullinger fust. Seems to me this here murderer didn't go fur enough."

"Meaning what?"

"Sh'u'd 'a' got rid of Pullinger, too. Then he'd 'a' been apt to go scot-free."

"You haven't questioned him?"

"Didn't seem jest the right time fur it," said Scattergood.
"Um. . . . What room did ye move him into?"

"Across the hall," said Mr. Carboy.

"I kind of figger he'll rare back about talkin' and dig in
his hoofs," Scattergood said. "If I was him, I calc'late I
would. Kind of assures him a good livin', don't it? All he's
got to do is state he don't know nothin' whatever, 'n' then
bear down on this party."

"Ah."

"Mebbe I better go talk to him," Scattergood said. He
got to his feet.

The seven remaining sat staring at one another, but they
did not have to remain in acute discomfort long, for Scattergood returned almost instantly.

"Pore feller," he said. "I opened up his door 'n' there he
lay fast asleep. Jest couldn't bear to stir him up."

"But —"

"He won't git away," Scattergood said. "Mebbe it'll do
me and all a sight of good to sleep on it fur the night.
Um. . . . Gittin' my bedtime, anyhow. Mandy, you look
tuckered."

"I be."

"G'night," said Scattergood.

"There'll be little sleep for any of us," said Carboy grimly.

"G'night, anyhow," Scattergood said.

When he got to his door he opened it for Mandy. "Snore
fur two," he said. "Lock yourself in and snore vehement."

"Shet up," Mandy said testily.

"I calc'late jest your usual, normal percedure'll be
aplenty," Scattergood said, and walked softly down the hall.

He entered a room across the passageway, removed his
shoes for comfort, wiggled his toes ecstatically, and turned
off the light. He moved a comfortable chair against the

wall, so that when the door opened it would conceal him from any intruder. Then he sat in silence.

The house became still. Night sounds without became audible. Dogs barked, a loon laughed on the lake, the eerie ululation of an owl came dolefully through the open window. Scattergood did not know the hour; he did not care. It might have been midnight—it might have been later— when the knob of the door turned stealthily. There was a pause; then the door opened slowly, softly. Scattergood did not stir. A dark figure passed between the old man and the dim window, and Scattergood, reaching out with his bare foot, kicked the door shut with a slam.

"Kind of figgered you'd come," he said. "Yeah. Ye had to, seems as though. Wa'n't no other way out of the mess, was the'?" He raised his voice. "Shine a light on him, Sheriff, 'fore he up and does a depredation."

A brilliant beam darted through the window and disclosed the intruder, standing over the empty bed with a weapon in his hand—not a knife, now, but a hammer.

"Moved Pullinger out whilst we was havin' dinner," Scattergood said. "Pore feller—he never knowed anythin', anyhow. To be sure. He's safe acrost in my room, with Mandy a-standin' guard. What a feller needs is a wife he kin trust, even after it gits dark. Never crossed my mind Mandy'd be what the papers call compromised."

Scattergood turned on the light. Carboy dropped the hammer. The sheriff and a deputy came through the window. Carboy did not speak.

"Knowed it must 'a' been you almost from the start-off," said Scattergood. "If it had of been sudden and unpremeditated-like, I mebbe wouldn't 'a' guessed. But this here was planned careful. Guests 'n' all. Placin' of guests. Sich plannin' couldn't be done by nobuddy but the feller that owned the house." He paused, then went on:

"How'd I know it was planned careful? Wa-al, fust off was that there college fraternity dingus. 'Twa'n't dropped. It was shoved careful and d'liberate under the Pullinger woman's skirts. Yeah. The only guess was it was put there to kind of cast suspicion onto somebuddy. And that somebuddy must be here to cast suspicion onto. Git the idee? From then on careful plannin' was the order of the day. Um. . . . Fust off I figgered mebbe this here murder was throwed in extry. It was plain Mandy and me was invited here fur a purpose, but when this killin' come along I guessed mebbe it had upset the plans."

"What plans?" asked the sheriff.

"The' wa'n't no other plans. Murder was the business before the meetin'."

"But why did Carboy want you here?"

"Wa-al," said Scattergood, "he wanted somebuddy local and kind of what you might call influential. To be sure. To jine in bein' suspected. And to git scared and sort of muddle the authorities. Yeah. He got the idee I was quite a feller, what with politics 'n' all, and that you wouldn't dast git too nosy with me one of the candidates. Might 'a' been a smart idee. But I calc'late his main idee in it was to have me diskiver a couple clues 'n' b'lieve 'em, 'n' be a highly regarded local witness ag'in' young Gowan. I was to do the convictin'."

"It didn't work," said the sheriff.

"On account," said Scattergood, "of askin' me for a visit without rhyme or reason. He wouldn't 'a' done that without a purpose. And, when I come to look into things, I seen the' wa'n't no other purpose besides this here murder. . . ."

Um. . . . G'night, Carboy. G'night, Sheriff. Calc'late Mandy an' me'll drive home."

He opened the door and stepped out into the hall. First he rapped at young Gowan's door and then at Linda Cate's. They stepped out into the hall.

"Jest wanted to relieve your minds some," he said. "Sheriff's got the miscreant. Seems as though Carboy was in the same boat as you. But he must've got desp'rate and tried the wrong way to git out. 'Course he never figgered anyone would guess he'd gone to her room after you did."

"Oh, Mr. Baines. We—we want to thank you," said Linda.

"You—I—" Gowan stumbled and was unable to finish what he had hoped to say.

Scattergood grinned. "You're startin' right," he said. "Kind of a valuable lesson. Fur married folks. Don't jump to conclusions even when all the evidence is ag'in'. Trouble with marriage is 't husbands 'n' wives seems t' be kind of eager to ketch each other at suthin'. Be more birds a-singin' 'n' flowers a-bloomin' if they kind of went out of their way not to ketch each other at suthin'."

He turned away down the hall. Before he entered his own door he turned and looked at them gravely.

"If," he said, "ye ever got to make a choice betwixt bein' exposed to suspicion or smallpox—pick smallpox. . . . G'night."

VII

Dancing Daughter

To SEE Scattergood Baines, of a hot summer afternoon, sitting in his specially reinforced chair on the piazza of his hardware store, one would not have guessed that he was a wealthy man, with political influence that reached as far as Washington. It would have been difficult for a stranger to understand how this fat, rugged-faced, rather shabby old man could be important in the world, or that, when he cared to do so or the need arose, he could control the political destinies of a sovereign state. Hardest of all to understand would have been that any man, with so much money and so much power, could content himself to sit day after day and lazily run a hardware store in a tiny village like Coldriver.

At the moment he was leaning back in his chair with his eyes closed and a bumblebee buzzing around his head. Deacon Pettibone, that dour, religious, harsh old man, sat on the steps. The bumblebee buzzed industriously and annoyingly, and Scattergood opened his eyes.

"Scat!" he said.

"Why don't ye swat him?" asked the deacon.

"He hain't meanin' no harm," said Scattergood. "He's like a lot of folks. Gits himself so excited over mindin' his own business that he irritates everybuddy he gits near. Um. . . .

117

Kind of nice to set and listen to bumblebees bumblin'
around a flower garden a couple of rods off. Soothin'. But
let them same bees go zingin' around your ears, and it's
like to set you crazy."

"So 'tis," said the deacon.

"Which brings a feller to the conclusion," said Scattergood, "that it makes a sight of difference if a thing happens
here or a hundred yards off."

He half shut his eyes and squinted down at the deacon.

"I was just a-thinkin'," he said.

"Politics?"

"Wimmin," said Scattergood.

"A man hadn't ought to let his mind run on wimmin,"
said the deacon severely.

"Beautiful wimmin was the ones I had in mind," Scattergood persisted. "I was jest kind of wonderin' why dum nigh
all the wicked wimmin you read about in the papers and in
hist'ry and what not is beautiful. Scrawny wimmin with
buck teeth runs mostly to virtue and good deeds. Fat
wimmin with whiskers gen'ally bog down into the kitchen
and bake apple pies, seems as though."

"Wimmin hadn't ought to be beautiful," said the deacon
harshly.

"Mebby we kin pass a state law ag'in' it," said Scattergood
mildly.

"It's the devil's doin's," said the deacon.

"If ye could make the people b'lieve that," Scattergood
said, "the devil 'ud git a lot of votes if he was to run fur
office. The's different kinds of beautiful wimmin."

"Snares and delusions," said the deacon.

"The's wimmin with beautiful faces; the's wimmin that is
beautiful from top to toe; the's wimmin with kind of homely
faces, and the rest of 'em is beautiful. Hard to say jest what

kind is the loveliest—but I got this here observation to make."

"Which one?" asked the deacon.

"It's the ones with perty laigs that creates the most disturbance."

"This hain't no talk fur a decent man."

"It's jest scientific," said Scattergood. "I'm inquirin' into a phenomenon."

"What fetched all this up?" asked the deacon.

"I jest happened to see Mark Goldie walkin' by a while ago. Set me to thinkin' about Prunelly. And thinkin' about Prunelly got me to thinkin' about beauty and inquirin' into it. Which, by nat'ral stages, brought me to the matter of laigs. Yeah, I calc'late Prunelly had about the sightliest set of laigs Coldriver ever see—that wasn't hitched to a thoroughbred hoss."

"She run off—didn't she?—and nigh busted Mark's heart."

"She run off," said Scattergood, "and the' hain't much doubt it was her laigs carried her. The' wa'n't no scope fur 'em in Coldriver. She could 'a' stayed around comfortable with her face, though it was kind of pert and interestin'. But them laigs was bound to start her lookin' fur."

"Lookin' fur what?"

"What every danged woman yearns fur," said Scattergood, "be she perty or homelier 'n a hedge fence; fur things to remember in her old age, and to look back on, and think about. I calc'late wimmin yearn to *live* more 'n what men does. They want fireworks a-shootin' off, and mysterious doin's, and minutes that bulge so they're like to bust. If a lot of fellers could git to look into their wives' minds they'd git fetched up with a turn. I bet ye, Deacon, the' hain't a saintly old woman with seventy year of noble deeds behind her that wouldn't up and swap it fur ten year of youth and a beautiful set of laigs."

"Prunelly Goldie was a headstrong gal," said the deacon. "She was bound to come to a bad end."

"So fur's I know," Scattergood said, "she hain't come to no kind of an end yit."

"She will," said the deacon tersely.

"G'-by," said Scattergood. "Um. . . . If godly folks 'ud only quit wishin' the worst 'ud happen to folks that hain't so godly, mebby them others 'ud figger bein' virtuous wa'n't like livin' on a diet of vinegar 'n' quinine. G'-by, Deacon."

Scattergood glanced up the street and saw Peter Haines taking Lottie Hamper into the drugstore for a soda. The old man frowned. He did not usually frown when a young man took a girl for a treat, but Peter was not so young, nor was Lottie, and the sight disturbed him.

But he settled back to his nap as the incoming train whistled. He knew that presently Pliny Pickett, who in ancient days had driven the stage and now was conductor on the one train operating over Scattergood's twenty-odd miles of rails, would appear to make his report. But it was not Pliny who arrived first. It was Johnny Bones, senior senator from the state, and an important man in the national capital. Johnny had been Scattergood's lawyer for many years until the old hardware man had elevated him to the Senate. He dropped into a chair beside Scattergood.

"How be ye, Johnny?" asked the old man.

"Bewildered," said Johnny.

"Don't blame ye, Johnny. But jest set tight. The crazier things look, the sooner they swing back to bein' sane. Um. . . . Any news?"

Johnny lowered his voice: "I was in the Egyptian Garden of the Metropolis Hotel last night in New York."

"Must be grand to be a senator," said Scattergood. "They git to see life. I envy ye, Johnny."

"Whom," asked Johnny, "do you think I saw there?"

"Hundred and twenty million folks in the country," said Scattergood; "it could 'a' been any of 'em. Hain't no sense to sich a question."

"Prunella Goldie," said the senator.

"Dew tell. Eatin' husks and clad in rags and tatters, mebby."

"You don't eat many husks in the Egyptian Garden," said Johnny. "They have what they call a floor show there. Prunella was dancing in it."

"Did she dance good?" asked Scattergood.

"She and her partner are a sensation."

"Partner? What partner, eh?"

"The man she dances with. The name of the team is Prunella and Serrano."

"Git paid fur it, does she?"

"Plenty."

"That'll be bad news fur the deacon," said Scattergood. "One of them hootchie-kootchie dances, was it?"

"It wasn't. It was what they call ballroom dancing. Her partner wore evening clothes and Prunella was dressed in a lovely gown."

"Didn't show her laigs?"

"You caught glimpses of them," said Johnny dryly.

"Be kind of a waste if ye didn't," said Scattergood. "How much you say she earns?"

"I heard the team were being paid a thousand a week."

"Shucks," said Scattergood. "The deacon'll bite himself. . . . Talk to her, eh?"

"She came over to my table and sat down, and we had a nice chat. She asked after you."

"Ask after her pa?"

"She says she wrote Mark and he was pretty harsh. Told her never to darken his door again, and that she'd lifted the cup and must drink it to the dregs."

"Beats all what comfort some folks finds bein' stiff-necked and hellish. Mark and the deacon believe strong in eternal damnation 'n' brimstone and hot pitch. But if the's wickedness, them two can't wait fur the devil to git to usin' his pitchfork—they got to elect themselves his handy men on earth. Um. . . . Meet this partner of hern?"

"Yes."

"What kind of a feller?"

"Handsome," said Johnny, "but he seemed to be rather interested in ham and eggs."

"I swan to man!" exclaimed Scattergood. "D'ye calc'late they're livin' in sin?"

"I didn't notice any marks. Prunella was lovely. I always liked her—she was so bright and eager."

"Must 'a' got it from her ma," said Scattergood.

"You know that big hotel they've built at Uncas Lake? She's going to dance there this summer."

"Huh. . . . Forty-four mile off, eh? Um. . . . Johnny, I dunno's I'd mention any of this here if I was you."

Johnny Bones grinned a very unsenator-like grin. "I'll settle back and be a spectator," he said, getting up to go.

It was not a half-hour later that the spare, bony, tall person of Mark Goldie crossed the bridge and would have walked by the hardware store had not Scattergood accosted him:

"How be ye, Mark, eh? How be ye?"

"In health," said Goldie. "I hain't got no complaint."

"Ye don't look over-cheerful, Mark."

"I'm wearin' sackcloth and pourin' ashes onto my head."

" 'Tain't much of an occupation," said Scattergood. "What's the idee of this ash-siftin' program of yourn?"

"My daughter has fetched my gray hairs with sorrow to the grave."

"Your hair hain't so gray as some," observed Scattergood. "Jest what dreadful thing has Prunelly up and done?"

"She left a God-fearin' home to live the life of an abandoned woman," said Mark.

"I never liked that description much," Scattergood observed. "Now, take me, I druther live in a God-lovin' home than a God-fearin' one. So Prunelly's become a wicked woman?"

"She's a-dancin' before Herod," said Mark.

"Um. . . . Now, let's suppose Prunelly went off to sing. Would it be wicked to sing?"

"Depends," said Mark.

"On whether she sung in a choir or in a theater?" asked Scattergood.

"Mebby so."

"Supposin' she went off to cook?"

"A gal's place is in her home, cookin' fur her father or fur her husband."

"Kind of complicated," said Scattergood. "If I foller your argument, Mark, almost anythin' a gal does kin be wicked if she don't do it jest when and how and in what place her pa picks out fur her."

" 'Honor thy father and thy mother,' " said Mark sententiously.

"Seems like the one that wrote that kind of neglected to put in a commandment sayin' parents ought to earn the right to be honored by their children. I never took to one-sided bargains."

"Never," said Mark, "mention her name to me ag'in. It's as if she was dead."

"Gosh," said Scattergood, "it must make a body awful miserable to be chuck-full of righteousness! G'-by, Mark."

On the Fourth of July Prunella and Serrano made their initial appearance at the Uncas Inn. On the morning of the fifth Coldriver found itself in a state of intense excitement, but not because of Prunella. It was because of another woman. Her name was Hamper—Lottie Hamper—and there had been whispers about her in the village. But there would be no more whispers, because she was dead. She was dead in her own back yard, where the butcher, on his rounds with his cart, had found her with a knife in her breast.

Before noon Sheriff Fox, moving rapidly, had identified the knife, had collected other corroborative bits of evidence, and had arrested for murder Lottie's next-door neighbor, whose name was Mark Goldie.

The sheriff sat on the step of the hardware store and made report to Scattergood: "Hain't no doubt it was Mark's huntin' knife. Last night, as a number kin testify, he drove Pete Haines away from her house when he was a-goin' in, and then had a back-bitin' quarrel with her."

"Dew tell," said Scattergood. "Pete Haines, eh? I swan!"

"When these here strait-laced fellers tumbles," said the sheriff, "they gen'ally pick out the wust kind of a woman."

"Mebby," said Scattergood, "it's lack of experience. Um. . . . Sure the evidence is clear? Mark didn't confess?"

"He jest sets in the jail kind of grim and silent, mutterin' and prayin'."

Early in the afternoon, Scattergood, who never would possess a motorcar, bargained for a ride to Uncas Lake,

where he arrived before the dinner hour. He registered at
the Inn.

"Hear ye got some special dancers here," he said to the
clerk.

"Prunella and Serrano. They dance at the tea hour, during dinner, and again at ten-thirty."

At the dinner hour Scattergood was led by the head-
waiter to an inconspicuous table, where he dined and
awaited the entertainment. Then Prunella and Serrano
danced in the open space in the center of the room. It was
beautiful dancing, graceful, light, gay, youthful. Scattergood studied Prunella's partner, an exotic young man whose
mysterious eyes and olive cheeks and perfect profile were
of the very essence of romance.

When the dance and encore were ended, Prunella and
her partner made their way through the tables toward the
door. Scattergood stood up and called, "Hey, Prunelly!
C'm here a minute."

She caught Serrano's hand and dragged him to Scattergood's table.

"This is a surprise," she said, and extended her hand.

"Set," said Scattergood. "Your young man kin set, too.
Name's Serrano, eh? My name's Baines. Um. . . . I drove
over special to see ye caper, Prunelly."

"That was nice, Mr. Baines."

"Married?" He glanced sidewise at Serrano.

"No."

"Goin' to marry this here young feller?"

"He's already married," Prunella said, with a gleam of
humor in her eye. "Tell Mr. Baines about the babies."

Serrano leaned across the table. "Pete's four," he said, "and
Gloria's almost a year. Now, Pete didn't have a bit of

trouble with his teeth. But Gloria—well, you wouldn't believe how hard they come through."

Scattergood grinned amiably. "Kind of a smart gal, hain't ye? Now, to look at him you'd think he was one of these here roués, wouldn't ye? Where's your wife and babies, Serrano?"

"Brooklyn," said the young man. "Rents are cheaper there, and it's quieter. . . . Gosh, I got to get along. I always call Nora up about now."

"Why don't you fetch her along?" asked Scattergood.

"Bad business," said Serrano. "If folks didn't think I wasn't married, I wouldn't be a draw. Want to see the babies' pictures, Mr. Baines?"

Serrano went on interminably about the children, his wife, the price of groceries. The old man listened with patience; then, suddenly, he terminated the interview.

"G'-by, Serrano," he said.

"Mr. Baines means he wants you to scram," said Prunella gaily. "Go and call up the wife and kiddies."

The young man withdrew eagerly.

Scattergood raised his heavy brows and waggled his head at the girl. "So ye hain't livin' in sin?"

"It couldn't be done with Serrano. No, Mr. Baines, I'm the same sweet little maid I was when I scampered out of Coldriver."

"Hain't had no news from your pa?"

"None," she said. "Father has washed his hands of me."

"If he was to kind of stand in need of ye, what would ye do?"

"Go like a shot," she said.

"Then," said Scattergood, "I calc'late ye better pack your traps an' come with me after your ten-thirty performance. Your pa's in a mess."

"What kind of a mess?"

"They arrested him for murderin' Lottie Hamper."

"I never heard anything so silly." She paused, and her eyes darkened with fear. "But he might have killed her," she said. "He—he might have killed her to stop her sinning. He might have worked himself up to think he was—God's avenger, or something like that."

"No need to say nothin' here," said Scattergood. "'Tain't but forty mile. Ye kin still keep your job 'n' drive over every day if you're needed. I'll drive ye tonight, and ye kin stay with Mandy 'n' me."

It was after midnight when they arrived in Coldriver. In the morning Prunella was eager to visit her father in the jail, and Scattergood accompanied her.

"I'll tell him you're here," said the old hardware merchant, and went down into the gloomy cellar, where he spoke through the barred door to Mark Goldie.

"Mark," he said, "Prunelly's here. She come to help."

"She's no daughter of mine," said Mark.

"You'll turn her away when she come to help?"

"She's no daughter of mine," Mark repeated.

"Looks to me like ye was perty stiffnecked," said Scattergood. "If ye don't move careful, Mark, they'll loosen it up with a rope."

"What men do to me don't matter," said Goldie. "It's God I'm concerned with."

"Mebby," said Scattergood, "He'll figger that bein' harsh to a gal that's got a right to your pertection is wuss 'n what murderin' a wuthless woman 'ud be."

Scattergood climbed the stairs to Prunella. "He won't see ye," he said. "What be ye a-goin' to do about it?"

Prunella smiled wanly. "He's my father," she said simply. "I'll stand by."

"Mebby the town'll take sides with him."

"That doesn't change my duty."

"I guess mebby we'll have to tinker with that there aspect of it," he said.

And tinker he did. By another morning Mrs. Serrano and her two babies were installed in Coldriver's hotel, and Serrano himself was brought over each morning to spend the day with them. Every afternoon Prunella and Serrano went back to the Uncas Inn to dance; each morning they returned to Coldriver.

"Git around," Scattergood said to Serrano, "and talk with folks."

So Serrano was seen with his plump little wife and his two babies—and, being a friendly soul, he speedily became acquainted. He even talked with the deacon.

But, while Serrano was boring the citizens of Coldriver, Scattergood was quietly going ahead with a plan of his own. He stopped Johnny Bones on the street.

"Know law, Johnny? Know lots of law?"

"Practically all of it."

"Um. . . . Includin' the rules of evidence and who kin testify, and to what?"

"I think I have a fair idea."

"Wa-al," said Scattergood, "I want Prunelly should testify."

"Testify to what?"

"Facts," said Scattergood. "Some of 'em kind of general and some p'tic'lar and havin' to do with the bank."

"The books themselves are the best evidence, but if Prunella happened to be working in the bank she could be appointed to bring the books and give evidence."

"Looks like Prunelly had her a job," said Scattergood.

So it came about that Prunella went to work in Scattergood's bank for a part of each day, in between her dancing engagements, and the town stared and wondered what the old hardware merchant was up to now.

"Wa-al," Scattergood said to the deacon a couple of days later, "you've had a chance to study the evil man that Prunelly's caperin' with. What's your idee, Deacon? Lewd and lascivious feller?"

The deacon snorted. "Him! Shucks. He looks like one of these here fallen angels but he's duller 'n a strip of tripe."

"Family man, hain't he?" asked Scattergood.

"Seems like I couldn't endure hearin' any more about them babies' teeth," said the deacon.

"So," asked Scattergood, "you're kind of prepared to admit a body kin dance and not turn over his soul to the devil?"

"That feller," said the deacon, "hain't never heard tell of wickedness."

And so public opinion veered. The women of Coldriver studied the situation and became sympathetic. Coldriver recognized dull virtue when it saw that commodity. . . .

It was a week after the death of Lottie Hamper before the prosecutor's office at the county seat was ready to hold the hearing. The hearing was to be held in the office of old Martin Bender, who had been Coldriver's justice of the peace for upwards of forty years.

The little office was jammed with spectators, and the street outside was crowded as the prisoner was brought from his cell and led to a seat at a table before the old justice. Johnny Bones was acting as counsel for the defense. A young man from the prosecutor's office acted for the State. Prunella and Scattergood sat in the front row of spectators.

The necessary preliminaries were accomplished; the State made out a damning prima-facie case, the principal item of which was Mark Goldie's hunting knife, but it· was supported by other evidence which seemed to show an association between Mark and the Hamper woman, almost daily calls, quarrels which were made to seem like the emotional outbursts of lovers. The young prosecutor succeeded in making it appear that Mark Goldie was jealous of the woman; that he threatened male callers with violence; that on the night of the murder itself he had so threatened Peter Haines. Upon this, the prosecution, feeling it had established sufficient motive, sufficient opportunity, sufficient evidence of the killing itself to justify the holding of Mark Goldie upon a charge of willful murder, rested.

Johnny Bones arose and addressed the old justice: "We shall call on one—possibly two witnesses, Your Honor. Will Miss Prunella Goldie take the stand?"

Prunella looked young and lovely and sad, but somehow competent, as she took the stand.

"Prunella," Johnny Bones asked, "what is your business?"

"I'm a dancer," she said simply.

"Remember, you are under oath."

"I know."

"Why did you run away from Coldriver?"

"I object," said the young prosecutor. "What's that got to do with it?"

"Mebby," said Justice Bender, "it hain't exactly got anythin' to do with the case, but it's an interestin' question."

"Because I wanted to dance. Because I wanted to make something of myself."

"And did you? How much do you earn?"

"My partner and myself are paid a thousand dollars a week."

"Now listen carefully: Is it necessary for a dancer to lead a fast or wicked life?"

"Dancing," said Prunella, "is work. To become a dancer you must work hours and hours a day. You have neither the time nor strength for foolishness."

"And after you have made a success?"

"You still must work. I must keep in condition, as if I were an athlete."

"Again I object to all this line of questioning," put in the prosecutor.

"I wish to establish the credibility of my witness," said Johnny with a smile. "Her character has been impugned."

"What we aims to do is git at the facts," said Justice Bender. "Go ahead, Prunelly."

"Is it a fact that your father refuses to have anything to do with you?"

"It is."

"Why?"

"Because he believes I am a bad girl."

"Are you?"

"Since the day I left Coldriver," said Prunella, "I have done nothing I would be ashamed to tell my mother, who is dead."

Mark Goldie sat stiff and erect in his chair, his eyes on his daughter's face.

"Prunella, since you came back to Coldriver, what have you been doing?"

"Working in Mr. Baines' bank?"

"You knew Lottie Hamper?"

"Yes."

"Has it been a part of your duty as a clerk in the bank to examine her account?"

"It has."

"What did you find?"

"That at intervals she deposited large sums of money."

"I will ask you to name no name at the moment, but was there another account that attracted your attention?"

"Yes."

"Why?"

"Because, every time Mrs. Hamper made a deposit, an identical sum was always withdrawn from this other account."

"It is reported that on the night of the murder your father quarreled with Lottie Hamper. Did you hear him quarrel with her at other times?"

"Frequently."

"What was the subject of these quarrels?"

"Her way of life. My father was worried about Lottie's soul."

"So if she quarreled with him on the night of the murder it was a quarrel such as you describe?"

"It could be nothing else," Prunella answered.

"And when your father drove a young man away from her door, it was a further effort to make her behave?"

"I'm sure of that."

"Your father," said Johnny, "believes evil of you. Do you not believe him capable of evil?"

"I do not. My father is a good man."

"Now, Prunella, why did you come back to Coldriver?"

"To help my father."

"What did you do to help him—besides working in the bank?"

"I searched for evidence to clear him."

"Where?"

"At Lottie Hamper's house."

"Are you familiar with your father's hunting knife, and where he kept it?"

"I am. It always hung in the summer kitchen, with his shotgun and rifle."

"Could it be stolen easily?"

"All you had to do was open the screen and reach in your arm."

"Did you find any article on Lottie Hamper's property?"

"I did. I found a newspaper crushed down in the middle of the big lilac bush."

"For what had the paper been used?"

"To wipe blood from a man's hands."

"I object—the witness—" This from the prosecutor.

"I calc'late Prunelly's entitled to her guess," said the justice.

"What paper was it?"

"It was a newspaper from the town of Pegler, Wisconsin."

"Do you know anyone who took such a paper?"

"Yes."

"Was it the same man," asked Johnny, "whose account you examined?"

"It was."

"What was his name?"

"Peter Haines," said Prunella.

There was a stir in the room near the door, a struggle. The huge form of Sheriff Fox stood erect and his great ham of a hand grasped a smallish man by the collar. "I got him, Scattergood," he said placidly.

Justice of the Peace Bender took off his glasses. "Case ag'in' Mark Goldie dismissed," he said.

Mark Goldie stood stiffly before his chair; his eyes, tortured, were fixed on Prunella's face. She walked toward him.

"Father," she said softly.

"I mistreated ye," said Mark humbly, "and ye come back and saved me." He moved his head uneasily. "I calc'late,

Prunelly, dancer or not, you turned out a better Christian 'n I be."

"Nonsense, Father," she said. "Let's go home."

She turned to Scattergood Baines and whispered in his ear.

"It was darling of you to let it seem as if I saved Father," she said. "It was—it was wonderful of you to let it look as if I found that evidence to clear him."

Sheriff Fox appeared in the door. "Hey, Scattergood, Pete Haines admits he done it."

"He's the kind that would," Scattergood said, and then to Prunella, "Calc'late ye better make your Pa go to the Uncas Inn and see ye cavort."

"Do you think he would?"

"I figger," said Scattergood, "that Mark's got him a start on an eddication today. Leave him hear Serrano talk about them babies' teeth." He paused and rubbed his nose. "I dunno jest why bein' doggone dull is a kind of a guarantee of virtue. Me, seems as though, if I was a-goin' to be all-fired good, I'd go at it in a kind of a caperin' and cheerful way."

"Maybe you do," said Prunella.

"I hain't jest built fur caperin'," said Scattergood, "but I kin wiggle my toes with the best of 'em."

VIII

Scattergood Ties a Knot

SCATTERGOOD BAINES leaned forward in his specially re-inforced chair and peered at a young woman who came slowly across the bridge toward the hardware store, on whose piazza he sat. It was his custom to sit in that place on fine days and to study the life of the village of Coldriver. It was much better than a newspaper.

He had been sitting there for more than a generation; and from that seat he conducted his affairs, the affairs of the village, and in large measure the affairs of the state. It was his pretense that he was a hardware merchant, and possibly he believed it himself; but his interests were many and important, for he was a rich man even by the standards of more urban communities than this little mountain town.

The girl walked slowly, not with that spring of youth to which she was entitled. Her face was grave. Even at her age it was beginning to set itself into lines of worry. It was apparent that she took no joy in the day. Scattergood squinted as she drew near and waggled his big head in displeasure. As she came abreast of him he spoke, and she lifted her eyes.

"Mornin', Lucy," he said. "Mornin'. How be ye?"

"Good morning, Mr. Baines."

"Goin' some'eres, or jest walkin'? Eh?"

"I was going home."

"Um. . . . Calc'late it'll be there yit if ye was to put it off mebby ten minutes. I been watchin' ye go past nigh every day, Lucy, and ye kind of got onto my mind. What ails ye? Huh?"

She dropped down upon the top step and leaned against the post. "It's so hopeless," she said wearily.

"What's hopeless? And who says so? I been a-hangin' around fur a consid'able spell, Lucy, and I dunno's I recall any situation that was what ye might call slam-bang without hope."

"Everything," said Lucy.

"Kind of general indictment, that, seems as though. This here sunshine hain't hopeless. I venture I could set here for an hour and read off a list of things that hain't hopeless nor even nigh to it."

"It's Con and I," she said.

"Have a quarrel? Git to bickerin'?"

"No."

"You sick of him, Lucy?"

"No."

"He tired of you?"

"No."

"Then jest where does it ache?" asked Scattergood.

"Con and I have been engaged as long as I can remember, almost. Since before he went to college. It was nine years ago he went away to college."

"You was fifteen then, wa'n't ye?" Scattergood knew the age and weight of every man, woman, child, cat, and dog in Coldriver.

"Yes. He was away at college four years. I wanted him to go. He was so ambitious, and finding the money was pretty hard. He had to earn the money as he went—but he did it, and he graduated. We thought then we could be married in a couple of months, because the power company had promised him a job. That's why he studied to be an engineer—because he knew he could get a fine start with them."

"And then," said Scattergood, "along come this here Deepression, and the' wa'n't no job."

"Nor has there been a job for five years. Five long years. And I'm getting older, and Con is getting older—and—and losing his grip. He's getting in a state of mind I'm afraid of. Sort of despair. And he's tried so hard to get placed—so hard. At first he kept studying. But you can't go on for five years. Now he is getting the idea he's no good. He's bogging down. In a couple more years he'll be nothing but an odd-job man."

"It's been a bad stretch of years fur young men," said Scattergood. "And all the time we keep on manufacturin' more young men and eddicatin' 'em and shovelin' 'em out into the world. It's been bad fur a million boys besides Con."

"It's only Con I'm interested in," she said. "It looks now as if we'll never be able to marry."

"Ever consider marryin' him anyhow, kind of figgerin' that the responsibility of a wife 'ud be good fur him—might compel him to git up and git?"

"I've offered to marry him a thousand times, but he won't have it. Mr. Baines, I haven't heard him laugh for months. He talks about the world not wanting him. He's getting around to where he's always saying 'What's the use?' Discouragement. He says when jobs open up they'll be given to boys who graduate this year and next—that nobody will want the boys who have been forced to sit and sit and go to seed for five or six years."

"A body kin kind of git his p'int of view," said Scattergood.

"He's not lazy," said Lucy fiercely. "He'll do anything.
He has done anything. But people are calling him a loafer—
and he knows it."

"Trouble with this world," said Scattergood, "is that young
folks hain't got no patience and old folks hain't got the time
to use it. Um. . . . G'-by, Lucy."

"If you could—" Lucy started to say, but Scattergood was
inexorable. "G'-by, Lucy," he repeated.

When she was gone the old man got up and ambled over
to the post office, where he collected the mail for himself,
for his bank, for his lumber company, and for his railroad.
He chatted for a moment with various people, and trudged
back to his piazza, which he commenced to litter with open
envelopes. Presently Pliny Pickett, the conductor of Scattergood's passenger train, came across the bridge. He stopped
at the steps.

"How be ye, Pliny?" Scattergood asked.

"No complaints, Scattergood, not to speak of."

"Then don't go mentionin' 'em," said the old hardware
merchant. "Huh. Got a letter from the B., A. & Q. jest now
relative to and touchin' on that there claim we made ag'in'
'em fur damage to a car of pulp. The upshot of it is they
say I kin go and jump in the crick."

"Dew tell," said Pliny.

"Four hunderd and thutty-one dollars 'n' eighty-seven
cents," said Scattergood. "Gone up the flue. I kind of wish
they'd settled it so's I kin sit reposeful 'thout figgerin'."

"Perty small potaters," remarked Pliny.

"Can't let nobuddy, much less a gobblin' railroad, do
me out of all that cash, Pliny. Can't tolerate it."

"Seems as though," Pliny agreed. "Don't blame ye none."

"Goin' anywheres special, Pliny? Eh?"

"Home, mebby."

"Pass Johnny Bones's office, don't ye?"

"Calc'late to."

"If ye was to pass ye might take a notion to go upstairs, mightn't· ye?"

"I might."

"If ye did," said Scattergood, "and ye happened to see Johnny would ye have any idees occurrin' to ye?"

"I'd tell him you was settin' on this here piazza," said Pliny, with caution equal to that of his employer.

"G'-by, Pliny," Scattergood said in dismissal.

"G'-by, Scattergood."

Very shortly Senator Bones, a distinguished and important man in Washington, but still "Johnny Bones" to Scattergood, came and sat on the top step.

"Got any time to practice law, Johnny?" Scattergood asked.

"I could find some if necessary."

"I want," said Scattergood, "you sh'u'd git me up a corporation."

"What for?"

"Jest figgered I might need one layin' around handy."

"What kind of a corporation?"

"Sort of general-like. Might be a buildin' corporation. One that's empowered to build anythin' from a barn to a Panama Canal."

"Just what are you up to, Scattergood? A lawyer is entitled to the confidence of his client."

"Have to know to make this here corporation legal, Johnny?"

"Not exactly."

"Then I calc'late I'm satisfied with how much ye know

about it," Scattergood said dryly. "Um. . . . Johnny, b'lieve in helpin' your feller man?"

"In moderation," said Johnny.

"It's a good idee," said Scattergood, "specially if you kin git fur yourself consid'able more profit out of the dicker 'n what ye bestow onto him." He closed his eyes and settled back in his chair. "G'-by, Johnny," he said.

The senator grinned at the abrupt dismissal, got to his feet, and walked down the street, a dignified and distinguished figure of a man.

Ten minutes later a ten-year-old, barefooted, came shuffling his toes luxuriously through the dust of the road. Scattergood hailed him: "Hey, bub!"

The boy stopped and looked up expectantly.

"D'ye wish ye had a nickel?" asked Scattergood.

"You bet you."

"Be ye acquainted with Con Price?"

The boy nodded.

"Could ye find him fur a nickel?"

"I know right where he is."

"It's a deal," said Scattergood. "Come and git it."

He handed a coin to the boy.

"What'll I tell Con?" asked the boy.

"Smart boy, hain't ye? What might ye tell him?"

"That you wanted to see him."

"Didn't say so, did I?"

"No."

"G'-by, bub," said Scattergood. . . .

It was a bit past lunchtime when Con Price appeared at the hardware store. He was a tall, lean young man with a good head and eyes that would have been keenly pleasant but for the commencement of a sort of hangdog look in them.

"How be ye, Con?" asked the old man.

"Alive," said the young man.

"Um. . . . It's still counted an asset. Huh. Got your surveying tools yit, Con?"

"Yes, Mr. Baines."

"Forgot how to run a line?"

"If I haven't," said Con, "it's not because I've had any use for my knowledge."

"Want to do some surveyin'?"

"I do."

"Need a feller to carry the rod and chain, won't ye?"

"Yes, Mr. Baines."

"Have him here in the mornin'," said Scattergood.

"What ——?"

"D'ye mean what wages do ye git? I'll tell ye. Ye git what I've a mind to pay ye."

"Suits me," said the boy with spirit. "I'll take that or less."

"I dunno," said Scattergood after a pause, "but mebby you're wuth the trouble. G'-by, Con. Tomorrer, early. And, Con, if I was you I wouldn't do this here surveyin' secret. I'd be kind of open and notorious about it. G'-by, Con." . . .

Next morning the young man, with his surveying gang of one, was at work before even early-rising Coldriver was about its daily tasks. He surveyed diligently for days. In that locality, where news is scarce and any unusual conduct on the part of any individual is of interest to the community, the fact of the survey was discussed and commented upon. When you add to that the efficient manner in which Con made a display of his work, it is not to be wondered at that news of the project traveled about the countryside and presently reached the ears Scattergood desired it to reach.

Not more than ten days elapsed before a well-dressed stranger disembarked from Scattergood's train and was driven to the hardware store. He got down from the taxi and crossed the walk, while Scattergood eyed him motionlessly.

"Mr. Baines?" asked the stranger.

"I answer to that name," said Scattergood.

"I am T. A. Gibson, of Boston."

"Railroad lawyer, I calc'late."

"Yes, sir."

"Pick out a step and set onto it," invited Scattergood. "What fetched ye to Coldriver? Hain't changed your mind about that there freight claim?"

"Freight claim? No, Mr. Baines. I knew of no freight claim."

"Sh'u'dn't be s'prised if ye heard of it before we git through," Scattergood said. "Sh'u'dn't be a mite astonished. If ye didn't come about that, why did ye come?"

"You are the owner of a railroad that runs from this village to the Junction."

"I be."

"The officials of the B., A. & Q. have been informed you are making surveys."

"I'm allus makin' suthin' or other," said Scattergood. "Got to keep my mind occupied."

Mr. Gibson smiled. "This survey has been keeping our minds occupied," he said. "May I ask the purpose of it?"

"Jest kind of enquirin' into the lay of the land," said Scattergood.

"Between this village and Amityboro," said the lawyer significantly.

"My curiosity runs in that direction."

"I'll put a direct question, Mr. Baines: Are you planning to extend your railroad to Amityboro?"

"I'll give ye a direct answer, Mr. Gibson," said Scattergood. "Mebby I be and mebby I hain't. It depends."

"My railroad," said Mr. Gibson, "would view such a project with concern."

"Dew tell! Um. . . . I dunno's the concern of the B., A. & Q. is one of the things that'll keep me layin' awake nights."

"The North Branch of the B., A. & Q.," said Mr. Gibson, "passes through Amityboro."

"So I hear tell."

"It proceeds eastward to Moxham," said Mr. Gibson, "where it joins our main line."

"To be sure. So freight 'n' passengers comin' from the north has to ride forty mile to Moxham 'n' then change cars, or git switched around 'n' ride down the other side of the triangle fur fifty mile to the Junction. Hain't no way acrost."

"That is the position."

"The news come to me in a roundabout way," said Scattergood, "that the's another railroad up there that they call the Amityboro & Northern. It ends kind of abrupt, and freight 'n' passengers has to ride from there on the B., A. & Q."

"Exactly."

"An' down to the Junction's a crossin' of the C., M. & G.," said Scattergood, "which goes scootin' off south towards New York."

"True."

"So," said Scattergood, "if the' was a direct connection betwixt them two railroads it 'ud save some fifty mile of haulin', 'n' avert them changes of cars 'n' cut down runnin'

time consid'able. And the'd be a heap of freight 'n' passengers the B., A. & Q. wouldn't enjoy the patronage of
any more."

"You state obvious facts."

"Wa-al," said Scattergood, "looks to me like it wouldn't
take much thinkin' to hit on the idee of buildin' twenty
mile of track to furnish that connectin' link."

"Frankly," said Mr. Gibson, "I am here because we do
not wish this railroad to be constructed."

"Back in this here wooden country," said Scattergood,
"we kind of do what we aim to 'thout askin' outside permission."

"No doubt. But surely you do not want to antagonize the
B., A. & Q."

"I druther have a skunk fur a friend than an enemy,"
said Scattergood agreeably. "I wouldn't go out of my way
to irritate even a slivercat. Antagonizin' is one of the wust
businesses a feller can go into."

"I'm delighted we agree upon that point."

"But," said Scattergood, "ye allus got to take into consideration if the other feller's got a right to be antagonized.
If, f'r instance, the B., A. & Q. was to git antagonized because I do suthin' I got a perfect right to do, and it's a good
thing to do, and I kin make more money 'n' friends by it
than by jest settin' supine and retainin' your friendship,
why, seems as though, that's a cat of another color."

"It will be a very expensive project."

"I figgered the cost. Allus do that."

"You will have to buy right of way. Suppose we were to
step in and overbid you for two or three pieces of land.
We could make the cost prohibitive."

"Mebby," said Scattergood, "you never heard of a thing
lawyers call the right of eminent domain. A railroad kin

kind of take what right of way it's got to have, and then fair-minded men awards to the property owner an honest price fur his land."

"But not," said Mr. Gibson, "until the legislature grants you the right to build your road and bestows that authority."

"Prob'aly you're right," said Scattergood.

"No such bill has been introduced into the legislature. I have investigated. And I fancy the B., A. & Q. could block the passage of such a measure."

"When did ye look?" asked Scattergood.

"During the past week."

"Um. . . . The' was other weeks and other legislatures," said Scattergood. "Mebby if you was to hunt the records back in 1925 you'd see where sich a bill was passed, and I got me the right to build jest sich a railroad. An' that there right has been kept alive."

"Is this a fact?" asked Gibson.

"I hain't given to much useless mendacity," said Scattergood. "When I set out to tell a lie it's the kind I won't be ketched in by jest consultin' a record of proceedin's."

"Nevertheless," said Mr. Gibson, "this road must not be built. The B., A. & Q. will not tolerate it. On the contrary, if we can come to an agreement, the B., A. & Q. will place its political resources behind you in this state—which to a man interested in politics is of vast importance. We can make you all-powerful in this state."

"Um. . . . Make me a present of the state, eh? Wa-al, I swan to man. Read the Bible much?"

"I'm familiar with the Scriptures."

"Then you read where the devil took a Man up on top of a high mountain where He could see all the kingdoms the' was on earth. And the devil he says to the Man, 'If

You'll drop Your present business and take up mine I'll make Ye a present of the whole kit and bilin'.' Recall?"

"I remember," said Mr. Gibson.

"Wa-al, the' was a joker in it all the time."

"I don't understand."

"Joker was," said Scattergood mildly, "that the devil didn't own a foot of the territory he was showin' off."

Mr. Gibson smiled wryly. "You're a difficult man to deal with," he said. "I don't want to threaten you. But the B., A. & Q. —"

"Never deal in threats, myself," said Scattergood. "Um. . . . But statin' possibilities hain't threatenin', not to speak of. It's jest referrin' to what might up and happen. Now, if the B., A. & Q. was to go meddlin' in my affairs and git troublesome, it might jest occur to the legislature that your railroad needed investigatin' fur tax purposes. Includin' an appraisal of property. And includin' also inquirin' into two, three deals and who got the profits. I heard of an instance once where sich a searchin' investigation made a couple of railroad officials skedaddle fur Paris."

Mr. Gibson smiled loftily. "It couldn't be done."

"The governor we got needs him a hullabaloo to stir folks up around election," said Scattergood. "If you figger it hain't possible, jest set while I call him up and kind of suggest it. Yeah. And tell him he'll have the backin' of sixty-seven per cent of the members of both Houses."

"Do you mean you would dare fight the railroads for control of the state legislature?"

"Calc'late so."

"It would turn the state upside down."

"Turnin' a state upside down's a good idea about once in so often."

"It would seem that this discussion is fruitless."

"Has been so fur."

"You insist upon building this piece of road?"

"Hain't even said I calc'lated to build no road. Hain't said so, have I?"

"Actions speak more loudly than words."

"Anyhow, they're more convincin'," said Scattergood.

"I will report your stand to the board," said Mr. Gibson.

"I bet you they'll be int'rested," said Scattergood. . . .

Mr. Gibson went back to the city and Scattergood continued to sit peacefully on his piazza. Con Price surveyed overtly, and Scattergood even put in a few teams to swamp out along the projected right of way. A week passed before Scattergood received a telegram inviting him to the city for a conference with railroad officials. He replied succinctly that he did all his conferring on his own piazza. Consequently, two days later, Mr. Gibson reappeared, accompanied by a high official of the road.

"Mr. Baines," this urbane gentleman said, "I've come to see if we can't find some way out of our difficulty."

"Hain't aware of no difficulty myself."

Mr. Bowker smiled tolerantly. "The difficulty seems to be on our side," he admitted. "What can we do to change your mind about building this strip of track?"

"I been studyin' politics," said Scattergood, "'n' I've been watchin' and broodin' over national finance."

"What has that to do with the matter in hand, sir?"

"I got to thinkin' about the general condition of things, as ye might say. Now, take jobs. Lots of folks hain't got jobs. So they can't spend money. So fact'ries 'n' stores can't make money. Yeah. Trouble at the minute is too many folks an' too few jobs. Affects us local. I call to mind a boy, name of Con Price, that hain't been able to git a job for a long stretch. Now, if he hadn't of been born, he wouldn't be a prominent member of the unemployed."

"True, but——"

"So I got to thinkin' about how to avert the next depression and spread some government money around to help cure this one. Can't fail. Jest pay every fambly a good sum of money not to have any babies. Then, next time the's a shortage of jobs, these here babies that wa'n't born can't be unemployed. Fix everythin' up nice."

"Yes, but Mr. Baines, how does that impinge on our problem?"

"Just a-leadin' up to it," said Scattergood. "When I was around earnin' money it was kind of the rule you got paid fur doin' suthin'. But styles changes. We old folks had the cart in front of the hoss. Nowadays you git hired to refrain from doin' suthin'. Yeah. You git paid fur not raisin' hawgs and fur not raisin' wheat, and so on and so forth. It gimme a new outlook on life."

"But still I don't follow you, Mr. Baines."

"Railroads that is built don't make money."

"They're not rolling in wealth at the moment. And that is why we wish to prevent the building of this line."

"To be sure. So it kind of occurred to me the way to make money out of railroads was not to have 'em. Like in this here instance. Mebby this road I'm a-goin' to build won't pay."

"It will not," assured Mr. Gibson.

"So," said Scattergood, "I might consider takin' up a gover'ment policy. Bein' patriotic and imitatin'. I calc'lated," said Scattergood, "I might git paid fur *not* buildin' a railroad."

"Ah," said Mr. Gibson. "You are frank."

"But I kin build a road," said Scattergood. "And I will build a road."

"But you are willing not to build a road," said the official, "providing that ——"

"You took the words out of my mouth, seems as though."

"It's a matter of money?"

"Money 'n' sentiment 'n' resentment 'n' charity," said Scattergood. "My motives is mixed. Money comes to the tail end. But I like my good deeds to git paid fur. A monument over a feller's grave must set heavy on his stummick."

"How much?"

"Twenty-five thousand four hunderd and thutty-one dollars 'n' eighty-seven cents," said Scattergood.

The two visitors eyed each other. They had feared worse.

"Yeah, I calc'late to sell ye the stock in my construction comp'ny fur that figger, carryin' with it all its assets and its liabilities."

"Why the odd figure, Mr. Baines?"

"We'll come to that later."

"For this sum you sell to us your company with all rights and appurtenances and privileges?"

"To be sure. But no dickerin'. That's my figger. Fust, last 'n' final."

"We are prepared to pay that amount. I don't see how we can help ourselves. In fact," said Mr. Bowker, "I came armed with a certified check for twenty-five thousand."

"And mebby another if I'd stood out. To be sure. But plenty's enough. I'll take that check and another fur the four thutty-one, eighty-seven."

"I'll give you my personal check for that sum."

"And, in a jiffy, I'll transfer to ye the stock in the construction comp'ny. Nothin' to do but hand it over, with the rest of the papers that's included, so's you'll have everything! Got 'em all signed."

He got up and lumbered in to his safe, from which he extracted a sheaf of documents. The check was placed in his hand and the papers in Mr. Gibson's.

"A nice deal," said Gibson. "We're stung, but we harbor no resentment."

"Good idee," said Scattergood.

"But what was the four hundred odd dollars for?" asked Mr. Bowker.

"I told ye I had conflictin' and various motives fur engagin' in this here dicker," said Scattergood. "Fust was a claim ag'in' your road fur a damaged car of pulp. Your claim department wouldn't pay it. I jest couldn't endure to stand that loss. So I set me to thinkin'."

Gibson pursed his lips. Here was a case where being penny-wise had turned out to be pound-foolish.

"What else?" he asked with interest.

"Wa-al, ye might call it charity. Ye might call it lendin' a helpin' hand. But the's a young feller here, name of Con Price, that wants to git married to a gal, name of Lucy. Engineer. Good boy. But couldn't git no job."

"I see. But how does this help him?"

"I give him a job," said Scattergood, "surveyin'. Yeah, a permanent job, all fixed and settled in a contract. Coverin' a period of five year. He's workin' fur you folks now under that there signed and sealed agreement. So him 'n' Lucy kin marry. You got the contract there, havin' assumed it when you bought me out."

Gibson clucked.

"Ye git a good boy," said Scattergood. "Fur the fust year you pay him two hunderd a month. The second two hunderd and twenty-five. The last year he gits four thousand a year. By that time, I calc'late, he'll be so valuable to you that you'll do your own salary raisin' as deserved. Yeah, them's my two reasons fur embarkin' on this deal."

"You mean you started to build a railroad, would have gone through with it—involving this whole state in a political battle—and—" Gibson sighed. "Is that what you mean?"

"To be sure," said Scattergood. "I jest had to have back my four hunderd and thutty-one dollars. An' Lucy 'n' Con had to git married. Reasons enough, seems as though."

"But with a tidy profit to yourself."

"The laborer," said Scattergood gravely, "is worthy of his hire."

He paused a moment. "Hold your hosses," he said, as he drew a pen from his pocket and wrote on the back of the check for twenty-five thousand dollars. He held it out for Gibson to see. The endorsement read, "Pay to the order of the Town of Coldriver." Scattergood cleared his throat:

"Only way to teach some folks a lesson is to make it expensive. But I don't calc'late to benefit none by it myself—except to git back my four hunderd and thutty-one dollars. Yeah. Goin' to be a heap of discussions durin' the next year. Taown Hall's dilapidated. This here'll put it in shape, with all the fixin's. Nothin' a taown needs these days like a place to gather an' discuss. . . . G'-by, Gibson, 'n' remember never to kick the wrong feller's dawg."

IX

Scattergood Encounters Science

SCATTERGOOD BAINES sat on the piazza of his hardware store in Coldriver talking earnestly with Pliny Pickett. Pliny had once been a stage driver between the village and the junction twenty-five miles away, but when Scattergood built the little railroad he became conductor of its lone passenger train. Pliny dropped in at the hardware store every noon to make his report.

Scattergood, as was his custom in good weather, sat outside in his specially reinforced armchair. It needed to be reinforced, because the old man was a weighty occupant. He was weighty not only in flesh but in fortune, for, as everybody knows, he owned the railroad, he owned sections of timber, he owned lumber mills; his safe-deposit box bulged with excellent securities—and he was the dominant political figure in his state.

But conducting the hardware store was the real business of his life. It was close to him and dear to him.

At the moment, however, he was not interested in hardware or railroads or politics. His mind was running on more abstruse matters.

"Book agent come along this mornin'," he said. "Smart feller. Knowed a lot."

"What kind of a book was he peddlin'?" asked Pliny.

152

"Had a name I can't recall," said Scattergood, "but it was all about minds. Yeah. The' was hunks of it about subconscious minds, and hunks about conscious minds. Kind of intricate."

"Buy one?" asked Pliny.

"Didn't jest seem to need one," said Scattergood, "'n' the longer I listened to this here feller the less I needed it. Ever hear tell of psychology?"

"Not's I call to mind."

"It's what makes your wheels go round. It's what makes ye act like ye do. It's what makes your wife nag ye, and it's what makes some fellers wuthless sots and other fellers noble citizens."

"Kind of a disease?" asked Pliny.

"Ye git born with it," said Scattergood. "Near's I kin gather psychology is the science of why folks does things the way they do and of what they kin contrive to do about it."

"About what?" asked Pliny.

"This and that," said Scattergood. "I gather from this here book agent your mind's kind of like an unbroke colt. Ye kin live all your life and let it run wild in the pasture, or ye kin break it to harness. This here book also gives ye an inklin' how to manage other folks."

"Handy knowledge," said Pliny.

"It tells ye," said Scattergood, "how to git more work 'n' better work out of your brains. Yeah. So's ye kin be a big success. Interestin'. But the more this here feller gassed the more I seen I didn't require to own no sich book."

"Why?"

"On account," said Scattergood, "it wa'n't nothin' but human experience put into fancy words. Take me. I been livin' and observin' and dickerin' fur a sight of years. Yes, sir. Wa-al, everythin' this here peddler told me in fancy language had happened to me in plain words. I knowed it all from kiver to kiver—'thout ever realizin' before how eddicated I was."

"Don't seem likely," said Pliny.

"I calc'late ye hain't never appreciated me as is my due," said Scattergood.

"The' was a section of it about gittin' in rapport. Know what that is?"

"No idee."

"It's like makin' a telephone connection," said Scattergood. "It's gittin' in touch with your own thinkin' machine. The's special ways to do it. In the book you got to take exercises, like layin' onto your back and kickin' up your laigs till you're tired. 'N' then you jest doze off, like, and then, fust ye know you've thought out whatever 'tis you're tryin' to think out."

"Don't b'lieve a word of it," said Pliny.

"It's true as Gospel," said Scattergood. "The best way to git a thing is to want it hard. If ye want it so hard ye jest can't endure to be lackin' it, then, b'jing! you've got it. I found that out forty year ago."

"Sounds like magic," said Pliny. "I bet 'tain't religious."

"Ever hear of ambition?" asked Scattergood.

"To be sure."

"That's one of the barnyard names fur it. Ambition is jest wantin' suthin' mighty hard."

He leaned back in his chair and closed his eyes. "G'-by, Pliny," he said.

"G'-by, Scattergood."

"If ye see me settin' with my eyes closed, don't never disturb me, Pliny. I'm tunin' in on the Infinite. G'-by, Pliny."

"Don't ye have to do nothin' to git suthin' but jest pine fur it?"

"A mite of hard work on the side don't harm none to speak of," said Scattergood.

The old man leaned back and, with eyes half shut, went about the job of getting himself in tune with the Infinite.

The connection, if it had been established, was broken by a customer. Scattergood served her, and then availed himself of the opportunity to chat.

"How be ye, Maggie?" he asked.

"I don't like to be called Maggie. My name is Margaret."

"Dew tell. Dunno how I kin contrive to humor ye in sich a matter, Maggie," said the old man. "'Tain't good fur ye. It's humorin' ye. Psychology says it's bad to humor folks when they git a highfalutin complex."

"Goodness!" exclaimed Margaret Noyes.

"Hain't seen ye around with Clif lately. Hain't had no quarrel, have ye?"

Miss Noyes compressed her lips. "Clif avoids me," she said.

"Funny way fur a young feller to act," said Scattergood. "What ye done to spite him?"

"Nothing," she said. "It's Clif. It's—Mr. Baines, I'm terribly worried about Clif. He's lost his grip."

"What did he have a-holt of?"

"I mean he's going to pieces. He's lost confidence in himself—and you can't blame him."

"I don't git in the habit of blamin' folks till the evidence is all in," said Scattergood.

"He thinks he's no good. He thinks he'll never amount to anything. And that's why he's avoiding me. How would you like to work your way through college and earn an engineering degree, and then go more than two years without a job?"

"It's a kind of an epidemic jest now," said Scattergood.

"You don't understand. He feels the fault is with himself. He's ashamed. He can't look people in the face. He believes everybody thinks he doesn't want to work. He's getting to a point where he'd be afraid to tackle a good job if it came to him."

"Huh," said Scattergood. "This here's the wust p'int of the depression. Yeah. The effect it has on young folks."

"And when jobs come," said Margaret, "it's going to be the boys fresh out of college who get them."

"That's Clif's idee," said Scattergood. "Um. . . . A hinge that gits oiled reg'lar don't grow rusty."

"How's he going to oil his hinges," demanded Margaret, "by doing day labor on the road or by getting odd jobs in the garage or by driving a truck once in a while?"

"So what d'ye calc'late to do about it? Eh? Got any notions?"

"I talked and I talked. I told him he was foolish. I told him I had all the confidence in the world in him." She paused. "I even told him I'd prove it by marrying him right now and taking a chance."

"But he wouldn't?"

"He said he wouldn't let me marry a man who was nothing but a failure."

"Sounds like one of them there case hist'ries the book agent was talkin' about. Um. . . . If ye was passin' here tomorrow shortly after the noon hour, what d'ye calc'late you'd do?"

"Why," she said, "I'd stop and speak."

"Two o'clock was when I mentioned, wa'n't it?"

"Two o'clock."

"G'-by, Maggie.". . .

That evening when Pliny came along to make his nightly report Scattergood took up the matter of psychology again. "Ye have to search back," he said. "Take you, f'r instance; you're a civilized feller, but you got impulses that derives from savages."

"I hain't nuther," said Pliny.

"You're full 'n' runnin' over with 'em," said Scattergood. "You hain't nothin' but a thin veneer stretched over the primitive."

"My gosh!" exclaimed Pliny.

"Um. . . . Acquainted with Pete Strake, be ye? Eh? Know him when ye see him?"

"Calc'late to."

"That hain't him loafin' by the pust office, is it?"

"Sure's shootin'."

"Goin' past that way, Pliny?"

"I be."

"If Pete's still standin' there might ye speak to him?"

"No reason fur not," said Pliny.

"Mention me, would ye? Wouldn't occur to ye to say you guessed I'd be settin' right here fur half an hour?"

"I'll git him here," Pliny said.

In five minutes Pete Strake, a heavily built man who looked as if Mackinaw jackets were his natural covering, stopped at the foot of the steps. "Want to see me, Mr. Baines?"

"Dunno's I do, but now you're here 'twon't do no harm to stop. Um. . . . Want to be straw boss this winter, Pete?"

"You bet you, Mr. Baines."

"Kind of a healthy-lookin' feller."

"Hain't many stouter 'n me."

"Ever have a fight, Pete? Eh? Kind of enj'y fightin'?"

"It gives a body exercise," said Pete, with a wide grin.

"Mind gittin' licked, Pete?"

"I druther do the lickin'."

"But ye do want to be straw boss, eh?"

"I calc'late I could contrive to lose."

The conversation veered to technicalities of the lumber camps and to other subjects, but Scattergood managed to make clear his desires. He 'dismissed Pete in his customary way.

It was an hour before Scattergood stirred. Then he got up and ambled over to the hotel, where he seemed rather surprised to see a Mr. Walter Falkner, from Boston, sitting on the piazza.

"How be ye?" he asked. "When'd ye git in? Eh?"

"Noon train," said Mr. Falkner.

"Fishin' or business?"

"Fishing," said Mr. Falkner, so Scattergood knew it was business.

"Hope ye git 'em," Scattergood said, and made as if to pass on. "Calc'late to be kind of busy myself tomorrer," he said, "but if it turned out you wanted to talk to me about anythin' I'd be settin' in front of the store right after two o'clock."

He walked down the steps again and along to the garage, where he saw young Clif Morton hunched in a disconsolate attitude. Clif looked a bit shabby.

"Busy tomorrer, Clif?" asked Scattergood.

"Busy loafing," said the young man bitterly.

"Couldn't manage to help me out?"

"Just the odd-job man, that's me."

"Come around in the mornin'," said Scattergood. . . .

Next day Scattergood invented labor in his hardware store, which used up the morning. Clif went to lunch and returned shortly after one o'clock. Then he shifted stoves on the second floor until Scattergood called him down. The young man compressed his lips as he saw Margaret Noyes sitting on the top step. It was two o'clock.

"Clif," said Scattergood, "I wisht you'd take this here paper over to Johnny Bones's office."

"It takes a college degree to fit a man for running errands," Clif said, and did not look at Margaret.

"I'm going that way," she said. "I'll walk along with you."

There was no avoiding it, so Clif, with bad grace, walked up the street with her and across the bridge. As the young people strolled away, Mr. Falkner was walking from the hotel to keep his appointment. Scattergood welcomed him, but kept the corner of his eye on Clif and Margaret. Presently he saw them stop before the post office. It looked as if Pete Strake had accosted them.

Pete seemed in a vicious humor. "Can't ye find nobuddy better 'n that to walk with?" he asked, and then laughed disagreeably. "Hain't nothin' so comical as a college dude with a patch on his pants."

Clif flushed, but was proceeding on his way without taking notice. Pete addressed Margaret. "I guess you hain't got good sense," he said.

Clif was white. The humiliation was more than he could bear—and to have Margaret a witness to it added acutely to the torture. He turned swiftly and swung at Pete's jaw.

"Looks like a fight," Scattergood said to Mr. Falkner. "Might be amusin' to watch."

The first blow had landed glancingly, but Clif followed it up with venom. Pete backed away, covering himself with the skill of a rough-and-tumble fighter. Then he launched a counterattack and the two men, one burly, powerful, the other slender, but young and wiry, stood and exchanged wild blows until Clif found himself sitting on the sidewalk with his head ringing.

He leaped to his feet, and was sent down again. Again, but more slowly, he stood erect. But blind rage was gone now. Caution had been knocked into him. He fought more warily. But to the spectators it seemed an unequal contest. Again the boy was knocked down. Once more he got up, and now he backed away with Pete following but seeming to lack the skill to profit by his advantage.

Twice more the boy was knocked prostrate, but each time he came back. He was tiring, but it seemed also that Pete's great arms were growing weary. Clif sparred.

Suddenly he saw an opening and put into a blow all he had. It landed flush on Pete's jaw, and the man, though not knocked from his feet, staggered back. Clif followed swiftly with right and left, and, as Pete threw up his arms to protect his chin, lowered his attack to the body. It was a desperate flurry. His fist drove into Pete's stomach and the man's guard dropped, and the boy, settling flat on his feet, drove a solid right to the big man's jaw. Pete went down and stayed down.

"Clif! Are you hurt?" cried Margaret.

"It didn't do me any good," said the boy, but, for all that, his shoulders were more erect than they had been for months.

"You were splendid," said Margaret.

Clif turned and climbed the stairs to Johnny Bones's office.

Mr. Falkner was shaking his head. "Man, what a fight! He knocked that kid down five times. Count 'em? Five. But the youngster got up every time. That's grit, b'jing! That kid's got it."

"Seems as though," said Scattergood.

An hour later Scattergood was alone and Margaret came
again to the steps.

"It was awful," she said. "I—I could hardly stand it."

"He done good, didn't he? Eh?"

"Oh, he was wonderful."

"Um. . . . Sh'u'dn't be s'prised if he kind of thought so
himself. Huh. . . . A man kin make twenty millions. He
kin write a great book. He can git to be president. But none
of them things gives him sich deep and abidin' satisfaction
as lickin' a man bigger 'n him. Cliff'll be more contented
with himself 'n what he was."

"It was a hard way," said Margaret.

" 'Tain't fun to cut a boil," said Scattergood, "nor to chop
out one of these here appendixes. This here was jest a kind
of a preliminary psychological operation."

"But," said Margaret, "it doesn't get him a job."

"Main thing's to make him git some respect fur himself.
Calc'late he can't help it now. He licked the stoutest feller
in the caounty."

"Now what?" asked Margaret.

"Time to strike," said Scattergood, "'s when the iron's
hot. G'-by, Maggie."

The old man went to the stairs and called up to Clif.

The young man came down, marred as to manly beauty,
but with a look in his eyes that had not been there in the
morning.

"Set," said Scattergood.

"Yes, sir."

"I got to make up my mind about suthin'. I hain't got
no time to go 'n' apply fur advice. It's got to be decided
ker-pop."

"What about, Mr. Baines?"

"This here's important. I got to decide right. If I give

the wrong answer nobuddy knows what it'll cost me. Mebby couple hundred thousand. I got to rely on you, Clif."

"On me! But I—you haven't any right to put it up to me. The responsibility—suppose I answer wrong."

"Then," said Scattergood, "it'll be perty awful. But I got to trust ye, Clif. The' hain't nobuddy else. I got to rely onto you. It's up to you 'n' nobuddy else whether I make a sight of money or lose a terrible chunk. Jest you."

"I won't do it. You can't put anything like that on me."

"Licked Pete Strake, didn't ye?"

"Yes."

"Figger a feller 't kin do that is no good? Eh?"

Clif was silent, and Scattergood nodded. "I trust ye, because I got to. But I figger a feller 't kin git knocked daown five times, 'n' then stand up and whallop the feller 't knocked him, is perty gritty. He hain't so yaller he won't dast express an opinion even if 'tis important. In addition to all that there, I wouldn't ask ye if I didn't think ye was fitted to answer."

"Do you mean that, Mr. Baines?" Clif was breathing deeply. His lips were compressed and white. But his shoulders were not slouched, and in his eyes was a sort of joy, a surprised, almost savage joy.

"Every danged word."

"What's the question?" asked Clif.

"One summer while ye was in college ye done surveyin' up the East Branch. Kind of familiar with that region?"

"I know every foot of it."

"Know where it forks?"

"Naturally."

"Here's what I done, Clif: I got me thousands of acres of land on option up both them branches. I got to exercise one of them options. I dunno which, 'n' you got to tell me. If I exercise the wrong one it's a-goin' to be bad."

"But why?"

"I got wind the power comp'ny's a-goin' to build a storage dam. Got to give 'em even flow of water durin' the summer when the streams dries up. So I optioned me that land—two locations. They got to flood one of 'em with the storage lake if they build a dam. I dunno which. And my options is expirin'. If I pick the right location I sell to the power company fur a heap of profit. If I pick the wrong one I lose all I put in. You got to decide. You're my consultin' engineer."

"I—I can't do it," Clif said hoarsely.

"If I didn't b'lieve you was capable of givin' the right answer I wouldn't of asked ye," said Scattergood. "I got confidence in ye, Clif. Ye can't disapp'int me. I hain't got nobuddy else to rely on."

Clif threw back his head and looked Scattergood in the eye. "How soon?"

"Now."

Clif walked back into the store and Scattergood could hear him pacing up and down. Five minutes passed.

"Wa-al?" demanded Scattergood.

Clif came out. His face had a drawn, tired look, but his chin jutted out. "The West Fork," he said, and then sat down on the top step.

"Be ye sure?" asked Scattergood.

The young man leaped to his feet. "Sure!" he said a bit wildly. "I know my business, don't I? I know the country. I've surveyed it. I am sure. I've got to be right. I'm right because I know my job."

"Maybe Falkner won't know you're right."

"Who is Falkner?"

"Chief engineer of the power company. Come along with me."

"Where?"

"Falkner's to the hotel. You got to convince him."

"Me. Convince a great engineer!"

"If you're right and you know you're right ye kin convince the Emperor Napoleon. You do the talkin'."

Clif followed Scattergood in a sort of daze. This could not be true. It was not happening to him. It was a sort of nightmare. He was terribly afraid, yet, somehow, exalted. He had proved his manhood on Pete Strake—his primitive, basic manhood. He had come up to scratch. He had not quit. Against odds he had won. He had taken punishment, bad punishment, and remained steadfast. Therefore there must be something to him. He was not contemptible. And now he had faced an emergency. He had dared to give a momentous answer. But, more than that, he had been trusted. A man had put his fate in his hands. Had relied upon him to give an answer involving hundreds of thousands of dollars! Then the world could not think he was a bum.

They mounted the hotel steps and climbed the stairs to Falkner's room.

"Falkner," said Scattergood, "this here's Clif Morton, my consultin' engineer."

Falkner shook the young man's hand. "You're the lad I just saw in a fight," he said.

"Couldn't avoid it," said Clif.

"Lad," said Falkner, "you have what it takes to make a great engineer. The basic thing: Courage! I'm glad to meet you."

"Falkner," said Scattergood, "you come up here to make

the final decision—whether you'd build your dam on the East Fork or the West Fork."

"You get too much information."

"Calc'late to hear things," said Scattergood. "Clif says West Fork."

"I don't agree," said Falkner.

"Mr. Falkner, you're wrong," said Clif firmly. He spoke as one having knowledge and authority. "I know this country, every inch of it. I've surveyed it. I don't know what reports you have had, but any man who recommended the East Fork to you is incompetent."

"Strong language, boy. We've had good men up here."

"There's one place to build a storage dam, and one method," said Clif. "Across Dover Notch, and an earthwork dam. I worked it all out. It was a problem that interested me. It's a matter of cost, a matter of efficiency, a matter of water supply. I'm right. Anybody who gives you a different opinion is wrong—or dishonest."

Clif launched into an exposition of flowage, of storage area, of elevations, of the sources of water in the two debatable areas. He propounded methods of construction, pointing out the advantages and economies of the West Fork. He was clear and exhaustive.

"Young man," said Mr. Falkner when he paused for breath, "I'd call that an able exposition. I'm going over the ground myself."

"Guess that'll be all, Clif," said Scattergood. "G'-by."

"Good afternoon, Mr. Baines."

"Much obleeged, Clif. G'-by."

When Clif was gone Falkner turned to Scattergood. "Surely that isn't the young man you spoke about: Lack of confidence. Inferiority complex. Losing his grip."

"It's him," said Scattergood.

"I guess you didn't understand him. That's a lad of parts. I'm not easily impressed, but he impressed me."

Scattergood smiled widely. "Amazin' what science'll do. Now, you wouldn't think smackin' another feller in the jaw would turn a man topsy-turvy. Nobuddy would if he wa'n't a student of this here psychology. Um. . . . I kind of appreciate your seein' him and lettin' him talk. I calc'late we kin go ahead now 'n' settle the details of our trade. But you listen here to me, Falkner; that there boy mustn't ever find out it was all settled to build the dam on the West Fork."

"He shan't," said Falkner. "What are you going to do with him?"

"He's my consultin' engineer."

"So you tell me. But he can't go far with you. I know he must be useful, but you wouldn't stand in the boy's way, would you? Mind—I'm not going around hiring good men away from their employment. But I liked that young man."

"I kind of hate to part with him," said Scattergood.

"I wish," said Falkner, "you'd let me have him—as a part of the deal."

"If you put it that way," said Scattergood, "I dunno how I kin refuse. But good men hain't so plentiful. What you figger to offer him?"

"I'd like him on this job. He knows the country; he knows the people here and their ways. Would you say he'd be interested in, say, twenty-five hundred a year?"

Scattergood went out presently. As he reached the street he saw Clif coming from the store and Margaret crossing the bridge. The young man did not avoid her. Instead he walked to meet her.

"Listen," he said; "I've been dodging you. I was afraid to face you. It was because I love you and I was ashamed.

I was afraid—afraid of the future. Well, I'm not dodging you any more. I'm not licked. I don't know how long it will take. I don't know how long I'll have to wait—but I'm going to be somebody."

"Clif!"

"Can you take it on the chin a while longer? I mean, will you wait?"

"A thousand years," said Margaret.

"You won't have to. Not ashamed to be engaged to a loafer?"

"I never was. Never. It was you."

"This morning seems a long way off," he said. "It was in another life. I was somebody else. I feel as if I had been sick, out of my head. But I'm conscious again. I'm alive. Do you love me?"

"Heaps."

"Marry me?"

"Today, if you say so."

Scattergood coughed. "Hey, Clif."

"Yes, Mr. Baines."

"Goin' past the hotel? Eh? Figger to walk that way?"

"I could."

"Um. . . . Know where Falkner's room is? Remember which number?"

"Of course."

"Hadn't any idee of goin' up to see him ag'in, had ye?"

Clif's eyes twinkled. "I could."

"Would ye be int'rested to take Maggie with ye?"

"If it would do any good."

"Wa-al, wouldn't be goin' right naow, would ye? This here minute?"

"It's a good minute."

"I'll be onto my piazza when ye come out from seein' him," said Scattergood.

It was more than half an hour before the young couple reappeared. You would not have known them. They owned the earth.

"Do you know what?" he called as soon as he was within earshot. "He offered me a job. Engineering job. On the new dam. Twenty-five hundred a year. I—I don't understand how it could happen. Twenty-five hundred a year—and big prospects of advancement. It's a miracle."

" 'Tain't no miracle," said Scattergood. "Jest science. D'ye know, I kind of wisht I'd bought me that there book the agent was a-sellin'. Not to study, mind ye. Not to read. Jest to keep around."

"I don't understand," said Clif.

"Jest to kind of keep me reminded what a heap of amazin' scientific stuff a feller knows 'thout ever knowin' he knows it. Clif, I calc'late a college eddication consists mainly in learnin' long names to call what you allus knowed by the title of Common Sense. G'-by, Clif."

"Thank you, Mr. Baines," said Margaret softly. She understood, but her husband would never know.

X

Life of the Party

Old Mrs. Miggle was well off. She owned the little white house in which she lived, and she had an income which amounted to the considerable sum of $2 for every twenty-four hours in the year. Upon this she lived very well indeed, and even laid a little by after supplying herself with such luxuries as she considered desirable.

She was of comfortably cushioned figure and was very proud of her snowy hair, which she washed regularly in a solution of bluing to make it appear more silvery. Her married son and daughter watched over her more vigilantly than she liked, but for all that she went on an occasional spree as far as Higgins Bridge, where she went to the movies, gorged on ice cream and cake, and generally demeaned herself in a regrettably profligate manner. Her children could do nothing about this.

She never missed a service in the Congo Church, nor a sociable nor a missionary meeting. She was a confirmed attendant at funerals, there was always a settin' of tea on the kitchen stove, and she could count a cribbage hand as quickly as any man in Coldriver.

Her age was seventy-two years.

Scattergood Baines was passing her house one afternoon when he heard a triumphant voice on the front stoop exclaim, "Fifteen—eight and fifteen's twenty-three—'n' out!"

"Drat it 'n' doggone it!" said another voice whose owner had apparently reached the limit of human endurance. "I never see sich a woman! I hain't a-goin' to endure it no more. I hain't a-goin' to set here every day and git the tar licked out of me with jest bullheaded luck. Pick up twenty-three in the dummy! I'm a-goin' home and I don't calc'late to come back, neither."

Scattergood, who, as may be remembered, was the owner of the hardware store in Coldriver, and of the railroad and of about everything worth owning in the valley—in addition to being political dictator of the state—put his hand on the latch of the gate and entered.

"Mr. Toomey hain't lost his temper ag'in, has he?" he asked. "He hain't gone and flew all to pieces once more?"

"He's allus doin' it," said Mrs. Miggle tranquilly. "Wust disposition of a man I ever see."

"I hain't nuther," declared Mr. Toomey excitedly. "I'm one of the calmest fellers ye ever see, but I can't abide settin' here day after day 'n' watching you pick twenty-three hands out of the dummy."

"I wouldn't of picked this one out," said Mrs. Miggle, "if you hadn't of put in a four and a six."

This seemed to render Mr. Toomey frantic. "How'd I know you was a-goin' to put in two fives and then git another one turned? Eh? Tell me that."

"One of Mr. Toomey's deefects," said Mrs. Miggle to Scattergood, "is that he hain't spry at envisionin' the future. He don't set back and calc'late on the consequences of puttin' in a four 'n' a six."

"The's two kinds of folks," said Scattergood. "There's the foreseein' folks and the trustin' ones. I dunno which gits the best of it. The foreseein' ones is wrong mebbe half the time, and the trustin' ones is right fifty per cent. Both of 'em has a habit of forgettin' the occasions when they was wrong."

"Jest the same I'm a-goin' home and I hain't a-comin' back," said Mr. Toomey.

"I was kind of thinkin' a cup of tea 'n' some ginger cookies 'ud be sort of fortifyin'," said Mrs. Miggle placidly.

"Wa-al, g'-by, Mr. Toomey," said Scattergood, with expressionless face. "I calc'late I'll set with Mrs. Miggle 'n' eat your share."

Mr. Toomey's face fell and his blue eyes darkened with a pathetic, baffled expression. His prominent Adam's apple went up and down. He got laggingly to his feet, too proud to surrender, and limped resolutely toward the steps.

"Come to think of it, though," said Scattergood, "the' was a matter I wanted to take up with ye."

"Sich as?" asked Mr. Toomey, with suddenly blossoming hope.

"Matter of politics," said Scattergood. "Kind of wanted your advice."

"Guess I kin linger long enough to help ye out, Scatter-good," said Mr. Toomey.

Mrs. Miggle got up unobtrusively and ambled into the house. Mr. Toomey's eyes followed her wistfully.

"I jest wanted to git your idees," said Scattergood, "on this here goin' off'm the gold standard."

Mr. Toomey cleared his throat. "Now, you take the time General Grant was president," he said importantly. "That there was a time when a body had to think about gold. Yes, sir—what with Jay Gould 'n' Jim Fisk 'n' them tryin' to bamboozle the govamint. You can bet your bottom dollar. 'N' then the' was Bryan 'n' his sixteen-to-one. Now, you take Bryan: He was a mighty handsome feller and he come close't to bein' elected." He sat back and looked very wise.

"Lucky you come to me, Scattergood. I understand them things. So I've give' ye the hull gold situation in a nutshell, hain't I?"

"I was kind of bewildered," admitted Scattergood, "but you up 'n' cleared things fur me so's I kin see what stand I ought to take. Um. . . . Mr. Toomey, why don't ye marry her?"

"Who? Me? Marry who?"

"Mrs. Miggle," said Scattergood.

"Ye hadn't ought to make sich jokes," said Mr. Toomey, after a short pause.

"I thought mebbe you was figgerin' on it," said Scattergood.

"I'm seventy-four."

"Methuselah was a sight older."

"'N' the's another p'int," said Mr. Toomey. "She's a rich woman, Mrs. Miggle is. Me, I hain't got nothin'." He drew himself up. "Besides, I hain't a-goin' to have people traipsin' around sayin' I married fur money." He paused and considered. "'N' on top of that her childern 'n' my childern wouldn't let us."

"I git your p'int of view," said Scattergood soberly. "A feller like you couldn't abide to have his feller townsmen gossipin' he was a fortune hunter. No, siree."

"I don't git my hands onto fifty dollars a year," said Mr. Toomey hopelessly. "My childern give me my board 'n' keep, but I hain't able to work much on account of my back." Mr. Toomey's back had prevented him from working much for as long as Scattergood could remember, which was more than a generation. "When my back went lame on me," Mr. Toomey said, "I should 'a' gone into politics. Fitted fur it, that's what I be. I understand them things. But I jest didn't git around to it."

"Seems kind of too bad. Mrs. Miggle's perty lonesome by herself in this here house, 'n' you're kind of lonesome."

"I kind of had it in the back of my mind," said Mr. Toomey, "to marry Mis' Miggle twenty-five, thutty year ago when she fust got to be a widder. But somehow I never got around to it."

"Calc'late Mis' Miggle 'ud agree?"

Mr. Toomey drew himself up, threw out his chest, and stared fiercely at Scattergood. "The' was a day," he said, "when I could 'a' had my pick of the wimmin in this here caounty."

"Huh. . . . Most folks still figgers you're a fine, up-standin' man," said Scattergood.

"Only thing ag'in' it," said Mr. Toomey, "is I couldn't up 'n' go home when I git mad."

"But, on tother hand," Scattergood argued, "you'd git to eat Mis' Miggle's cookin' three times a day."

"Can't be done," said Mr. Toomey dolefully. "Fust, I won't live off'm no woman. Second, our childern wouldn't tolerate it."

"I dunno which is the wust," said Scattergood; "childern stickin' their noses into the lives of their parents, or pa's and ma's meddlin' with the lives of their childern."

"My son-in-law, him that I live with," said Mr. Toomey, "is allus a-talkin' about me movin' off some'eres." He swallowed and his old eyes grew dark and troubled. "Two, three times he's kind of hinted about the Old Folks' Home."

"Um. . . . Ye wouldn't like that idee, Mr. Toomey? Eh? Ye wouldn't like all the comp'ny there'd be to the Old Folks' Home?"

"I been a proud man, Scattergood. I couldn't endure to be eatin' the bread of charity. I druther starve in a dawg-kennel. . . . And that hain't all, nuther. Mrs. Miggle's daughter's allus talkin' how it hain't fit fur her to be livin' here alone. Says she ought to have somebuddy in the house with her. She gits to talkin' about it bein' wasteful to keep two houses a-goin' when only one's necessary."

"Mrs. Miggle, she wouldn't like that?"

"Even old folks," said Mr. Toomey, "likes to have a foot of earth they kin call their own. Ye never git so aged you're willin' to bog down and git bossed mornin', noon, and night. Even if 'tain't more 'n a room, ye want it fur yourself, where ye kin shet the door and be on your own proppity. Makes ye feel like ye amount to suthin'. Young folks don't figger old folks got any feelin's or desires nor nothin'. Jest on account of a body's nigh eighty don't mean he's content if he gits his meals. Aged folks, Scattergood, hain't shadders. They're alive just as much as they was when they was twenty. They don't want to be pushed and shunted. I hain't sure but dyin' seems jest as distant 'n' remote to a man like me as it does to a young feller. By dad, Scattergood! Old folks is people; they hain't jest things with arms 'n' laigs to git shunted around regardless."

Scattergood nodded. "Seems as though," he said. "It hain't so good to be old 'n' dependent. Bad enough to git old. Um. . . . Here comes Mis' Miggle 'n' them refreshments."

"Younger folks," said old Mr. Toomey, "don't put no value on us old ones. We hain't nothin' but a nuisance. The's times when I jest set and spend the hull day a-feelin' helpless."

Scattergood ate generously of the fat sugar cookies supplied by Mrs. Miggle, and took his leave thoughtfully. He returned to his hardware store, where business was not brisk, and seated himself on his specially reinforced chair on the piazza. It was a vantage point from which he could watch the affairs of Coldriver, and there was little that missed his keen old eyes. ·

If you knew him well you would know he was confronted by a problem that baffled him. Presently his hand stole downward and unlaced his right shoe. He kicked it off, closed his eyes, and twiddled his toes. It seemed his mind could not function at its most efficient with his feet imprisoned.

After a time the afternoon train whistled its way into the station—the train on Scattergood's twenty-five-mile railroad. Pliny Pickett, who, in ancient days, had driven the stage along the road now occupied by rails, and was now a uniformed train conductor, came across the bridge to make his daily report.

"Afternoon, Scattergood," he said.

"Afternoon, Pliny."

"I seen Ham Stanley hobnobbin' with Jonas Plummer from Gainesboro. A-standin' on the platform down to the junction with their heads together."

"Dew tell," said Scattergood.

"The's talk Plummer's kind of plannin' on controllin' the legislature follerin' election."

"Ye s'prise me," said Scattergood. "Um. . . . How's it feel to be aged, Pliny?"

"How'd I know?" demanded the conductor belligerently. "I hain't but seventy."

"What keeps ye young, Pliny? Eh? What keeps renewin' your youth?"

"Hain't never had time to git old."

"I calc'late," said Scattergood, more than half to himself, "it's that there uniform with the brass buttons does it. Yes, siree. I betcha it's that. Makes ye feel important. When ye git along in years it's mighty needful to feel important. Better 'n money."

"Mebbe so."

"Yeah. When you're jest a boy, the most soul-fillin' thing in the world is this here emotion folks calls love; when ye git middle-aged, it's money; when ye git old, it's havin' folks deferrin' to ye 'n' thinkin' ye amount to suthin' in spite of your years."

"What's that got to do with politics?" Pliny demanded.

"Nothin'. I jest got to thinkin'."

"Wa-al, ye better git to thinkin' about what schemes Jonas Plummer's contrivin' to upset your applecart."

"G'-by, Pliny," said Scattergood.

"G'-by, Scattergood."

The old hardware merchant sat watching the comings and goings on the street. Just before five o'clock he saw James Leader come out of Sam Kettleman's store and cross the street.

"How be ye, Jim?" asked Scattergood. "Country run to suit ye?"

"Suit me better if I could git away from here," said Leader sourly. "Suit me better if my wife didn't have so many relatives."

"Hain't got but one, has she?"

"That's more 'n enough. Drag onto me. If Ol' Man Toomey'd only be content to go to the Old Folks' Home I could git to goin'. The's an openin' down to Brampton I could fit into. Danged ol' coot. I've wrote and, if this here place's open, he's a-goin' to go whether he's content or not."

"Hain't much expense, is he?"

"I git sick of seein' him underfoot."

"Um. . . . Give ye another forty year 'n' you'll be aged, yourself."

"Mebbe, but, by dang, I won't be dependent onto my daughter's husband."

Scattergood grunted. "G'-by, Jim," he said in dismissal and closed his eyes.

After a while he got up and ambled across the road to the livery barn, where his old mare was hitched and waiting for him. He had never taken to the motorcar. Slowly he drove out to the edge of town, where Mandy would have supper ready.

"I was to a missionary meetin' to young Mis' Miggle's this afternoon," she announced.

"I bet ye talked 'em deef and blind," said Scattergood.

"I done my share," said Mandy placidly. "But I done some listenin', too. Mis' Miggle was goin' on about her ma livin' alone. She's goin' to shet her house and move in on the old woman."

"Calc'late that's their business," said Scattergood.

"Whenever was it you give a darn whose business anythin' was?" asked Mandy. "You better do suthin' about this. It'll kill the ol' woman. Takin' away her independence like that! . . . You stick your nose in plenty things. Now go 'n' stick it into this."

"What kin I do? Eh? Tell me that."

"That," said Mandy, "is fur you to contrive." Her tone was one of finality.

"I got my hands chuck-full, what with election a-comin' on."

"Wa-al, you got 'em fuller now," said Mandy, and disappeared into the kitchen.

Scattergood, following his custom when there was nothing of importance to keep him out of his bed, retired shortly after nine and slept until the extraordinarily late hour of six in the morning. He ate a quite astonishing number of flapjacks drowned in maple sirup, hitched the old mare, and drove down to the hardware store. He opened up, then took his seat on the piazza ready to receive custom.

Young Ware Newton came out of the hotel and walked toward his place of business in the post-office building. Ware was a lawyer, recently graduated from the state university, and was seeking to make his professional fortune in Coldriver.

"Mornin', Ware," said Scattergood. "How be ye?"

"First rate, Mr. Baines. And you?"

"No complaints. Huh. Interested in politics, Ware?"

"Yes, sir."

"Ambitions?"

"Mr. Bones got to be United States senator," Ware said with a grin.

Johnny Bones had started life much as Ware was starting it; he was and had been for years Scattergood's attorney.

"Never kin tell," said Scattergood. "Depends. Um. . . . Like to run fur the legislature, Ware? Eh?"

"Against Ham Stanley?" asked Ware.

"I calc'late he'll want the job ag'in," said Scattergood. He paused. "I said *run*, Ware. Didn't say nothin' about bein' elected."

"You mean you want me to be a candidate in opposition to Ham?"

"Didn't say so, did I?"

"No, Mr. Baines."

"Um. . . ."

"I would like to make the campaign against Ham," said Ware with a grin.

"Might come out so's you wa'n't altogether disapp'inted," said Scattergood. "G'-by, Ware."

"Good morning, Mr. Baines."

"I noticed in politics," said Scattergood, "that the feller that gits to campaignin' fust and loudest don't make no mistake."

"If you listen," said Ware, "you'll hear a young man start running for the legislature in about ten minutes."

"G'-by, Ware," said Scattergood.

Ware was as good as his word. He stopped at the newspaper office and wrote out an announcement of his candidacy, and ordered a supply of placards with his picture on them, to be distributed about the countryside. He paused long enough in the post office to announce to the citizens gathered there for the morning mail that he was.going to oppose Ham Stanley. Then he went upstairs to plan his campaign.

Before noon Ham Stanley was standing on the bottom step of Scattergood's piazza.

"What's this I hear about Ware Newton runnin' against me?" he asked.

"Hain't been out of this here chair this mornin'. Dunno what you heard."

"He's goin' to run."

"Dew tell."

"Now, listen, Scattergood. I been stickin' to you. This here hain't your doin', is it?"

"I hain't got no reason to be dissatisfied with ye, have I? Hain't give' me no cause to distrust ye?"

"No, siree."

"Then ye ought to be contented," said Scattergood. "G'-by, Ham."

In Coldriver the nomination for member of the state legislature was made in caucus, and the caucus was, in effect, a town meeting. Nomination was equivalent to election, because the opposition party was practically nonexistent in the village. So the campaign was internecine strife, and strife it was, because young Ware Newton proved himself a campaigner of remarkable energy and skill.

Nobody knew exactly what was happening, and Scattergood did no enlightening. He sat quiescent on his piazza and took no hand. Citizen after citizen applied to him, but they might as well have questioned the town pump.

"Looks like the boys was scramblin'," he said. "If one or tother of 'em don't win, the way they're goin' at each other, hammer and tongs, I calc'late to be amazed."

"Hain't ye takin' sides?" asked Deacon Pettibone.

"Don't see no call to mix in," Scattergood said.

A few days before the caucus he wired Johnny Bones in Washington. His telegrams always pleased the senator.

"If you have nothing better to do," the telegram read, "there is a caucus here on the eighteenth. Folks say one of two candidates is going to get the nomination."

Johnny read this, and wrinkled his brows. It is true he was a senator and an important man in Washington, but he knew Scattergood placed events in Coldriver above events in the national capital. Scattergood was up to something—that was clear; and Johnny wanted to see what it was.

So he took train to Coldriver and, before he was driven to his home, stopped at the hardware store.

"How be ye, Johnny?" said Scattergood. "Lookin' well."

"Feeling well, Scattergood. What's in the wind?"

"Wa-al," said Scattergood, "it seems Jonas Plummer's figgerin' on acquirin' the state legislature. Yeah. Accordin' to signs 'n' tokens he's up and acquired Ham Stanley. Hide 'n' tail. So it come about that young Ware Newton got the idee of runnin' ag'in' Ham."

"Odd," said Johnny.

"Wa'n't it, now?"

"Where do I come in?"

"Looks like a close fight," said Scattergood. "You're a kind of a diplomatic feller. Mebbe, if ye set your mind to it, ye kin contrive suthin' to soothe all hands."

"Except Ham?"

"Fur some reason or other I hain't concerned about Ham."

"The caucus is Friday?"

"As usual," said Scattergood. "G'-by, Johnny. Folks'll be s'prised to see ye. Didn't come home fur no political reason, did ye?"

"Just came," said Johnny, "to see how the garden was getting along."

Hardly had the senator passed out of sight when old Mr. Toomey stopped before the hardware store.

"Jest come to say good-by," he said, and his old face was stricken. "M' son-in-law, he's got an openin' off some'eres and they're a-sendin' me to the Old Folks' Home come Monday."

"Dew tell!" exclaimed Scattergood.

"Seems like I can't bear it," said the old fellow. "But I guess I hain't no good. I'm jest a burden 'n' a nuisance."

"You don't look like no burden to me," said Scattergood. "You still got time to marry Mis' Miggle 'n' avoid it."

"I got my pride," said Mr. Toomey. "But even if I didn't have 'twouldn't be no use. No, Scattergood. The wust has happened to Mis' Miggle, too. Her daughter's shettin' up the house and movin' in with her. Won't have a place to call her own. Her that's been independent all these years. I could endure it if it was jest me, but I can't a-bear the thoughts of Mis' Miggle."

"Kind of fond of her, Mr. Toomey?"

"We been a-playin' cribbage together fur forty year,"

said Mr. Toomey. "I git exasperated with her. But she kin cook like all git out."

"Um. . . . Got to go Monday, eh?"

"In the mornin'," said Mr. Toomey.

"Anyhow," said Scattergood, "you'll git to see the caucus Friday night."

"Hain't int'rested in no caucuses."

"Kind of take your mind off your troubles if you was to go," said Scattergood. "Goin' to be a squabble."

"My squabblin' days is over," said Mr. Toomey, as he turned away.

Scattergood watched the heartbroken old man move off across the bridge and turn to the right toward Mrs. Miggle's. The old hardware merchant compressed his lips. He did not like to see aching hearts in Coldriver.

Senator Bones apparently took no part in the furious campaigns. Scattergood sat inert and watched. But every day when Pliny Pickett reported on the condition of the railroad he was given oblique instructions. These, as a trustworthy lieutenant, Pliny carried out to the letter.

At home Scattergood did not fare so well. Mandy gave him no peace.

"I told ye to do suthin' about them two ol' folks. Ye hain't made a move."

"I got a p'litical campaign on my hands. Hain't got no time fur side issues."

"Ye better have."

"Mebbe Mr. Toomey'll be better 'n' happier to the Home. Mebbe Mis' Miggle ought to have somebuddy livin' with her. Mebbe it's all fur the best."

"Any time anythin' unpleasant's done to old folks," said Mandy, "their childern says it's all fur the best. It hain't never all fur the best to do suthin' cruel. If ye don't contrive suthin', ye better git your mouth puckered up to eat to the hotel. I won't cook fur ye."

"I hear tell the hotel's got a perty good cook," said Scattergood placidly.

He got up from the breakfast table and drove to the village. It was Friday. At eight o'clock the caucus would be called to order by Sheriff Fox, and the voting would commence. Shortly after noon business in town was suspended. The candidates were making final speeches. Young Ware Newton stopped for a moment at Scattergood's store.

"I think I've got Ham licked, Mr. Baines," he said hopefully.

"Which is better," Scattergood asked, "to be a member of the lower or the upper house in this here state legislature?"

"To be a senator, of course."

"Um. . . . Then ye won't be so disapp'inted in case ye lose."

"I don't believe I can lose."

"Funny things happens. Happen to hear old Senator Graham was ailin' 'n' meanin' to resign? Means special election. Now, a feller that's had good practice a-runnin' for representative ought to be about ready to make a run fur senator. Eh? If it was to turn out you lose."

"Would I have your backing?"

"Hoss, foot, 'n' artillery." Scattergood paused and eyed Ware. "But keep on electioneerin' like all git out."

At seven o'clock the square was crowded; at half past the town hall was full. It was plain that there would be more than a hundred voters. At eight o'clock the sheriff pounded on the table and called the meeting to order. Here was democracy functioning at its best—a meeting of citizenry, members of a political party, to choose in open meeting the candidate to represent them on election day.

"Caount the hands fur Ham Stanley fust," had been Scattergood's only instructions.

As the meeting opened it might have been noted that Pliny Pickett and perhaps a dozen men loitered in the hall outside the main chamber.

Nominations were made and seconded. The voting commenced.

"All in favor of nominatin' Ham Stanley," called the sheriff, "hold up their right hands."

Arms sprouted like asparagus all over the room, and the count was made.

"Fifty-six votes fur Ham Stanley," announced the chairman. "Them in favor of Ware Newton raise their right hands."

He counted aloud, reaching "Fifty, fifty-one, fifty-two."

Pliny pushed four men from his group into the hall, and they lifted their arms.

"Fifty-six," said the sheriff, "and it stands a tie."

The meeting was in an uproar. It was fifteen minutes before order could be restored, and once again the vote was called. It resulted in fifty-eight votes for Ham Stanley— and then, impossibly enough, fifty-eight votes for Ware Newton. Three more ballots were taken. Each time, Pliny Pickett, standing in the door, pushed into the room just enough of his group to make the vote a tie.

Then Senator Bones mounted the rostrum.

"It seems impossible to break this deadlock," he said. "It may result in bitterness which will injure the party. I suggest, therefore, that we compromise upon a third candidate. A compromise candidate. I have in mind a man who will bring honor to the office, who will endow it with mature wisdom and experience and dignity. A man who will worthily represent this town of Coldriver. He is a man with a host of friends and no enemies. He does not seek this office—it seeks him. I am proud to place the name of this splendid citizen before you. Maximus H. Toomey."

There was an astonished silence, broken by Ware Newton.

"Mr. Chairman," he shouted, "I withdraw in favor of Mr. Toomey."

"How about you, Stanley?" called the sheriff.

Pliny Pickett whispered in his ear, "It's better to withdraw 'n' to git licked. Think you 'n' Jonas Plummer's got a chance't in Coldriver?"

Stanley arose, scowling. "In the interests of party unity," he said sourly, "I withdraw in favor of Mr. Toomey."

"There bein' no other candidates before this meetin'," declared Sheriff Fox, "I declare Mr. Toomey the candidate of his party for the office of state representative."

There was a shout. Old Man Toomey sat paralyzed in his chair. Friendly and excited hands raised him to his feet.

"Speech! Speech!" was shouted in his ear.

"It hain't so," said the old main in a low voice. "It jest can't be so." He looked about him in bewilderment. "You folks is jokin'. Me in the legislature. Me an important feller like that! D'ye mean it?"

"You are the nominee of your party," said Senator Bones, "and we are proud of you."

The old man blinked. Quiet tears ran down his leathery cheeks.

"I don't have to go to no Old Folks' Home," he said unbelievingly.

"Indeed not," said Johnny. "Why, you'll get a salary of twelve hundred dollars a year—and mileage."

"More 'n twice't as much as what Mis' Miggle has a-comin' in," the old man whispered. "But 'tain't the money. It's amountin' to suthin'. It's not bein' on the shelf. Why, folks, I hain't no dodderin' old fossil no more! I'm a man ag'in!"

He drew himself up, and the old voice took on strength and timbre.

"Feller citizens," he said, "I'm obleeged to ye. I'll do my best. You won't never have no call to be ashamed." He cleared his throat. "I'm a man of years 'n' experience—that's what I be."

It was not easy to extricate him from the hall, but after a while he found himself in Johnny Bones's car with Scattergood and the senator.

"Where we a-goin'?" he asked.

"We figgered mebbe Mis' Miggle 'ud like to hear. She'll be glad to know you're fixed, even if she's a-goin' to lose her own independence in her own house."

"Who says she is?" demanded Mr. Toomey. "I'll show ye. I'll show all of ye. I'll show them sons 'n' daughters. I calc'late to put 'em in their places."

The car stopped before the white house, and Mr. Toomey sprang out.

"Mis' Miggle! Mis' Miggle!" he called.

"What's wanted?"

"You be," said Mr. Toomey precipitately. "By Dad! I'm a-goin' to perty nigh run this here state, and a feller in my position's got to have a wife. I don't want to hear a word out of ye. Git on your shawl 'n' bonnet. We're goin' to git married!"

"Married! Be ye crazy?"

"Mis' Miggle, you're speakin' to the representative from Coldriver. I don't want no sass."

"But our childern . . . my daughter . . . she's a-movin' in on me next week."

"Hain't nobuddy a-movin' in on ye but me. I'll show 'em.

I'm a-goin' to have twice the income you got. I'm a-movin' in, and bein' your wedded husband, b'heck, nobuddy's movin' into my wife's house 'thout I say so."

"Why, Mr. Toomey!"

"I'm an important man, I be. Calc'late to buy a silk hat. And my wife's an important woman. Git that bonnet on."

"They'll stop us. They'll pervent it."

"Senator," asked Mr. Toomey, "how fast kin this here car go?"

"Possibly eighty miles an hour."

"Squeeze her up to ninety," said Mr. Toomey. "Mis' Miggle 'n' me's elopin'. Head fur Higgins Bridge 'n' a minister."

The shaken but agreeable Mrs. Miggle was seated in the car beside Mr. Toomey and, with the senator and Scattergood for wedding attendants, drove pell-mell to Higgins Bridge. They were married.

Mr. Toomey was majestic. "Mis' Miggle," he said, "you hain't Mis' Miggle no more. You're Mis' Representative Toomey. So act accordin'."

"Yes, Mr. Toomey."

He was silent a moment. "I was chose," he said, "on account of my age 'n' experience. I want to tell ye it's a perty fine and satisfyin' thing to be along in years. Folks looks up to ye."

"Mr. Toomey," said his wife, "you're a fine figger of a man."

"I be," said Mr. Toomey. "Wait till ye hear me makin' a speech in the Capitol." He thought a minute. "The best part of it all is bein' able to tell every young 'n' middle-aged human bein' in the world to go to tunket."

"Amen," said Mrs. Toomey. "Amen to that."

XI

Scattergood Prescribes for the Doctor

,SCATTERGOOD BAINES watched the young man alight from the train. The stranger must have been two inches above six feet. His face was thin, not with illness, for he gave the impression of strength and health, but with something that seemed to Scattergood to indicate a troubled mind; He was not handsome, but he was arresting. His was the sort of face which seems to have lost the ability to lighten with a smile.

The stranger stood in some uncertainty, then slowly turned his head to look about the platform. His eyes came to rest upon Scattergood and he took two strides in the direction of the old hardware merchant.

"There is a hotel?" he asked in a deep, pleasing voice.

"Calc'late so," said Scattergood. "Was the last time I looked. How be ye?"

The young man seemed a bit surprised. "Very well, thank you, sir," he said. "How does one reach the hotel?"

"Sime'll take ye. . . . Drummer?"

"I have nothing to sell. Are you familiar with this locality?"

"Who? Me? Famil'ar with Coldriver? Hain't lived here more 'n fifty year, but I'm commencin' to git acquainted."

"Would there be a small house to rent?"

188

"Figgerin' on stayin' some time?" asked Scattergood.

"Well," said the young man, "I expect to make my home here."

"Huh. . . . My name's Baines—Scattergood Baines. What's yourn?"

"Fort—Eber Fort."

"Heard wuss names," Scattergood said sententiously. He turned his head. "Hey, Sime, ketch holt of Eber's trunk. He's goin' to the hotel temp'rary. G'-by, Eber."

"Good afternoon, Mr. Baines—and thank you."

Eber Fort found himself in Sime's truck moving along the road.

"Is it a good hotel?" he asked.

"Best we got," said Sime. "That," he went on, "was Scattergood Baines."

"Indeed. And who is Mr. Baines?"

"Pertends to run the hardware store," Sime said. "Fact is he runs ever'thin'. Richer 'n Rockefeller. Got the hull state in his pocket when it comes to politics. Owns this here railroad, too."

Eber was silent. Sime spat over the mudguard. "Goin' to settle here, eh? What in tunket fur?"

"It seemed like a good place," said Eber.

"Good place to bog daown 'n' rot. Nothin' ever happens 'n' nothin' ever will happen. No, siree!"

"Do you guarantee that?" asked Eber.

"Guarantee printed plain on every bottle."

"Then I seem to have found what I wanted," said Eber.

Sime delivered Eber and his heavy trunk at the hotel and drove away morosely considering the eccentricities of humanity.

Eber did not unpack his trunk, but presently he went down the stairs and out upon the street. He turned to the

right toward the bridge, the post office, and the bank, and
soon was passing a frame building with a piazza two steps
above the walk. On this piazza dozed the fat old man Eber
had encountered at the depot. But as the young man passed,
Scattergood opened his eyes.

"How be ye, Eber?" he asked.

The young man stopped.

"Speakin' about a house, wa'n't ye?" asked Scattergood.
"I got a kind of a rig. Took it in dicker, lock, stock, 'n' barrel.
Dunno's I made any profit. Stands off by itself, kind of.
Single man, be ye?"

"Yes."

"Mebbe ye better stay to the hotel, then."

"I'd prefer a place of my own," said Eber.

"Kitchen, dinin'-room, parlor, 'n' bedroom. Up yonder on
top of the hill. Furnished 'n' all. I kin let ye have it fur, say,
fifteen dollars a month."

"I should like to see it," said Eber.

Scattergood squirmed, managed to insert a huge hand in
his trousers pocket, and extracted a key. "Ye climb that
road till ye come to a kind of a white place 'thout any barn.
Mebbe half a mile." He grunted. "If the key don't fit when
ye git there you've come to the wrong house. G'-by, Eber."

Eber blinked. He was not accustomed to doing business
in this manner, nor to renting furnished houses for $15 a
month.

"Calc'late to do fur yourself?" asked Scattergood.

"You mean a servant?"

"Don't run to servants around here. Mostly we have hired
help. Now, there's the Widder Brant. Calc'late she'd be
willin' to come to ye fur four-five dollars a week."

Eber climbed the hill, walking slowly and without interest, even though his surroundings were strange to him

and though it was here he proposed to live. At last he reached the top and could see the valley in which nestled the town. It was peaceful, distant from life, drowsy—a backwater of the world where one might lose himself and find oblivion.

He walked on with head down until suddenly he was aware of the pad of feet, and an enormous animal launched itself upon him. He found himself lying in the dust looking up at the largest and most genial puppy he had ever seen. The puppy backed off, crouching with all the coy grace of an elephant.

"Did he knock you down?" asked a voice.

"No," said Eber a trifle ironically. "I was taking a nap here and he just happened along."

"Oh," said the young lady, "you're angry!"

He was conscious of appearing exceedingly absurd when his effort to rise brought an enthusiastic pounce from the St. Bernard puppy.

"Not angry," said Eber. "He seems to mean well, but he's a bit unexpected. If you would attract his attention I might be able to get up."

The young lady called the puppy and Eber got to his feet and looked down upon her. She was slender, young, and pertly beautiful.

"I'm glad you're not going to make a fuss," she said. "So many people make a fuss when he knocks them down."

"I'm rather used to it," he said, and the somber expression returned to his face. "Good morning."

"But I want to apologize."

"Quite unnecessary."

"I never saw you before," she said with directness.

"I only arrived by the latest train."

"What are you doing here?"

"I have come to live."

"Goodness! What for?"

"People up here ask strangers a good many questions," he said.

"Oh, you must have met Mr. Baines! Isn't he a honey?"

"Quite possibly. It has been an experience to encounter you, Miss—" He hesitated briefly, but before he could go on she announced her name.

"Pangborn," she said.

"—and your dog," he concluded.

He lifted his hat and strode onward resolutely. She, on her part, stood stock still and peered after him. Then she spoke to her dog. "Darling," she said, "there is a distinct improvement in Coldriver."

Eber found and inspected the little house. It was isolated, neat, comfortable, exactly what he had hoped to find, so he returned to the village, where Scattergood still sat on his piazza.

"I shall be very glad to rent your house, Mr. Baines," he said.

"Aim to swell our pop'lation, eh? Goin' into business?"

"I am going," said Eber, "to think."

"Calc'late to work at it long?" asked Scattergood.

"Until," said Eber, "I reach a conclusion."

"I'm kind of int'rested," said Scattergood. "Be ye jest a-goin' to think kind of general, or be ye a-goin' to think about somethin' p'tic'lar?"

"About myself," said Eber.

"Interestin' topic," said Scattergood, "but the' hain't much money into it."

Eber expressed his thanks and walked on toward the hotel. Scattergood stared after him. Something was wrong here. A young man, obviously of education and ability, who was running away from something; surrendering the life he had known, giving up his ambitions, his friends, to secrete himself in Coldriver. Scattergood puzzled over it. From what was the young man in flight? He did not act, to Scattergood's way of thinking, as a fugitive from justice would act.

Eber moved into his cottage; the Widow Brant took charge of his household; and Coldriver, as was its habit, stood aloof but observant.

Mrs. Brant reported that he was a nice young man and easy to do for. He did not seem to care what he ate. He arose early, had nothing to say about himself, read a great deal, and took long walks. Gradually the knowledge permeated the village that Eber kept irregular hours. He was encountered tramping the roads after midnight. He was seen by early risers prowling about the countryside before dawn. And what Coldriver does not understand it is suspicious of. Lights were seen in his house at impossible hours. It seemed he never slept. And so he found the villagers looking at him askance. Though he seemed to be unaware of people, he could not but be aware of the spirit of antagonism that commenced to surround him.

Then Vigo Payne's little dog disappeared; for three days it remained unaccounted for, and then it was found down by the East Branch, and it was dead. It had not died peacefully. Coldriver inspected the little dog and gritted its teeth. A week later Palmer Crafts' dog was missing, and days afterward it was found dead in the same manner.

It was recalled in the post office that Eber, though he frequently did not notice human beings who greeted him, never failed to pause to exchange the time of day with a friendly dog. This was magnified until it became significant evidence.

"It stands to reason," said Elder Hooper to Scattergood, "that somebody done these here depredations. Nobody ever done 'em till this here Eber come to taown. Allus makin' up to dawgs, hain't he? Proba'ly he's one of these here fiends you read about in the Bostin papers."

"If pattin' a dawg makes a feller a fiend," said Scattergood, "I calc'late I'm kind of the kingpin of all of 'em."

"What's he allus a-prowlin' at night fur? It hain't fur no good."

"What I like about you religious folks, like you 'n' the deacon," said Scattergood, "is ye kin detect evil so fur and read it so plain. Calc'late it's a gift, hain't it?"

"We got eyes to see," said the elder. "This here taown's gittin' aroused ag'in' this young man. If he hain't careful he'll be gittin' himself a ride on a rail with feathers a-sproutin' out of him."

So, thought Scattergood, this was the sort of talk that was going around! Tar and feathers!

"Elder," said Scattergood, "if I was a feller in your position I'd be a-smoothin' down instid of a-stirrin' up, seems as though."

"He's got idle hands," said the elder grimly, "and Satan he up 'n' finds work fur idle hands to do."

"G'-by, Elder. Seems as though I hain't got patience to talk with ye today. Havin' lived in this here world a consid'able spell I got an idee Satan finds jest as much work fur busy hands to do as he does fur idle ones. And the busy ones is more industrious performin' it, because they hain't lazy. G'-by, Elder."

The elder walked away morosely and Scattergood went on considering the problem. As he sat with half-closed eyes an enormous young dog led a petite young lady across the bridge and stopped in front of the hardware store.

"Mr. Baines," she demanded, "have you heard all this terrible talk that's going around about that new young man, Mr. Fort?"

"Jest been a-listenin' to a sample," said Scattergood.

"I've never done so much walking in my life as I have in the past two weeks," she said.

"What fur?"

"To pounce out at him," she confessed. "He doesn't like it. But I told him he'd get to like me when he knew me."

"Know anything about him, Melissa? Any p'tic'lars?"

"None. He won't answer questions. All I know is he's just chock full of knowledge about bones and insides. He calls different parts of people by the most outlandish names."

"Um. . . ."

"He doesn't like himself," said Melissa.

"If I was a little girl with kind of romantic notions," said Scattergood, "I'd kind of work 'em off readin' books. It hain't considered safe to go chasin' after young fellers ye don't know."

"I know a great deal about him," she said promptly.

"Sich as?"

"He is very sad. He wouldn't hurt a mouse. Something terrible has happened to him, and he's afraid. He's got a smile that makes you want to cry. If he ever fell in love with a woman he wouldn't ever be able to see anybody else. And I won't have him tarred and feathered—so there!"

"Calc'late we can't have that happen," said Scattergood. "Have you told him you've kind of chose him?"

"I've hinted," she said, "but he's so abstracted and all he doesn't seem to notice."

At this point the puppy lumbered off up the street, dragging his young lady protesting behind him.

Toward midafternoon Vigo Payne, accompanied by three

other somber men, stopped at Scattergood's piazza. "Scattergood," said Vigo, "they jest found Mis' Ware's dawg.
Dead like the rest of 'em."

Scattergood breathed deeply.

"I got me a letter from Bostin," said Elmer Ruddy, peer-
ing up at Scattergood out of his single eye. "Yes, sir. I
kind of figgered from things that this here Eber Fort come
from there, so I wrote. What I heard was aplenty."

"Sich as?" asked Scattergood.

"Kicked out of the hospital where he was aworkin' fur
doin' suthin' so low down that nobody don't dast talk about
it," said Elmer. "Doctor—that's what he was. Naow, we figgered it was a doctor killed them dawgs the way they was
killed."

"High-class figgerer, hain't ye, Elmer? Did ye go so fur's
to figger what fur a doctor 'ud want to kill dawgs?"

"We done so," said Vigo. "We figgered he's one of them
vivisection fellers. Only wuss. I mean mebbe it's right to
cut up dawgs scientific. But it hain't right to cut 'em up
fur fun. Scattergood," Vigo went on, "I'm one of them that's
lost a dawg. I'd like to lay hands onto the one that done it."

"Don't blame ye," said Scattergood. "But ye wouldn't
like to lay hands onto the one that didn't do it."

"It's why I'm a-hesitatin' and kind of holding the boys
back. So fur the' hain't no evidence fur the law. I'm a law-
abidin' citizen, Scattergood, but the's times a thing happens
the law can't git at."

"Never heard tell of one," said Scattergood. "If ye kin
git proof to convince a hull taown a man ought to be tarred
'n' feathered it's evidence enough to give to a jury, seems
as though. If ye can't convince twelve decent men in a
courtroom, then ye ought to set still 'n' move ag'in' no
person."

"So I have argued, Scattergood, but the boys don't agree with me. But I've talked 'em into settin' a watch. We got sev'ral that's volunteered to set up nights 'n' foller this Eber Fort 'n' watch until we ketch him in the act."

"Or ketch somebuddy else," said Scattergood.

"The' hain't nobuddy else to ketch," Elmer declared. "Nobuddy else in taown 'ud commit no sich depredation."

Scattergood puffed. "And who," he asked, "is a-goin' to watch the watchers?"

"The watchers," said Elmer, "don't need no watchin'."

"G'-by, boys," said Scattergood.

"Hain't got no advice fur us?" asked Vigo.

"I've already give' it," said Scattergood. "G'-by."

Scattergood ambled across to the livery barn and had his mare hitched to his ancient buggy. Then he drove up the hill toward Eber Fort's.

Presently he saw three figures coming toward him and became aware that Melissa had been successful in that day's quest, for she and her huge puppy were walking along beside Eber Fort. The old hardware merchant drew up and nodded.

"How be ye, Melissa? How be ye, Eber?" he greeted them. Then he frowned down at Melissa, "Scat!" he said. "Eber 'n' me's got business."

She looked up at him and he saw how worried her eyes were. "Will it really be a good idea if I scram?" she asked.

"If scram means clear out," Scattergood said, "it'll be as good an idee as you've had today. G'-by."

The old man sat silent in his buggy until she was out of earshot. Then he asked, "How be ye, Dr. Fort?" he asked.

The young man raised his eyes slowly, and they were stricken eyes. His lips twisted in a smile. "So it's caught up with me already?" he asked.

"A feller," said Scattergood, "can't run away from himself, because he's got to lug himself along. You wa'n't a-runnin' from whatever it was ye done as much as ye was tryin' to escape from yourself."

"How do you know?"

Scattergood did not answer that question, but asked one himself: "D'ye calc'late it 'ud be a good idee to tell me about it?" He paused. "The tale that's goin' around could be improved consid'able by the truth. Was ye kicked out of the hospital for committin' an atrocity?"

"I was not dismissed from the hospital," said Eber. "I resigned."

"To forestall bein' kicked out?"

"No. Not for what happened, but for what might happen next time."

"Somebuddy died on account of your heedlessness? Eh? Was it like that?"

"No. I was supposed," said Eber, "to be a surgeon. It is not immodest to say I was gaining a reputation. I was in the operating-room. A child was on the table. The anesthetic had been given. It was a mastoid. I reached out my hand to the nurse for the instrument I required and she handed it to me. Then I dared not operate. I was afraid, I tell you. I stood there trembling, afraid to touch the patient. I—" He paused and his face twisted. "I lost confidence in myself. I remember telling them I could not operate, and walked out of the room. Then I was sitting in a chair and I was crying—crying from fright. So I resigned. I was no good. I was a coward. . . . That's the story."

"Um. . . . Int'rested in vivisection?"

"It never had my approval," Eber said.

"Dew tell. And so ye let go and come to hide yourself here?"

"To see if I could think of anything to do with my life," said Eber.

"I'll drive ye back home," said Scattergood. "Git in." Eber obeyed with an odd docility. "Huh. If I was you I'd kind of stay around the house fur a spell," Scattergood said. "I wouldn't do no walkin' to speak of. Especial not at night."

"Why, Mr. Baines?"

"Because," said Scattergood cryptically, "they won't take my advice to watch the watchers." They arrived at the cottage. "G'-by, Eber," said the old man.

Scattergood drove back down the hill and presently was dozing again on the piazza of his hardware store. After a time Pliny Pickett came strutting along in his uniform as conductor of Scattergood's passenger train, which ran back and forth to and from the Junction some twenty miles down the valley.

"How be ye, Pliny?" Scattergood asked.

"Rheumatiz troublin' me," complained Pliny. But he brightened. "Hain't so bad off as Doc Boyle, though. Hisn's got him daown. Can't turn over in bed."

"Hope the' don't no babies come along tonight, then," said Scattergood, for the venerable Doc Boyle was Coldriver's sole physician. "How's traffic?"

"Six passengers 'n' consid'able express. The boys is riled up, Scattergood."

"Hear any talk, Pliny? Hear any talk?"

"They aim to set a watch on this here Eber Fort, and then git word to the boys quick if they ketch him at anythin'. Plan to deal with him vig'rous."

"G'-by, Pliny."

The old hardware merchant went home to his supper and sat down to make believe he was reading. At nine-thirty he yawned. It was his bedtime. But as he slipped his galluses down over his shoulders the telephone rang. The tearful voice of Melissa Pangborn came to him over the wire.

"Oh, Mr. Baines, my puppy has disappeared. I can't find him anywhere."

Scattergood frowned. He slipped his galluses up over his shoulders again and reached for his hat.

Melissa, too, could not remain in the house. She drove her little car into the village, driving slowly, stopping frequently to whistle. But there was no sign of the puppy. She turned up the hill into the road past Eber Fort's house. There was a light, but she did not draw up there. Every now and then she stopped to whistle. Her headlights illuminated the road, and presently they fell upon two approaching figures. One was a man; one was a dog. She brought the car to a screeching stop. It was her big St. Bernard, and there was a rope around his neck and he was being dragged along unwillingly by Eber Fort.

She leaped from the car, snatched the rope from his hand, and blazed at him: "You—you—oh, it was true after all! Give me my puppy, you dog-murderer! Oh, I hope they tar and feather you!"

She cuffed the puppy into her car, and before Eber could open his mouth she whizzed down the road.

Because she felt the need to unbosom herself to someone, Melissa continued through the village to Scattergood's house. He was just descending the steps. "I caught him!" she cried. "He was dragging the puppy along the road on a rope! He was going to—to do what he did to those other dogs."

"Who was?" asked Scattergood.

"That Eber Fort," she said. "I want them to hurt him! I want them to do dreadful things to him!"

"Hush!" said Scattergood. "Ye don't want nothin' of the sort."

A second car stopped at the gate, and Melissa's heart missed a beat because there arose from it a thin, terrible wail, almost a scream, of baby agony.

"Who's that?" demanded the old man.

"Vigo Payne," came a man's hoarse voice. "It's my leetle Mary. She's took terrible bad. I'm carryin' her to Doc Boyle. It's her head ag'in, Scattergood."

"Git along," Scattergood said. "We'll foller."

A quarter of a mile brought them to the home of Dr. Boyle. The old man marched into the doctor's bedroom, where Boyle lay groaning. The old doctor, as best he could, examined the patient.

"Vigo," he said, "it's like what I feared." He pointed back of her ear. "It's a hospital operation. Even if I was up and around, I couldn't do it. I'm no surgeon. Only hope is to get her to a hospital."

"Can't ye do nothin', Doc?"

"Vigo, I'm nothing but an old country doctor. I haven't the skill."

Scattergood leaned over the bed. "Gimme that baby," he said grimly.

Surprised, uncomprehending, Vigo and Melissa followed him. "Up to Eber Fort's house," he commanded.

The car roared up the hill, sped down the road, and stopped at Eber's door. Scattergood, the baby in his arms, kicked the door open. Eber sprang to his feet.

"Doc," said Scattergood, "you got a case. Boyle says it's got to be operated."

"But I ——"

"Life or death," Scattergood snapped. "Be ye a man? Be ye a-goin' to set by and see a baby die fur want of your skill?" He thrust the child into Eber's arms, and the young man stared down at it.

"Got your tools?" Scattergood demanded.

"Yes."

"Use 'em," Scattergood said. "Whatever 'tis it's jest behind her ear."

"Mastoid!" It was exactly this operation he had flunked. It was this that had made his nerve crumple and caused the ruin of his career. . . . Suddenly Eber stiffened. "Light all the lamps," he said crisply. "Clear the dining-room table. You—girl—" he seemed to have forgotten Melissa's name. "Ever administer an anesthetic?"

"Never."

He sighed. "Do as I tell you, then—and don't fail me."

Thus, crudely, on a hard table lighted insufficiently by oil lamps, he prepared to work. A sort of cheer that was more a roar sounded from the not distant village. It sounded from the throats of a score of young men who had lingered hopefully in the cribbage club—to which had come Elmer Ruddy. Elmer had a dog in his arms, and the dog was freshly dead.

"I ketched him!" he shouted. "I ketched him in the act—'n' there's the evidence!"

So, stirred to vengeful rage, the twenty young men roared out of the cribbage club and marched grimly up the hill. The night was no longer still. The score of young men approached noisily. So deep was Eber's concentration that he did not hear, but Scattergood heard and Melissa heard. At last even Eber was forced to hear, but he did not turn his head.

"Stop that noise," he snapped, as his deft hands went about their task.

"Keep a-goin', Doc," said Scattergood. "I'll see if I kin quiet 'em."

"Yes, yes! Stop them!" It was a cry wrung from Melissa. "They're coming for Eber. Maybe to lynch him."

Eber's hand paused ever so slightly. "Lynch me?" he asked vaguely, as if he did not comprehend, as if he were too deep in concentration to understand. He was muttering to himself as he worked. "Keep them quiet ten minutes."

Then the mob was at the door, shouting grimly for Eber to come out. The young man was fully conscious of the mob's presence now. It had come to do something to him, for some unknown reason. He glanced once at Melissa and shook his head.

"They sha'n't hurt you!" she said through clenched teeth.

"Pay attention," he snapped.

Minutes passed. Five minutes, ten minutes. Eber worked swiftly, deftly. The smell of ether and of disinfectants filled the room. Now the terrible work was done. Eber sighed and stood erect. "There," he said. "There. The rest is beyond a surgeon's art." He stared across at Melissa. "Put her in my bed," he said. And then, "I did it! And I didn't crack."

"You were wonderful—wonderful."

He walked to the door, and a low, angry growl greeted him. Scattergood stepped before him. "Boys," said the old man, "Eber's jest been savin' the life of a baby. Hain't it fair ye sh'u'd kind of give him a chance to clear himself? Eh? What fetched all this on? He didn't do nothin' to Melissa's dawg."

"He killed Pete Wayland's setter," said Elmer.

"Where 'n' when?"

"Clearin' daown by the East Branch. He was seen."

"What time, eh? What time?"

"Hour ago."

"Who seen him?"

"Elmer. Elmer fetched in the dawg."

"Elmer, eh? M'lissa, come here. Where was you an hour ago?"

"On this road a quarter of a mile down."

"Who'd you meet?"

"Eber Fort—leading my dog."

"Hear that?" asked Scattergood. "East Branch's a mile 'n' a half away, hain't it? Eber was here, boys. But some-buddy else was there. Who's got a reppitation for beatin' his hosses? Who was it busted a horn off'm a cow this here spring? 'Twa'n't Eber. Wa'n't but one feller where this dawg was killed, and that feller couldn't 'a' been Eber. Elmer'll bear a lot of lookin' into, seems as though."

There was a silence, an odd silence. "Give ye a hint to watch the watchers, didn't I? Eh? Who was a-watchin' Elmer?" demanded Scattergood.

"Ye can't prove it!" shouted Elmer.

"Kind of go through his pockets, boys."

The men seized their neighbor. In a pocket was a hunting knife—bloodstained.

Scattergood said, "Don't go committin' no more errors this here night. Elmer's pa had to be shet up, didn't he? Wa-al, tomorrer we'll kind of institute an inquiry into if Elmer wouldn't be better off shet up, too. . . . G'-by, boys."

He turned his back on them and went into the house. Eber followed, and Melissa.

"Done it, didn't ye, Doc?" Scattergood said. "Yeah. With a growlin' mob outside. Don't look like no lack of nerve to me."

Eber's face was radiant. "Fear is gone," he said. "It will never return. I'm going back. I'm going to live again."

"Calc'late we'll miss ye," said Scattergood. "Um. M'lissa done splendid tonight, Doc."

Eber smiled down at her. "I found the puppy lost in the woods," he said.

"I'm ashamed. It—I thought it had broken my heart."

Eber looked into her eyes. "Did you really mean it when you pursued me all over the township?"

"Like everything," she said.

"You'll never have to pursue me again—because I'll always be at your heels," he said. "If you want me there."

"I dunno," said Scattergood, "but I better clear out."

"Yes, do," said Melissa.

"Huh. . . . Kind of fort'nate, seems as though. Lots of fellers goes to pot on account of they don't never git no chance to git acquainted with themselves. Yeah. Scairt of themselves because they don't have the luck to git tested. Um. . . . Wa-al, Eber, you give yourself the right answers. G'-by."

"And don't come back," said Melissa. "Not for an hour."

XII

Scattergood Deals in Dreams

SCATTERGOOD BAINES was of an inquiring disposition. Nothing was so minute as to fail to arouse his curiosity, and no human activity was too trivial for him to meddle with. So, when he passed the white, fence-enclosed house of Urban Downs, he stopped and sniffed, because an exceedingly pungent and disagreeable odor assailed his nose. He endeavored to identify the smell, but it was beyond him, and because his nature was such as it was, he simply could not go along about his own business until he found out about the smell.

So he opened the gate and walked around to the kitchen door, where Mrs. Downs was standing over her cookstove. "Mornin', Em'ly," said Scattergood. "How be ye?"

"Middlin', Scattergood."

"Em'ly, what in tunket you cookin'? Eh? When I was passin' I got a sniff of it. Kind of a new dish fur these parts, seems as though. Got a kind of a foreign smell to it."

Mrs. Downs compressed her lips. "No sich stink as that ever come out of my kitchen," she said tartly.

"I was wonderin'," Scattergood said. "'Tain't an odor that makes one think natural of cookstoves. Kind of clingin' 'n' penetratin'," he observed, and put his nose up in the air to sample it again. "Suthin' die under the house?"

206

"It's young Urban," said Mrs. Downs wearily.

"Ye better git him off to a doctor," said Scattergood.

"He's inventin'," said Urban's mother.

"Inventin' suthin' to make the neighbors move away, eh?"

"It's scientific," she said. "I forgit how many millions he calc'lates to make out of it. So fur all he's made is to make me sick to the stummick."

"Kind of clings to ye, don't it? Where's the source of it— in that there old tool shed out in the back yard?"

"Urban he fitted it up to be one of them there laboratories," she said. "Four year in college, and what does his pa 'n' me git out of it? I'll tell ye, Scattergood Baines. What we git out of that there boy's eddication is to be stunk out of house 'n' home."

"Em'ly," said Scattergood, "I'm all-fired cur'ous to diskiver what kin create sich a stench. Urban out there a-brewin' it now?"

"He's a-brewin' it all the time, when he hain't a-brewin' suthin' wuss," said his mother.

Scattergood ambled away from the kitchen door and, without hesitating to inquire if he would be welcome, walked toward the door of young Urban's workshop. The door stood open, the better to allow the escape of malodorous fumes. Scattergood coughed and snorted, but was not to be daunted. He stood in the open door and surveyed young Urban, who was so surrounded by gadgets and lights and trays and retorts and wires as to be all but invisible. He cleared his throat, and Urban turned.

"Morning, Mr. Baines," he said.

"I kind of got attracted to this here spot like a bee gits attracted to a flower garden," said Scattergood. "Mebbe you didn't take note of it, Urban, but this here locality is a bit high."

"So Mother says," replied the young man. "You get used to it."

"How long does that take?" asked Scattergood. "I dunno's I could wait, or if it'd be wuth while. Gettin' used to a smell is a kind of hard work that don't pay enough wages. What ye up to, anyhow?"

"Television," said young Urban.

"What say?"

"Television," repeated Urban with some patience. "The transmission of pictures in the same way that radio transmits sound."

"Who wants to see 'em?"

"Everybody," answered Urban.

"Everybuddy but me," Scattergood rejoined. "I dunno's I crave to have no pictures transmitted to where I kin see 'em."

"Wouldn't you like to sit in your home and be able to see the President making a speech in Washington?"

"Druther see him 'n I would hear him," said Scattergood.

"Or watch an actual battle while it's going on over in Europe?"

"Never took much delight in carnage," Scattergood said.

"It'll revolutionize the world," said Urban.

"World's been revolutionized too darn' much as it is," Scattergood said. "Um. . . . The Lord He manufactured the hull world in six days 'n then he rested up. Ever since then human bein's has been revolutionizin' it without botherin' to rest. I read in the Good Book the Lord He was kind of contented with His job, but human bein's is harder to satisfy."

"One of the big radio companies," said Urban, "offers a check for a million dollars to the one who can solve it."

"Solve what?"

"The problem," said Urban, "of amplifying light the way they can amplify sound. They can send pictures now a few miles and make them perfectly visible. But only about the size of a post card. To make it practicable we must find a way of sending them indefinite distances and of exhibiting them in any size desired."

"And you're pursuin' that there million-dollar check?"

"Yes, sir."

"How you progressin'?"

"I'm not discouraged," said Urban.

"Got time to kind of explain it to me?" Scattergood asked, and Urban launched upon his hobby. He not only talked, he showed drawings and recited formulas; and the old hardware merchant listened, with his astute old eyes fixed upon the young man's glowing, enthusiastic face. Scattergood nodded gravely from time to time, but at the end he was not encouraging.

"Don't seem as though," he said, "any good could come to humanity out of sich a stink. G'-by, Urban."

"Good-by, Mr. Baines."

Now, Scattergood, whatever you may say of him, was not a graceful individual. He required almost as much space to turn in as an ocean liner. As he swung about to face the door his elbow encountered a jar of the liquid which seemed to be giving off a major part of the aroma that ladened the air. The old man snatched at it, but too late. Half its contents poured over his lined and splotched and freckled hand. "Doggone!" he exclaimed regretfully and perhaps a little apprehensively.

"No harm done," said Urban. "Don't worry, it won't hurt you."

Scattergood, lacking a towel, waved his hand in the air to dry it. "Trouble with the world," said Scattergood, "is too many inventions. Yes, siree. Too many inventions givin' mankind speed the Lord never intended it sh'u'd have."

"The world must progress," said young Urban.

"All the time man saves by speedin' he uses fur some purpose he hadn't ought to. . . . G'-by, Urban."

With that, the old man who had ruled Coldriver for two generations, who was the most powerful political figure in the state and one of its richest citizens, ambled out of the laboratory and made off down the hill toward the hardware store which he pretended was the real business of his life. He was shaking his head and grumbling to himself about people in a hurry.

Before he had walked a hundred feet he was interrupted in his reflections by a young contralto voice which said insistently, "Oh, Mr. Baines!"

He stopped and turned, and when he saw a pretty girl he smiled that smile which was so hard to resist.

"How be ye, Mittie? How be ye? How's your pa? What ye want?"

"Mr. Baines, have you been to see Urban?"

"Kind of follered the scent, like ye might say, and found him to the end of it."

"Is it the Selectmen?" she asked.

" 'Twa'n't official. Jest curiosity."

"Oh, I was afraid Father had complained. He said he was going to."

"Dunno's I'd blame him," said Scattergood. "Not if the wind was blowin' this way. Is your pa calc'latin' to go on the rampage?"

"He doesn't like Urban any more," she said sadly. "He thinks Urban isn't any good and he's forbidden me to have anything to do with him any more."

"Dew tell—and I figgered it was to all intents and pu'poses all settled betwixt you."

"It was," said Mittie Savage. "But Father gets things wrong sometimes. He knew Urban was studying chemistry in college and got it into his head that meant he was going to come home and work in a drugstore. Somehow he got his heart set on Urban being a druggist—you know how he is."

"He gits notions," Scattergood admitted.

"But Urban studied a lot of other things, like electricity and engineering, and he never meant to work in a drugstore. I tried to explain to Father that an engineer was too important to work in a drugstore."

"What'd he say?" asked Scattergood.

"He said to wait till I got a stomach-ache and then I'd know how important a drugstore is."

"Sounds kind of like him," said Scattergood, with a grin.

"But when he heard Urban was inventing, that was the capsheaf," said Mittie.

"How do you calc'late to feel about it?"

"I admit I'd rather Urban went to work," said Mittie, "but then maybe he knows best, and, whatever he wants to do, I want, too. And if anybody can make this invention he's got his heart set on, why, Urban can."

"And then you git a million dollars 'n' set the world on fire."

"I don't care about the million dollars, Mr. Baines. It would frighten me. All I want is Urban." She paused and bit her trembling lip. "If Father makes a complaint to the Selectmen they'll stop Urban."

"Um. . . . Wa-al, Mittie, I got to be moggin' along. G'-by, Mittie."

"But—but can't you do something?"

"I'll go 'n' cogitate some," he said. "I'll kind of set and review the testimony fur and ag'in' smells. Um. . . . G'-by, Mittie."

The old man plodded along, down the hill, past the bank, and across the bridge until he reached his dingy hardware store, where, on the piazza, his especially reinforced armchair awaited his bulk. It squeaked its protest when he settled into it, and then was silent as he eased back comfortably and closed his eyes. It was not long before Pliny Pickett, conductor of Scattergood's train, which ran twenty-five miles down the Coldriver Valley to the Junction, arrived with his midday report.

"How be ye, Scattergood?" he asked, in imitation of his employer's manner.

"How be ye, Pliny? Eh? Public travelin' spry? Overrun with traffic?"

"'Leven passengers 'n' a travelin' man," said Pliny. "Travelin' man complained on account of the cars wa'n't air-cooled."

"Seems like I'm allus a-buttin' my head ag'in' human progress," said Scattergood. "'Tain't enough to pervide folks with means for gittin' from place to place—ye got to fly in the face of nature. Hot days is made to compel folks to sweat. Huh. Any rumors spreadin' around taown about smells, Pliny?"

"Young Urban Downs is creatin' 'em wuss 'n a tanyard," said Pliny.

"How long's folks a-goin' to endure 'em 'thout kickin' up a rumpus?"

"It's brewin'," said Pliny. "The deacon 'n' the elder was conferrin' last night."

"Kind of figgered them two would be injectin' themselves into the situation," said Scattergood.

"They kind of allowed he was committin' a nuisance," said Pliny.

"G'-by, Pliny," said Scattergood.

"G'-by, Scattergood," Pliny replied. It was after lunch that Homer Savage came hurriedly out of his drugstore—a drugstore in which he sold—in addition to drugs—wallpaper, paints, canned goods, and a number of other commodities. He diagonalized across the street to the hardware store, where Scattergood sat, and there was a telegram in his hand. "Jest got some bad news, Scattergood," he said.

"Sich as?" asked Scattergood.

"Brother Anthony was killed last night in an automobile."

"That's bad hearin', Homer. You'll be a-goin' out to Michigan?"

"Calc'late I'll have to. Scattergood, I'm kind of worried."

"Most folks is," said Scattergood. "It's the main business of the human race."

"If," said Homer, "you back a feller's note and the feller dies—then what?"

"Then," said Scattergood, "you most gen'ally wish you hadn't never learned to write. You back a note fur your brother?"

"Fur eight thousand dollars," said Homer.

"Um. . . . Calc'late he's got it?"

"I dunno. If he hain't, 'n' if they come onto me fur it, I lose my store."

"Better come to the bridge 'fore ye cross it," Scattergood said. "Huh. Hain't noticed young Urban Downs a-settin' onto your front stoop evenin's lately."

"I forbid him," Homer said shortly.

"Ye s'prise me," said Scattergood. "Folks kind of figgered it was settled for him 'n' Mittie to marry 'n' settle down."

" 'Twas," said Homer, "till the boy took up with inventin' 'n' makin' evil smells."

"Them things," said Scattergood, "didn't leave no blot on his character, did they?"

"I planned—him bein' college eddicated and all—that he'd come into the store 'n' git ready to take it over when I pass on."

"Ever strike ye," asked Scattergood, "that Pa's and Ma's do a sight of plannin' 'n' schemin' fur their childern 'thout givin' them much say in the matter?"

Homer's mouth set stubbornly. "If he gives up inventin' and comes into the store he kin have Mittie. Not otherwise."

"Mebbe, if you're patient," said Scattergood, "he'll git cured of inventin'. When ye a-goin' to Michigan?"

"Tonight," said Homer.

"Hope ye find ever'thin' workin' out fur the best," said Scattergood. "G'-by, Homer."

Homer Savage was absent from Coldriver nearly a week. While he was gone Scattergood sat, for the most part, on the piazza of his hardware store and dozed. But he seemed to have acquired a new habit. For years his fellow townsmen had watched him, in moments of deep thought, remove his shoes and wriggle his toes. Now he added to that eccentricity the new one of twiddling his fingers. He would sit for minutes staring at his hand, and then he would work his fingers as if he were playing a piano.

He evinced an unusual interest in Urban Downs's experiments, though the boy seemed to be making scant progress toward his goal. Money for supplies was not plentiful, nevertheless he labored day and night.

When he was not combining chemicals to cast a malodorous pall over the neighborhood, he was sitting at his drafting table making diagrams; and Scattergood would sit in the doorway, and pore over these drawings and listen to Urban's technical patter, by the hour.

"How about you 'n' Mittie?" he asked.

"Eh?" The boy looked up from his work and shook his head. "Oh, Mr. Savage has kicked me out. As soon as I get this million he'll feel different."

"Seems as though," said Scattergood. "But s'posin' ye don't quite contrive to git this here million?"

"Mittie'll marry me anyhow."

"Ye don't know Mittie as well's a feller should that figgers on makin' her his wife. She's a good gal that's been trained in obedience. I warn ye, Urban, if Homer don't give his permission Mittie won't never marry ye."

"I'll make her," said Urban.

"Usin' what fur tools?" asked Scattergood. "Um. . . . Seems like ye been combinin' these here drugs a number of times. What's the main purpose 'n' object of it?"

"If it works," Urban said, "it's pretty nearly the key to the problem."

"Ye s'prise me," said Scattergood.

On Monday Homer Savage returned from his brother's funeral and, early in the day, came across lugubriously to talk to Scattergood. "Scattergood," he said, "d'ye calc'late the bank could contrive to lend me eight thousand dollars?"

"Hain't give it no thought—yit," said Scattergood. "Why?"

"Wa-al, that there note I backed fur my brother—seems like I got to pay it. He didn't leave practically nothin'."

"Folks that goes around gittin' other folks to back their notes," said Scattergood, "most gen'ally don't. Almost seems like the's jest two kinds of people—them that saved up money and them that borrows it from 'em 'n' loses it."

"That don't help none. Kin I borrow?"

"Eight thousand is a snag of money," said Scattergood.

"I don't need to be told that, nuther," said Homer.

"It'll require some thinkin' over," Scattergood said, "but I'm kind of dubious."

"They'll sue me," said Homer, "'n' then take my store away from me."

"The time," said Scattergood, "to think about that was when ye got so free 'n' easy with your signature. Um. . . . G'-by, Homer. I'll kind of mull it over in my mind. Let ye know. G'-by, Homer."

Savage plodded back across the road heavily, and Scattergood lifted himself out of his armchair and walked around the corner to the other drugstore, a dusty old place, conducted by old Pylon Jones more as a habit than to gain a livelihood.

"How ye progressin'?" he asked.

"Slow but sure," said the ancient druggist. "What in tunket d'ye calc'late to do with this here perscription?"

"Mebbe p'ison mice," said Scattergood. "Be ye fond of mice, Pylon?"

"Never give 'em no thought," Pylon said.

"Even mice," said Scattergood, "is cunnin' when they're babies. Makes a body think it hain't so much how ye start out in life as how ye *turn* out that matters. Now, take mice. If mice kept on bein' pink 'n' cunnin' all their lives, folks 'ud kind of have compassion onto 'em. Or if, when they growed up, they didn't git to be mice gnawin' holes in the woodwork."

"Mice," said the druggist, "is foreordained to be mice."

"Ye got a p'int of argyment there," said Scattergood, "but it makes a body wonder why. Why, f'r instance, does a mouse have to be a mouse, 'thout no choice in the matter? Must be some reason."

"I quit searchin' fur reason thutty year ago," said the druggist.

"Longer I live," said Scattergood, "the nearer I come to guessin' the' hain't much reason fur things; the's jest laws compellin' 'em."

"Anyhow," said the druggist, "barrin' accidents, strikes, boycotts, furrin enemy, and act of God I'll have this here perscription finished fur ye in the mornin'."

On his way back to the store Scattergood encountered Elder Hooper and Deacon Pettibone, and they wore the satisfied faces of two men who had seen their duty and done it.

"What ye two ol' coots been up to?" asked Scattergood. "Eh? Ever' time I see ye a-lookin' so doggone righteous I figger you've done a meanness."

"We're obliged, bein' who we be," said the elder, "to take matters into our hands."

"So ye done what?" asked Scattergood.

"We lodged a complaint with the Selectmen ag'in' young Urban Downs."

"Deacon," asked Scattergood, "d'ye ever call to mind bein' less 'n seventy year old? Eh? Remember back that fur?"

"What's that got to do with a fool boy a-drivin' folks out of house 'n' home?"

Scattergood did not answer this question directly. "When ye was along about twenty-one or -two or sich a matter," he asked, "did ye ever dream 'n' see visions?"

"What foolishness be you leadin' up to, Scattergood?" asked the elder.

"Didn't ye ever, when ye was a boy, have no dream about leadin' armies to vict'ry, or diskiverin' a new world like Columbus, or contrivin' some great act fur the good of humanity, or rescuin' a gal in distress, or accomplishin' some deed 't would make the world rear back onto its haunches 'n' praise your name?"

"Don't recall no sich nonsense."

"I done so," said Scattergood. "I had them dreams, and they was perty splendid. I dunno but they made the best part of my life. It don't do no ol' man credit to set about destroyin' the dreams of a boy."

"Shucks!" exclaimed the deacon tartly.

"Them dreams fades quick enough," Scattergood said, "'thout some ol' coot a-kickin' holes into 'em. Now, take Urban here. He's dreamin' a dream, but he's also creatin' a stink. The stink won't last long, but the dream'll go on forever, on account of he'll remember it till his dyin' day and how rosy the world looked and all—when he figgered he was able to move maountains. Mebbe he'll be a big man; mebbe he won't never be nothin' but jest Urban Downs. But it does kind of seem to me like we ought to let him fiddle with that there dream till it unravels or till it jells."

"We lodged our complaint 'n' we calc'late to stand by it," said the elder.

"Sometimes," said Scattergood, "I kind of hope, when you two ol' scalawags git to heaven they won't let you play on no harps. I git to wishin' they'd assign ye to the piano-movin' department."

With that, he trod away solidly.

Not an hour later young Urban Downs came hurriedly down the hill to tell his troubles to Scattergood—as everyone in Coldriver always did. "Mr. Baines," he said, "I don't know what to do. The First Selectman just came to my workshop and ordered me to stop. He said I was committing a nuisance and the town couldn't tolerate it. Can't anything be done?"

"'Tain't stinks 't bothers 'em," said Scattergood. "It's unpractical stinks. Now, take the pulp mill. When the wind's right it's like to turn your nose inside out. But the pulp mill makes money 'n' pays wages. Your smell, Urban, don't pay nothin'."

"But haven't I a right to do scientific research? Can't you do something, Mr. Baines?"

"I'm afeard the Selectmen has got the legal right of it, Urban."

"Then," said Urban valiantly, "I shall leave town. I shall go away where I can work. I won't be persecuted."

"Youth," said Scattergood, "is allus persecuted by age— or that's how it looks to youth, till it takes its own turn at being age and persecutin' the next batch of youth. What about Mittie?"

"I'll come back for her when ——"

"When the universe is acclaimin' your name," Scattergood interrupted. "Mebbe. Young Feller, it's easier to stay back in the fust place 'n what it is to come a-sneakin' back with your tail betwixt your laigs. Lots of young fellers goes away like you purpose to do, and then the pride that's in 'em keeps 'em from ever comin' back to git twitted with failin'. Better set 'n' think a spell, seems as though. G'-by, Urban."

"I'm going to pack and go," said the boy.

"Talk to Mittie fust," said Scattergood.

"She won't talk to me," said the boy heavily. "Her father won't let her. He's forbidden her even to speak to me."

"D'ye want Mittie, Urban?"

"More than anything in the world."

"Huh. Then mebbe your case hain't hopeless," said Scattergood. "G'-by."

After the noon mail came in Scattergood walked across

to Savage's drugstore and went behind the screen, where the proprietor sat over a newly received letter.

"They're a-goin' to sue me," said Mr. Savage.

"And when they git jedgment they'll sell your store over your head."

" 'Tain't fair," said Mr. Savage.

"The feller rented the money to your brother, didn't he?"

"Yes."

" 'N' you promised to pay it back if your brother didn't?"

"Yes."

"Then it hain't so doggone unfair," said Scattergood.

"How about lendin' me the money?"

"How'd ye ever pay that much back?" asked Scattergood. "How would ye? 'Tain't my money in the bank. It's other folks' money. What prospect ye got to pay back eight thousand dollars?"

"Not much, Scattergood," said Mr. Savage. "Not much, I calc'late."

"Then," said Scattergood, "ye hain't got no right to ask me to lend. Um. . . . How's Mittie?"

"Cryin'," said Mr. Savage.

"On account of Urban?"

"I won't have her takin' up with no loafin' young spriggins," said Savage.

"Don't calc'late to change your mind on that p'int?"

"I don't," said Mr. Savage, and Scattergood nodded.

"Sorry I can't contrive to help ye out," he said. "G'-by to ye."

So matters stood for a number of days. Business called Scattergood from town. Urban Downs went ahead with plans for shaking the dust of Coldriver from his feet. Mr. Savage became the defendant in an action to recover $8,000, and Mittie's eyes were red with constant crying. On a

Tuesday Scattergood came home, and he was accompanied by an obviously city-bred man of businesslike aspect. This gentleman was deposited in the hotel, and Scattergood settled down in his strong chair on the piazza of his hardware store.

Presently along came a small boy whistling, and Scattergood called to him. "Hello, bub," he said.

"Hello, Mr. Baines."

"Figger ye got time to run a couple errands, eh?"

"Got time," said the boy.

"I'll give ye a dime," said Scattergood.

"It's a dicker," said the boy, approaching the steps.

Scattergood felt in his pocket for a coin and extended it to the boy. "Hm. . . . Ever see a new kind of a spinnin' top I got?" he asked.

"What kind?"

Scattergood went into the store and returned with a very superior top in his hand. "Try her once," he invited.

The lad wound the top, hurled it to the walk, and watched it gyrate.

"'Tain't but a dime," said Scattergood.

"I want it," said the boy, and passed back the coin.

"Skedaddle," said Scattergood. "Ye might tell Urban Downs 'n' Mr. Savage 'n' Mittie that I'll be settin' right here at two o'clock."

"And ye want them to come?" asked the boy.

"Didn't say so, did I? Didn't speak no sich words. Skedaddle."

At two o'clock Urban Downs and Mittie and her father arrived at Scattergood's store—and the stranger from the hotel. Scattergood introduced him as a Mr. Withers. Savage eyed Urban with an unfriendly eye. Mittie bravely restrained her tears.

"Urban," said Scattergood, "I hear tell of a feller who shot him an arrow at a star, but it didn't hit no star. It come down into the roof of a smokehouse. Jest how disapp'inted d'ye figger that feller was? Eh? He hit suthin'. 'Twa'n't as lofty a target as he aimed fur, but it was a hit. And the' was hams in the smokehouse."

"I don't understand," said Urban.

"Um. . . ." Scattergood turned to Mr. Savage. "You're set ag'in' Urban, hain't ye? Because he's kind of wuthless and don't make no money and won't git to be a drug clerk instid of an inventor."

"No wish to talk about it," said Savage.

"Urban," said Scattergood, "Mittie's Pa's in trouble. He calc'lates to lose his store on account of signin' a note fur eight thousand dollars. Be ye glad?"

"Of course not, sir."

"Pervidin' ye had eight thousand dollars, d'ye calc'late you would take any steps?"

"Mittie," said Urban, "could have anything I own—always."

Again Scattergood turned to the druggist.

"Would ye sell a half-interest into your store fur eight thousand? Eh?"

"You know durn' well I would."

"Urban, if ye had that much, and could buy a partnership with Mittie's Pa and own half of a drugstore, is the' any reason ye couldn't go on dreamin' 'n' inventin'? 'Twouldn't be no bar, would it?"

"Of course not. But I have no money and no way to get any."

"Mr. Withers, here, he represents a firm down to Bostin that sort of specializes in makin' folks beautiful to look at.

He claims manufacturin' lipsticks 'n' creams 'n' this, that, 'n' tother is one of the biggest industries in the country."

"It is," said Mr. Withers.

"Most as many folks wants to git beautiful as wants to git rich, and mebbe more. Mr. Withers he says a feller that kin find some sort of a makeshift to render a woman pertier 'n what she was, is apt to make him a fortune."

"True," said Mr. Withers.

"So," said Scattergood, "I kind of got to ponderin' over my hand."

"What," asked Savage tartly, "is all this leadin' to?"

"Freckles, spots, 'n' blemishes," said Scattergood. "I jest sot here fur days and kind of stared at my hand, and then, all to once, it come over me how much more beautiful, as ye might say, my right hand is than my left hand. Hain't no comparison." He held up his two hands, with their backs toward his audience. "Look at this here paw," he said, waggling his left. "All freckled, hain't it? Dang nigh obscured by spots 'n' blemishes. Yeah. And look at this here right hand. Hain't sca'cely a spot, and, as fur freckles, they jest don't exist no more. Which set me to calc'latin'."

"What of it?" asked Savage.

"Urban," said Scattergood, "I calc'late ye would be took down in your pride if ye turned out to be an inventor of suthin' less world-shakin' 'n television."

"I don't know. Why?"

"Or if, when ye was aimin' at them there stars and, by accident, didn't hit nothin' loftier 'n a smokehouse roof. Um. . . . Recall I spilt some of that smellin' fluid over my hand fust time I come to see ye?"

"It couldn't have harmed you," said Urban. "Those were harmless chemicals."

"Better 'n harmless," said Scattergood. "Them chemicals

was downright beneficent. They give me a beauty I hain't possessed fur years. The' wa'n't no towel and I didn't have no handkerchief to wipe my hand off with, 'n' I didn't want to take no chance of sp'ilin' my pants wipin' it on the seat. So I jest waved her 'n' let her dry."

"I see no p'int to this," said Savage.

"P'int is, when I woke up next mornin' 'n' took a look at that there hand, them freckles 'n' all was dum nigh faded out. I'm a feller fur puttin' two 'n' two together, so I kind of hung around Urban's shop 'n' I contrived to smear some more of that there smellin' fluid onto me. What's the result, eh? Freckles gone."

"And then," said Mr. Withers, "he came to me with a bottle of it he had made up. The odor was terrific. But that we eliminated by adding flavoring."

"So," said Scattergood, "nobody kin say practical good didn't come out of your inventin'. Mebbe lots of great things come into the world by accident. Seems as though you stubbed your toe over a beautifyin' liquid, Urban. Willin' to sell it?"

"Why—why—who would buy it?"

"Mr. Withers," said Scattergood. "I dickered with him consid'able. Yeah. He calc'lated finally he was willin' to pay ye daown, fur the patent rights to this here formula, a lump sum, 'n' a royalty, continuin'. Eh, Withers?"

"It is cheap to manufacture. Tests have proved its efficacy. We will give you ten thousand dollars cash, and five cents a bottle on every bottle sold. It probably will amount to a handsome sum annually."   .

"What say?" Scattergood asked Urban.

"I—why, I don't know what to say." He looked at Mittie; he looked at Mr. Savage, and his face lighted. "Mr. Savage," he asked, "will you sell me a half-interest in your store for eight thousand dollars—including Mittie in the deal?"

"You mean," demanded Savage, "this young spriggins's gittin' that much money for makin' them evil odors?"

"Seems as though," said Scattergood.

Savage drew a deep breath. "Urban," he said, "I calc'late I misjedged ye. I didn't know ye was workin' on suthin' practical. It's a deal, if ye say so."

"How about it, Mittie?" asked Scattergood. "You're part of the consideration."

She reached out shyly and placed her hand in Urban's but said no word.

"I figger that settles it," said Scattergood. "Got that check, Withers?"

"Here it is, Mr. Baines."

"Urban, you step to the bank and sign some papers 'n' it's yourn," said Scattergood. "G'-by, ever'body."

They rose, and even Savage seemed happy. Perhaps Urban was more bewildered than joyful. "I don't know how to thank you, Mr. Baines," he said slowly.

"When ye don't know what to say," said Scattergood, "keep your mouth shet."

They rose to go, but the old man spoke again: "Um. . . . If only they was allus somebuddy around to pick the practical parts out of the dreams of dreamers, mebbe dreams 'ud have a better repute. I dunno." He paused. "Urban, you go 'n' have more dreams. If the's practical bits in 'em, that's good. Dreams," he said, with a waggle of his old head, "is their own dividends. G'-by."

XIII

Scattergood Studies Human Nature

SCATTERGOOD BAINES always interested himself in new-comers to Coldriver; sometimes directly, with a cross-examination carried on in his own peculiar way; at other times by watching closely and listening shortly. In the case of John Sand and James Sand he chose the latter method.

He would sit on the piazza of his hardware store, which he liked to pretend was his principal interest in life, and let the news drift to him. From that piazza he ruled the politics of his state; he operated his twenty-five miles of railroad; he ran his bank; he carried on his divers operations in timber. As he sat there, often shoeless, twiddling his bare toes in the sunshine, he had nothing of the look of a very wealthy man. But Scattergood did not go in for appearances.

It is surprising how much he learned about John Sand and James Sand in a very few days—and how little. The two men had come to town unheralded and rented furnished the little house which Old Man Challoner had just vacated by death. John Sand was a big, hearty man with a great yellow beard, and James Sand was a big, taciturn man with a great brownish beard. Although Coldriver, even in this day, possessed a number of bearded citizens, the Sand brothers quite outdid them on length and luxuriance.

It was guessed that they were twins, though there was no sure information on this point; and it was estimated that they were in the neighborhood of forty years old, though there was no record to verify the guess. They appeared to have no regular occupation, though nobody could accuse them of laziness. They toiled from early morning until late afternoon in their garden, and took turns in coming downtown for their daily supplies. It was noted that neither ever called at the post office.

John Sand was the sort of man who got acquainted with dogs. He also got acquainted with small boys. It was commented upon that, before he became acquainted with a single adult resident, he was on excellent terms with the juniors. He called them all "Bub," and it was a speedily established custom to take half a dozen of them into the drugstore and buy each of them a stick of sugar candy or an ice cream cone.

James Sand, on the contrary, never spoke to a dog and he ignored children. He ignored everybody as much as was possible, and did his shopping tersely. It was not that he was stand-offish, but rather that he did not seem to notice people. He seemed always to be thinking about something. John laughed a great deal, and loudly. James was never seen to smile. John would stop to chat with anybody upon the least encouragement, but the town had heard James speak no more than the few curt words necessary in giving his order to the grocer.

But John, garrulous as he seemed to be, never talked about anything definite. He never gave the smallest crumb of information. Never, by any chance, did John mention James, or where they had come from or why they had settled in Coldriver. No inferences could be drawn as to the previous business of the brothers, or whether they were rich or poor or if they had left a family in some distant place. Coldriver knew that on a certain day they had disembarked from the train—but they might as well have dropped from Mars. Their history began with their entering the train at the Junction, and even Pliny Pickett, the conductor, did not know if they had reached that point of departure from the East or from the West.

They did not do business at the bank, but they seemed to have ample cash. They ran no bills, paid for what they purchased on the spot, and there you were. They did not attend church, though they suspended work in their garden on the Sabbath. They never went to the movies. They took no newspaper.

All of this information came to Scattergood, but for once he knew no more than his fellow townsmen. It puzzled him, and he did not like to be puzzled. There was no real reason why he should delve further into the affairs of the brothers, because they were always well behaved. They set the world an example in minding their own business and, adroit as he was, Scattergood could find no excuse for questioning or meddling.

It was more than two months after the arrival of the Sand brothers that Pliny Pickett, aged and rheumatic conductor of Scattergood's train, contributed one more strand to the mystery. He stopped at the hardware store to make his noontime report. "How be ye, Scattergood?" he asked.

"About the same, seems as though. How be you, Pliny?"

"Feller come up on the train today," Pliny said. "Dark-favored feller with a kind of a weasel face."

"What's int'restin' about him, Pliny? Eh?"

"Questions he up 'n' asked. He was all-fired curious about twins. Kep' askin' about 'em. Wanted to know if twins ever rode onto the train."

"What kind of twins?"

"Growed-up men," said Pliny, "with whiskers."

"Um. . . . Whiskers, eh? Could ye make out his attitude of mind towards them beards—if it was friendly or unfriendly?"

"Couldn't make out nothin'," said Pliny, "savin' and exceptin' that this here feller didn't look like he'd be friendly to nobuddy."

"What'd ye tell him, Pliny?"

Pliny looked hurt at the question. "I didn't tell him nothin'. Ever' time he asked me suthin', I up 'n' asked him a question back. I hain't one to be peddlin' information to no strangers. No, siree. I jest says to him, 'Mister, what's your interest into twins?' And the like of that."

"What become of him? Didn't git off'm the train here?"

"Got down to Higgins Bridge."

"Um. . . . Feller didn't mention where he come from?"

"Didn't mention nothin'."

"G'-by, Pliny."

Scattergood sat and pondered this new development. A sharp-faced man was looking for twins with beards. This man had not impressed Pliny favorably, and Pliny was a judge of character. A sharp-faced man might be anything. He might be a nephew; he might be an enemy; he might be a lawyer. Or, thought Scattergood, he might be a detective. He considered this latter possibility. A suspicious individual might, watching the arrival and the conduct of the Sand brothers, have arrived at the conclusion that they were in hiding. If they were in hiding, it must be for a reason. And, if they were in hiding, it was possible, even probable, that someone would be searching for them.

While the old man was marshaling these possibilities he saw John Sand come out of the drugstore followed by four or five small boys and girls, each sucking a striped stick of candy. The big man said something jovial to the children, and turned to cross the bridge. He had a broken implement in his hand and Scattergood judged he was on his way to the blacksmith shop. As Sand came abreast of the hardware store Scattergood spoke to him. "How be ye, John?" he asked.

John Sand stopped and turned his head in some surprise, for Scattergood had never hailed him before. "Good afternoon, Mr. Baines," he said courteously.

Scattergood wondered what the man's face looked like underneath that great yellow beard and what tale of years it had to tell.

"John," he said, "I'm a feller that asks a sight of questions. Formed the habit. The's times when it's jest givin' my habit it's head and allowin' it to gallop, but the's times when I ask 'em on puppose."

Sand nodded his head, but made no audible reply.

"This here time," Scattergood said, "I got a cravin' to ask a couple, and they hain't from idle curiosity."

Still John Sand made no reply, but his big, amiable blue eyes twinkled.

"John, be you 'n' your brother twins?"

"It has been guessed we are," said John Sand.

"Kind of noncommittal, hain't ye? Dunno's I blame ye. But the's allus a time to speak and a time to keep silent. Wouldn't care to tell me how ye come to pick Coldriver fur a home?"

"Isn't it a lovely, peaceful little place?" asked John Sand.

"Where few strangers come," added Scattergood. "Listen, young feller, I hain't a body that hates folks. I don't call to mind ever runnin' around and gittin' all lathered up strivin' to do nobuddy an ill turn."

"I am willing to believe that," said John Sand.

"If a feller or a fambly moves to Coldriver," said Scatter-good, "I git a kind of an interest into 'em. I kind of like to see ever'body in Coldriver git along."

"Why," asked John Sand, "do you think my brother and I may not be getting along?"

"John," said Scattergood, "fellers that is secretive mostly have suthin' to hide."

"Every human being has something to hide."

"Ye wouldn't care to tell me about what you're concealin'?" asked Scattergood.

"Is it not possible," asked John in return, "that my brother and I are eccentric?"

"It could be," said Scattergood. "Wa-al, I calc'late we won't git no place. Jest one more question. Be ye acquainted with a dark-complected feller with a weasel face that's got a kind of a hobby fur searchin' out twins with beards?"

The smile faded from John Sand's blue eyes, and his face stiffened and aged. The piece of steel he grasped in his hand fell with a clang to the sidewalk. He did not speak, but abruptly he turned on his heel and strode back across the bridge. Scattergood watched his broad shoulders until they passed out of sight up the hill. Then he got up from his seat and heavily descended the steps to the sidewalk, where he bent and gingerly picked up the implement John Sand had been carrying to the blacksmith. He bore it inside the store and sat down at his littered desk and wrote a letter to an individual of authority in Boston.

"Dear Friend Matt," it said. "I hear tell there's a place down to Washington where they store up fingerprints. There will be some on this tool. I wish you'd go about it private and find out if you can who they belong to, and oblige."

A few days later Scattergood received his reply by wire: "These prints belong to no known criminal."

That was a Tuesday in the morning. The noon train arrived and brought with it quite the most beautiful young lady Scattergood had ever seen—a beautiful young lady accompanied by a young man so handsome that Pliny Pickett decided he must be a motion picture star. The couple were driven to the hotel, where they registered as Howard Brush and Winifred Mason. Directly after their midday meal they emerged and walked to the hardware store, where Scattergood sat dozing.

"Is this Mr. Baines?" asked Miss Mason.

"Allus was up to now," said Scattergood. "How be ye?"

"I am Winifred Mason," said the beautiful young woman. "This is Mr. Brush. We were told that you would know all about everybody living in Coldriver."

"Mebbe not ever'thin'," said Scattergood, "but a sight more 'n some folks guesses."

"I have come a long way to find two young men named John and James Sand," she said. "They are large young men, twins, and wear beards. Can you give me news of them?"

"What kind of news?" asked Scattergood.

"Any news," said Miss Mason, "but preferably good news."

"Friend of these here fellers?" he asked.

"She's not," said Brush sharply. "A young woman such as Miss Mason is not a friend to a pair of forgers. She came here out of foolish sympathy."

"Don't call to mind a piece of sympathy," said Scattergood, "that was ever foolish. These here fellers is forgers, eh?"

"Beyond a doubt," said Brush.

"Not beyond my doubt," said the young woman quickly. "I refuse to believe until I have it from John's lips."

"They cashed the forged check, didn't they? They got and used the money?"

"Yes," admitted Miss Mason. "But until John tells me so I will not believe they forged their uncle's name."

"All the same," said Brush, "if their uncle hadn't refused to prosecute, they would be in the penitentiary, where you wouldn't have to hunt for them."

"What kind of a defense did these here twins make when they was accused, eh?" Scattergood asked.

"They denied the check was a forgery. Said their uncle sent it to them by mail," said Brush.

"But he didn't, eh?"

"No. It was a traced signature."

"I sort of gather," Scattergood said, "that you don't feel as kindly to'ards 'em as Miss Mason?"

"I look at the facts," said Brush.

"I've knowed folks before," said Scattergood, "that never looked at nothin' but the facts. Gen'ally they was uninterestin' and mostly they was disagreeable."

He eased himself back in his especially reinforced chair and regarded Winifred Mason gravely. "Um. . . . Winnie," he said, "them twins is here."

"Where? How can I find them?"

"If I was you," said the old man, "I dunno's I'd go a-rompin' in onto 'em rash 'n' regardless. Um. . . . Did ye know another feller was a-searchin' fur 'em?"

"No. Who?" demanded Brush.

"Dark-favored feller with a kind of a weasel face," said Scattergood. "Hain't acquainted with his name."

"Trost!" exclaimed Brush, and scowled. "What's that shyster doing in this mess?"

"No friend of yourn?" Scattergood asked Miss Mason.

"No. I can't imagine what his interest may be."

"Gits kind of complicated," observed Scattergood. "Now, when things gits complicated a good thing to do is to set 'n' ponder 'n' wait fur what's a-goin' to happen. Be ye the kind of a gal, Winnie, that ever takes advice?"

"I'll wait," she said. "Do you always make people do what you want them to?"

"Off and on," said Scattergood dryly. "I've had some luck with it." His hand reached down for his shoe. "G'-by," he said in abrupt dismissal.

When they were gone he removed his shoe and disclosed a sockless foot, at which he gazed with some affection. Then he closed his eyes comfortably and commenced violently to twiddle his toes. Scattergood Baines was concentrating. . . .

It seemed that Scattergood was right in his surmise that when affairs became complicated events were apt to be generated by the working of a tangled set of forces. His knowledge of resultant catastrophe came from none other than Sheriff Fox, who pounded upon Scattergood's door at the hour of five o'clock next morning.

Scattergood thrust his head out of his bedroom window. "What's ailin' ye, Sheriff? Eh?"

"Len Small, he up 'n' found a body," said the sheriff.

"Dew tell! Name of who?" asked Scattergood.

"None of us ever seen him afore," said the sheriff. "Little skinny feller, black hair 'n' swarthy skin."

"Um. . . ." said Scattergood. "Where'd this here body git itself found?"

"Edge of the orchard adjoinin' where them two twins with the whiskers lives."

"Death come nat'ral?"

"Evidence p'ints to he was choked."

"In that there case," said Scattergood, "I better git my pants on."

The old man could be amazingly spry when need required and it was a matter of moments before he was walking down the road with Sheriff Fox. Five minutes of trudging carried them to the orchard, where a deputy stood guard over the body of a smallish, dark man.

Scattergood regarded him. "Don't seem like he was real nice-lookin' even when he was alive," he said. "Any idees, Sheriff?"

"Nary," answered the officer, who did not relish being confronted with problems.

Scattergood surveyed the locale. A hundred yards away and slightly downhill was the little house occupied by the twins. "Um. . . . While you set things to whizzin'," he said, "I calc'late I'll stroll down 'n' see if them Sand brothers heard or seen anythin' helpful."

He rapped loudly on the back door, and dour James Sand appeared.

"Mornin'," said Scattergood. "Up early, hain't ye?"

"I am an early riser," said James.

"Mebbe you're a light sleeper, too, eh?"

"I am," said James.

"Wa-al, when ye was a-sleepin' light did ye hear any sounds or see any sights that might have a bearin' on a feller man bein' strangled adjacent to ye?"

James hesitated briefly and stared straight into Scattergood's eyes before he replied. Then it was with a brief "No."

"Huh. Too bad. Naow, could you 'n' your brother mog along with me 'n' kind of see if you ever see the corpse before?"

"What has it to do with us?" asked James.

"He's a stranger," said Scattergood; and then John appeared at his brother's side.

"What is it, Mr. Baines?" he asked.

"Murder," said James. "He wants us to go see."

"If ye can identify the body," said Scattergood.

The brothers glanced inquiringly at each other. James shrugged. "Why not?" he asked, and, hatless, they followed Scattergood up the hill and presently were standing beside the remains.

"Familiar face?" asked Scattergood.

"No," said James.

"Mebbe ye better stoop closer," Scattergood advised. "I wouldn't want nobuddy to make a mistake. This here body wouldn't be a feller by the name of Trost, now? Lawyer feller?"

"It would," said John.

"What's he doin' here?"

"I couldn't tell you, Mr. Baines."

"He was searchin' for a pair of twins with whiskers. What was his idee?"

"Since you told me such a man was making inquiries, I have wondered," John said. "I don't know the answer."

"Nice feller, was he?"

"I never had beyond a speaking acquaintance with him. His reputation was that of a shady and not successful lawyer."

Scattergood wriggled his heavy shoulders. "John," said he, "when a thing like this happens, questions has to be asked that otherwise could be let to lay."

"Quite so."

"And things have to be pried into public that might better be left private."

"You mean that James and I will be required to explain ourselves?"

"That's the ticket," said Scattergood. "You're kind of mysterious, like. This here Trost comes spyin' around after ye. He gets himself killed. The hull thing sort of calls fur explanations."

"I agree," said John wearily. "Will you come to the house?"

"C'mon, Sheriff," said Scattergood; and presently they were seated in the Sands' little neat parlor.

"What was your callin' before you up 'n' moved here?" Scattergood asked.

"We were on the faculty of Fillmore College," said John. "Engaged in certain research work."

"'N' then," said Scattergood, "up pops this here mess of the forged check fur ten thousand dollars."

The room was suddenly silent. John stiffened; James became tense. Then both big men sighed. "It did," said John.

"Ye might kind of enlarge, seems as though," said Scattergood.

"We have an uncle who is wealthy," said John. "The college was not rich. We required money for laboratory equipment and to carry on our experimentation. Uncle declined to assist us. He was not without a certain eccentricity. One morning a check unaccompanied by letter came in the mail. It was not uncharacteristic. James and I carried it to the bank and obtained the money, which we used as I have indicated. It seems the check was a clumsy forgery. Our uncle had never sent it to us. He contented himself by making the matter public, but declined to prosecute. We resigned from the faculty and came here, seeking a spot where people did not stare and believe us to be criminals."

"Interestin'. Then you claim you didn't trace this here uncle's signature?"

"We did not."

"No idee why this here Trost come pokin' around?"

"I can't," said John, "see how he comes into it at all."

Sheriff Fox was growing restless. "Shall I take 'em in?" he asked.

"Dunno's I would—yit," said Scattergood.

John's face was puzzled. "Take us in?"

"Sheriff's got a notion you done away with this here man Trost."

"But why should we? We scarcely knew the man!"

"So ye say," said the sheriff grimly. "Anyhow, ye did know him some, 'n' nobuddy else around these parts ever see him before. It stands to reason he wa'n't killed by no complete stranger. 'N', besides, this here story ye tell hain't convincin'—not to me."

"Sheriff's got some right onto his side," Scattergood observed. "Still and all, I don't figger the p'int's come when he kin do any arrestin'. Nope, Sheriff, I wouldn't be hasty. These here twins can't git away."

He turned his head as someone rapped timidly on the front door, and Sheriff Fox strode to open it. Past his obstructing bulk Scattergood could see a young woman who spoke tensely. "I—I wanted to see Mr. Sand," she said.

"C'm in, Winnie," called Scattergood. "The boys is here."

She stepped into the room and paused, young, slender, proud, apprehensive. The old hardware man gave her only a glance, turning his eyes quickly to study the faces of the Sand brothers. James's face was wooden, expressionless; John's cheeks were suddenly gray and his lips parted as if, through some curtain of agony, he were looking upon unattainable paradise.

"John," she said, and had eyes for no other.

The man rose and stood motionless.

"Why did you run away from me?" she asked, and came a little closer. "Didn't you know, John, that I wouldn't believe unless I heard it from your own lips? John, didn't you know that I love you?"

John Sand spread his hands. "How was I to know?" he asked simply. "I only knew, Winifred, that I worshiped you. I never dreamed—" He paused. "I could not bear to stay and meet your eyes and see shame in them."

"There would have been no shame, John. They told me these things about you, but I don't believe them. I told your uncle and Howard Brush that I never would believe any of it until I had it from your own lips. John, did you forge your uncle's name to that check?"

"No," he said.

She nodded her head. "I did not need to ask," she said, "but I had to put the question. I made Howard Brush bring me here to ask it."

"I always thought," John said, "that you would marry Howard."

She smiled. "John dear," she said, "when you take your eyes from a microscope in a laboratory they see very little."

"A-hum," interrupted Scattergood. "Winnie, ye hain't asked enough questions, seems as though. It takes two to make a pair of twins. Yeah. I calc'late ye better kind of inquire what James knows about that check."

Winifred turned to him and shook her head. "John answered for both," she said.

"Thank you, Winifred," James said, and his eyes were kindlier than Scattergood had ever seen them. "Yes, Mr. Baines," he went on, "Miss Mason answered for both of us."

"Dew tell! What fetched ye here so early, Winnie?"

"I couldn't sleep. So I came out for a walk—and I felt I must come here."

"Nothin' special fetched ye? No tidin's about a feller named Trost?"

"What news about Mr. Trost?"

"He come to a bad end," said Scattergood.

For a moment she seemed puzzled; then she gasped. "Are you saying that someone has killed the lawyer Trost?"

"Complete 'n' final," said Scattergood; "which puts another set of complexions onto the case."

"Murder?" exclaimed Winifred.

"Ye might call it that," said Scattergood, "and not commit no error."

"But who ——?"

"Sheriff Fox here's got his mouth all fixed up to arrest these here twins."

"No," she said.

"Nobuddy here but them—'n' you 'n' Brush—got any knowledge of Trost. Folks don't kill off total strangers."

"But—but it's utter nonsense!" she exclaimed. "Why should they kill Trost?"

"I been askin' myself that," said Scattergood. "I been kind of runnin' up one side of that there question and down tother. I been askin' myself also why this Trost feller come here a-tall. Um. . . . Seems like the' was quite a congregation from your taown here all of a sudden. Got any idee why Trost come?"

"None," said Winifred. "He was a miserable little shyster, a despicable little man. But what he could have had to do with this affair I cannot imagine."

"Kind of clear he come to find the twins," said Scattergood. "He was huntin' fur 'em by description. Looks like he found 'em. Huh. Havin' seen his face only in death I

dunno's I kin jedge character exact. But he didn't look to
me like a feller that would waste his time doin' a friendly
errand or one that didn't do himself no advantage."

"Mebbe," hazarded the sheriff, "he found out suthin' and
come moseyin' along to git him some blackmail. Now, take
it like I see it, Scattergood. We got two twins here. We got
a forged check. We got a murder."

"Correct so fur," said Scattergood.

"Wa-al, mebbe both these here twins forged that check.
But, on tother hand, mebbe only one of 'em did. Mebbe
John done it and mebbe James done it. Git the idee?"

"I kind of see what you're drivin' at," Scattergood said.

"If James done it, he wouldn't want John to know, and
vicey versy. But this Trost he found out which and come to
collect on what he knowed. So, looks to me, all we got to
do is find out which of 'em was roamin' around last night
and met Trost where we found him."

"Neither of us left the house last night," said John.

"One of ye could 'a' sneaked out whilst tother was asleep,"
said the sheriff. "But doggone if I see how we're a-goin' to
prove which. Not unless we hunt out somebody that seen
him."

"And if ye do," said Scattergood, "a good lawyer'd make
a jury b'lieve your witness wa'n't sure which he seen. Dark
night, wa'n't it? Both got whiskers. Both same size, and all."

"What d'ye advise doin', Scattergood?" asked the sheriff.

Scattergood did not reply, but asked a question of Winifred. "This uncle that the check was forged of," he asked,
"is he perty wealthy? Eh? Rich?"

"Yes," she answered.

"He was a-goin' to leave his money to these twins when
he died? Will it to 'em?"

"Everyone supposed so," she said. "They were his only real relations."

"But he won't leave it to 'em now. Who'll it go to?"

"To me," said Winifred.

"Sakes alive!" exclaimed Scattergood.

"I'm a sort of connection," she said, "and he is fond of me."

Scattergood waggled his head and clucked. "All the same," he said to himself, "I dunno's I kin jest see you stranglin' a feller."

"She could 'a' hired somebuddy," suggested the sheriff hopefully.

"Never see sich a mess," Scattergood complained. "Um. . . . Don't seem like the twins had no motive fur murder; and Winnie, havin' a fust-class motive—mebbe—hain't my idee of a ruthless 'n' ravin' strangler."

"What ye mean by the mebbe?" asked the sheriff.

"The mebbe," said Scattergood, "referred to the chance that the twins—neither of 'em—did this here forgin'; and that Trost knowed who did and come to strike a bargain. They'd pay, most likely, to git proved innocent. And somebuddy prevented it. Only sensible conclusion to come to, only it don't make no sense."

"Yit somebuddy done it," said Sheriff Fox.

"So somebuddy else had to have a motive," Scattergood said. He got up and lumbered to the door. "Wouldn't arrest nobuddy yit, seems as though," he said. "Calc'late I better git back to the store."

"Hey," said the bewildered sheriff, "I dunno what to do next."

"In sich a case," said Scattergood mildly, "I'd jest set. Yeah, Sheriff, I'd jest set 'n' reflect 'n' kind of let my soul stretch its j'ints." He smiled at Winifred. "Also, Sheriff, I'd do my settin' out on the front stoop with James."

He ambled down the road and into town, stopping first at the post office and then opening up the hardware store for business. After which, leaving the store unlocked and alone, he went to the hotel for his breakfast. He was through his second stack of griddlecakes and sirup when Howard Brush came to the door.

"Mornin', Howie," said Scattergood. "Lookin' fur somebuddy?"

"Has Miss Mason been in to breakfast?" asked the young man.

"She hain't been," said Scattergood, "'n' she won't be."

"What do you mean?"

"Seen her a-turnin' into the house where them twins live," said Scattergood.

The young man shrugged his shoulders and approached Scattergood's table. "She's so infernally headstrong," he said.

"Wimmin is that way," Scattergood said.

"I feel responsible," said Brush. "She would come here. I must prevent her from doing anything to ruin her life."

"That," said Scattergood solemnly, "is what a body might call a noble intention. Pervidin' they know what is ruinin' a life 'n' what hain't." He smacked his lips over the last morsel of griddlecake. "Looks kind of certain these here twins forged that check."

"No doubt of it," said Brush. "But Winifred won't be convinced."

"Naow," said Scattergood, "I've noted a thing about folks 'n' dawgs. Pervidin' they do a thing once they're perty sure to do it ag'in. If a dawg kills him a hen, he hain't goin' to rest content till he's killed more hens."

"Meaning what?" asked Brush.

"Meanin' that mebbe ye can't convince a woman that a man's done a thing once, but if he does it ag'in right smack under her nose she can't dodge no further. Yes, siree. Forgin's a act that gits to be a habit. Once a feller's forged he gits to be a kind of an addict. So, if I was you 'n' had Winnie's best int'rests to heart, I'd kind of obstruct and set around 'n' wait fur the habit to git habitual."

Brush frowned and considered. "Perhaps you're right," he said reluctantly, "but I can't stay here forever, and Winifred is apt to do something reckless."

"Chance ye got to take," said Scattergood. "The' was excitement in taown this mornin'."

"What excitement?"

"That feller Trost was found murdered."

"Trost! What happened?"

"All's I know's he was found in the sugar orchard adjoinin' the twins' house," said Scattergood. "Looks kind of dark fur 'em I'd say." He pushed back his chair. "Calc'late they'll be needin' money. Mebbe fur lawyers 'n' sich. From what I hear tell they hain't got a good deal of it." He grinned dryly. "Hope, if they decide to do any forgin', they won't pick onto me, bein' the only feller in these parts that's got much cash into the bank."

He walked back to the hardware store and there, throughout the day, he conducted himself as if nothing out of the normal had occurred in Coldriver. Once, in the morning, he had a long talk with Deputy Pilkinton, who went straightway to the house of the twins and remained there.

It was not until just before dinnertime, which was noon, of the following day that the old man stirred himself. He sat in his reinforced chair on the piazza of the store until he saw Howard Brush and Winifred Mason emerge from the hotel and come down the sidewalk toward him. As they drew abreast he spoke to them: "Mornin'! Seasonable weather, eh?"

"No weather will be seasonable until this dreadful thing is cleared up," said Winifred.

"Um. . . . I was calc'latin' to walk up 'n' talk things over with the twins," said Scattergood. "Got a kind of a sort of a notion. Um. . . . Goin' that way?"

"Yes," said Winifred promptly, as Brush started to shake his head.

So, silently, they walked up the hill together and to the little cottage, where Scattergood rapped on the door. It was opened by Deputy Pilkinton, and sitting in the room were the twins.

"Johnny 'n' Jim," said Scattergood gravely, "I been a-puzzlin' over ye. I been figgerin' out what I'd do if I was in your place."

"And what conclusion," asked John, "have you reached?"

"Wa-al," said Scattergood, "it's like this. Evidence shows you boys forged a check. Common sense says ye got to have more money jest now. Question is, how'll ye git it? Foller me? So when I got to mullin' over this here question the answer come to me. Ye'd be apt to git that money like ye got tother money ye needed. By forgin'."

"Mr. Baines!" exclaimed Winifred.

"Now, a body don't jest up 'n' forge a name. He's got to kind of practice writin' it. Got any objection if we kind of run through the house 'n' see if we kin run onto any of that there practicin'?"

"None in the least," said John.

"Dep'ty," said Scattergood, "git to scratchin' around."

So, under Winifred's protesting eye, they rummaged the house, but nowhere was there found a sign of illicit penmanship. Scattergood waggled his head. "I was plumb hopeful," he said ruefully, and then he slapped his knee. "Doggone!" he exclaimed. "We hain't tried the barn yit. Got kind of a workshop out there."

"A very primitive, makeshift laboratory," said John. "Help yourselves."

They all went out to the barn. In one end it had been painfully fitted up with such insufficient apparatus as the twins had been able to secure, and the deputy made a lumbering search of this locality. He looked in boxes, pried into pages of notes, lifted whatever was liftable, but it was not until he raised the top of an old-fashioned desk that he made the discovery.

"Hey, Scattergood!" he said.

The old hardware merchant went to him, looked at the papers in his hand, and turned to peer at John and James. "Jest how," he demanded, "do ye calc'late to explain these here? Fur what reason would ye be a-writin' my name about a hundred times. Um. . . . 'N' what I'd like to know is what ye calc'late to do with this here check on my bank, with my name signed to it, fur $1,817.11?"

The room was still. Then Winifred's voice, unbelieving, vibrant with fear and agony, cried, "Oh, John! John!"

"Kin ye explain?" asked Scattergood.

"I cannot explain this, as I cannot explain the other," said John.

"How about you, Jimmy?" asked Scattergood.

James only shook his head.

Scattergood cleared his throat. "Like I said," he told them, "folks is critters of habit. They repeat. It's one of the things ye kin rely on, especially if ye give it a mite of urgin'. So, with things tangled up like they be, I figgered to give human nature a chance't to work 'n' see if it wouldn't do our solvin' fur us. Yeah. Either you twins done these things, includin' murder, or ye didn't."

"John!" said Winifred again, and moved to his side and clasped his arm.

"So, dependin' onto human nature, I kind of give it a push. And it went jest like a hoss turns a corner when ye pull on the rein. Yeah, I kind of furnished the idee and waited fur it to ketch. Um. . . . Howie, was ye out of the hotel last night?"

"No."

"Funny," said Scattergood. "Now, who was the feller come down your fire escape along about two o'clock in the morning?"

"Nobody," said Brush, with a shrug.

" 'N' crossed the river on them stones below the bridge; 'n' sneaked around back to this here barn; 'n' got into it; 'n' put a mess of papers into this here desk? Who was that there feller, Howie?"

"How should I know?"

"Calc'late I'll have to tell ye," said Scattergood, "because ye was watched constant 'n' follered. Ye was seen every step of the way. Ye was even seen, yestiddy, when ye was alone in your room, a-workin', a-slavin', and a-copyin' my name off one of the national bank notes issued by my bank. 'N' whilst ye was eatin', the sheriff he went in 'n' got him a few examples fur evidence." His face was sad as he turned to the door, in which stood Sheriff Fox.

"I guess ye kin take him away, Sheriff. A feller that figgers on a life of crime hadn't ought to have sich a sight of human nature in his stummick. He hadn't ought to ever repeat. Too bad ye was compelled to kill this here Trost. Um. . . . Too bad Trost figgered he could git more money out of the twins 'n' what he could out of you."

"But, Mr. Baines—" commenced Winifred.

"Worryin' about why he done it? Wanted to marry you,

didn't he? Knowed you was in love with Johnny. First forgin' was to git Johnny 'n' Jimmy out of the way, kind of. Ruin 'em. Fix it so's their uncle's money 'ud come to you. 'N' then marry ye when ye got over grievin' about Johnny. Ample 'n' reasonable motive. . . . Take him off, Sheriff, 'n' keep him safe. A feller as chuck full of human nature as he is'll do what it's human to do. Yeah. Ye kin depend on his breakin' down 'n' confessin' complete. Kind of a feller he is."

Scattergood, when they were gone, turned to Winifred and John and James and sighed heavily. But then he smiled. "Human nature allus works," he said, "but a body gits a sight more pleasure out of seein' it work good than work bad. And more of it does. Like laigs. More of 'em walks straight 'n' firm than walks with a limp. Um. . . . Jimmy, I calc'late you 'n' me better go out 'n' watch the crops grow a spell while Winnie 'n' Johnnie gives their human natures a chance to express themselves all cozy 'n' private."

At the door he turned. "Johnnie," he said, "when Winnie asks ye to shave off them whiskers don't git stubborn. Shave 'em. G'-by, Johnnie. G'-by, Winnie. Um. . . . I got an idee ye kin train human nature like ye kin a setter pup. Or ye kin take a chance on lettin' it train itself. But this ye kin depend on—it's a-goin' to repeat what it's learnt. G'-by, folks."

XIV

Coldriver Capers

COLDRIVER was torn asunder; it was divided into two acri-
monious camps; and that harmony which had made the
village so restful a home of contentment, seemed to be
shattered without hope of repair. Deacon Pettibone was the
leader of one faction; Elder Hooper of the other. These
two old patriarchs who had marched grimly side by side
in matters of public morals for more than fifty years were
estranged, and more than estranged. They were open, active,
and vindictive enemies. When kinfolk fall out, the quarrel
can be more malignant than any squabble between strangers; civil war is more bitter than any belligerency between
two nations; but when an altercation arises in a church,
touching upon matters of religion and governance of the
body, then you have warfare without mercy, one which will
divide neighbor from neighbor for a generation.

It had its inception when the Reverend Matthew Sims
resigned to go to a larger church. Unfortunately he chose a
moment to take this step when Elder Hooper was on his
first visit to Florida, and Deacon Pettibone thus became
the final authority in the hiring of the new pastor, a young
man by the name of Wilbur Jepson.

On the Monday following the new minister's first sermon
in the church, the deacon dotted his way to the piazza of

Scattergood Baines's hardware store, setting down his peg leg on the sidewalk with firmness and a certain testy clump.

"Mornin', Scattergood," he said to the old hardware merchant, who was also the owner of Coldriver's bank and railroad and of most of the surrounding timber, and who, from his specially reinforced chair on the hardware store porch, exerted benignly autocratic sway over the politics of the state.

"Mornin', Deacon," said Scattergood. "How be ye? Eh?"

"Hearty," said the deacon, and came directly to the point: "Hear the new minister yestiddy?"

"Nope," said Scattergood. "When I went past the church he wa'n't talkin' loud enough so's I could hear."

"It was a movin' discourse," said the deacon. "He's a splendid eddicated young man. I calc'late he's a-goin' to be more pop'lar 'n the last one."

"Had any word from Elder Hooper on that p'int?" asked Scattergood.

"He's down to Floridy. He wasn't consulted."

"Shouldn't be s'prised," said Scattergood, "if he consulted himself when he gits to hear about it."

"If he stayed to hum where he b'longs, instid of gallivantin' off, his opinion 'ud git asked," said the deacon testily.

At this moment a young man emerged from the post office and strolled across the bridge toward the hardware store.

"Who's that there?" asked Scattergood.

"That's preacher," said the deacon.

Scattergood stared with interest. "What's that he's got into his mouth?" he asked.

"Losin' your eyesight?" snapped the deacon. "What's it look like?"

"It looks like a pipe," said Scattergood, "but mebbe it's some kind of a sacred music instrument."

"What's ag'in' pipes?" demanded the deacon.

"Nothin', so fur's I'm concerned. Does he wear them clothes habitual? They hain't black."

This was an accurate statement. The new pastor didn't wear the black frock coat which Coldriver was accustomed to see on the backs of its ministers. He wore, on the contrary, a well-cut sack coat of rather natty plaid.

"I swan to man!" said Scattergood.

"How he dresses," said the deacon, "is his own business."

"'Tis," said Scattergood, "till the elder gits home."

"If that ol' coot," said the deacon, "kicks up a fuss, he'll git showed how to keep in his place."

Scattergood wagged his head, half with amusement, half with apprehension. He was not one to extend a hearty welcome to germs of trouble entering the village of which he was so fond. "Wa-al," he said, "if ye was goin' in fur suthin' newfangled ye sure picked a suitable time fur it."

By this time the young minister was abreast of the steps and Scattergood, without waiting for an introduction, spoke to him affably. "Mornin', Reverend," he said. "Me 'n' the deacon was discussin'. Name of Scattergood Baines. How be ye?"

"Very well, sir. I've heard of you, Mr. Baines. But I missed you in church on the Sabbath."

"Did ye, now? Um. . . . How d'ye like Coldriver as fur's ye got?"

"It seems a lovely little village—with opportunities for service. I think I shall be very happy here." Then he smiled boyishly. "I hear that the fishing is very good."

"Fust-class," said Scattergood.

"I must get some of the boys to show me the good

streams," said Mr. Jepson. "By the way, I hear there isn't a baseball team in Coldriver."

"Hain't been fur two-three year."

"We must organize one. Baseball's one of my major vices."

"Mebbe you play, yourself?" suggested Scattergood.

"Pitch," said Mr. Jepson.

"Hum. . . ." Scattergood yawned. "Life's a-goin' to dawn on ye all of a sudden, seems as though. Name's Wilbur, hain't it? Yeah. What with one thing 'n' another and with this 'n' that 'n' tother you're a-goin' to be interduced to new experiences. G'-by, Wilbur. G'-by, Deacon."

It was his usual form of curt dismissal when he had exhausted the present possibilities of his company. The deacon and the pastor moved off together. As they got a couple of yards away Scattergood called after them. "If ye think up any more capers," he said, "I'd kind of like to hear about 'em. Gives a body suthin' to mull over. It's int'restin' to have things different on account of they hain't the same. Yeah. Seems like they vary the monotony."

Coldriver, like most remote New England villages, has a habit of waiting. It gives newcomers plenty of rope to hang themselves without interference; or to prove themselves acceptable as neighbors and friends. In due time it makes up its mind and acts accordingly. But even Coldriver is allergic to propaganda. If someone starts something Coldriver will take sides.

So it sat back on its haunches and waited to see what the Reverend Wilbur Jepson was going to do, and whether they liked the results.

All of which might have resulted in pleasure and profit to all individuals concerned if Elder Hooper had decided to pass the remainder of his years in sunny Florida and had not come home, to find installed a minister whom he had not helped to choose and upon whose coming he had not set the seal of his approval. But he did come home, and, unfortunately, upon a day when the Reverend Wilbur's baseball team was playing its first game with Higgins Bridge, with Reverend Wilbur himself in the box, in what was undoubtedly a baseball uniform. Also, the elder could look out upon the baseball field from his back stoop and see and hear, and the things he saw and heard caused a convulsive twitching in the very marrow of his brittle old bones.

When an elder among his people hears a crowd at a ball game bellowing with might and main to its pitcher in language which contains such phrases as "Burn 'im over, Preacher!" "That's the old soupbone, Reverend!" he is apt to be a bit bewildered, if not baffled. He encounters head-on a fact that he has kept resolutely in the background for fifty years, namely, that a minister of the Gospel is an actual, veritable human being and not one set apart in a sort of sacrosanct vacuum. The shock is tremendous and the reaction is likely to be malignant.

So the elder put on his best black coat and his derby hat—a ceremonial dress—and betook his tall, spare frame to make official call upon Deacon Pettibone. The deacon sat on his front porch and eyed the elder's arrival with belligerence. He knew what was coming.

"Back, be ye, Elder?" he asked.

"And high time, seems as though," said the elder. "What's been a-goin' on durin' my absence, Deacon?"

"A sight of things," the deacon replied noncommittally.

"I'm referrin' to the church," said the elder.

"Attendance's been good."

"What," interrupted the elder, "about the preacher?"

"We got a new one."

"Picked out by who?"

"The members of the Session that stayed to hum where they b'longed," said the deacon.

"Was that him," asked the elder grimly, "a-throwin' the ball up in that there baseball diamond?"

"Calc'late so," said the deacon.

"D'you, a deacon of the church, give your approval to sich monkeyshines?"

Up to that moment the deacon had disapproved heartily, but now, faced by his adversary, he experienced a sudden change of heart. He had to approve whether he wished to or not, and to stand stubbornly behind his approval. "You bet your bottom dollar," he said, "I do."

"Then," said the elder, "all I got to say is, you're a dodderin', backslidin', irreligious ol' coot. In all my born days I hain't never seen sich teetotal irreverence, not to say blasphemous conduct, on the part of a ordained minister of the Gospel."

"Why, ye spindle-shanked, ornery, narrer-minded ol' *sport!*" The deacon emphasized the last word venomously. "You that goes off to enj'y riotous livin' on them beaches full of nekked wimmin in Floridy! Ye hain't got enough firm religion in your hull rack of bones to kiver the up end of a ten-penny nail."

"'Attaboy, Preacher,'" quoted the elder harshly. "'Sock the ol' apple, Reverend.' Them's words I heard applied to him."

"A-doin' the Lord's work in the way his hands find to do," said the deacon.

"I calc'late," said the elder with brittle irony, "we'll be havin' prize fights in the church basement instid of strawberry sociables."

"If 'twould lead the young into ways of righteousness I'd be fur it," said the deacon uncompromisingly.

"As fur me," said the elder, "I'm callin' a meetin' of the Session to diskiver if sich capers is sound doctrine."

"Call 'n' be danged to ye," said the deacon, and, rising, he clumped into the house and slammed the door after him. . . .

The elder was not one to let an unpleasant duty stand and grow stale, especially if the duty was to be unpleasant to someone else. He circulated and he discussed. He launched philippics and within a short twenty-four hours he had the town in a turmoil of argument which grew bitter to the point of vituperation. As was inevitable he worked his way at last to the piazza of Scattergood's store.

"Scattergood Baines," said the elder, with the venom of one about to make an accusation, "what I want to know is how be you standin' on this here preacher matter?"

"Up to now," Scattergood said, "I calc'late I'm kind of settin'."

"This here preacher hain't nothin' but a blasphemous, irreligious, game-playin' runagate."

"Wa-al, wa-al," said Scattergood, "calc'late he's bad as that, hey? Um. . . . Listenin' to you, I'd figger he was somebuddy runnin' fur sheriff on the Democratic ticket instid of a feller a-ministerin' to the spiritual needs of his fellow men."

"A bla'guard a-runnin' fur sheriff wouldn't be half such a peril to the salvation of this here taown."

"I hain't what ye might call a stiddy churchgoer," said Scattergood, "but I hain't ignorant complete and teetotal of what's contained into the Scriptures. That there Book's divided into two pieces, hain't it?"

"You know well it is."

"And the fust half is full of hatin' 'n' slayin' 'n' vengeance 'n' sich."

"Fur I thy God am a jealous God," said the elder.

"Yeah. To be sure. But the court kind of reversed itself in the second half, seems as though. I call to mind somethin' about bein' kind to them that despitefully uses ye, and there bein' more joy over a mis'able scamp comin' to repentance than over a passel of folks bein' noble 'n' virtuous from the start off. And, if I hain't furgot, the's quite a sight of sayin's about lovin' your neighbor. Now, Elder, hain't you goin' back of the returns, like a body might say? You're a-rulin' out that chunk about suffer little childern to come to me and reinstatin' the one about vengeance is mine."

"The' hain't no compromise with—" commenced the elder, when he was interrupted by a sudden crash of glass, and one of Scattergood's ancient and seldom washed windows ceased to be. Scattergood did not stir, but his keen, shrewd old eyes swept the terrain and caught a glimpse of a wiry little body ducking from the concealment of a lilac bush to the fancied safety of the livery stable. He recognized the boy, but he did not voice his recognition.

"Um . . ." he grunted, as if nothing had caused a break in the conversation. "Seems to me, Elder, your job calls fur healin' 'n' smoothin' over instid of irritatin' 'n' tearin' apart."

"I know my duty, Scattergood Baines," said the elder.

"So did the Old Testament," said Scattergood, "but when it was took up on appeal it got reversed by the Higher Court." He closed his eyes. "G'-by, Elder," he said.

"Hain't ye a-goin' to take no stand?"

"G'-by," repeated Scattergood, and after a furious look at that placid face the elder betook himself up the street toward the post office.

It was midafternoon when Scattergood saw a small boy

come swaggering down the road, marching past the hardware store with an exaggerated air of bravado.

Scattergood addressed him. "How be ye, Bub?" he asked.

The boy stopped, and assumed that blank look which is the protection of youth when confronted by some unexpected conduct on the part of an elder. "How be ye?" he responded.

"Got a Barlow?" asked Scattergood.

"The' hain't no more Barlows," said the boy.

"I got knives better 'n any Barlow ever was," said Scattergood. "Want to see 'em?"

Plainly the boy was bewildered and uncertain, but Scattergood's grin reassured him and he approached the steps.

"Set," said Scattergood as to an equal. "Took grit, didn't it?"

"What took grit?"

"Marchin' past here like you just done. The fellers dared ye, eh?"

"How'd ye know?" asked the boy.

"Wa-al, ye kind of had the gen'al appearance of a feller that was showin' what he dast do. Huh. How'd ye come to pick a time to do that there depredation jest when your grandpa was a-standin' here?"

"I didn't pick it," said the boy. "The buckshot up 'n' bounced off'm a rock."

"'N' busted my winder," said Scattergood. "Winder glass is costly."

"Ye kin put me in jail if ye want to," said the boy.

"Hain't no fishin' in jail," Scattergood said. "I been a-hearin' a sight about ye, Bub. Fur the life of me, I don't jest see where a boy gits the time to do all the mischiefs you git blamed with."

The boy was silent. He made no denials. Scattergood liked that.

"Folks," he said, "is prophesyin' you're a-comin' to a bad end."

"I hain't," said the boy. "What you calc'late to do with me?"

"I was kind of turnin' over in my mind if you'd druther have a knife with a screw driver 'n' a gimlet in it, or jest one with a blade that's big enough to skin a deer?"

"Hain't no use drutherin'," said the boy. "I hain't a-goin' to git neither."

"Um. . . . Know the new minister?"

"I seen him. Grandpa don't hold with him."

"Seems as though," said Scattergood. "That there knife's got fust-class steel into it. Um. . . . Be ye able to ketch trout?"

"Sure."

"Preacher's been a-wishin' to go fishin'. But he wouldn't have no luck unless somebuddy showed him. It could be somebuddy with a new knife with a blade longer 'n that." Scattergood measured the length with his square fingers.

"D'ye mean," asked the boy, "that you'll give me that there knife if I take Preacher a-fishin'?"

"Didn't say so, did I? No. But s'posin', now, I went into the store and come out with a knife and kind of laid it down close't to you, and didn't say nothin' about money."

"Or busted winders," added the boy.

"To be sure. Yeah, and when ye got up I was to say, 'Bub, hain't that there your knife slipped out of your pocket?' What would ye do?"

"I calc'late," said the boy, "I'd go ask Preacher to go a-fishin'."

"I didn't hire ye to, did I? Eh? No bargain betwixt you 'n' me?"

"Nary," said the boy.

Scattergood went into the store and returned with a gigantic knife, which he laid on the steps. "G'-by, Bub," he said, and then, as the boy moved off, "Hain't ye lost your knife out of your pants pocket?"

"Dummed if I hain't," said the boy, and was gone in a cloud of dust.

This was the day when Merton Springer and Floyd Baker had a fist fight in front of the post office, with the new preacher as the *casus belli*, marking the fact that the Great Schism was in full swing and that anything might be expected. That night two events occurred, one during an informal meeting of the anti-preacher faction at the elder's house, the other in front of Sam Kettleman's grocery and ice-cream parlor.

Some twenty or thirty men and women who shared the elder's views met in his little home to voice their rancor and lay plans for ousting the Reverend Mr. Jepson from his pulpit. They were gathered in the small parlor when, stealthily, a window was pushed up from the outside and no less than five uninvited guests entered, or were pushed in by willing hands—the five being large and rangy and frightened tomcats.

One thoroughly frightened tomcat can be very effective in a crowded room; five enraged and terrified toms can work a miracle of confusion. There was a communal bolt for the front door. But the door would not open, because someone had taken down the elder's clothesline and with it had tied the knob of the front door to the knob of the back door, thus causing a situation puzzling and unpleasant for those inside.

One of the less decrepit men bethought himself at last of a window, through which he climbed and untied the door. But the meeting was distinctly over for that night. And next day Coldriver laughed—at least, that part of it laughed which either had no interest in the church and its squabble or was on the side of Deacon Pettibone and the new preacher.

The second happening was the breaking and looting of the gum machine that hung beside Sam Kettleman's front door.

Naturally, the cat episode was blamed on the deacon, or at least upon his party of supporters of the Reverend Mr. Jepson. The gum machine outrage caused, at first, only a ripple. But the next night someone broke into Wade Lumley's store and stole $1.30 from the till. This was followed by a couple of other petty thieveries, with the result that Deputy Pilkinton, large with authority and importance, took charge of an investigation.

His first step was to lay his problem before Scattergood Baines. "Scattergood," he said impressively, "this here taown's in the middle of a crime wave."

"Dew tell!" exclaimed Scattergood.

"Robbery follers robbery," said the deputy, "and I got to lay hands onto the miscreant."

"Seems as though," Scattergood agreed.

"Now, take these here crimes, they hain't the work of a expert," said the deputy. "Scattergood, I come to the conclusion they was the deeds of a boy."

"Could be," said Scattergood.

"So," said the deputy, "I kind of mulled it over 'n' give consideration to what boy was likeliest. In this here position of mine I git around, Scattergood. I git to hear things.

The wust boy in this here tarnation taown's that there grinnin' imp of a grandson of Elder Hooper's."

"Got any evidence that p'ints?"

"Not what ye'd call proof," said the deputy, "but if 'tain't him, who is it?"

"Dunno's I ever see a feller that could reason out things more logical 'n you," said Scattergood admiringly. "But, Dep'ty, before I acted I'd sort of have things all tied up neat with a piece of string."

"Calc'late you're right. Dunno's I want the elder daown around my ears—unless I kin prove it."

"G'-by, Dep'ty," said Scattergood.

The next person to disturb Scattergood's leisure was the minister himself. "Mr. Baines," he said, "you are not a member of my congregation, but I've come to you for advice."

"Concernin' what?" asked Scattergood.

"The heartbreaking situation that has arisen in my church. I do not understand it. I do not know how to conduct myself nor what is my duty."

"My advice to a feller that don't know what to do next," said Scattergood, "is not to do anythin'."

"But I must do something. My congregation is divided into bitter cliques, one demanding my resignation as their pastor, and the other approving, apparently blindly and in anger, anything I may do."

"Figger out what lays to the root of this here squabble?"

"Elder Hooper," said the preacher, "disapproves of my clothes. He considers it impious that I smoke a pipe. It is blasphemous for me to encourage the boys and young men in this town in engaging in clean sports such as baseball."

"Object to your preachin'?"

"He refuses to come to hear me."

"This here village," said Scattergood, "is kind of off'm

the beaten track. The kind of preachers we're used to is stern, uncompromisin' fellers that allus draws the conversation around to suthin' religious, and that hain't got a notion which end of a baseball bat you hang onto. Them's the kind we allus had. Them's the kind we allus expect."

"But times have changed, Mr. Baines, and the duties of pastors have changed with them. My conception is that the extra-church activities of a minister are vastly more important than his sermons on the Sabbath. Our duty is to try to reach with friendship persons we cannot reach with words inside the church. Our job, if I may call it so, is not to bring sinners to repentance, but to head them off from being sinners. When a boy is playing a good game he isn't in mischief. He learns his minister is human, and can be a friend and companion. He becomes reachable."

"Yeah," said Scattergood, "but the elder hain't caught up with sich newfangled idees. On top of which, he was in Floridy when you was hired."

"But shall I resign? Shall I bring peace by stepping aside?"

"Think you're right?" asked Scattergood. "Be ye convinced you're actin' like a preacher should act? Eh?"

"I am," said the minister.

"Folks is by the ears," said Scattergood. "If you was to go, the squabble 'ud still remain. They got to hatin' one another 'n' they enjoy it an' they'll keep it a-whizzin'. You won't, seems to me, cure nothin' by lettin' go of the wildcat."

"Do you think I can work a reconciliation?"

"Dunno. Um. . . . Hear ye been a-fishin' some."

"Yes, Mr. Baines."

"Along with that there young scalawag that's the elder's grandson?"

"He certainly knows the streams."

"Preacher," said Scattergood, "the elder's a proud old skeezicks. Unbendin'—but he could bust. A thing that might bust him would be fur some disgrace to overtake him or his fambly."

"Are you hinting at something, Mr. Baines?"

"Um. . . . See consid'able of this here young spriggins, don't ye?"

"He seems to have formed an affection for me."

"Judgin' from what you seen would ye state he was a low, sneakin' crim'nal?"

"What utter nonsense!" exclaimed the minister. "He's a bright, unusually mischievous boy, who requires handling. That type can be pushed wrong, but they must be pushed. I've a real fondness for him."

"Um. . . . Keep it 'n' work at it," said Scattergood.

"You have something in mind," said the minister.

"Figger he'd steal?"

"Absurd," said the minister, and then paused, with wrinkled brows. "He wouldn't steal as the law and as adults understand stealing. But to play a game—I don't know. To pit his brains and skill against someone—I don't know. He might steal something as a man in baseball might steal a base. Am I being clear?"

"Clear to me," said Scattergood, "but it would be mighty unpenetrable to the sheriff. Um. . . . G'-by, Preacher."

"But, Mr. Baines, what are you getting at?"

"G'-by, Preacher," Scattergood repeated. "Once I heard of a feller goin' through the woods 'n' he seen a track in the mud. He reasoned out it couldn't be a hawg, 'n' mebbe it was a deer. He was the kind of a feller could take a hint. G'-by."

For the next several days Scattergood watched with acute misgivings the spreading of the schism and the increase of bitterness. He saw men and women who had been born within a few rods of each other and who had been friends for a lifetime pass upon the street without speaking. He saw how the thing affected the business of the village as much as its social life. Wade Lumley was a partisan of the preacher's. For days not a member of the anti-preacher party had entered his store. Sam Kettleman was of the elder's party, and so lost the custom of every inhabitant who adhered to Deacon Pettibone. Old friends, between whose back yards had been gates always open, nailed them up. And so Coldriver was divided as it had never been divided before. It was a condition such as Scattergood had never been asked to face; a problem such as he had never been required to solve.

Matters were approaching the climax of a church meeting, which Scattergood wished to avert if that were possible; because, if that divided congregation met, bickered, and quarreled within the four walls of their edifice dedicated to worship, there could be no healing.

And all the while Deputy Pilkinton, not concerned with matters of religion, prowled about the village. "I been a-shadderin' that there Hooper brat," he confided to Scattergood. "He hain't sca'cely made a move I hain't aware of. Calc'late to ketch him red-handed. Jest missed him last night when he sneaked a dollar-twenty out of the cash register over to the garage."

"You're a-doin' your duty splendid," said Scattergood, "but if I was you I wouldn't do too much of it too quick."

"Slow 'n' sure is how I allus act," said Mr. Pilkinton.

Scattergood closed his eyes, and then, automatically, his big hand went down to meet his foot and he unlaced his shoe, which he kicked off onto the boards. For a long, apparently somnolent period, he sat wriggling his toes in the sunshine. So Coldriver knew he was not asleep but was concentrating. It was almost noon when he opened his eyes and scanned the streets. In the course of a day every citizen not bedridden was sure to pass under his eyes. It was only a question of waiting until the right one came along.

It was not until midafternoon that Bub Hooper came down the middle of the road. Abreast of the hardware store, he turned to grin at Scattergood.

"Hey, Bub!" called Scattergood.

The boy came over to the steps.

"Set," said Scattergood.

"I been fishin' with Preacher," said Bub.

"Bub, ever hear about that there Dutch boy that rammed his thumb in the dike 'n' prevented the hull country from bein' flooded?"

"Yeah."

"What d'ye think of him, eh?"

"He was perty slick," said Bub.

"The's different kinds of heroes," said Scattergood.

"Fellers that fight like this here Sergeant York, 'n' fellers that ketch crim'nals, and fellers that dive into the water after folks. Seems like a body here don't git no chance to be no hero."

"Yeah. Them kinds of heroes is good. But I got a sneakin' idee the slickest kind of a hero 'ud be one nobuddy knowed was a hero but himself 'n' maybe a couple of friends. Kind of a secret hero. And, seems as though, part of bein' a hero is sufferin' suthin' fur somebuddy else and grittin' your teeth and never lettin' on."

"Kind of like one of them martyrs Grandad reads about."

"Yeah, only he'd come out all right in the end and wouldn't git b'iled in oil or anythin'. Um. . . . I been kind of lookin' around fur suitable material fur a hero. I got an idee, Bub, you're the kind of a feller a body could ride the river with."

"Aw, shucks," said Bub.

"'Tain't everybody gits a chance to save hunderds of folks from suthin' wuss 'n a flood.' A taown, Bub, kin be destroyed jest as bad by hatin' 'n' despisin' 'n' vindictiveness as it kin by a fire. Be ye old enough to kind of understand what I'm a-gittin' at?"

"You're figgerin' over this minister squabble," said Bub.

"Yeah," said Scattergood, "I'm a-figgerin' about the minister squabble, and I don't see no way of savin' this here village from bein' ruined except to git me a hero."

"I allus wanted to be one," Bub said.

"G'-by, Bub," said Scattergood.

"But what'll I have to do ——?"

"G'-by, Bub," Scattergood repeated.

The church meeting was called for Thursday night. On the morning of that day the village noted that the new preacher talked for quite a half-hour with Scattergood Baines, and wished it could know what the conversation was about.

"Preacher," said Scattergood, "things comes to a kind of a climax tonight."

"And, hard as I have tried," said the preacher, "I can effect no reconciliation."

"Calc'late to go the meetin', don't ye?"

"I shall be present to defend my conduct."

"Yeah. Um. . . . But ye got to perform some conduct in the meantime. Consid'able. Preacher, you got no idee what a sight of things a body sees by jest a-settin' and notin'.'"

"No doubt," said the young man.

"Um. . . . If ye can't heal a sore by applyin' soothin' medicines," Scattergood said, "ye sometimes got to use a hatchet, without givin' chloroform to the patient. Seems like the elder's afflicted with sich a sore. Preacher, 'fore ye go to that there meetin' tonight I want ye should stop fur a minute 'n' git a suggestion."

"Very well, Mr. Baines. But I cannot see what good it will do."

"Can't never tell. I hain't one to give orders, Preacher. Allus held by hintin' 'n' makin' suggestions. But I'm givin' out orders naow. From this here minute till the meetin's over you do what you're told, 'n' nothin' else. Nothin'. Now, if I was you, I'd put in the rest of this here day a-playin' baseball with the boys."

Hardly had the preacher walked heavily up the street when Deputy Pilkinton approached. "Calc'late I've collected my evidence," he said smugly. "I hain't scarcely let that young rip out of my sight fur days. He's been spyin' around every place there's apt to be some cash a-layin' loose. I got him dead to rights."

"Um. . . . Kind of sad, eh? Can't hardly abide the thought that the elder's grandson turned out to be a scalawag. Hain't seen Bub around fur some time."

"He kind of give me the slip," said Pilkinton.

"Ye kin depend on him comin' home fur his supper," Scattergood said. "If ye feel ye got to capture him I dunno's there'd be a more fittin' time 'n jest when the evenin' meal's over."

So it came about that just as the elder was rising from his table to carry his wrath to the meeting in the church, Deputy Pilkinton pounded on his door.

"What's wanted?" snapped the elder.

"I come fur that there grandson of yourn," said the deputy.

"My grandson! What do you want with him?"

"Got to arrest him, Elder. Got to arrest him fur thievin' 'n' stealin'.'"

The old man stared at Bub, who stood with hanging head. "Thievin' 'n' stealin'," said the old man slowly. "Dep'ty, what you're a-sayin' is a doggone lie."

"I got the evidence," said the deputy, "and he's got to come along."

"Ye aim to take him to jail?" The old man's voice quivered. "A Hooper took to jail!" Then he drew erect his thin old shoulders. "Tonight hain't no night fur private sorrows," he said grimly. "I got my duty to the taown 'n' the church. If this here grandson of mine has sinned, he's got to suffer." The hard old man did not look at his grandson.

He muttered, but his words were not audible. What he said to his own tortured soul was, "More 'n I kin bear, seems as though." Then, turning away with a sort of Spartan determination, he walked out of the house.

The church was already full to overflowing, and the elder marched up the center aisle to take his place with the Session upon the platform. They were all there, the old men who had managed the church for more than a generation—all were there save the minister.

The church was still. They waited—waited for the coming of the minister, the minister who was to be the center of the coming struggle. Minutes passed.

At last the elder could contain himself no longer. He got to his feet, grim, spare, unbending, and spoke. "This here meetin'," he said, "was called by me fur the purpose of puttin' on trial before this congregation the man that was hired durin' my absence to be shepherd of this here flock. I'm chargin' him with ways 'n' conduct that's scandalous 'n' impious in a minister of the Gospel. I'm chargin' he hain't fit ——"

Upon these words the front doors of the church were opened and the minister entered. Behind him were three of the larger boys of the town, who held roughly by elbows and shoulders a fourth boy who was almost a man—a fourth with matted, unkempt hair and unpleasant face. And him they marched down the aisle to the table before the pulpit. And then the congregation saw Scattergood Baines, who did not enter, but placed his bulk in the opening of the doors and remained there impassive.

There was a rustle and clatter of curiosity and excitement, which stilled as the preacher turned, not mounting his pulpit, and held up his hand for silence.

"Members of the Session and Congregation," he said, "it is not fitting I should be tardy in attendance upon my own trial without proper cause. I will state that cause."

He paused and their attention centered upon him, for there was that in his voice which dominated them.

"The grandson," he said, "of a respected, perhaps revered, member of this community, has but now been arrested for theft."

The elder jerked in his chair.

"The heart and the pride of that old man," went on the minister, "is breaking. It seemed to me more important that his head should not be bowed in shame and in sorrow than that I defend myself against the accusations which have been brought against me."

There followed a silence deep and tense.

"I speak," said the preacher, "of the grandson of our Elder Hooper."

The old man sat motionless as death.

"A part of the charges brought against me," said the minister, "is that I have demeaned my office by playing games with the boys of this village. But, through those games and that intimacy, I have come to know them. And my judgment was," he went on, and a faint smile altered his face, "that Bub Hooper was a young scalawag, who might toss tomcats into a meeting, but that he was incapable of meanness or of dishonesty."

Again he paused. "I have established friendship with the boys of this village, and they trust me. And I have come to know which of them are worthy of trust. So, knowing that Bub Hooper was worthy, it seemed right to delay you while I cleared him of this charge."

The elder's figure seemed to grow shorter, to lose its rigidity. There was a look of pathetic eagerness in his eyes.

"And so," said the preacher, "that all men might know, and that no shadow of doubt could ever remain, I went hastily to find the real culprit and to expose him before your eyes. I rejoice to say to you that Bub Hooper is cleared of any charge and that this unfortunate young man has confessed to each recent theft."

He turned to the three youths who held secure the culprit. "You may take him away now," he said gently, and then, to the congregation, "The meeting may now proceed with its business."

Again there was silence as he mounted the platform. The silence became painful, and then the elder, gripping the arms of his chair, hoisted himself to his feet. His lips moved, and at first no words were audible, but then he mastered himself and spoke so that all could hear.

"I'm jest a cantankerous old man," he said, and paused. "Before this here congregation I confess to the sins of envy and jealousy and onreason and vindictiveness. Urged on by these here vices, I stirred up this here squabble and set brother ag'in' brother." He halted, and swallowed. "I despitefully used Preacher, but he returned good fur evil.

Times change, but I hain't been able to change with 'em.
I been stiffbacked and harsh. I been wrong, and I led a
part of ye into wrong paths. Now I'll be beholdin' to ye
if you'll foller me back to where ye b'long. I want them that
sets on the left of the church to git up and shake hands
with them that sets on the right of the church—in friendship 'n' forgiveness 'n' forgetfulness of what's happened
due to me. And then I'm a-goin' to ask the Preacher to lead
in prayer before we—before we adjourn."

For a space there was no movement. Then Wade Lumley rose and shook hands with Sam Kettleman, and suddenly they lost their dignity and pounded each other on
the back.

After that there was no left side and no right side, but
only a congregation, relieved, sometimes tearful, happy that
things should be again as they were. The minister looked
toward the door, but Scattergood Baines was no longer
there. He might have been seen far down the street with a
small boy, barefoot, trudging along at his side.

"How's it feel to be a hero, hey, Bub?"

Bub considered. "Dunno's it seems to make a body feel
much different," he replied.

"The best kind of a hero," Scattergood said, "is the one
that don't feel different after he gits to be one. . . .
What'll ye have, eh? Choc'late or vaniller?"

"Both," said Bub.

"I'll be dummed," said Scattergood, "if ye hain't entitled,
'n' to strawberry 'n' consequent bellyache besides."

XV

The Young Spriggins

"I HEAR tell," said Scattergood Baines, as he sat approximately on his shoulder blades in the chair that had been specially constructed and reinforced to sustain his weight, "that the Brookses is goin' to have a vendue."

"Sellin' off the hull kit 'n' b'ilin'," said old Pazzy Doakes glumly. "Lock, stock, 'n' barrel."

"Be a nice job fur ye," said Scattergood. "Take three-four days auctionin'."

"I hain't a-goin' to git it," said Pazzy.

"What say? Hain't you the auctioneer in these here parts, eh? Got to have one, hain't they?"

"They're a-fetchin' up one from Newton or some'eres. Young Brooks told around I was a back number 'n' they calc'lated to have somebuddy younger 'n' spryer 'n' more up to date."

Scattergood waggled his great head and frowned as Pazzy continued.

"'Tain't so much the money, Scattergood," said the old fellow; "it's a kind of a stroke to my pride, as ye might say. Fur forty years the' hain't been a vendue in this caounty that I hain't run—and to folkses' satisfaction. Now these here Brookses, that hain't nothin' but summer visitors anyhow, has got to haul in somebuddy furrin 'n' newfangled." The

272

old man paused and then said plaintively, "And I'd got me up more 'n a dozen new jokes."

Old Pazzy moved heavily away and Scattergood gazed after him sympathetically. It was not a big problem or a big sorrow, but it was big to Scattergood Baines, for it affected one of his people, a man he had known for two score years. And anything that touched an inhabitant of Coldriver touched the old hardware merchant, whose very comfortable fortune had been built up in that valley. He had acquired timberlands and a small railroad there. He owned the bank. Commencing in Coldriver, he had built up a political power that now ruled the state. Yet any grief or joy that touched one of his immediate people was of greater moment to him than something which might be of importance to the whole commonwealth.

He realized how badly the old auctioneer was wounded. He knew the old man's pride in his art, for Pazzy regarded himself as an artist, a public figure, a person elevated and set apart by a peculiar genius. Scattergood resented what the Brooks family had done, but it was too late to interfere.

Presently handbills were being spread about the countryside announcing the auction and, in flamboyant type, advertising the name of the auctioneer who was to preside—a name new to Coldriver. "Dynamite Dan," he called himself, "The Vendue Man."

"Hear him talk! Hear him joke! Watch him sell!" advised the handbills. "The greatest auctioneer since P. T. Barnum. He'll make you laugh! He'll make you cry! He'll make you buy!"

There was more of it, and none derogatory to the abilities of Mr. Dynamite Dan.

Scattergood read one of the bills and made a little noise in his throat. "Feller hain't got a mite of vanity, seems as though," he said to Pliny Pickett. "Dunno when I see a body so humble 'n' self-effacin'."

"Fetched ol' Pazzy's granddaughter up on the train to-day," said Pliny, who was conductor on Scattergood's twenty-four miles of railroad that wended its way down the valley to the Junction.

"Name's Reva, hain't it?" asked Scattergood, who knew well the name of every man, woman, child, cat, dog, and pet rabbit in the county, but who never openly admitted knowing anything.

"Yeah. Must 'a' cost the old feller a perty penny eddicatin' her up like she looks to be. What was it she went to learn how to play onto? A pianner?"

"I calc'late the school also taught some g'ography 'n' figgerin'," said Scattergood. "But kep' 'em kind of in the background. Look healthy?"

"Pertier 'n a calendar," said Pliny.

"Keepin' comp'ny with Tobias Newton, wasn't she—'fore she went a-traipsin' off?"

"Folks claimed they was a-goin' to marry," said Pliny.

"Wa-al," said Scattergood, "he better git to it before that there eddication gits a chance't to set. Bein' learned in flats 'n' sharps and sich musical didos has ruined many the good cook. Trouble with learnin'," the old man said reflectively, "is that some folks never kin forgit they got it."

"Folks is kind of lookin' forrud to this here vendue," said Pliny. "It's a-goin' to be well attended."

It was well attended. The handbills had done their work, and Coldriver turned out in holiday humor to enjoy a free show.

On the morning of the sale there arrived in Coldriver a single motorcar which did its utmost to make itself appear a parade. It was not an expensive car and it might not even be new, but it was painted white, and on each side in flamboyant letters appeared this bit of information: "DYNA- MITE DAN IS PASSING YOU." In this car sat a young man, also dressed in white, with a large, also white, hat of the size and shape dear to the hearts of inhabitants of the state of Texas. He was tall. When he removed his sombrero his hair was thick and black and curly. No one could deny that he was handsome, nor would any man deny that he was vain. He was one of the few people in the world who could strut sitting down behind the wheel of an automobile. There was a radio in his car which played loudly as he came to a stop before the inn, so that Dynamite Dan seemed to make his entry to the accompaniment of a brass band. He sprang down, leaving his radio to blare, and strode into the lobby of the inn, where he took off his hat with a flourish.

"Dynamite Dan is here!" he announced.

Now, Coldriver is a curious place—not curious in the sturdier portions of New England, but curious in the country at large. It doesn't meddle—not at first. It lets strangers assert themselves without let or hindrance. It permits them to assume importance and even authority, while it sits back on its haunches and watches. A man can show as much wisdom as he chooses, or make as huge a fool of himself as his capacities permit, without a restraining hand being placed upon his shoulder. Coldriver believes in letting every- body run his course. If things turn out all right, very well. If the newcomer lands on his nose, it sweeps up the pieces and goes on its way placidly. But the newcomer never realizes he is putting on a one-man show and providing amusement to spectators.

Coldriver received Dynamite Dan as if he were the con- sequential person he asserted himself to be.

"Dew tell," said the proprietor when Dan made his announcement. He slewed the register around, and the auctioneer wrote in it with a flourish, signing himself not "Dan Smiley," his actual name, but "Dynamite Dan."

Ovid Nixon, now proprietor of the hotel, regarded this autograph tolerantly.

"Best room in the house," said the auctioneer. "Nothing too good for Dynamite Dan."

"Seems as though," said Ovid. "Number Six. Up them stairs 'n' two doors to the left."

Dynamite Dan started for the stairway with the key in his hand.

"Ye hain't got your satchel," said Ovid mildly.

"Have the bellboy bring it."

"Hain't no bellboy," said Ovid. "Folks that wants their satchels up most gen'ally carries 'em."

"Have someone bring it," said Dynamite Dan over his shoulder, and mounted to his room.

Ovid Nixon relaxed into his chair and did nothing. The suitcase remained on the floor where the auctioneer had dropped it. So far as Ovid was concerned it would still be there next Christmas. . . .

The sale was an event, as all vendues are in that locality, a combination of picnic and bargain hunt. A couple of hundred farmers and villagers gathered early on the place to make a day of it and to enjoy whatever sort of show the new auctioneer meant to provide. He provided a good one. The man had undoubted genius for his peculiar business— a great, not unmusical voice, broad humor, plausibility, and salesmanship. He interspersed his auctioning with sleight-of-hand tricks, and he played on the banjo and sang comical songs. Besides which he looked boisterously handsome in his white suit of clothes and he was able to put himself across. He appealed. But he appealed especially to the women.

He knew how to ingratiate himself with a crowd, and during the noontime recess, when coffee and sandwiches were served, he circulated among the people, exerting a sort of charm with which they had hitherto been unacquainted.

For days Coldriver talked about the vendue and about Dynamite Dan, and there was no little ripple when he made the announcement that it was his plan to make Coldriver his headquarters.

"Curious," said Scattergood to Pliny Pickett. "A body wouldn't think the' was room in Coldriver fur him to swing his talents around."

"Mebbe," said Pliny, "he's got him an idee."

"And mebbe," said Scattergood, "it's suthin' else."

"I'd admire to know," Pliny said, "if he calc'lates to wear them white clothes all the time."

"It might turn out," said Scattergood, "he's got him some red ones or yaller ones, which would be entertainin' to see. Consid'able agreeable to the women, hain't he, eh?"

"They kind of gather around him like cows around a lump of rock salt," said Pliny.

"Wa-al," Scattergood said, "it's an observation of mine that when ye git a feller the women pounces onto and follers around, while the menfolks chaw terbacker 'n' wisht they could spit onto his shoes, that ye better maintain an open mind—'n' wait to see what comes of it."

Dynamite Dan did something to the ladies of Coldriver. It is always women who rush to worship idols, which, in general, seems to speak badly for the qualities of the menfolks at home.

Probably it has something to do with romance and

glamour. The ladies pursue it even in the hope of catching it by proxy or in some sort of mental debauch. Possibly a husband with a two-days stubble who smells faintly of the barn or of gasoline has something to do with this. Glamour in the home is not so common as are eggs for breakfast, and who can blame a bored and ardent lady for trying to get her share of it vicariously?

Young Tobias Newton went about his business of driving the big oil truck with a face that grew more and more set as the days passed and as he saw Reva Doakes skittering about the country in Dynamite Dan's white car. All the ladies liked Dan, but Dan seemed to have settled his attentions upon Reva.

"'Tain't enough," Toby said to Scattergood, "that this here play-actin' pup comes a-buttin' into taown 'n' steals away Pazzy's business, but on top of it he's got to go a-tamperin' with his granddatter."

"Mebbe," said Scattergood, "he hain't tamperin'."

"I dunno if ye know it," said Toby, "but the ol' man up 'n' put a mortgage onto his place to send Reva off to git sp'iled with that highfalutin nonsense. How's he a-goin' to pay it off now? Tell me that."

"Mebbe Reva'll earn the money a-playin' on the pianner."

Tobias snorted. "She gits a dollar a Sunday fur playin' the organ to the church," he said.

"Still like her, Toby?" Scattergood asked. "Eh? Hain't turned ag'in' her?"

"I hain't turned ag'in' the Reva that was," said the boy, "but I'm a-gittin' perty disgusted with the one that is."

"Um. . . . Dunno's I'd feel that way, Toby. Wimmin is like weather—different on different days. Around about Reva's age, nobuddy kin perdict if they'll rain or hail or kick up a thunder squall or jest shed sunshine. The's jest two things to do, Toby, seems as though. One's to set 'n' be patient, and tother's to cuff 'em up to a peak. Only cuffin' up to a peak never done no good except to relieve a man's feelin's."

"But she's lost her head about this Dynamite Dan. I've a dum good mind to dynamite him."

"Good idee," said Scattergood, "if ye want every woman in the caounty to up 'n' weep over his black eye."

"Then what?" demanded Toby. "Want I sh'u'd jest set 'n' endure it?"

"If so be ye kin contrive to manage it," said Scattergood.

"Ol' Pazzy'll never git him another vendue," Toby said.

"If ye feed a feller enough cake," said Scattergood, "he'll git him a upset stummick. I'd kind of abide 'n' let nature take its course, like ye might say, 'n' then one day it'll git to a p'int where ye kin sort of shove in your hand 'n' give it a suggestion how it kin act for the best int'rests of all. . . . G'-by, Toby."

"G'-by, Scattergood." . . .

For the next month the *status quo* was pretty well maintained in Coldriver. Dynamite Dan labored unceasingly to ingratiate himself with the people, and not without success, for he had a certain kind of personal charm. His undoubted success with his first auction brought him other business that would inevitably have gone to Pazzy Doakes. And in each instance Dan gave the countryside a good show and realized excellent prices for the vendor. It seemed he was established.

And then Mr. Simeon J. Bolster let it be announced that he was leaving Coldriver. Mr. Bolster owned the largest place on the Handle, that strip of lovely mountain country where the wealthiest of Coldriver's summer residents had homes.

Mr. Bolster's daughter was to marry and go to live in California, and old Simeon had determined to pull up stakes in the East and move to the Coast, so that he might be near the one person in the world for whom he appeared to hold affection. So Simeon was planning to sell out. And, to clean the matter up quickly, he ordained that everything should be sold at public vendue.

It was a plum for any auctioneer, such a plum as did not fall into the lap of a local man once in a lifetime. The commissions to be derived might add up to a sum ranging from five to ten thousand dollars!

"Taown's comin' to life," said Pliny Pickett, after he made his noontime report upon traffic on Scattergood's twenty-four miles of railroad. "Here we be with this here Bolster vendue in the offin' and with Old Home Week a-comin' on in ten days! Jest one thing after another, hain't it?"

"Seems as though," said Scattergood. "Hear any talk, Pliny? Eh? Hear any conjectures about who Simeon Bolster's a-goin' to hire fur auctioneer?"

"Everybody says it'll be this here Dynamite Dan," Pliny said. "Ol' Pazzy hain't got a chance."

"Looks like the old has to give way to the new," said Scattergood.

"Yep. And looks like this here Dynamite feller's takin' Pazzy's granddaughter away from Tobe Newton."

"The ladies," said Scattergood, "does seem to find Dynamite Dan agreeable. Um. . . . G'-by, Pliny."

"G'-by, Scattergood." . . .

That afternoon the old hardware man harnessed his mare to the dusty old buggy and drove out toward the Handle. As he passed the broad lawn of Simeon Bolster's estate he saw that dour gentleman inspecting flower beds with the air of one who has just found half a worm in the apple he is eating.

"Whoa," called Scattergood. "Whoa. . . . Afternoon, Simeon. How be ye? Flowers blossomin' perty fine, hain't they?"

"You can't eat flowers," Simeon said morosely.

"Not to speak of," agreed Scattergood, "but neither kin ye wear a beefsteak in your buttonhole. Um. . . . Hear tell you're movin' off to Californy."

Simeon nodded a grudging affirmative.

"Goin' to hold a vendue, be ye?"

"Yes."

"Calc'late ye'll have this here up-'n'-comin' Dynamite Dan do the auctionin'?"

"Maybe so. Maybe not."

"Matter of business," said Scattergood. "Sentiment don't enter into business to speak of. Now, some fellers, jest out of sentiment and fur old times' sake might stick to Pazzy Doakes. But this here Dynamite Dan gits high prices."

"I've not made up my mind," said Simeon.

"Wa-al, Old Home Week's a-comin' in ten days. Folks'll be took up with that. One thing at a time's a good motto, jest as you was sayin'. Um. . . . Them flowers is perty enough to take a prize to the State Fair."

"My flowers will take no prizes," snapped Simeon. "My cattle will take no prizes. My flowers and my cattle are my private business. Next thing," said Simeon grumpily, "they'll be offering a prize for the sleekest and fattest wife."

"Can't never tell," said Scattergood, and nodded toward the house, from which emerged a young woman. "How be ye, 'Melia?"

"Well," said Miss Amelia succinctly, her manner distinctly

resembling her father's. She was tall and rather thin and not beautiful.

"Um. . . . G'-by, Simeon. G'-by, 'Melia," said Scattergood, and clucked to his mare. He drove back to town and resumed his seat on the piazza of his hardware store. With eyes closed and shoes off, he wriggled his toes in the declining sunshine. To Coldriver this meant he was engrossed in some problem.

He got up presently, locked the store, and ambled up the road. In front of the post office he encountered Dynamite Dan.

"How be ye?" asked Scattergood. "Huh. . . . I was jest visitin' with Simeon Bolster. He's a-teeterin' betwixt you 'n' old Pazzy as to which he's a-goin' to hire fur his vendue."

Dan smiled confidently. "I'm not worrying," he said.

"All the same," advised Scattergood, "a feller ought to take his precautions. Got to ketch your trout before ye kin eat it. Dunno's I'd jest bog down in a puddle of confidence if I was you. G'-by, Dan."

With which he marched on up the street, and Dynamite Dan stared after him with puzzled eyes.

At noon next day, when Pliny Pickett reported at the store, Scattergood listened to his tale of passengers and grunted.

"Dynamite Dan," he said, "is kind of prominent in these here Old Home Week festivities, hain't he?"

"Practically runnin' 'em," said Pliny.

"Wants 'em to be a big success, I calc'late."

"So he kin git credit fur it," said Pliny.

"Um. . . . It might be you'd meet him kind of accidental today, mightn't it, Pliny?"

"I could," Pliny said.

"A feller that thinks he thinks up a suggestion is more apt to be fur it than if somebuddy else thinks it up," said Scattergood. "Huh. If Dynamite Dan was to think he thought up one about havin' a queen fur Old Home Week he might git enthusiastic about it."

"What kind of an idee would he have about that?" asked Pliny.

"He might think about havin' one elected," said Scattergood. "He might think up havin' some nominated on the openin' meetin' of the week in the Taown Hall. And the one gittin' the most votes would be queen fur the week 'n' git called Miss Coldriver."

"Hain't a bad notion," said Pliny.

"Didn't hear nothin' from me, did ye? I didn't make no suggestion?"

"Nary."

"G'-by, Pliny," Scattergood said, and settled down to await results.

A customer disturbed him. Up the steps of the store came heavily a girl who made up in weight what she lacked in beauty. She was not tall, but she was of astonishing girth. She panted from her exertions.

"How be ye, Huldy?" asked Scattergood. "Be lookin' fur a new job, won't ye? Um. . . . How long ye been a-cookin' fur Simeon Bolster, Huldy?"

"Two year. What I want's a nutmeg grater."

He served her and sped her departure. Scattergood liked Huldy Parker, but for once was in no mood for conversation.

That night Scattergood sat on the front stoop of his neat little home on the edge of the village and listened to Mandy, his wife, who was discursive on many subjects. Her tongue was tart.

"Men," said Mandy, "kin be dumb fools, but wimmin kin be dumber."

"I hain't prepared to argy the p'int," said Scattergood.

"Take the way they're a-preenin' and a-gogglin' over this young spriggins!" Mandy said sharply. "Take the way Reva Doakes is actin'!"

"What's the matter with Reva?"

"You know full well," said Mandy. "Look at how Pazzy put a mortgage on his place to git her taught a mess of high-falutin nonsense! Then take how this spriggins comes in and snaggles away Pazzy's business! Then take how Reva gives Tobe Newton the mitten! I hain't never been quite· so disgusted."

"Jest a lot of humans givin' free rein to their human nature," said Scattergood.

"I had it all planned out in my mind," Mandy said fiercely. "Fust Tobe 'n' Reva'd marry. Then Pazzy'd git this auctionin' job fur Simeon Bolster. Pay off his mortgage 'n' have money in the bank to boot. So Tobe 'n' Reva'd go to live with Pazzy in his house. But this Dynamite feller mogs in and busts it all to flinders."

"If you was let loose in the world," Scattergood observed, "Divine Providence could up 'n' take a long vacation. Um. . . . I hear tell Dynamite Dan's a-goin' to lay a proposition before the committee tonight. Yeah. And, observin' the young man, I sort of gather he's a one to go to lengths to git this here job of Simeon's."

"He ought," said Mandy, "to be circumvented."

"Seems like the's time," said Scattergood, "when you're in fettle to be a fust-class circumventer. You hain't a one to heave a stone 'thout calc'latin' on knockin' over at least two birds."

"Jest what you gittin' at?"

"I'm a-gittin' at conveyin' a suggestion," said Scattergood. "To Dynamite Dan."

"Sich as?" asked Mandy tersely.

"One that looks like it 'ud kind of solidify Dan with Simeon, and make that there job drop into his lap like it was a ripe plum."

"Be ye crazy?" she demanded.

"Some says so," admitted Scattergood. "I hain't jest sure myself. Um. . . . Ye could chance to meet Dan to the pust office tomorrer noon."

"I could," said Mandy, "but I shan't. I hain't nobuddy's cat's-paw. Least of all yourn." She paused and glared at him. "When I meet him," she said, "what'll I say?" . . .

That evening Dynamite Dan propounded to the committee his plan for a Miss Coldriver. The idea was accepted.

The news of the coming election of a sort of Queen of Love and Beauty was received by the town with interest. It came as an agreeable surprise to Reva Doakes, because she felt Dan had devised this whole matter for her personal glorification.

At twelve next noon the village was treated to the unusual sight of Mandy Baines ambling into the post office. Spectators observed that she blocked the way of Dynamite Dan and smiled upon him as she had been seen to smile upon few men, addressing him with a kindly, motherly air and even herding him into a corner for private conversation. And Dan listened and nodded, and strutted a little. And the villagers heard Mandy lift her voice a little at the end of their talk and say, "I'm allus a one to have the int'rests of young folks to heart. That's why I'm a-talkin' to ye, because I wouldn't like to see suthin' happen that hadn't ought to happen."

"I certainly am obliged," said Dan. . . .

In a few days old residents of Coldriver began to pour into their home village. They came on this decennial occasion from all states and localities. Houses were full of guests and the hotel was crowded. The town was gay with bunting and flags in honor of the visiting prodigals.

On Monday night the festivities opened with a get-together in the Town Hall, where there were to be speeches of welcome and music and an evening of general hand-shaking and renewing of ancient acquaintance. In the chair was Old Man Bogle, the First Selectman.

After a couple of bursts of oratory and a piano solo by Reva Doakes, the chairman arose and cleared his throat.

"Now," he said, "we're a-comin' to the p'int of the evenin' and that is the selectin' and electin' a lady out of our midst to be the queen of this here home-comin' week. She's a-goin' to be entitled Miss Coldriver, 'n' she's a-goin' to ride in a special decorated float in the p'rade. Be ye ready fur nominations?"

Instantly Dynamite Dan was on his feet. Reva Doakes, sitting beside the piano, blushed and looked rather lovely as she turned infatuated eyes upon the young man.

"Ladies and Gentlemen of Coldriver," he said, "it is only fitting and proper that, on such an occasion, when so many of you have traveled hundreds of miles to reach the town of your birth, that you should unite to pay a graceful compliment to one of your loveliest young ladies."

He paused, and gazed confidently about him.

"This thing of selecting a queen was my suggestion," he admitted, "and I want to place in nomination for the compliment and the honor the name of a gracious and delightful young lady who, by appearance and manners and popularity, is well entitled to be your queen. I feel myself signally honored by placing before you the name of Miss Amelia Bolster, daughter of one of our first citizens, Mr. Simeon Bolster."

For a moment he stood holding the silent audience with

his eyes until, from the depths under the balcony might have been heard Pliny Pickett's voice saying dryly, "I figgered he'd end up by sayin', 'Goin', goin'—*gone!*'"

As he returned to his seat he did not glance toward the piano nor see the suddenly pale cheeks of Reva Doakes, nor the hurt, humiliated look in her eyes, a look that slowly changed to scorn.

Before Dan was seated, a young man arose from the audience. "I got another lady to nominate," said Tobias Newton. "She hain't no summer visitor, but was born right here amongst us. Mebbe she hain't got quite the quality of looks as some, but she's got more of 'em, and she's the best cook in Coldriver. I'm nominatin' for queen Miss Huldy Parker!"

The audience sat quiet again, quiet and delighted, for it perceived something was happening.

"Move the nominations be closed!" bellowed Pliny Pickett.

Obviously Dynamite Dan was disturbed. He, too, familiar with audiences, saw that something was happening which he had not planned or reckoned upon. Who was this Huldy Parker? He thought he had met every girl in the town, but here was a name with which he was not familiar. Just what his feeling would have been could he have realized he had been jockeyed into the position of sponsoring Amelia Bolster in an election of this sort against her own cook, it is impossible to guess.

Joyously the audience carried the motion to close nominations. In the rear of the hall Simeon Bolster leaped to his feet and commenced to bellow, but Old Man Bogle declared him out of order.

"We'll now percede to the election," said the chairman, "and we'll do it by a count of hands. Them in favor of Miss

Amelia Bolster will h'ist their right hands." A scattering of arms were raised, which the old man counted carefully. "Now," he called, "them in favor of Huldy Parker." The room suddenly assumed something of the appearance of an asparagus bed on a lush morning. It bristled with hands. Old Man Bogle cleared his throat. "Hain't no need to caount," he announced. "The' was nineteen votes fur Miss Bolster, 'n' all the rest fur Huldy. So, folks, you've chose Huldy Parker to be queen of these here doin's. . . . Huldy, will ye come forward?"

Huldy, the whole two hundred pounds of her flushed red as a beet, came swaying and rolling down the aisle and climbed to the rostrum. There she stood, grinning, mammoth, good-natured, bewildered.

"Now," said Old Man Bogle, "I'm a-askin' the originator of this here idee to put on the queen's head the crown she's entitled to wear while the doin's is goin' on."

Dynamite Dan, flabbergasted for the first time in Coldriver's experience, struggled to his feet and clumsily placed on Huldy's head a gilded, pasteboard diadem. And the assemblage cheered.

Then the meeting was over. Dan could find no quick and private exit. He had to pass the piano where Reva sat, and he tried to smile at her, but her eyes would tolerate no smile from him.

"I never saw anybody as cheap and mean as you are," she said. "Don't ever speak to me again."

"But, Reva ——"

"You're something," she said, "that crawled out from under a rotten log."

Dan hurried on, but at the door he found himself confronted by a furious Simeon Bolster.

"So," said the crabbed old man, "you're the young man

who violated my daughter's privacy. You're the one that humiliated her in public. Beaten by her own cook! You did a good night's business for yourself, you—you—" He could find no apt epithet. But he could think of something that would hurt worse than epithets as his eye lit on the ancient, spare frame of old Pazzy Doakes. "Mr. Doakes," he called in a choked, apoplectic voice, "you come to my house in the morning. I'm appointing you to auction off my effects."

Scattergood sat beside Mandy waiting for the crowd to thin. He saw Tobe Newton lingering in the aisle, saw him intercept Reva Doakes. She tried to pass him with averted head, but he grinned and detained her and forced her to look up at him. And then her eyes filled.

"Oh, Tobe," she said. "I've been such a fool. Take me home. Take me home."

Scattergood grinned at his wife. "Mandy," he said, "I calc'late one stone done fur both of our birds prompt 'n' final. Um. . . . Calc'late we better mog home. I kin finish up that there pie with a peaceful conscience."

XVI

Scattergood Starts a Revolution

"I CALC'LATE," said Scattergood Baines, "that I hain't been a-payin' enough attention."

"To what?" asked Pliny Pickett, ex-stage driver and now conductor on Scattergood's railroad, which operated over twenty-five miles of track down Coldriver Valley.

"To young folks," Scattergood said succinctly. He settled back in his big chair, one that had been specially reinforced with iron rods to bear his weight, and looked with melancholy eye down the street of the village.

"What's the youngsters been doin'?" asked Pliny.

"Goin' away," said Scattergood. "Yeah. Pullin' up stakes and goin' away. Boys and gals. Their mas and pas git 'em raised up to where they hain't a nuisance no more—and off they skedaddle. Pliny, the' hain't enough young folks left in Coldriver to wad a gun."

"Do seem to be runnin' kind of sparse," agreed Pliny.

"Yeah. Come a few more years 'n' the' won't be nobuddy left here under eighty, seems as though."

"They come a-wanderin' back," said Pliny.

"Some does," admitted Scattergood. "Some does, draggin' their tails when the world's kind of up 'n' stepped on their faces. And them that does is the culls. The prime, A Number One, first-grade ones—they make a go of it, and we've seen the last of 'em."

290

"Wa-al, that's how things is," said Pliny philosophically.

"It's how things hadn't ought to be," said Scattergood. "Um. . . . What dum fool wants to leave these here green hills and them there valleys with brooks piddlin' down the middle of 'em—unless they got to? Eh? Who? What boy or gal with the sense God give geese wants to leave this here air and quiet 'n' peace 'n' go to live in smoke 'n' rumble 'n' clatter, where ye dassn't walk on the grass 'n' trees has got iron railin's around 'em?"

"Mebbe so. Mebbe not," said Pliny, declining to take a definite position on the subject. "What got ye off on this tote road, Scattergood?"

"Marty Sampter," said Scattergood. "She come a-mournin' around this mornin' because her boy Pete's gittin' all set to push off 'n' look for a job in the city. She wanted I should argue with him."

"Did ye? Eh?"

"I did not do so," said Scattergood.

"Whyn't ye?"

"Because," said Scattergood, "the' hain't no argiment to offer up. G'-by, Pliny."

"G'-by, Scattergood," Pliny said, and limped off up the street.

Scattergood did not close his eyes. Somehow he did not feel like cat-napping in the spring sunshine today. He was accusing himself—but vaguely. He could not quite figure out the wording of the indictment. Of what was he guilty?

He pinched his great cheek and whistled between his teeth, as his eyes peered up the street, across the bridge, and to the village square with its absurd traffic light on a post in the middle. He was not made easier in his mind when he recalled how the selectmen had ordained that light after a visit by one of them to the city, and how they had stationed the constable there on a tall, revolving chair, borrowed from Scattergood's bank, to direct the passing of the few dozens of vehicles which crossed that spot each day. The constable sat there now, wearing a pith helmet like an African explorer. Even when Scattergood recalled how Old Man Tingley, from the Handle, who was a mite nigh-sighted, had driven into town and, seeing the traffic post handy, had hitched his span of horses to it, he felt no lift of the spirit.

He recalled how he had come to Coldriver years ago, in his bare feet, squeezing the sand up luxuriously between his toes, and how, penniless, he had bamboozled the local merchantry into setting him up in a hardware store. He called to mind the days of his hard labor and scheming and battling—heavy years that had seen him rise to a position of almost supreme political power in the state, to the owner-ship of the bank, the railroad, square miles of timber, and to wealth that ran well above a million. It had been success, though he had never taken time to be proud of it. And today he was not proud. He felt that, somehow, he had failed.

"They wouldn't be migratin'," he said to himself, "if they wasn't pushed."

Presently a girl, who could not have been more than twenty, came stepping across the bridge. She was slender, erect, lovely. Not lovely in the way some women whom you see about night clubs and expensive restaurants are lovely, but she could have been. Her dress was in the mode—thanks to periodicals she had read—but it had been made by her own hands and lacked something of the zip of a Paris model. However, it was becoming.

Scattergood watched her approach, and as she neared the piazza of the hardware store he perceived that her lips were set and her eyes unhappy. "Mornin', Mettie," he said. "How be ye? Eh?"

"Well, thank you, Mr. Baines," she answered.

"Then what fur be ye a-shettin' your lips that way, Mettie? Huh?"

"I hate this place," she said furiously.

"Dew tell. What's Coldriver up 'n' done to ye now? Say."

"It's—it's a cemetery surrounded by an old people's home," she said bitterly.

"Funny," said Scattergood, "how folkses' minds run to the same subject. Thinkin' of leavin' us, Mettie?"

"You know I can't, Mr. Baines."

"So I do, seems as though. Ma hain't able to git out?"

"She never will be able," said Mettie. "If you and Senator Bones hadn't got me the job in the post office ——"

"Ne' mind about that, Mettie. Ne' mind. What fetched this here tantrum up all to once? Eh?"

"Harry," she said, "is going to Boston."

"They're comin' two to a hill," said Scattergood. "Pete Sampter's skallyhootin' too."

"They're going together," said Mettie.

"And you figger he won't come back?"

"Would you?" she countered.

"If you was a-waitin' fur me," said Scattergood, "seems as if."

"He won't," she said. "He'll go to the city, and if he has any luck he'll grow away from us. He'll be different. He'll see the difference between me and city girls, who buy their clothes instead of making them. We can't compete," she said.

"Why should ye?" asked Scattergood. "Ye use different kinds of bait fur different kinds of fish. Ye paint your toenails to ketch brokers 'n' bond salesmen. But ye bake pies to ketch widowers with a quarter-section of farmin' land."

"You're wrong, Mr. Baines. Men know how women should look nowadays. They see pictures and they go to the movies."

"But boys don't go traipsin' off to the city jest to ketch 'em a gal that looks like a movie star. What takes 'em away?"

"If you," demanded Mettie, "could see nothing ahead of you but odd jobs, or a chance to work the rest of your life in a garage, what would you do? Look at the men who have stayed. There's Henry over there. For twenty years he's been clerk in the grocery, and never will be anything else. Nobody ever gets to be anything else. There's nothing to do. The future holds nothing but monotony."

"Done a sight of thinkin', hain't ye?"

"I've had reason to."

"You figger they hain't a-goin' of their own free will 'n' accord, but because Coldriver's practically kickin' 'em out? Eh?"

"Precisely," said Mettie.

Scattergood sucked at his front teeth. "H'm," he said finally. "G'-by, Mettie."

Accustomed to this formula of dismissal, as was all of Coldriver village, Mettie proceeded on her way with staccato little steps. Scattergood stared after her. He looked about him for a possible messenger and saw a little girl coming primly down the walk.

"How be ye, Mary?" Scattergood asked.

"Nice," said Mary.

"Would ye like to have a dime, Mary?"

"Yes, Mr. Baines."

"Um. . . . Know Harry Knobs 'n' Pete Sampter?"

"Yes. They're in the barbershop."

"Aim to pass there?"

"Yes, Mr. Baines."

"If ye passed there 'n' seen 'em, what would ye say, Mary?"

"I'd tell them you were sitting on your piazza, Mr. Baines."

"Wouldn't tell 'em I wanted to see 'em?"

"You didn't say so," said Mary.

Scattergood was filled with admiration. "Your Grandpa 'ud be proud of ye, Mary. Here's a dime." He paused. "I got suthin' to show ye," he said, arising and walking into the store. Mary followed.

Scattergood took down from a shelf a tin toy stove. "Now, ain't it purty, Mary?"

"How much?" asked Mary.

"Only a dime," said Scattergood.

Mary regarded it longingly. "You hired me for a dime," she said.

"Yes'm."

"But," said Mary, "if I give you my dime for that stove you make a profit. How much?"

"Nigh four cents," admitted Scattergood.

"So you'd be getting your errand done for six cents instead of a dime," said the little girl. "'Tain't fair."

Scattergood beamed. "If Mandy 'n' me had a daughter like you, Mary, seems like we'd be tickled almost to death." He passed over the stove. "This here's a reward fur not gettin' ketched."

Presently Harry Knobs and Pete Sampter came walking down the street in obedience to the summons.

"What can we do for you, Mr. Baines?" asked Harry.

"Hear tell you're goin' away," said Scattergood.

"Yes, sir."

"Sot on it, be ye?"

"Yes, sir."

"Never does no good to argue with folks that is dead sot," Scattergood said. "So I hain't a-goin' to. D'ye *want* to go?"

"It's not a question of wanting, Mr. Baines. We've got to go—or rot. There's no place for us here—no future. We could go along the way some men have done, getting a job for a few days here and a few days there—and probably get enough to eat. But who wants to live that way?"

"Nobuddy," agreed Scattergood. "Would you druther live here than go traipsin' off to the city? Eh?"

"I don't know," said Pete. "What's here to interest anyone?"

"I managed to keep myself int'rested fur upward of fifty years," said Scattergood. "Wa-al, I jest kind of wanted to git your idees. Sorry to hear you're goin', boys, and good luck to ye. G'-by."

That night Scattergood discussed the matter with Mandy, and she made what might have seemed to anybody but Scattergood an irrelevant observation.

"My hens," she said, "scratches on my side of the fence."

"Dew tell!" exclaimed Scattergood. "What makes 'em do that?"

"I give 'em more entertainin' gravel to scratch," she said tartly.

"Them's hens," said Scattergood. "My trouble's with roosters."

"If," said Mandy, "a passel of hens wants to keep a rooster to home, they got ways of doin' it. One of the leadin' ways is fur a hen jest to stand around 'n' cluck her admiration at how he scratches his own gravel."

"Pervidin' the's gravel to admire bein' scratched," said Scattergood.

"I calc'late," Mandy said, "a rooster gits more vanity 'n'

satisfaction out of it if he gits it into his head he invented gravel 'n' pervided the supply. Jest like *you*, you ol' coot, practically b'lievin' ye invented apples so as you could gorge yourself on pies."

"Um . . . if ye wa'n't sich a cook, Mandy, I'd 'a' got me a better-natured 'n' more sightly woman long 'fore this."

"What with?" Mandy demanded.

"I calc'late," Scattergood said mildly, "I better toss out some gravel, 'n' your part'll be to git the hens to make the roosters believe it was their original idee in the fust place. Know Mettie Greer?"

"Was there when she was born."

"You 'n' Mettie better have a p'litical convention, seems as though," said Scattergood. "Takin' up in toto the subject of the Red Mill."

It was two days later that Scattergood, seated on the piazza of his hardware store, saw Mettie Greer and Harry Knobs cross the bridge, evidently in hot argument. The old man waited to speak until they came abreast of him. "Mornin'," he said.

"Good morning, Mr. Baines," said Harry.

"Mr. Baines," said Mettie sharply, "Harry's been arguing with me. He's got a perfectly crazy idea."

"It was just a kind of a thing I thought of," Harry said. "But all the same I bet you I could put it over."

"Huh. Crazy idee, huh? Most things was crazy idees in the beginnin'. Some keeps on bein' till the end, and others turns out to be airplanes. What's yourn?"

"I was just telling Mettie," Harry said diffidently, "that I bet I could build up a business here—a kind of a business, if it could be done my way."

Mettie winked at Scattergood.

"Which is what?" asked the old man.

"Well," said Harry, "there's ten or fifteen or twenty men around here, most of them young men with nothing regular to do. Like me. Well, it seemed to me we could get together."

"'N' do which?" asked Scattergood.

"A reason one man can't start a thing—say a factory," said Harry, "is he's got to have capital. I mean, to start off and keep him running until he begins to sell his stuff and make a profit. But if, instead of one man doing it, and having to pay everybody that worked for him, it was the other way around . . ."

"Meanin' jest what?"

"That everybody who worked there started it. I mean, went in together and did all the work—then there wouldn't have to be any wages paid. If, say, fifteen or twenty of us started to manufacture something I bet nobody could compete with us."

"Usin' what for machinery?" asked Scattergood.

"That was part of my idea," said Harry, and Mettie winked again. "I noticed the Red Mill was laying idle. There's water power. It's in pretty good shape, shafting and belting and three lathes, and saws and planers. A little fixing up and she'd run."

"But ye don't own it," said Scattergood.

"I kind of thought that out," said Harry. "It's just laying there eating its head off. The way it looked to me, we could rent it pretty cheap, and have an agreement to buy if we made any profits."

"Yeah. But how about timber, if you're a-goin' to manufacture suthin' wooden?"

"What we ought to make is something small that a great many could be sold of. Something that could practically be made from cull lumber or timber. Like clothespins, or those handles they give you in the store to carry home bundles. We could buy cull lumber practically for nothing, and we could buy timber along fences and bum timber from farmers. Enough to get a start, and probably on credit."

"Um. . . . Thought ye was a-goin' away."

"So I am," said Harry.

"Of course he is," agreed Mettie. "He couldn't make a go of a wild idea like this. It would be a lot better to get a job running an elevator in town and have regular wages. Harry just hasn't the organizing ability to do anything like this."

"Who says I haven't?" demanded Harry belligerently. "And who said anything about running elevators?"

"What other kind of a job could you get?" asked Mettie.

"You think I can't organize, eh? You think I'm no good for anything but running an elevator? That's what you think of me, is it? Well, I'll show you." He turned to Scattergood with a determined chin. "How about that mill?" he asked. "Will you rent it?"

"Might consider it," said Scattergood. "Might be willin' to sell. Tell ye what I'll do, me bein' conservative and not given to gamblin'. I'll lease you that there Red Mill, lock, stock, 'n' barrel, fur ten per cent of your profits, if any, and I'll agree to sell it to ye at the end of a year fur four thousand dollars— 'n' let the fust year's rent apply on the purchase price."

Harry looked at Mettie defiantly. "We've made a dicker," he said.

"What ye a-goin' to manufacture?" asked Scattergood.

"Plenty things," said Harry. "Come along, Mettie. I've got to get this thing to whizzing."

Whatever Harry may have lacked, it was not energy. His first recruit was Pete Sampter, and the pair of them talked up the scheme day and night. They put spirit into it. It was almost like organizing a baseball team. And they succeeded.

At the end of the week a dozen young men were at work in the Red Mill, putting such machinery as was there in shape for use.

Three old clothespin machines, lathes, and slotters, had been resurrected from the cellar and set up. The lathes were ready to turn out chair stock or drumsticks. Pete had bought on credit a couple of weathered piles of cull maple and birch from a lumber mill down the river, and they were ready to start. Their staple was to be clothespins.

But on the day they opened, a man appeared in town and called at the mill. He represented the clothespin manufacturers of the country, to whom had come word that three extra machines were about to throw their product on the market.

"Young man," he said, "the clothespin business is not what it once was. Every mill is running on quota. If you enter the business now you will upset the market. Prices will go to smash."

"With our plan," said Harry, "we can manufacture cheaper than anyone. If prices drop we'll be better off than anybody else."

"But to whom will you sell?"

"If they're cheap enough someone'll buy our pins," said Harry.

"We'll buy your machines," offered the stranger.

"Can't be done," said Harry. "We're going ahead."

"Sorry. But we can't have it. We'll have to drop prices to a point where even you can't manufacture and live. Think it over. I'll see you tomorrow."

Harry hurried down to the hardware store and told his tale to Scattergood, who nodded and puffed out his fat cheeks.

"Kind of expectin' it. Invadin' a staple market that's had

to be organized. Never had much faith in clothespins, seems as though. But ye kin create a disturbance. And any feller that kin create a disturbance is in a position to make a dicker."

"What sort of a dicker? We've nothing to trade."

"Ye got one of the best things to swap that the' is," said Scattergood.

"What's that, Mr. Baines?"

"Not doin' suthin'—like not raisin' pigs or not raisin' tobacco, or not manufacturin' clothespins. Now, you fetch that feller daown here tomorrow, and we'll kind of lock horns."

Next morning Harry and the representative of the clothespin manufacturers seated themselves on the steps of the piazza of the hardware store.

"I hear tell," said Scattergood, "you don't want the boys to start manufacturin' pins."

"And gave my reasons."

"Fust-class reasons," said Scattergood. "What ye got to offer? What'll ye swap?"

"I don't understand."

"What'll ye swap the boys for not makin' pins?"

"Why—er—I have no proposition other than to buy the machines."

"Um. . . . Kind of one-sided. You want the boys to not do suthin'. Wa-al, mebbe they'd trade not makin' pins for *your* not makin' suthin'. Hain't there suthin' you make that hain't important that all you woodenware mills'd quit makin'—and that the boys could make in a leetle mill?"

"It's a new idea."

"Cost ye a sight of money to drop prices 'n' go into a war."

"A lot."

"Wouldn't it be better 'n' wiser if ye was to agree to quit

makin' some little thing that the's a little profit in, in return fur peace and comfort and a steady market?"

"It sounds reasonable," conceded the emissary. "What have you in mind?"

"These here," said Scattergood, holding up one of those little handles for carrying packages which storekeepers give customers. "How about these here contraptions? Have to be tarnation cheap, because they're give' away. Can't be a sight of money in 'em for you manufacturers."

"Am I to understand that you will agree to refrain from manufacturing pins if we will give you the market for handles?"

"That's the idee," said Scattergood.

The man considered. "It appeals to me," he said. "Let me wire my principals." He did so, and returned later with his acceptance of the proposition.

"Now," said Scattergood to Harry, "you're in shape to start a-goin'. You'll have to fix ye a machine to bore a hole through the handle, and one to bend the wire. Let's see ye gallop."

While the boys adapted machinery and made ready, Scattergood had another interview with Mettie. "The girls, seems as though, hain't gittin' no advantage from this here thing. Familiar with Mis' Pease's maple cream?"

"Yes, indeed."

"Folks around here has only harvested maple sugar kind of haphazard," said Scattergood. "Yeah; and the same with apples that kin be turned into cider. In both cases cookin' is involved, especial if ye make apple butter 'n' apple jelly. Give ye a notion?"

"It does," said Mettie promptly. "Oh, a grand idea. We can put Coldriver on the map. Make the name stand for something."

"As how?"

"A Coldriver brand. Coldriver Products. No telling how far we could extend it—even to farmers' wives and house-wives in their spare time, and with garden stuff that would go to waste. Canned things. And have them special. Not only maple-sugar things and apple things, but, say, catsup, and advertise it as Mrs. Minturn's Own Recipe. And mustard picked by Mrs. Judson, and so on and so forth. Go to some of those big Boston and New York stores and sell to them exclusively. Put everything up in a dandy jar or package. Instead of having a canning factory, make the whole town one big factory, with everybody in it."

"Mettie," said Scattergood, "looks to me like ye got suthin' perty near sublime. . . ."

For years Coldriver had gone on about its drowsy affairs, decreasing in size, worrying about it, seeing no way out. Most people had lived in reasonable comfort, but none had a surplus for those things that make life attractive. It was hard for the town to move out of its rut. But even the skeptical were interested in watching how the boys came out with their co-operative mill. However, when Mettie leased every sugar orchard in the township and contracted for every apple she could find, she met with opposition. It was no way for a girl to act. It was not ladylike. It was meddling.

That first fall she could go at the thing in only a small way—except for her sugar. But she did convince a dozen housewives and farmers' wives that it would be just as easy to put up preserves and jellies and vegetables in special cans for her as to pile them on shelves in the basement. By snooping around glass manufacturers she found odd-shaped and attractive glass containers. She had Coldriver labels printed, and on each was a blank space where the cook who produced the contents was to sign her product, as if it were a painting.

Then, with her idea and with samples of apple butter and jelly and catsup and a dozen other things, she visited Boston and New York. She was astonished at the reception she met—that her idea met. Coldriver products, each can prepared by a skillful home cook! Each can autographed by its maker! Two great stores, one in Boston, one in New York, contracted to take her entire output.

And then the maple-sugar season came on and the sap commenced to run. Men from neighboring farms, without employment in these cold months, were glad of work in the sugar orchards. William Bard and Thomas Horley, famous sugar makers, undertook the job of boiling the sap and reducing it to luscious cakes of sugar, yellow as honey. The kitchens in the Congo Church basement and the Methodist Church basement became factories for making maple cream and maple candies. And all of it was packed in novel boxes bearing the Coldriver Products label.

The results were astounding. Mettie was kept busy day and night superintending and attending to correspondence, as private orders commenced to pour in.

A new life burgeoned in the town. Houses, long weathered, bloomed with new coats of paint. Fences were straightened, and they, too, gleamed white. The motion-picture house was compelled to run, not two nights a week, but six. For the money did not go into one pocket, but into the pocket of every man and woman in town who was willing to contribute labor and skill. Families were able to go to Boston for a few days' pleasure. Wives blossomed forth in new dresses and hats. Young men wore new and becoming suits. Money was flowing into Coldriver, not in a great flood but in a steady, deserved stream.

' As for the boys, they had commenced with fifteen on the job. By the first of January there were twenty-five. With what amounted to an exclusive market for handles they found the days were not long enough to satisfy the demand. And it was not alone they, themselves, who profited from this. Farmers with scrub timber profited, lumber mills that had not been able to get rid of cull lumber found a steady market. The grocery man, the butcher, the dry-goods merchant—all profited, because money was coming in and people were able to buy.

Scattergood, sitting one day in the bank, made some calculations based upon deposits and the increase in savings accounts. He knew that the boys in the mill, in the first six months, had paid to themselves satisfactory wages and had a surplus of $9,746.21 in the bank. Out of this they voted to pay for and own the mill and machinery. And their calculations were that their profit for the coming twelve months would, when divided, give to each of them more than he had ever dreamed of earning.

What with wages, and their dividends, there was no young man in that company who could not afford to marry, and there was no young man who wished to withdraw and go to the city. And people were drawn closer to one another; there was a spirit of mutuality abroad. Dwellers in Coldriver came to recognize that this prosperity which had come to the town was there because everybody had his shoulder to the wheel; that it depended upon no one of them, but upon all.

Such small financing as had been necessary Scattergood had done through his bank. It was not alone that the depression was over in Coldriver; it was that something much more deep-seated and ancient had come to an end. Coldriver was awake. It was not a scattered village now, but a

unit, self-conscious, industrious, proud because it realized
that what it had done had been accomplished by itself, out
of its own resources, without outside aid. . . .

It was on a chilly April day that Mettie sat in Scattergood's office in the bank.

"Wa-al, Mettie," Scattergood said, "everybuddy went to a
sight of trouble, seems as though, to keep your young man
from leavin' town."

"That did sort of commence it, didn't it?"

"Good a reason's any fur institutin' a revolution. Nothin'
more important to this here human race than marryin' and
givin' in marriage. Pervidin' the right ones git together.
Marriage is like one of these here duets to the singin'
school—awful soothin' if the right two people git together,
but awful annoyin' to all if they git to squeakin' off key."

Mettie looked at Scattergood and smiled. "Thanks for
reminding me," she said.

"Of what, eh? Remindin' ye of what?"

"Marrying Harry," she said. "We've both been so tarnation busy it's slipped our minds."

"Um. . . . It's one of them things ye don't need no
memorandum pad to remind ye of," said Scattergood. "And
'tain't the only way of increasin' the pop'lation."

"No?"

"I dunno if ye've noticed it," said Scattergood, "but the
Git-to-the-City movement has not only got itself checked,
but the flow's set in the other way. Yes'm. Since las' June,
when this thing got to goin', eleven young fellers under
thutty has hitched up their britches and come back from
the city to live."

"Really?"

"Five new houses built."

"True."

"Twenty-two folks paid off substantial on mortgages."

"How fine!"

"Savin's bank deposits increased up'ards of twenty-five thousand—and Wade Lumley's washed his store winders for the fust time in thutty year."

"Not a soul on relief."

"I calc'late to be kind of content," said Scattergood. "G'-by, Mettie."

She arose and walked toward the door, but halted as he spoke again.

"Proves," said Scattergood, "a feller kin lift himself by his own bootstraps. Yeah. A hull town kin h'ist itself. Mettie, I just thunk up a recipe that kin do any dummed thing in the universe."

"What is it, Mr. Baines?"

"Mix a good idee with plenty industry and serve while bilin'."

"It worked," she said.

"Jest one ketch in it," said Scattergood.

"What's that?"

"Findin' the good idee," said Scattergood. "G'-by, Mettie. Better git your marryin' done 'fore summer. Um. . . . Human bein's is at one and the same time the most helpless critters on earth—and the doggondest most surprisin'ly able 'n' resourceful. What makes 'em int'restin'. Every time I figger I know all's to be knowed about 'em, I find out I hain't graduated out of the kindergarten." He snorted. "G'-by, Mettie. Trouble with humans is that every time you up 'n' solve a problem they're jest doggone smart enough to contrive a wuss one. Like a snake allus a-tryin' to swallow himself by the tail."

"Which," said Mettie, "it can't manage to do."

"Nope," said Scattergood, "but it gits a sight of satisfaction and a sore mouth tryin'."